Degrassi

THE NEXT GENERAT

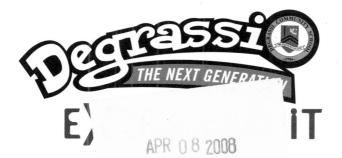

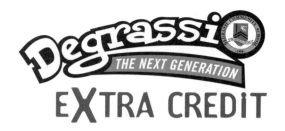

Degrassi THE NEXT GENERATION
EXTRA CREDIT

4 SAFETY DANCE

Story by J. Torres

Art by Steve Rolston

New York | London | Toronto | Sydney

A Pocket Books / Madison Press Book

POCKET BOOKS, a division of Simon & Schuster, Inc.
1230 Avenue of the Americas, New York, NY 10020

Library of Congress Cataloging-in-Publication Data is available.

ISBN-13: 978-1-4165-3079-4
ISBN-10: 1-4165-3079-7

First Pocket Books trade paperback edition May 2007

10 9 8 7 6 5 4 3 2 1

Manufactured in Canada
by Friesens

For information regarding special discounts for bulk purchases, please contact
Simon & Schuster Special Sales at 1-800-456-6798 or
business@simonandschuster.com

Produced by
Madison Press Books
1000 Yonge Street, Suite 200
Toronto, Ontario, Canada M4W 2K2
www.madisonpressbooks.com

PREVIOUSLY ON DEGRASSi...

Marco Del Rossi has had his ups and downs since coming out of the closet. He's lost some friends, but he's also found out who his true friends are. And though he's still struggling to gain his dad's acceptance, he's open about who he is at school. When Marco meets Dylan Michalchuk and falls in love with him, he learns just how much love can hurt when someone betrays you. And when he eventually decides to give Dylan a second chance, Marco finds out that it's often easier to forgive than to forget....

Ashley Kerwin went from being a popular student politician to the school pariah after trying the drug Ecstasy. Her friends, including on-again, off-again boyfriend Jimmy Brooks, turn their backs on her but she finds a kindred spirit in Ellie Nash. Her attitude, along with her look, changes with the times and she eventually finds a way to thrive through music. After a failed relationship with Craig Manning, she spends a year with her father in England. Once she's back home, she quickly rekindles her romance with Jimmy, but discovers it may take time to settle back into her old life....

ACT 1

"Sometimes it's very difficult to keep momentum
when it's you that you are following."

— Eva Peron in "Evita"

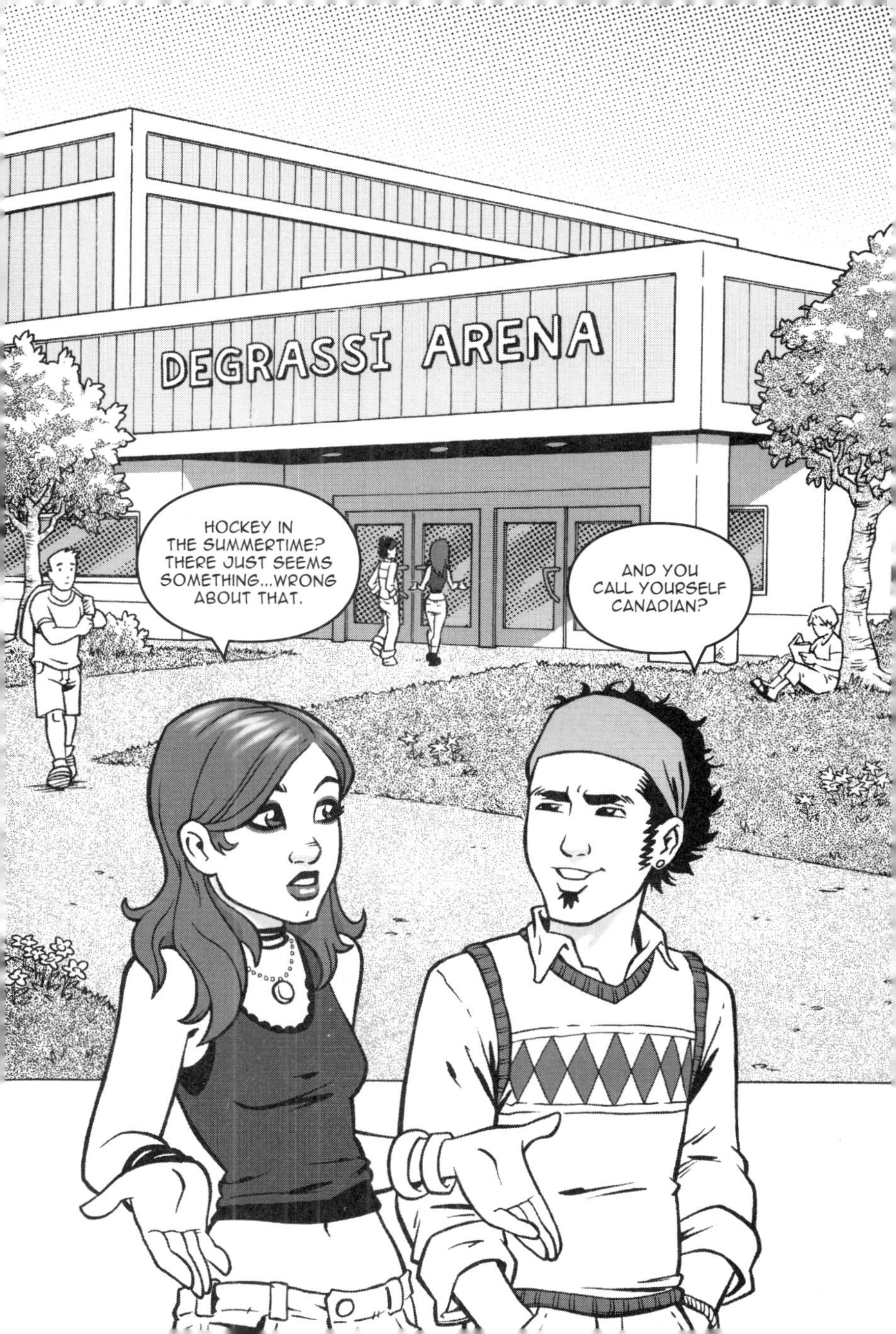
DEGRASSI ARENA
HOCKEY IN THE SUMMERTIME? THERE JUST SEEMS SOMETHING...WRONG ABOUT THAT.
AND YOU CALL YOURSELF CANADIAN?

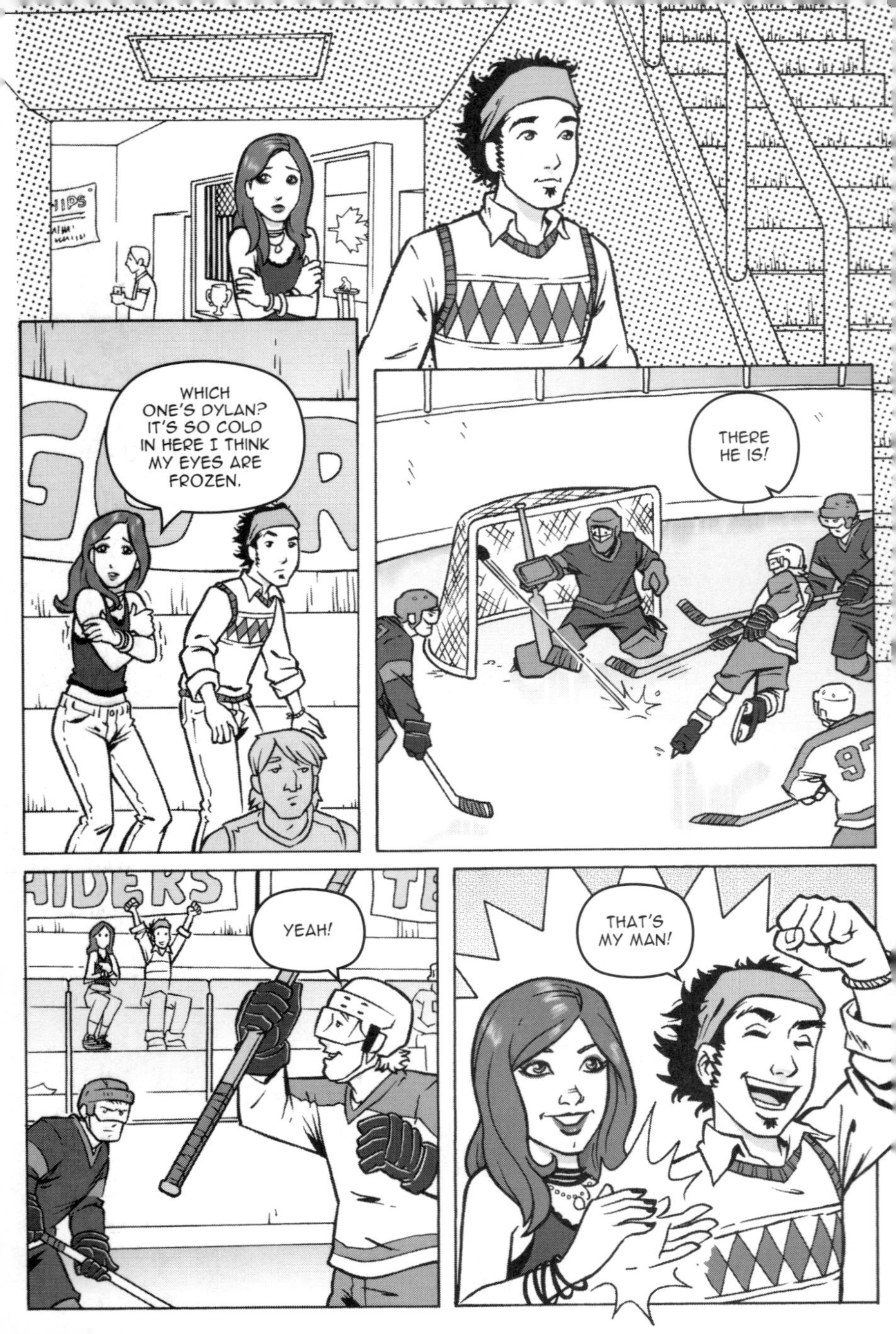

WHICH ONE'S DYLAN? IT'S SO COLD IN HERE I THINK MY EYES ARE FROZEN.
THERE HE IS!
YEAH!
THAT'S MY MAN!

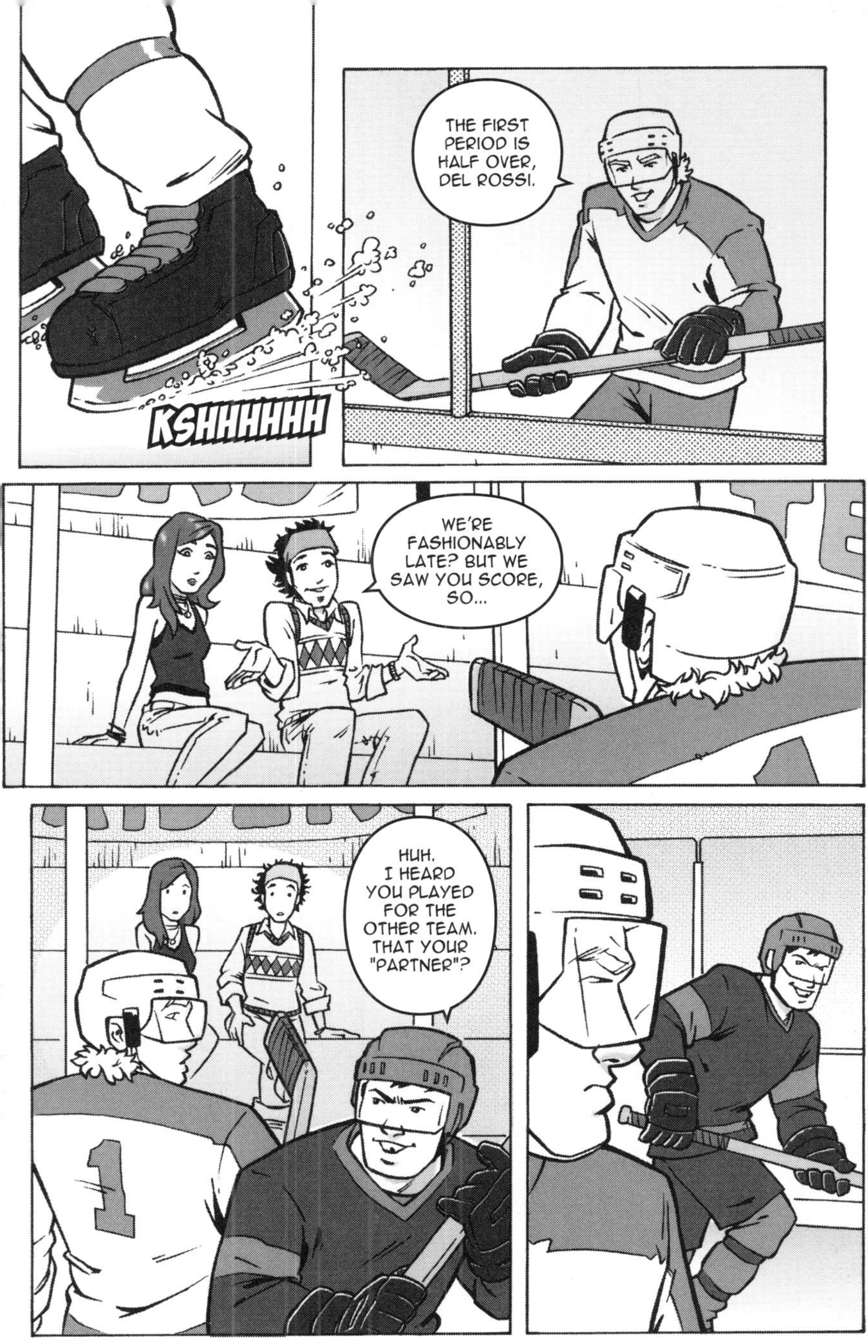
KSHHHHHH
THE FIRST PERIOD IS HALF OVER, DEL ROSSI.
WE'RE FASHIONABLY LATE? BUT WE SAW YOU SCORE, SO...
HUH. I HEARD YOU PLAYED FOR THE OTHER TEAM. THAT YOUR "PARTNER"?

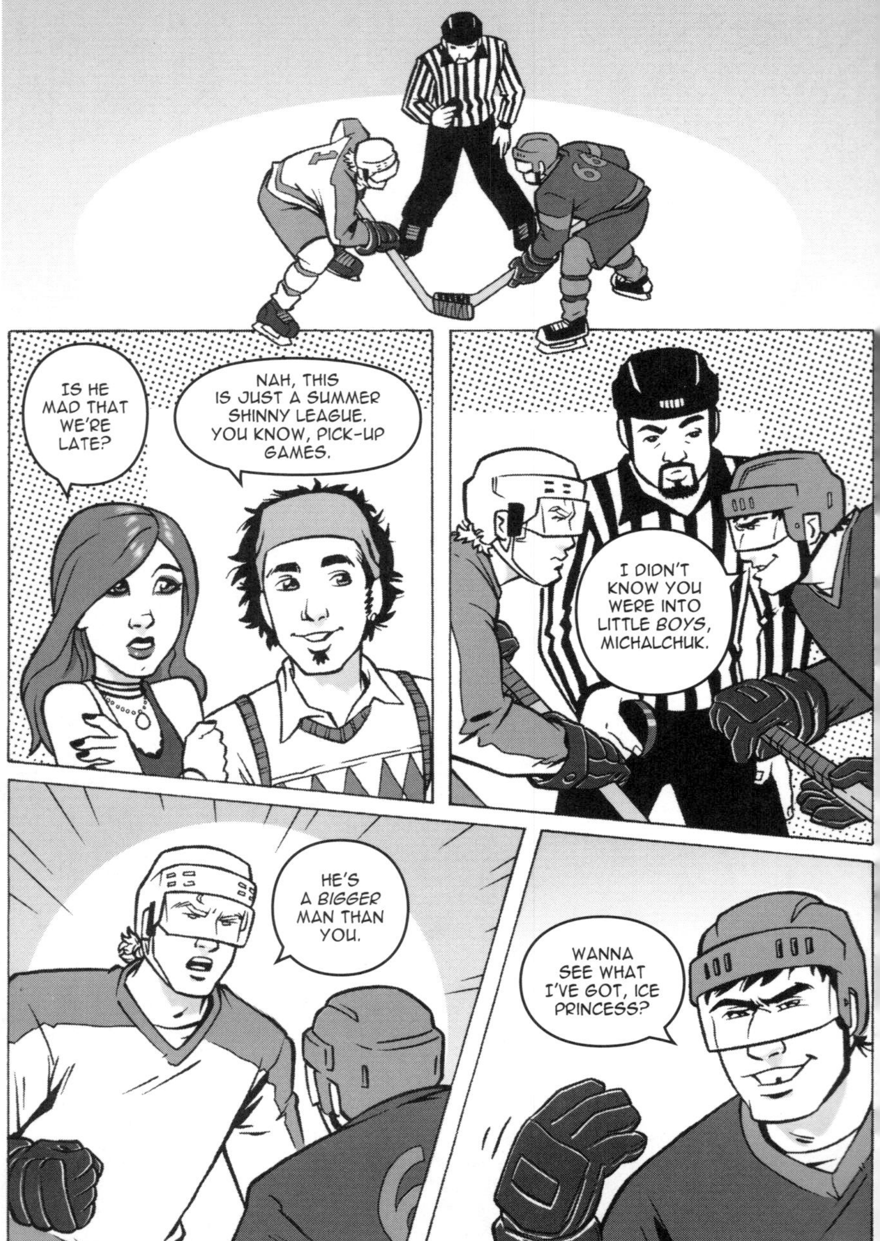
IS HE MAD THAT WE'RE LATE?
NAH, THIS IS JUST A SUMMER SHINNY LEAGUE. YOU KNOW, PICK-UP GAMES.
I DIDN'T KNOW YOU WERE INTO LITTLE *BOYS*, MICHALCHUK.
HE'S A *BIGGER* MAN THAN YOU.
WANNA SEE WHAT I'VE GOT, ICE PRINCESS?

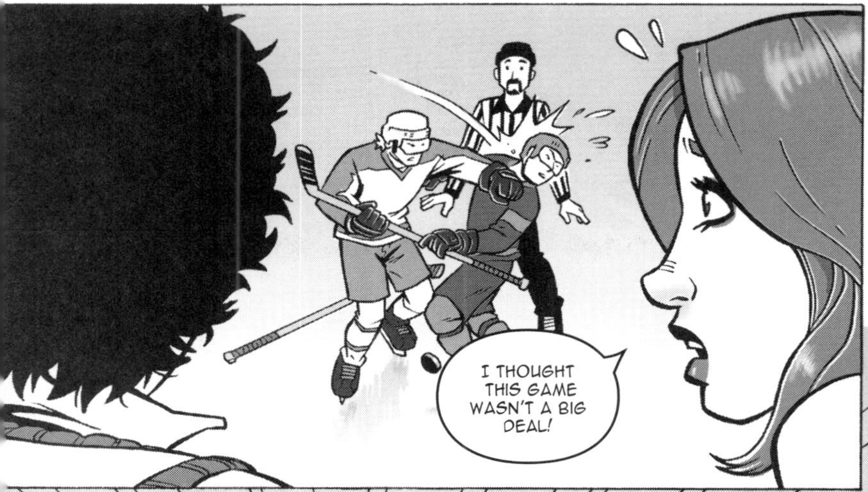
I THOUGHT THIS GAME WASN'T A BIG DEAL!

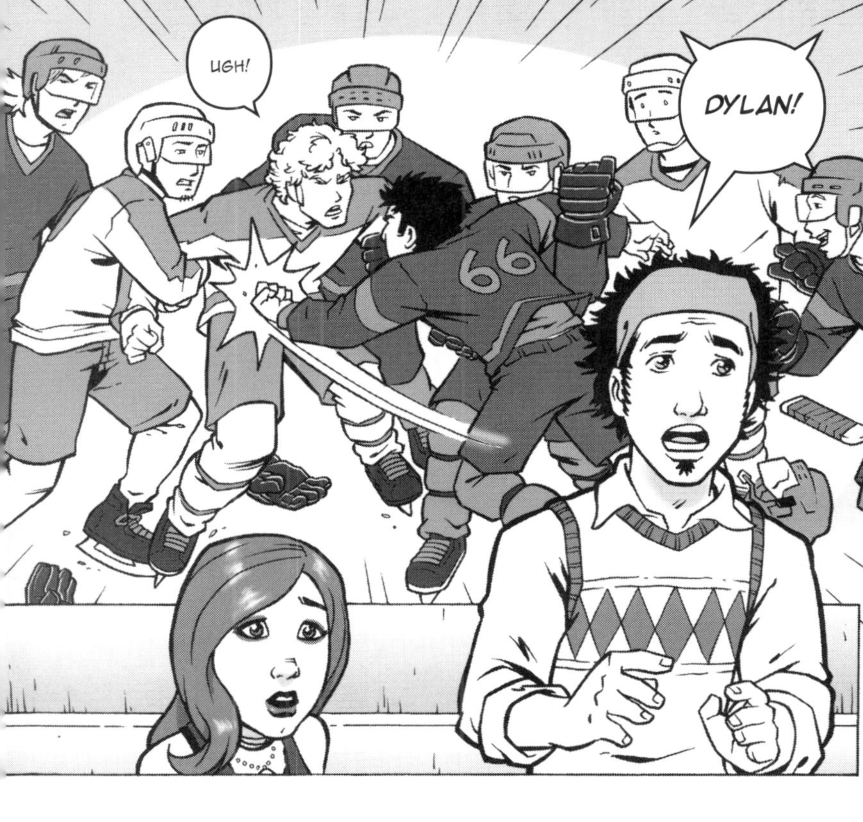
UGH!
DYLAN!

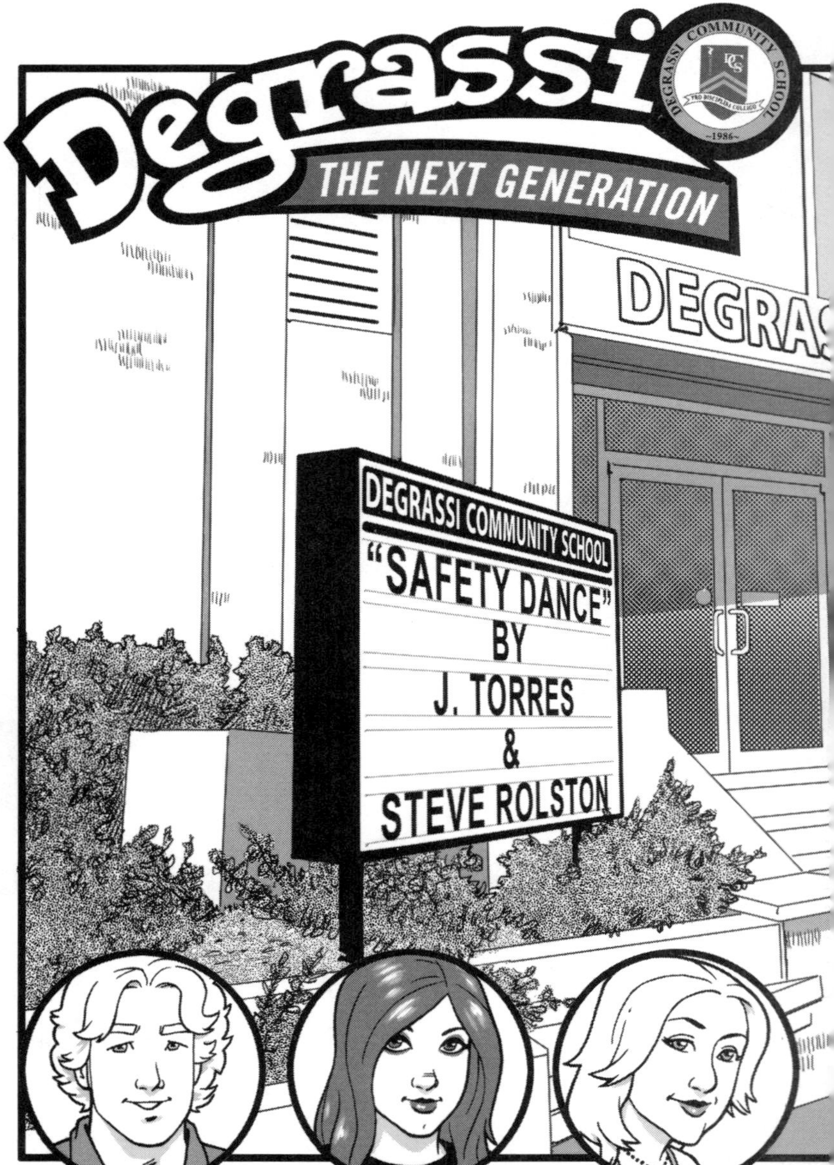

Degrassi
DEGRASSI COMMUNITY SCHOOL
PRO DISCIPLINA COLLEGO
-1986-
THE NEXT GENERATION
DEGRAS
DEGRASSI COMMUNITY SCHOOL
"SAFETY DANCE"
BY
J. TORRES
&
STEVE ROLSTON
DYLAN
ELLIE
PAIGE

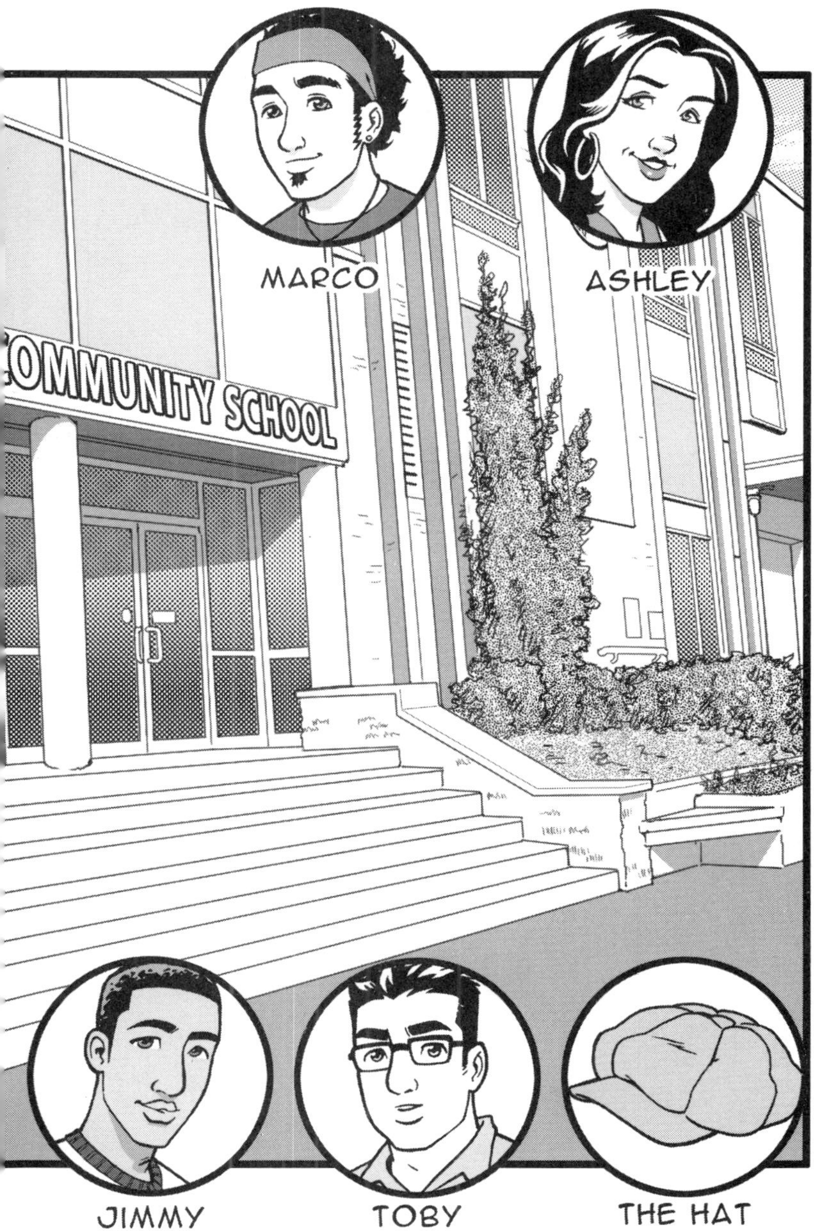
MARCO
ASHLEY
COMMUNITY SCHOOL
JIMMY
TOBY
THE HAT

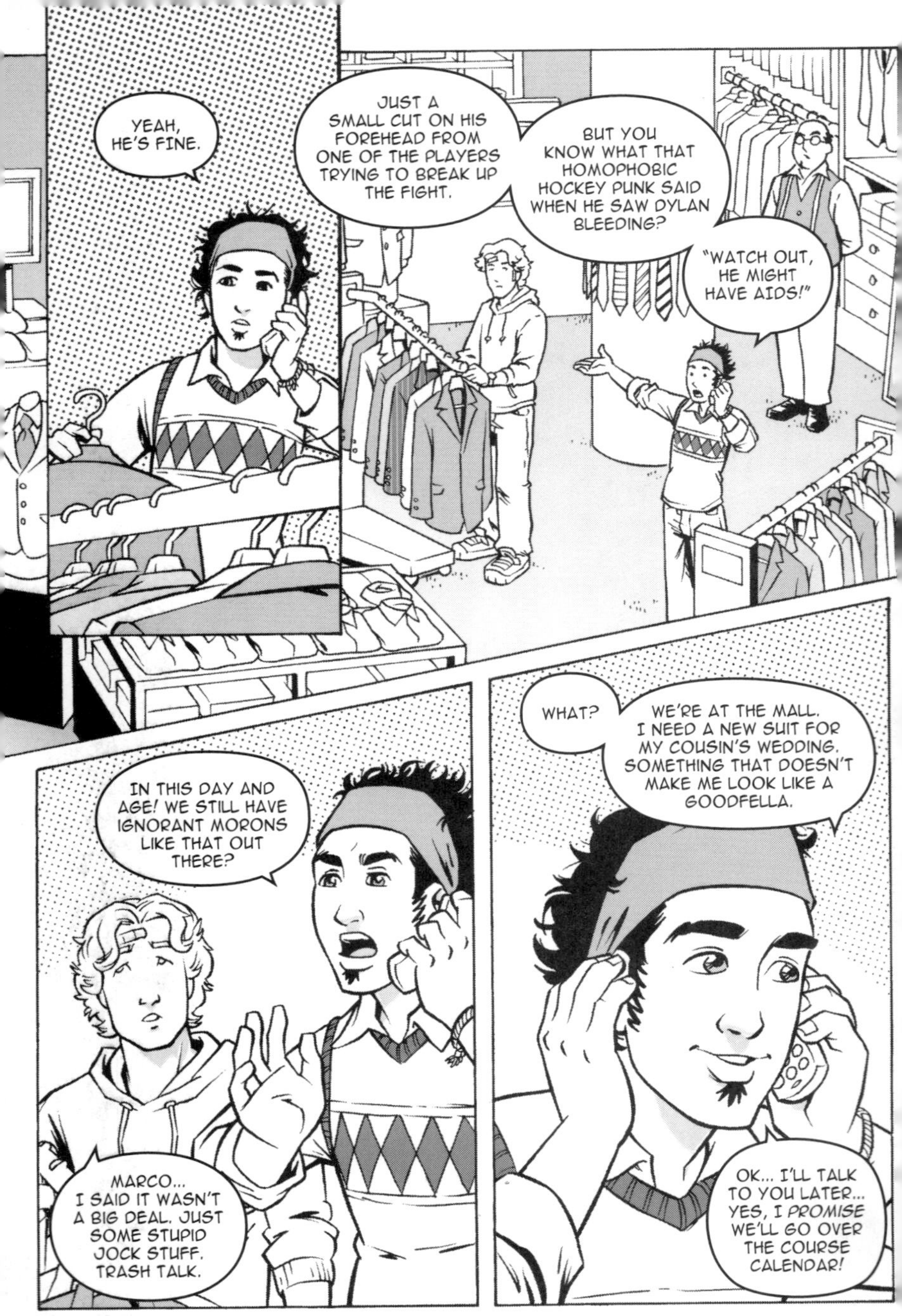
YEAH, HE'S FINE.
JUST A SMALL CUT ON HIS FOREHEAD FROM ONE OF THE PLAYERS TRYING TO BREAK UP THE FIGHT.
BUT YOU KNOW WHAT THAT HOMOPHOBIC HOCKEY PUNK SAID WHEN HE SAW DYLAN BLEEDING?
"WATCH OUT, HE MIGHT HAVE AIDS!"
IN THIS DAY AND AGE! WE STILL HAVE IGNORANT MORONS LIKE THAT OUT THERE?
MARCO... I SAID IT WASN'T A BIG DEAL. JUST SOME STUPID JOCK STUFF. TRASH TALK.
WHAT?
WE'RE AT THE MALL. I NEED A NEW SUIT FOR MY COUSIN'S WEDDING. SOMETHING THAT DOESN'T MAKE ME LOOK LIKE A GOODFELLA.
OK... I'LL TALK TO YOU LATER... YES, I *PROMISE* WE'LL GO OVER THE COURSE CALENDAR!

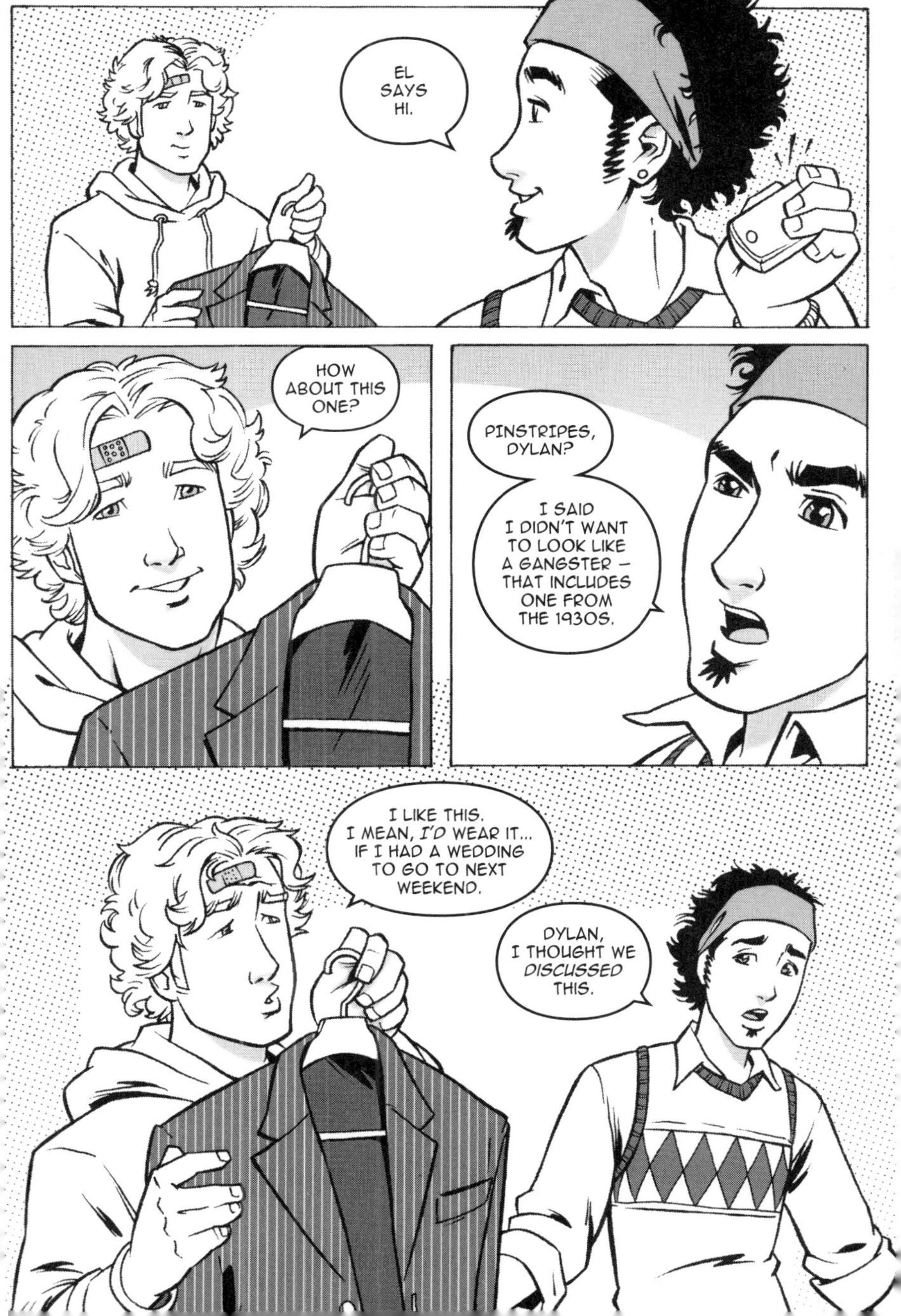
EL SAYS HI.
HOW ABOUT THIS ONE?
PINSTRIPES, DYLAN?
I SAID I DIDN'T WANT TO LOOK LIKE A GANGSTER – THAT INCLUDES ONE FROM THE 1930S.
I LIKE THIS. I MEAN, *I'D* WEAR IT... IF I HAD A WEDDING TO GO TO NEXT WEEKEND.
DYLAN, I THOUGHT WE *DISCUSSED* THIS.

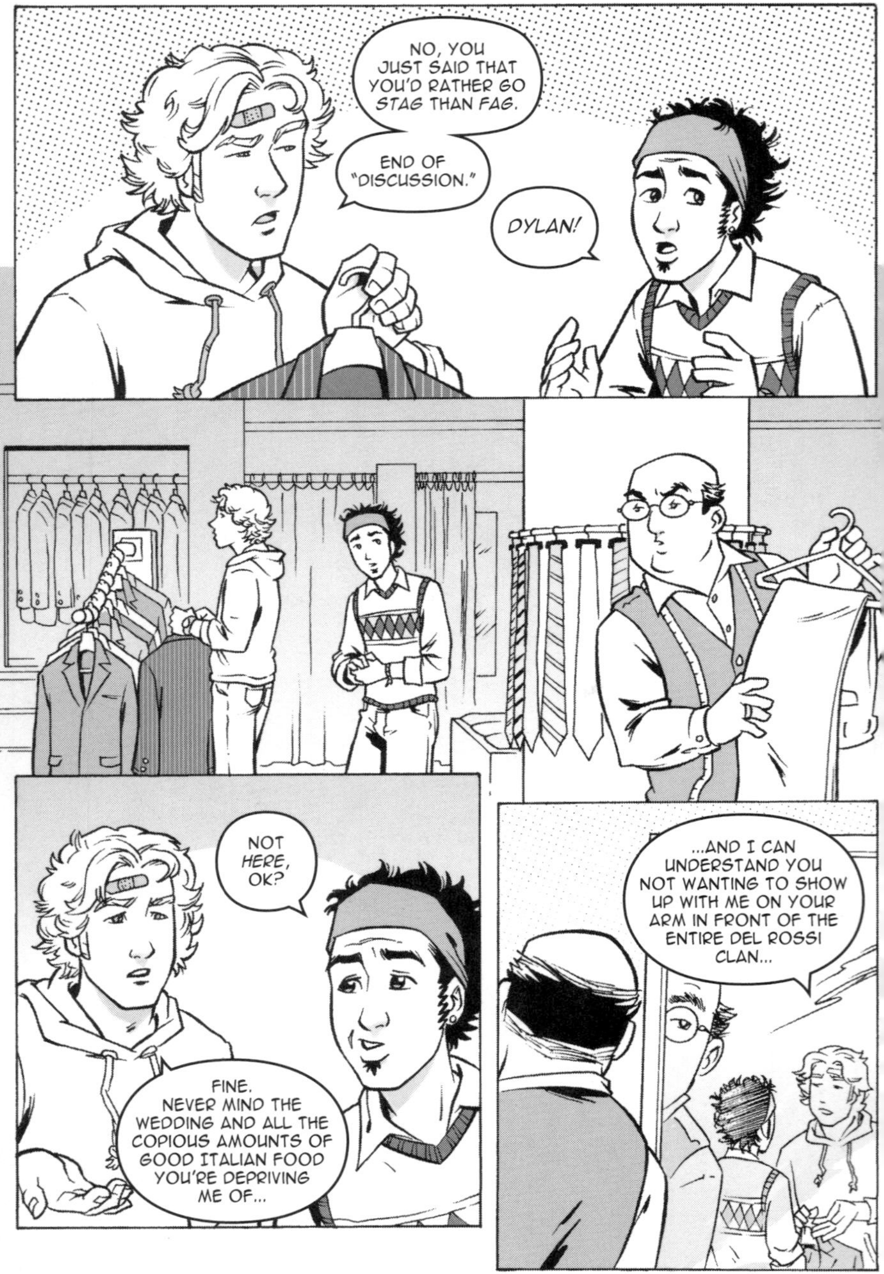
NO, YOU JUST SAID THAT YOU'D RATHER GO STAG THAN FAG.
END OF "DISCUSSION."
DYLAN!
NOT HERE, OK?
FINE. NEVER MIND THE WEDDING AND ALL THE COPIOUS AMOUNTS OF GOOD ITALIAN FOOD YOU'RE DEPRIVING ME OF...
...AND I CAN UNDERSTAND YOU NOT WANTING TO SHOW UP WITH ME ON YOUR ARM IN FRONT OF THE ENTIRE DEL ROSSI CLAN...

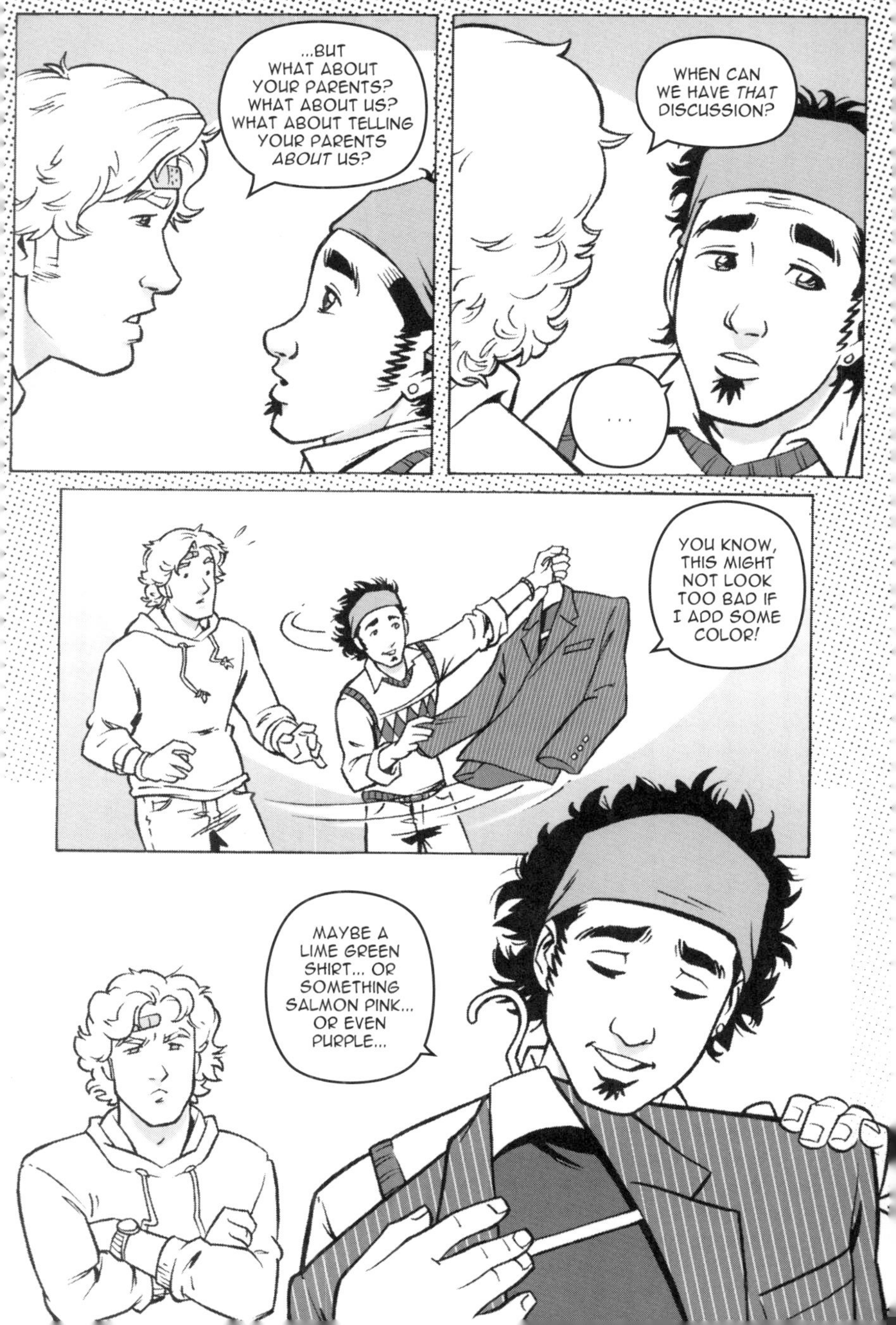
...BUT WHAT ABOUT YOUR PARENTS? WHAT ABOUT US? WHAT ABOUT TELLING YOUR PARENTS *ABOUT* US?
WHEN CAN WE HAVE *THAT* DISCUSSION?
. . .
YOU KNOW, THIS MIGHT NOT LOOK TOO BAD IF I ADD SOME COLOR!
MAYBE A LIME GREEN SHIRT... OR SOMETHING SALMON PINK... OR EVEN PURPLE...

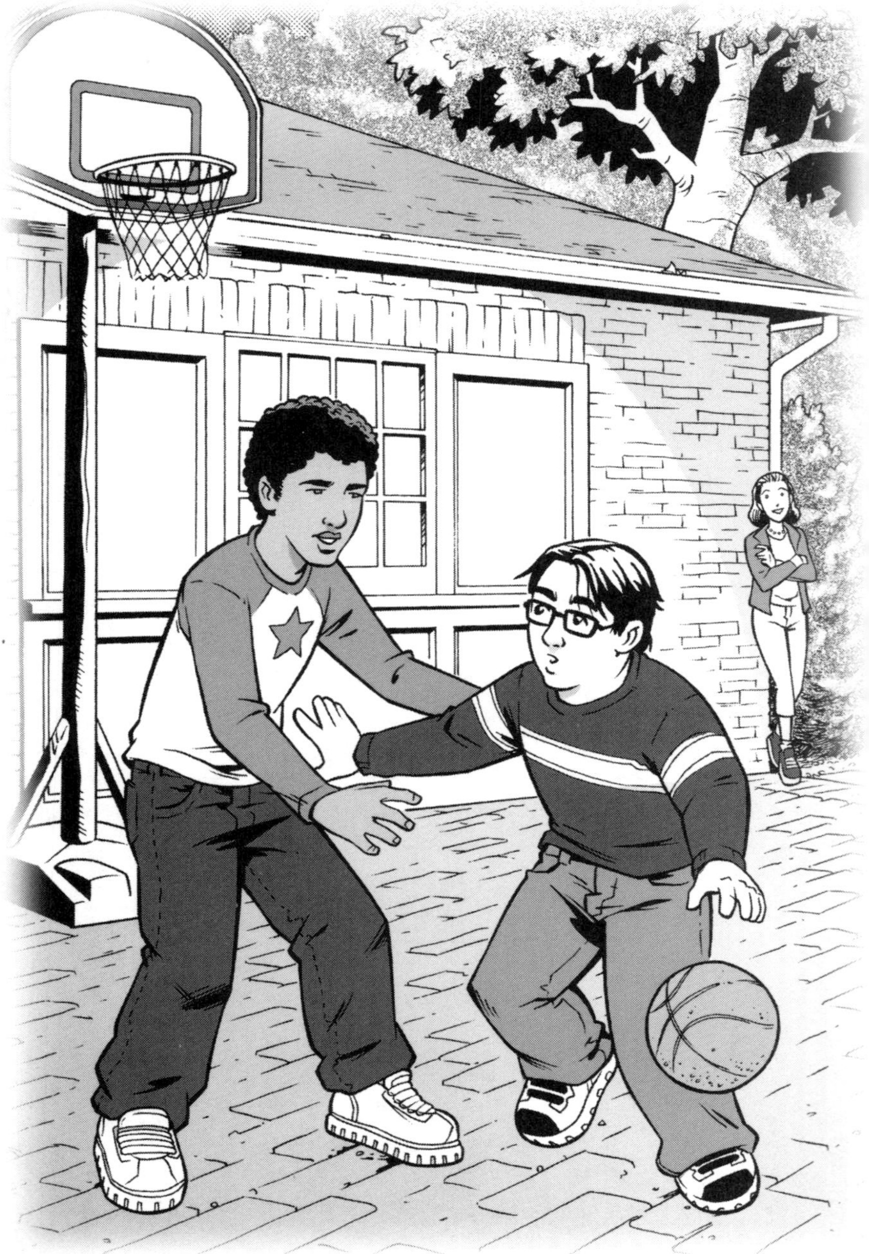

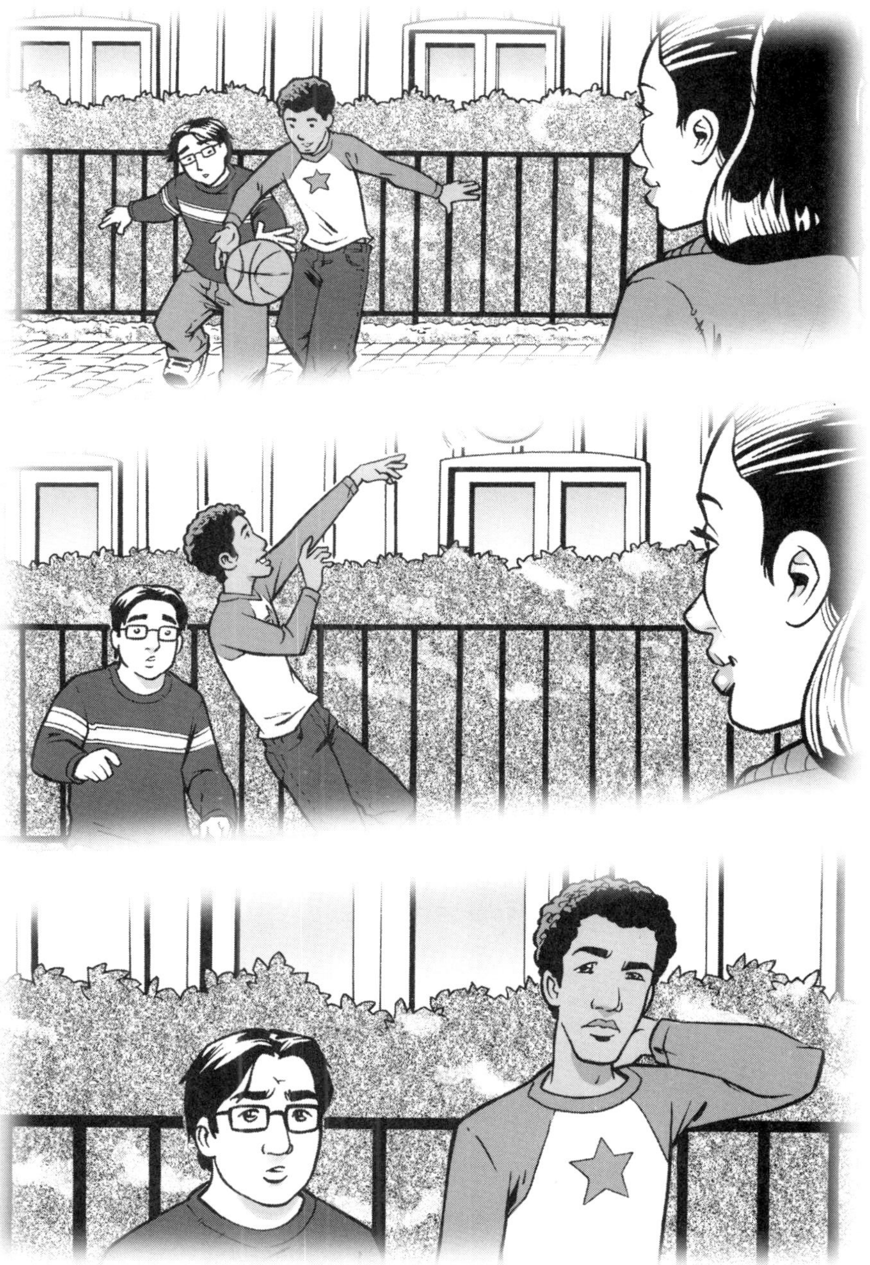

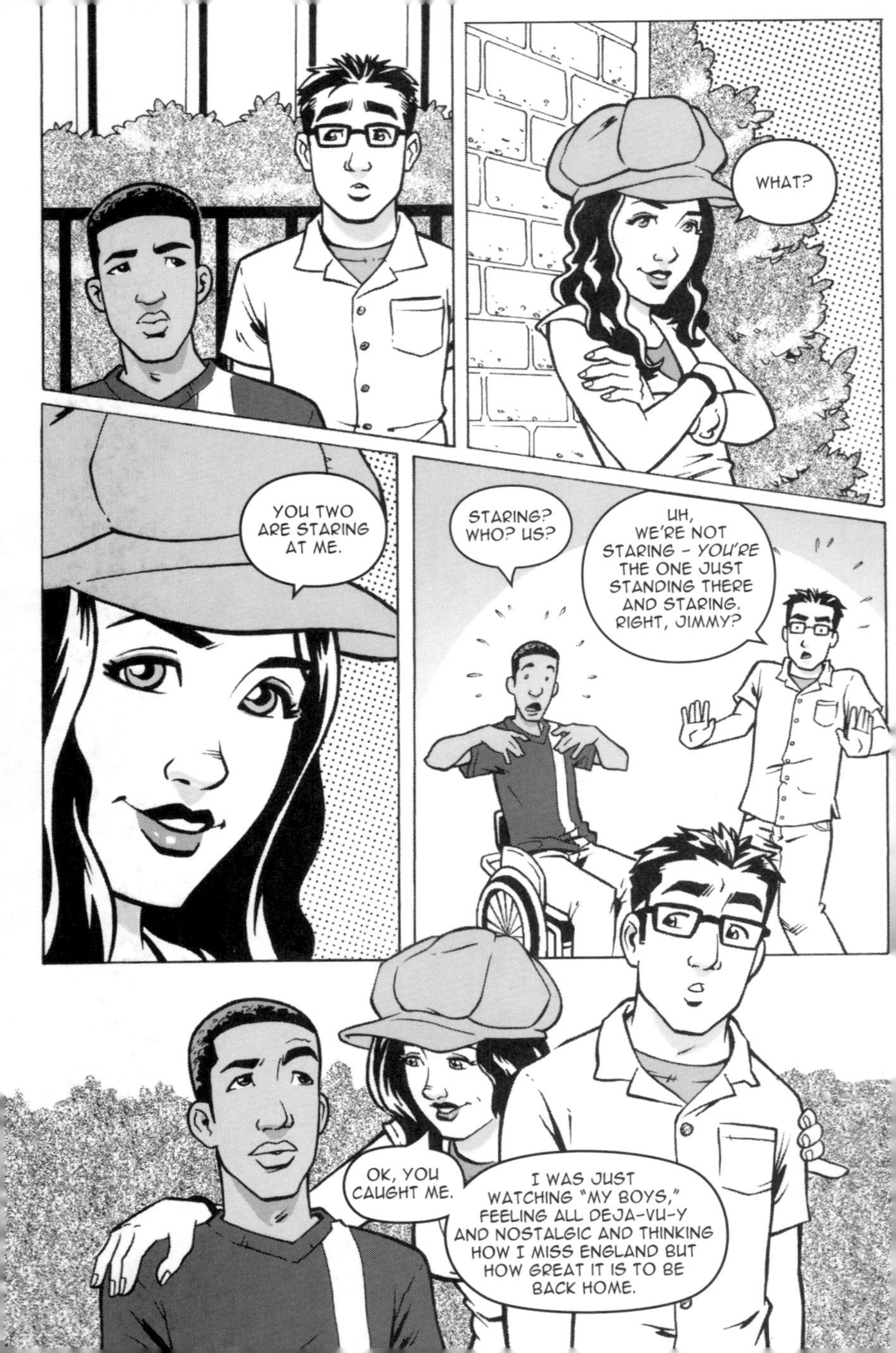
WHAT?
YOU TWO ARE STARING AT ME.
STARING? WHO? US?
UH, WE'RE NOT STARING - *YOU'RE* THE ONE JUST STANDING THERE AND STARING. RIGHT, JIMMY?
OK, YOU CAUGHT ME.
I WAS JUST WATCHING "MY BOYS," FEELING ALL DEJA-VU-Y AND NOSTALGIC AND THINKING HOW I MISS ENGLAND BUT HOW GREAT IT IS TO BE BACK HOME.

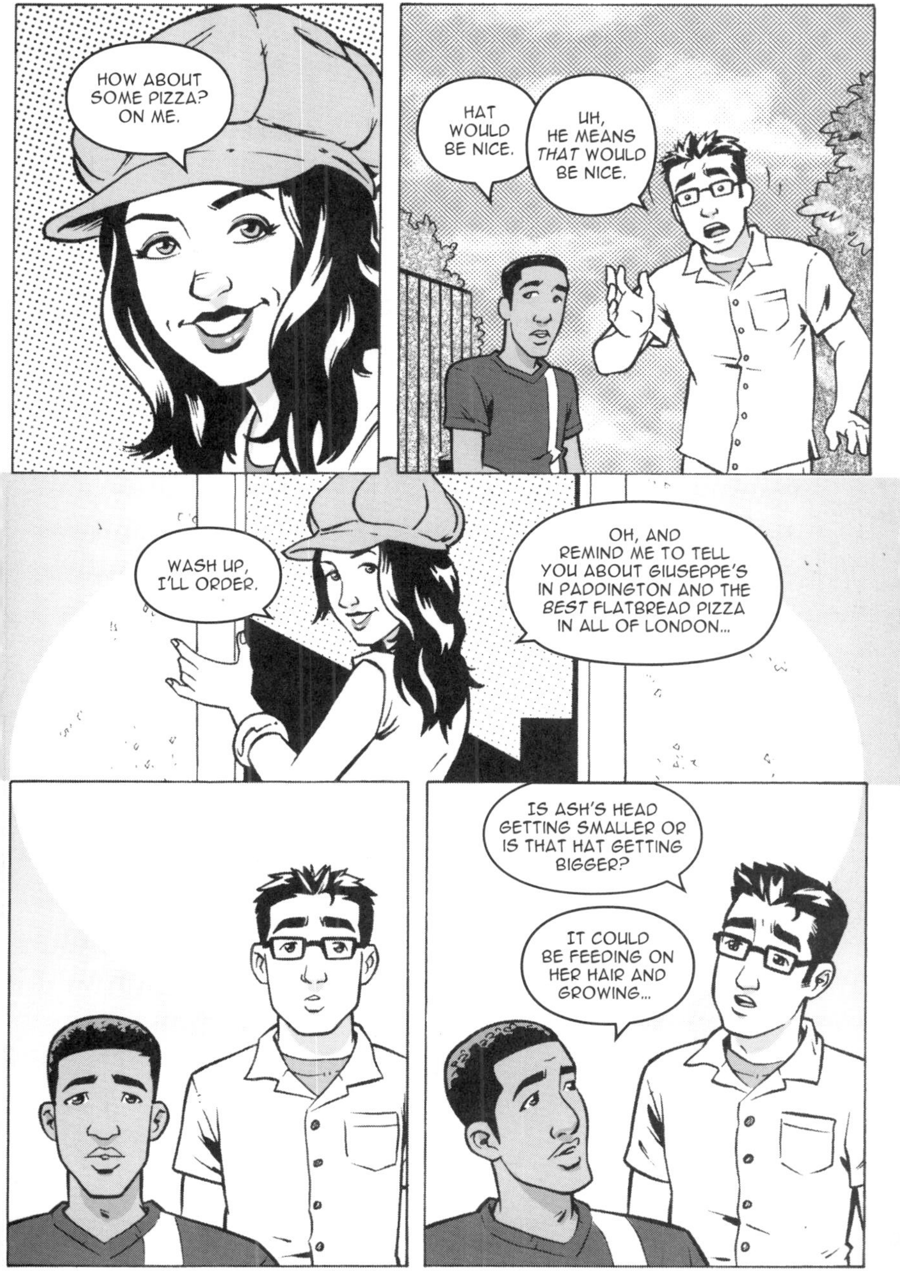
HOW ABOUT SOME PIZZA? ON ME.
HAT WOULD BE NICE.
UH, HE MEANS *THAT* WOULD BE NICE.
WASH UP, I'LL ORDER.
OH, AND REMIND ME TO TELL YOU ABOUT GIUSEPPE'S IN PADDINGTON AND THE *BEST* FLATBREAD PIZZA IN ALL OF LONDON...
IS ASH'S HEAD GETTING SMALLER OR IS THAT HAT GETTING BIGGER?
IT COULD BE FEEDING ON HER HAIR AND GROWING...

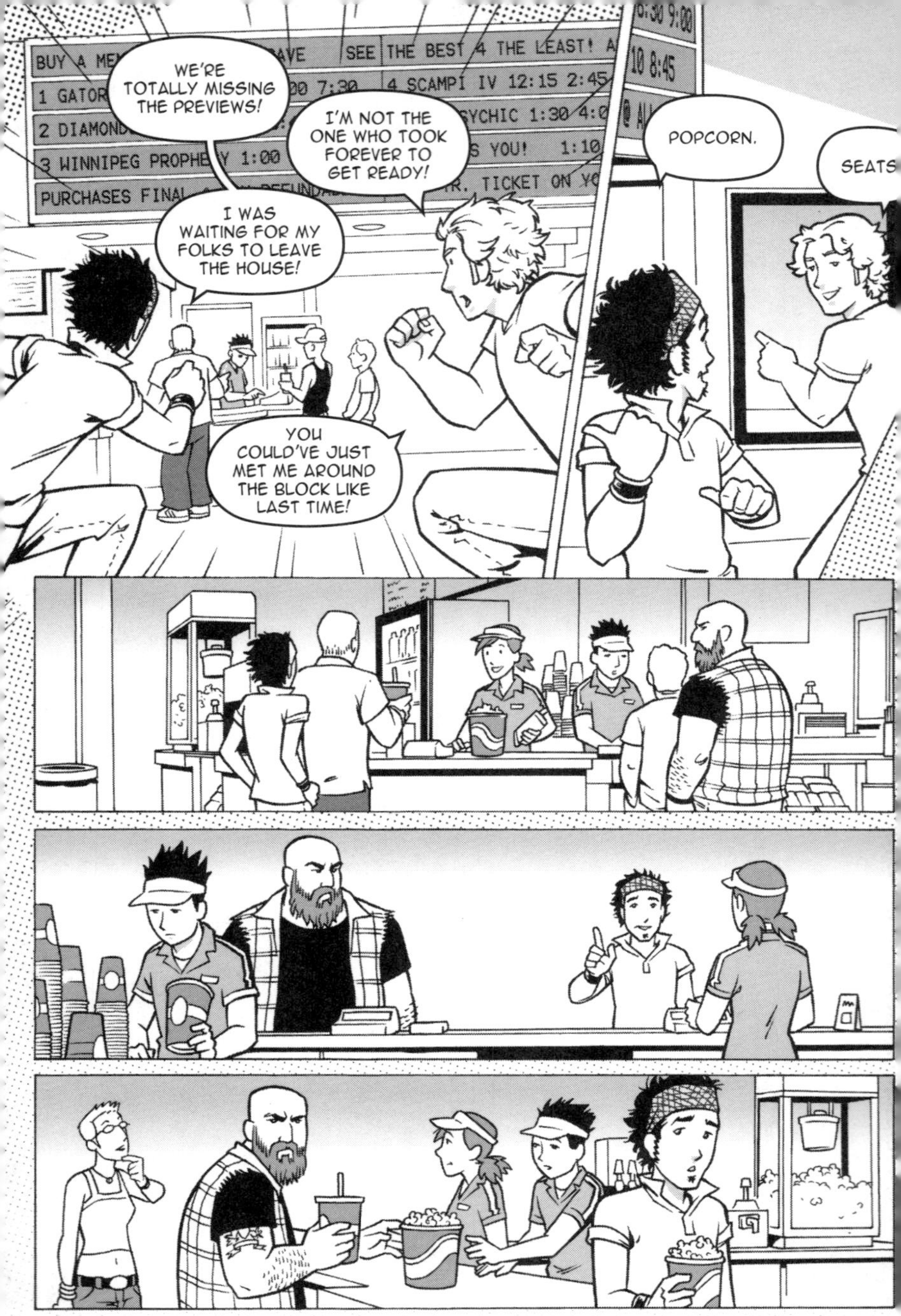
WE'RE TOTALLY MISSING THE PREVIEWS!
I'M NOT THE ONE WHO TOOK FOREVER TO GET READY!
I WAS WAITING FOR MY FOLKS TO LEAVE THE HOUSE!
YOU COULD'VE JUST MET ME AROUND THE BLOCK LIKE LAST TIME!
POPCORN.
SEATS

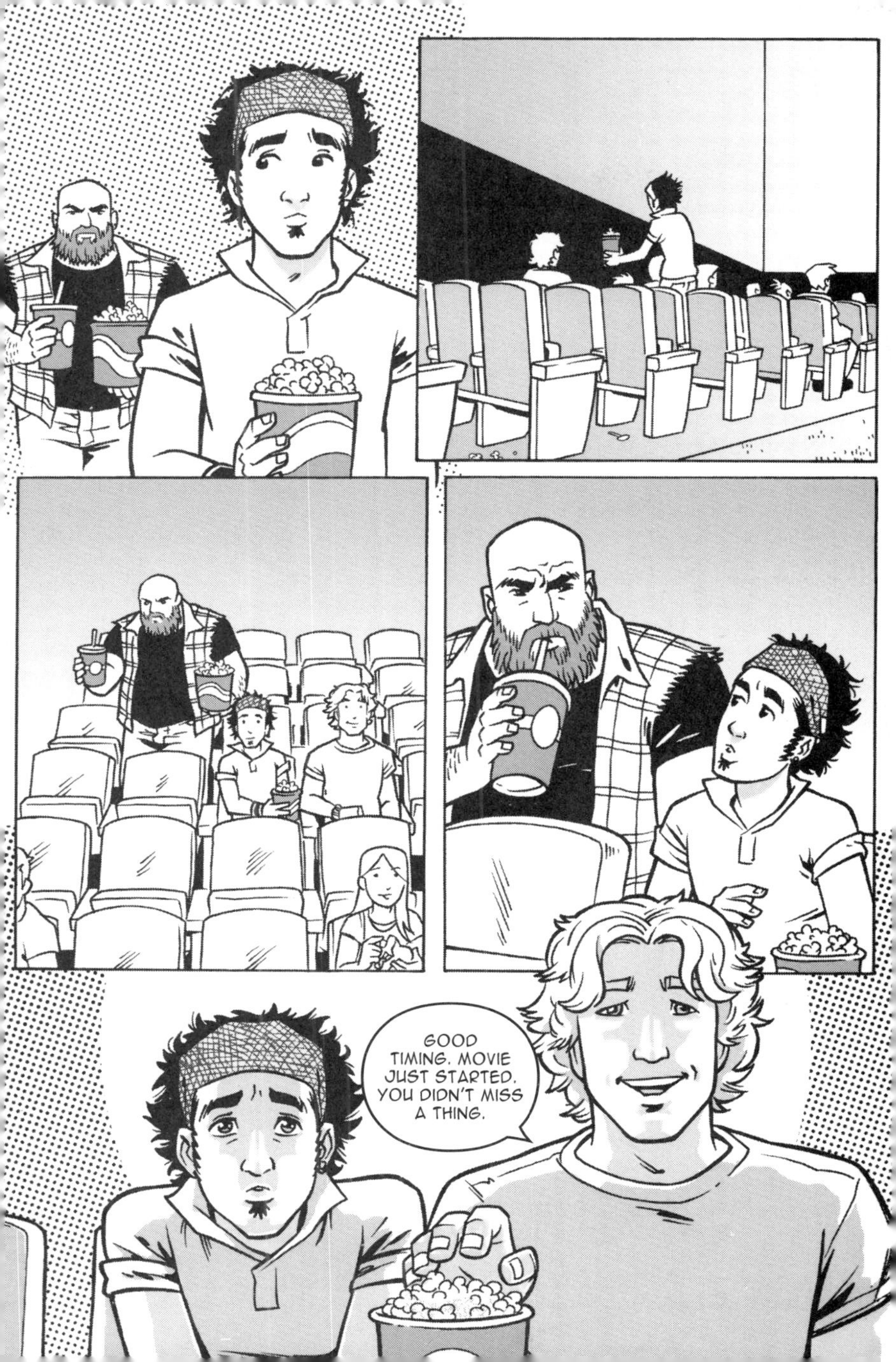
GOOD TIMING. MOVIE JUST STARTED. YOU DIDN'T MISS A THING.

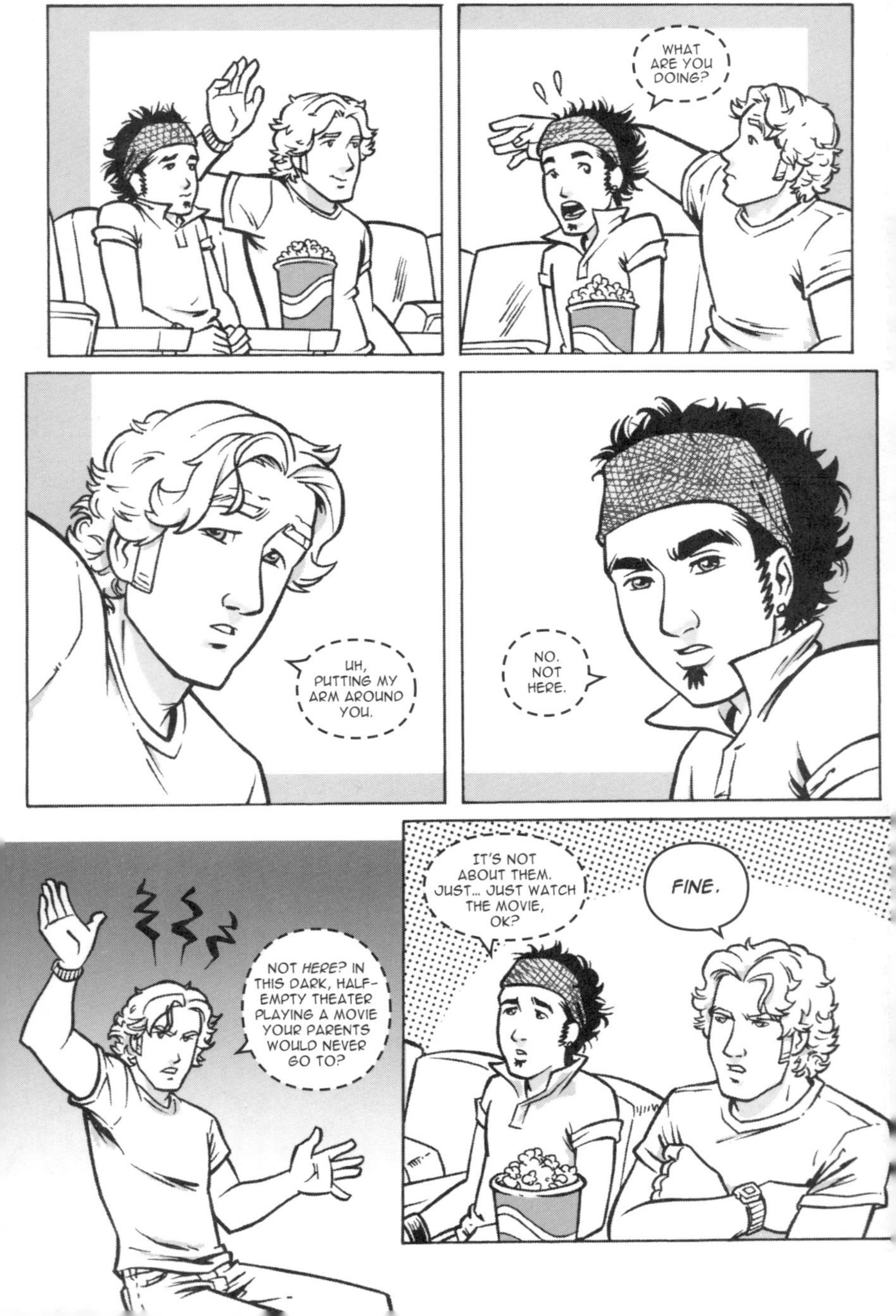
WHAT ARE YOU DOING?
UH, PUTTING MY ARM AROUND YOU.
NO. NOT HERE.
NOT *HERE*? IN THIS DARK, HALF-EMPTY THEATER PLAYING A MOVIE YOUR PARENTS WOULD NEVER GO TO?
IT'S NOT ABOUT THEM. JUST... JUST WATCH THE MOVIE, OK?
FINE.

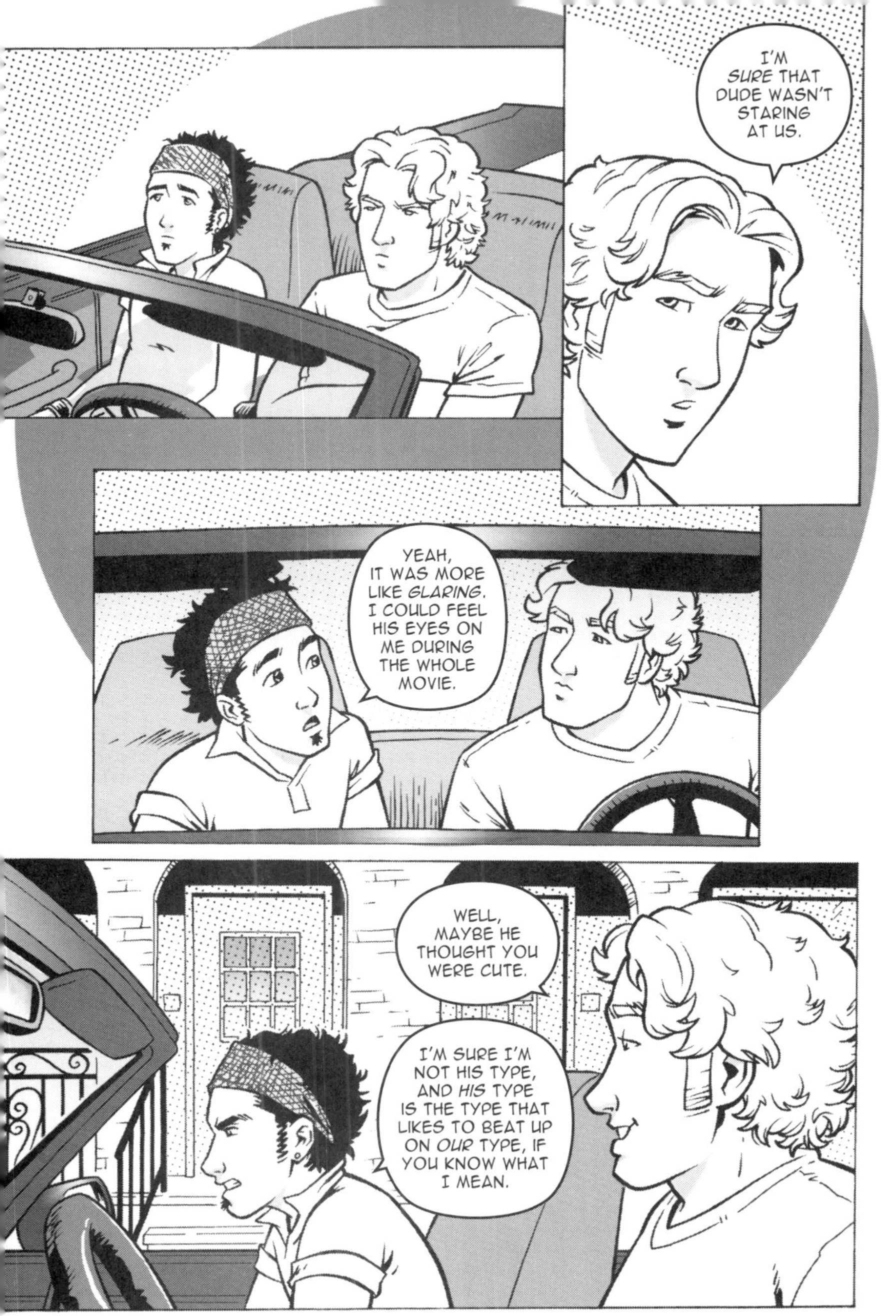
I'M *SURE* THAT DUDE WASN'T STARING AT US.
YEAH, IT WAS MORE LIKE *GLARING*. I COULD FEEL HIS EYES ON ME DURING THE WHOLE MOVIE.
WELL, MAYBE HE THOUGHT YOU WERE CUTE.
I'M SURE I'M NOT HIS TYPE, AND *HIS* TYPE IS THE TYPE THAT LIKES TO BEAT UP ON *OUR* TYPE, IF YOU KNOW WHAT I MEAN.

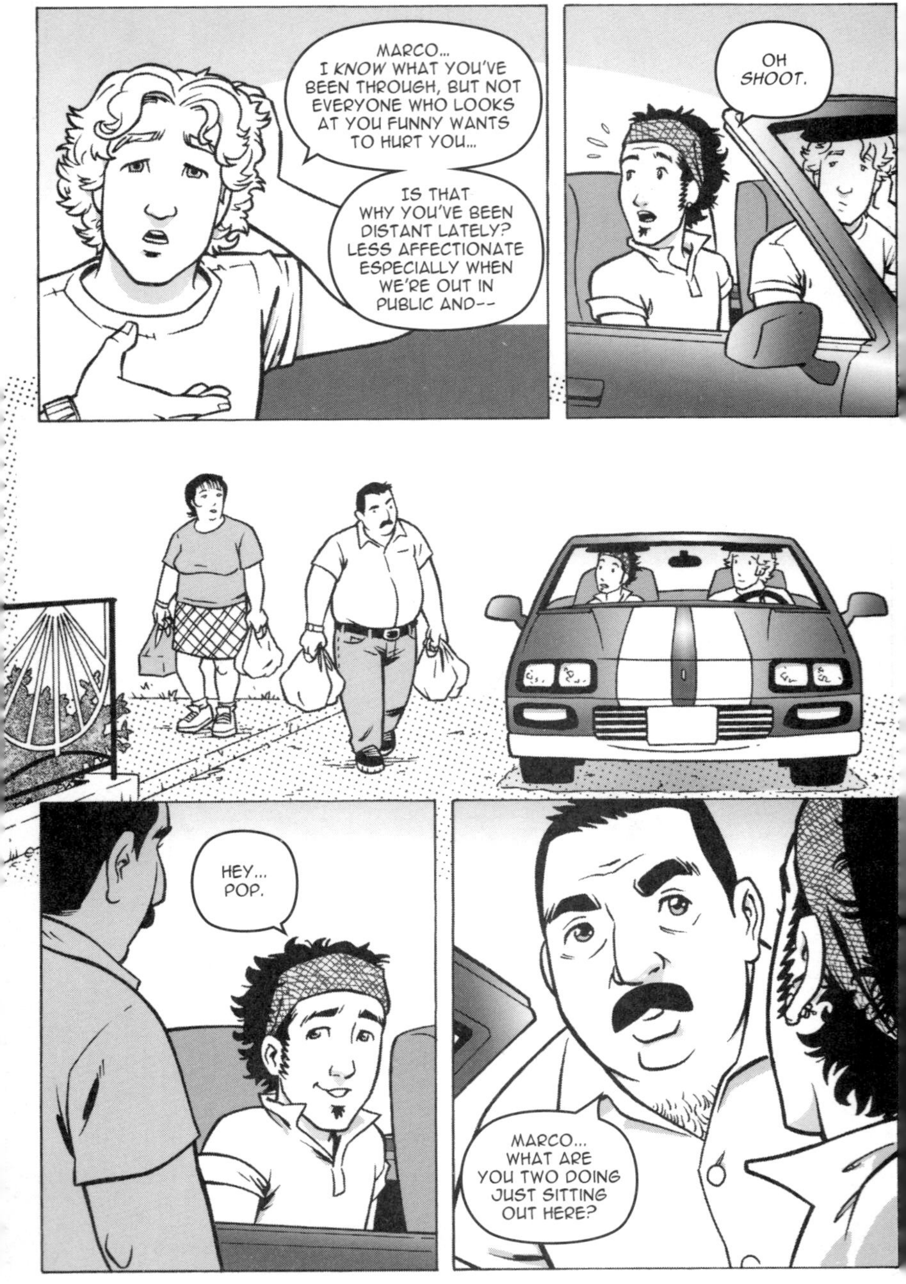
MARCO... I *KNOW* WHAT YOU'VE BEEN THROUGH, BUT NOT EVERYONE WHO LOOKS AT YOU FUNNY WANTS TO HURT YOU...
IS THAT WHY YOU'VE BEEN DISTANT LATELY? LESS AFFECTIONATE ESPECIALLY WHEN WE'RE OUT IN PUBLIC AND--
OH *SHOOT.*
HEY... POP.
MARCO... WHAT ARE YOU TWO DOING JUST SITTING OUT HERE?

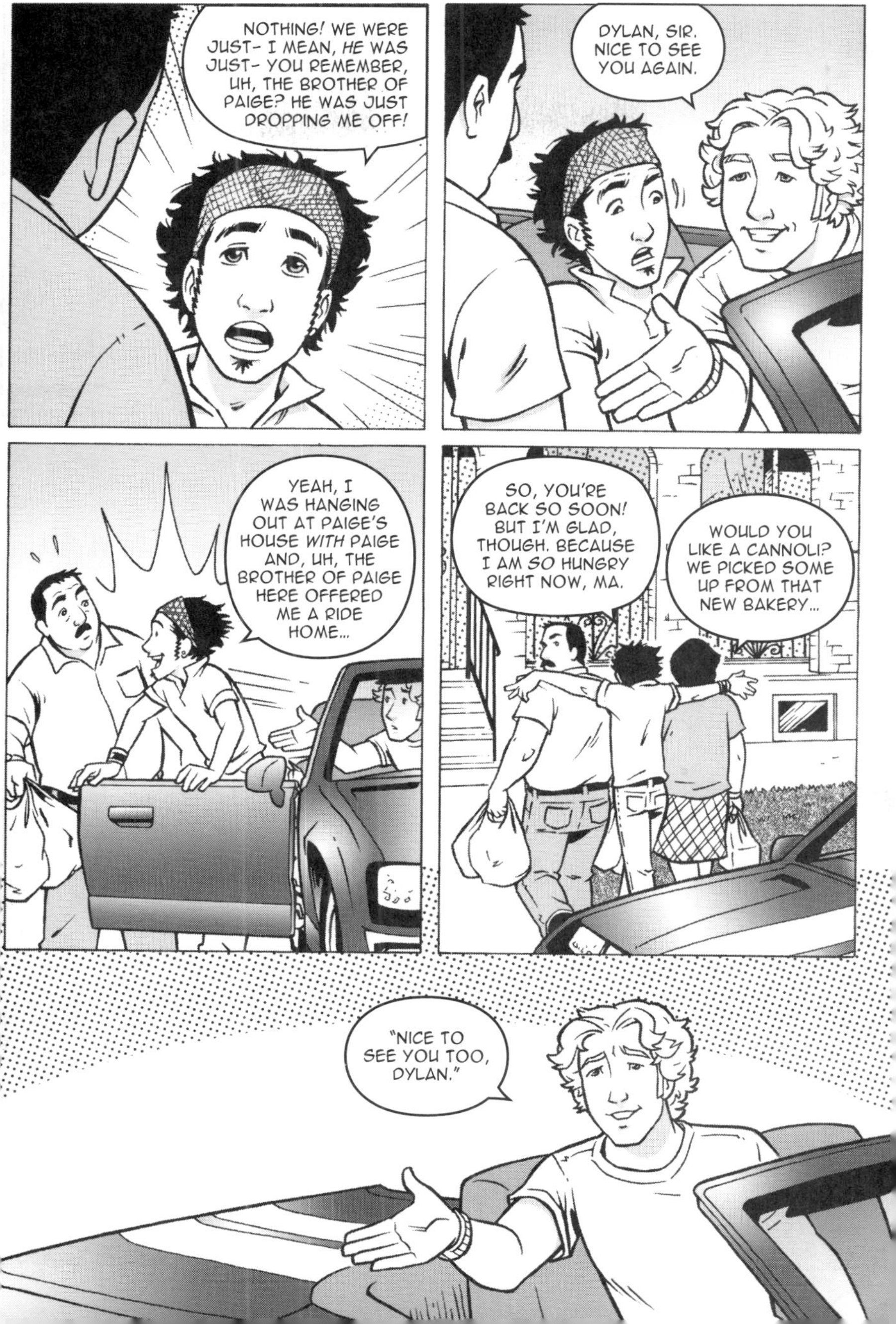
NOTHING! WE WERE JUST- I MEAN, HE WAS JUST- YOU REMEMBER, UH, THE BROTHER OF PAIGE? HE WAS JUST DROPPING ME OFF!
DYLAN, SIR. NICE TO SEE YOU AGAIN.
YEAH, I WAS HANGING OUT AT PAIGE'S HOUSE WITH PAIGE AND, UH, THE BROTHER OF PAIGE HERE OFFERED ME A RIDE HOME...
SO, YOU'RE BACK SO SOON! BUT I'M GLAD, THOUGH. BECAUSE I AM SO HUNGRY RIGHT NOW, MA.
WOULD YOU LIKE A CANNOLI? WE PICKED SOME UP FROM THAT NEW BAKERY...
"NICE TO SEE YOU TOO, DYLAN."

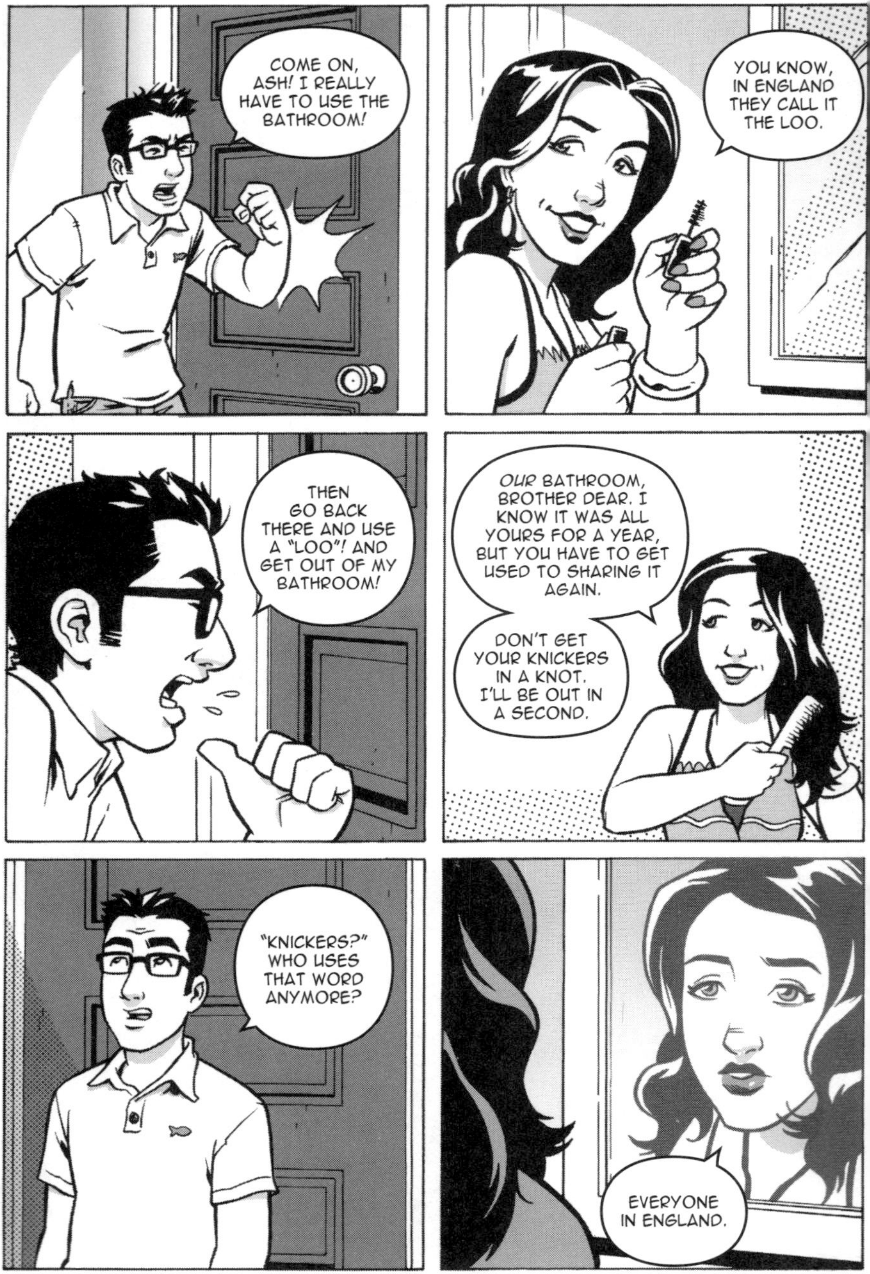
COME ON, ASH! I REALLY HAVE TO USE THE BATHROOM!
YOU KNOW, IN ENGLAND THEY CALL IT THE LOO.
THEN GO BACK THERE AND USE A "LOO"! AND GET OUT OF MY BATHROOM!
OUR BATHROOM, BROTHER DEAR. I KNOW IT WAS ALL YOURS FOR A YEAR, BUT YOU HAVE TO GET USED TO SHARING IT AGAIN.
DON'T GET YOUR KNICKERS IN A KNOT. I'LL BE OUT IN A SECOND.
"KNICKERS?" WHO USES THAT WORD ANYMORE?
EVERYONE IN ENGLAND.

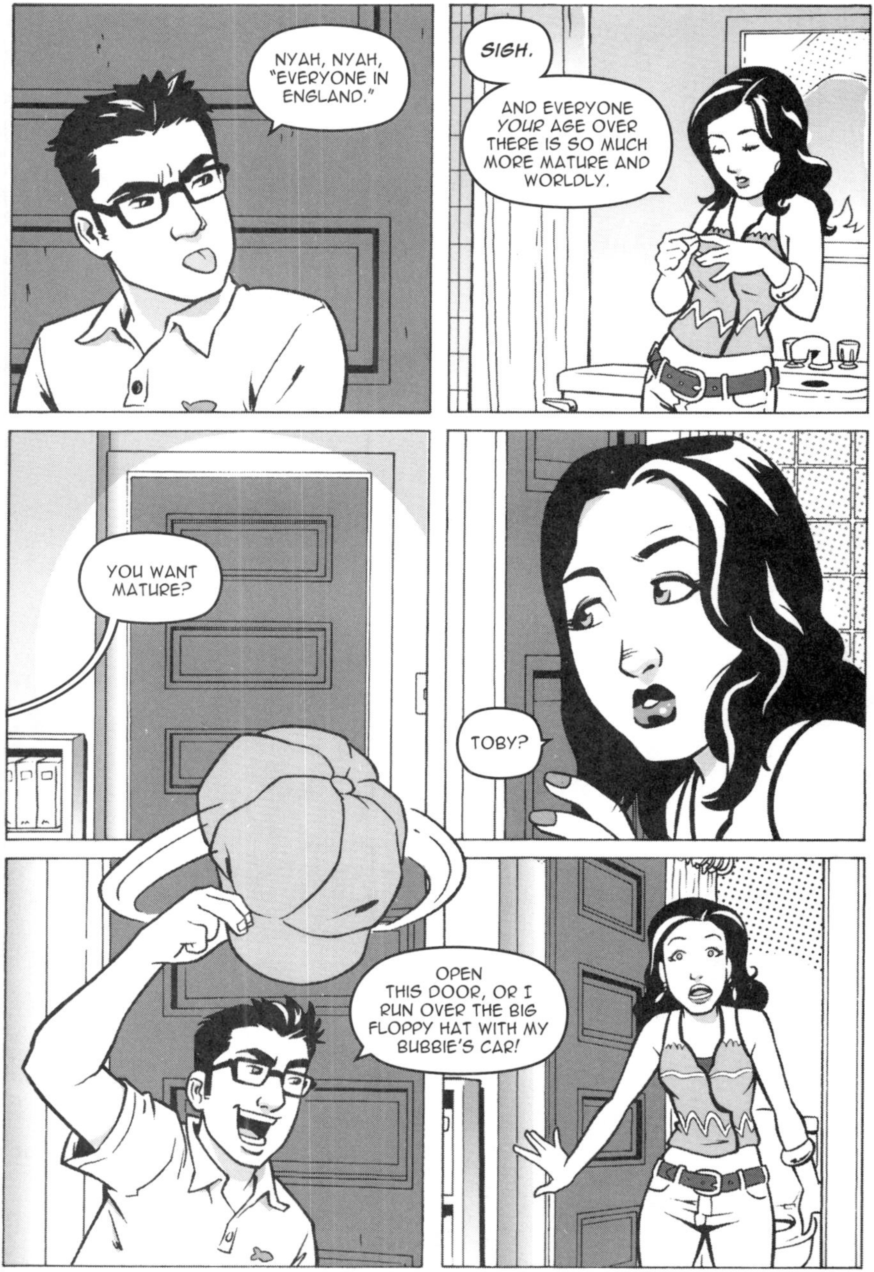

NYAH, NYAH, "EVERYONE IN ENGLAND."
SIGH.
AND EVERYONE *YOUR* AGE OVER THERE IS SO MUCH MORE MATURE AND WORLDLY.
YOU WANT MATURE?
TOBY?
OPEN THIS DOOR, OR I RUN OVER THE BIG FLOPPY HAT WITH MY BUBBIE'S CAR!

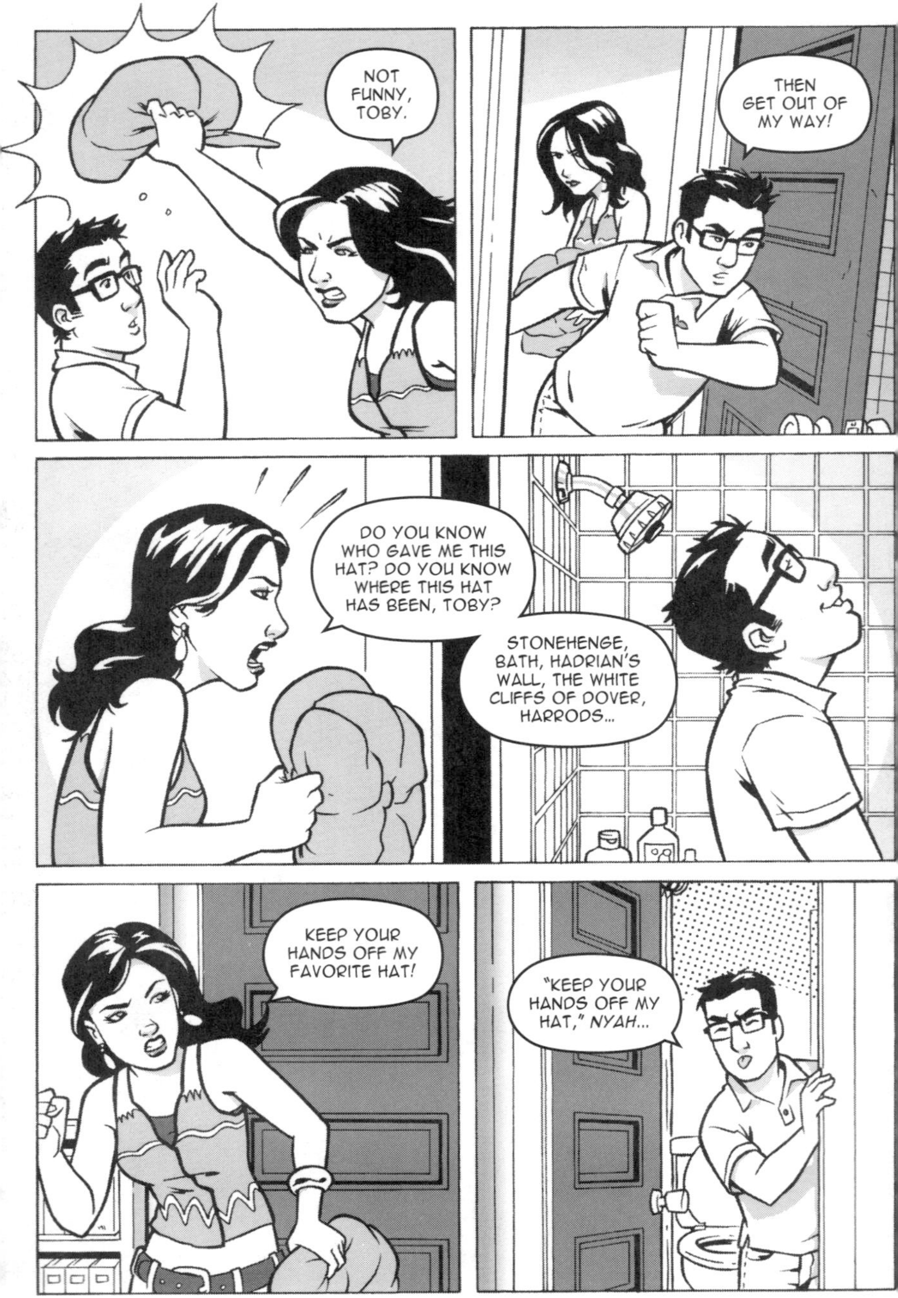

NOT FUNNY, TOBY.
THEN GET OUT OF MY WAY!
DO YOU KNOW WHO GAVE ME THIS HAT? DO YOU KNOW WHERE THIS HAT HAS BEEN, TOBY?
STONEHENGE, BATH, HADRIAN'S WALL, THE WHITE CLIFFS OF DOVER, HARRODS...
KEEP YOUR HANDS OFF MY FAVORITE HAT!
"KEEP YOUR HANDS OFF MY HAT," *NYAH*...

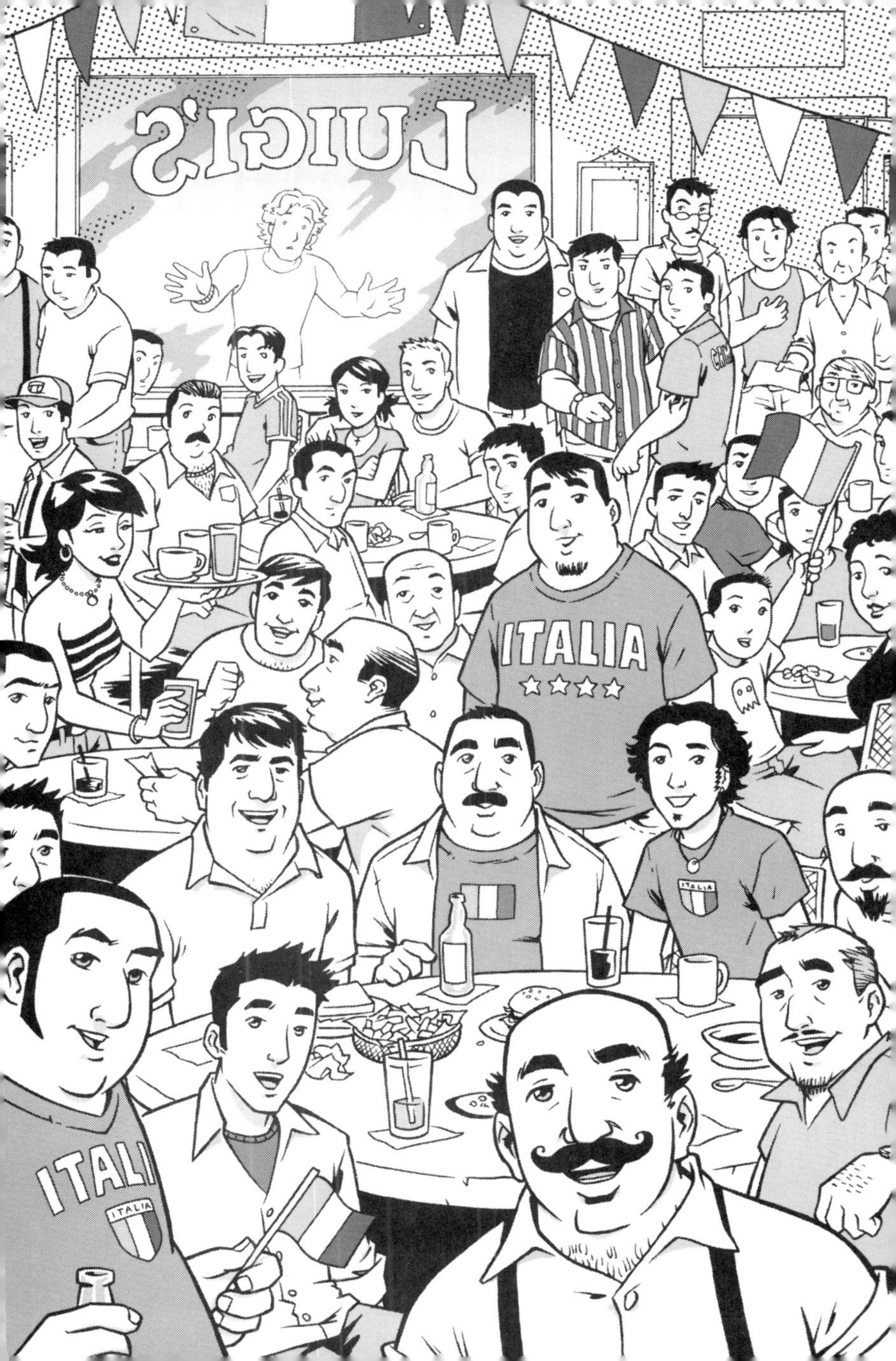
LUIGI'S
ITALIA
ITALI
ITALIA

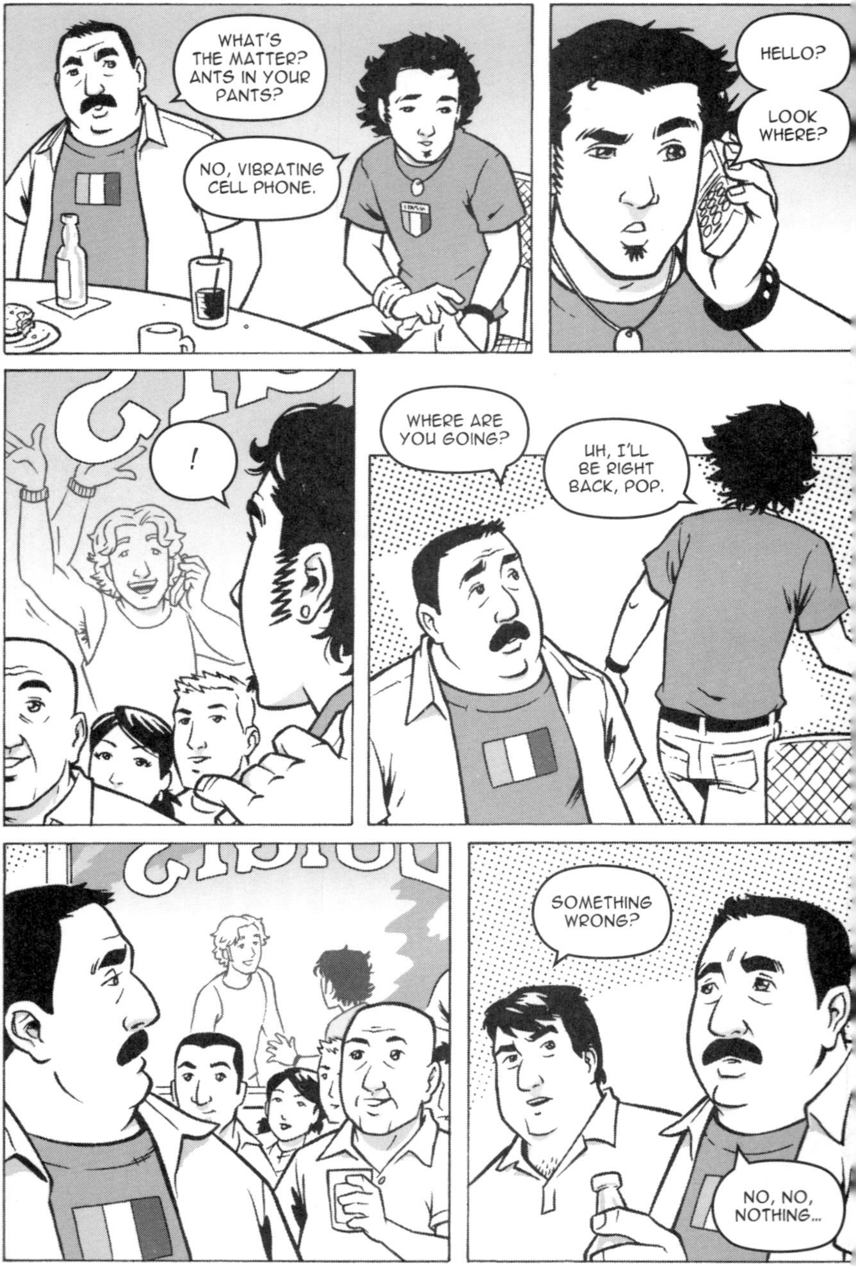
WHAT'S THE MATTER? ANTS IN YOUR PANTS?
NO, VIBRATING CELL PHONE.
HELLO?
LOOK WHERE?
!
WHERE ARE YOU GOING?
UH, I'LL BE RIGHT BACK, POP.
SOMETHING WRONG?
NO, NO, NOTHING...

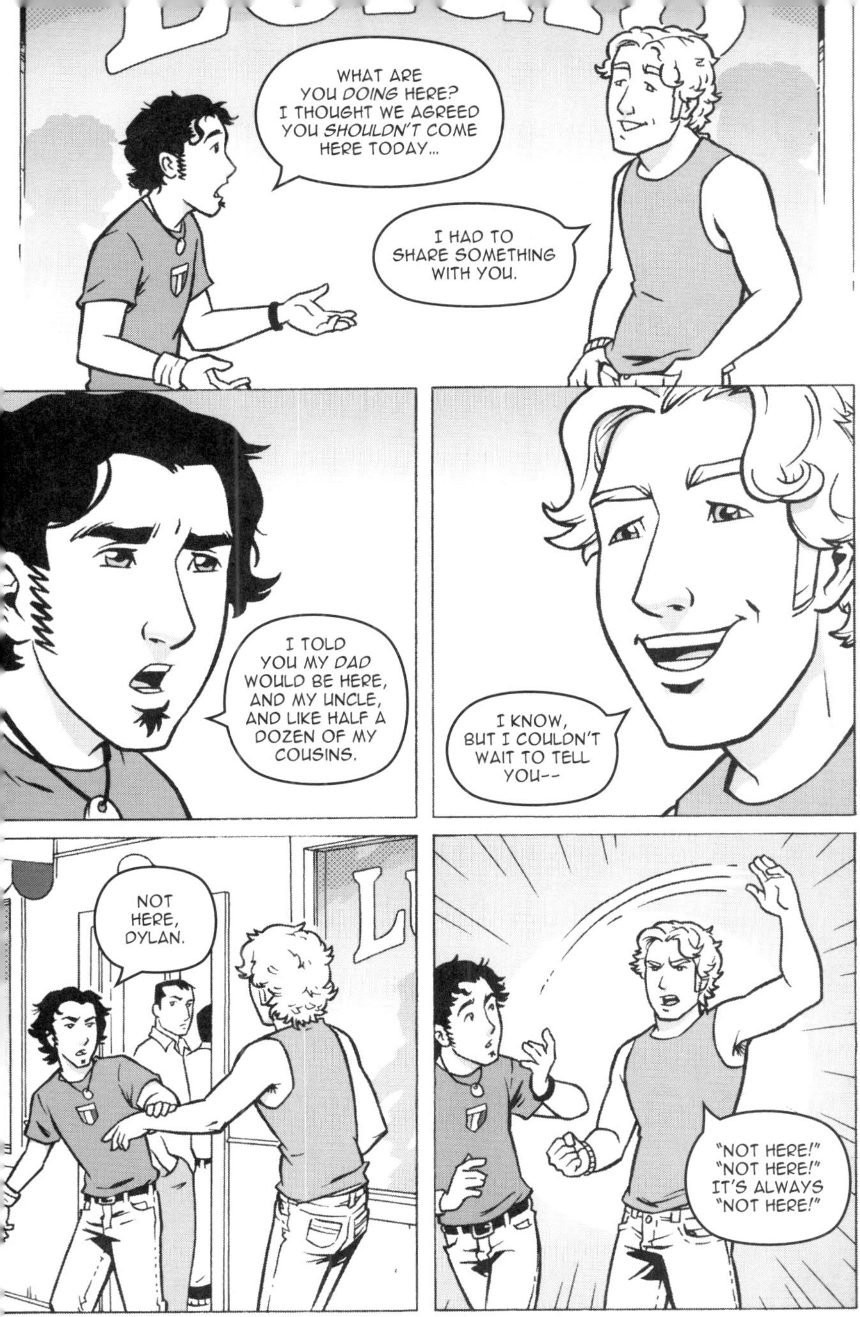
WHAT ARE YOU *DOING* HERE? I THOUGHT WE AGREED YOU *SHOULDN'T* COME HERE TODAY...
I HAD TO SHARE SOMETHING WITH YOU.
I TOLD YOU MY *DAD* WOULD BE HERE, AND MY UNCLE, AND LIKE HALF A DOZEN OF MY COUSINS.
I KNOW, BUT I COULDN'T WAIT TO TELL YOU--
NOT HERE, DYLAN.
"NOT HERE!" "NOT HERE!" IT'S ALWAYS "NOT HERE!"

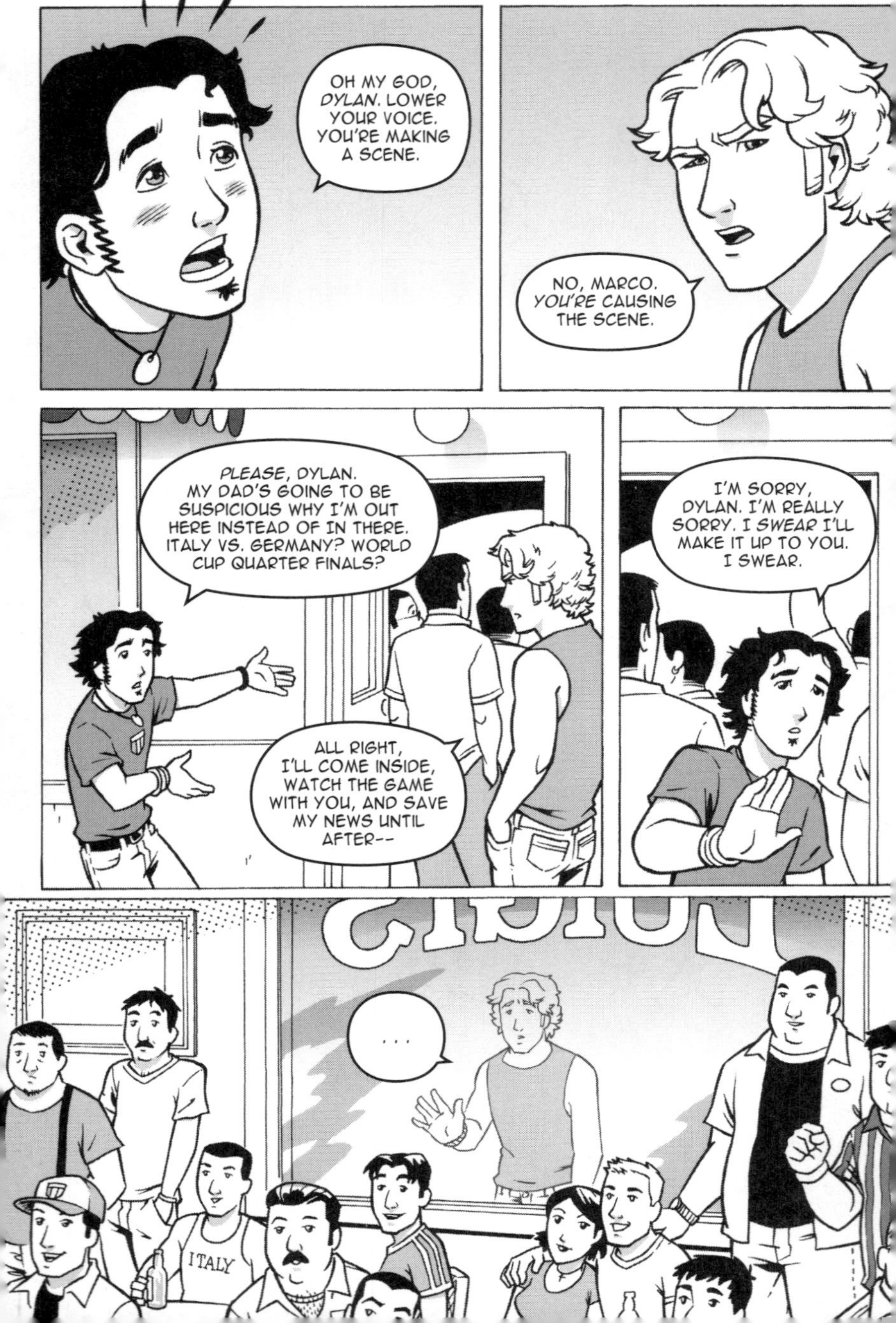
OH MY GOD, DYLAN. LOWER YOUR VOICE. YOU'RE MAKING A SCENE.
NO, MARCO. YOU'RE CAUSING THE SCENE.
PLEASE, DYLAN. MY DAD'S GOING TO BE SUSPICIOUS WHY I'M OUT HERE INSTEAD OF IN THERE. ITALY VS. GERMANY? WORLD CUP QUARTER FINALS?
ALL RIGHT, I'LL COME INSIDE, WATCH THE GAME WITH YOU, AND SAVE MY NEWS UNTIL AFTER--
I'M SORRY, DYLAN. I'M REALLY SORRY. I SWEAR I'LL MAKE IT UP TO YOU. I SWEAR.
. . .
ITALY

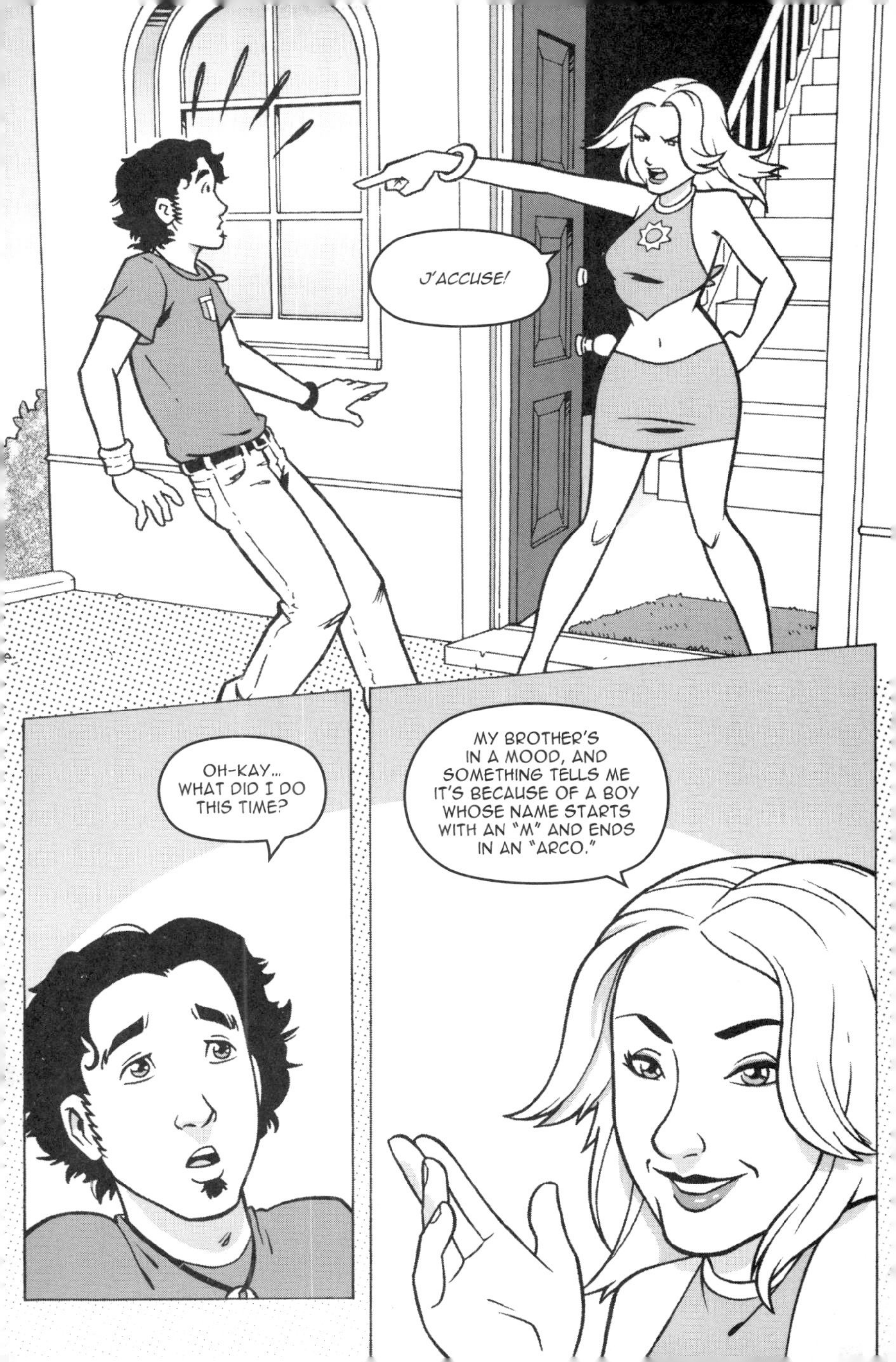
J'ACCUSE!
OH-KAY... WHAT DID I DO THIS TIME?
MY BROTHER'S IN A MOOD, AND SOMETHING TELLS ME IT'S BECAUSE OF A BOY WHOSE NAME STARTS WITH AN "M" AND ENDS IN AN "ARCO."

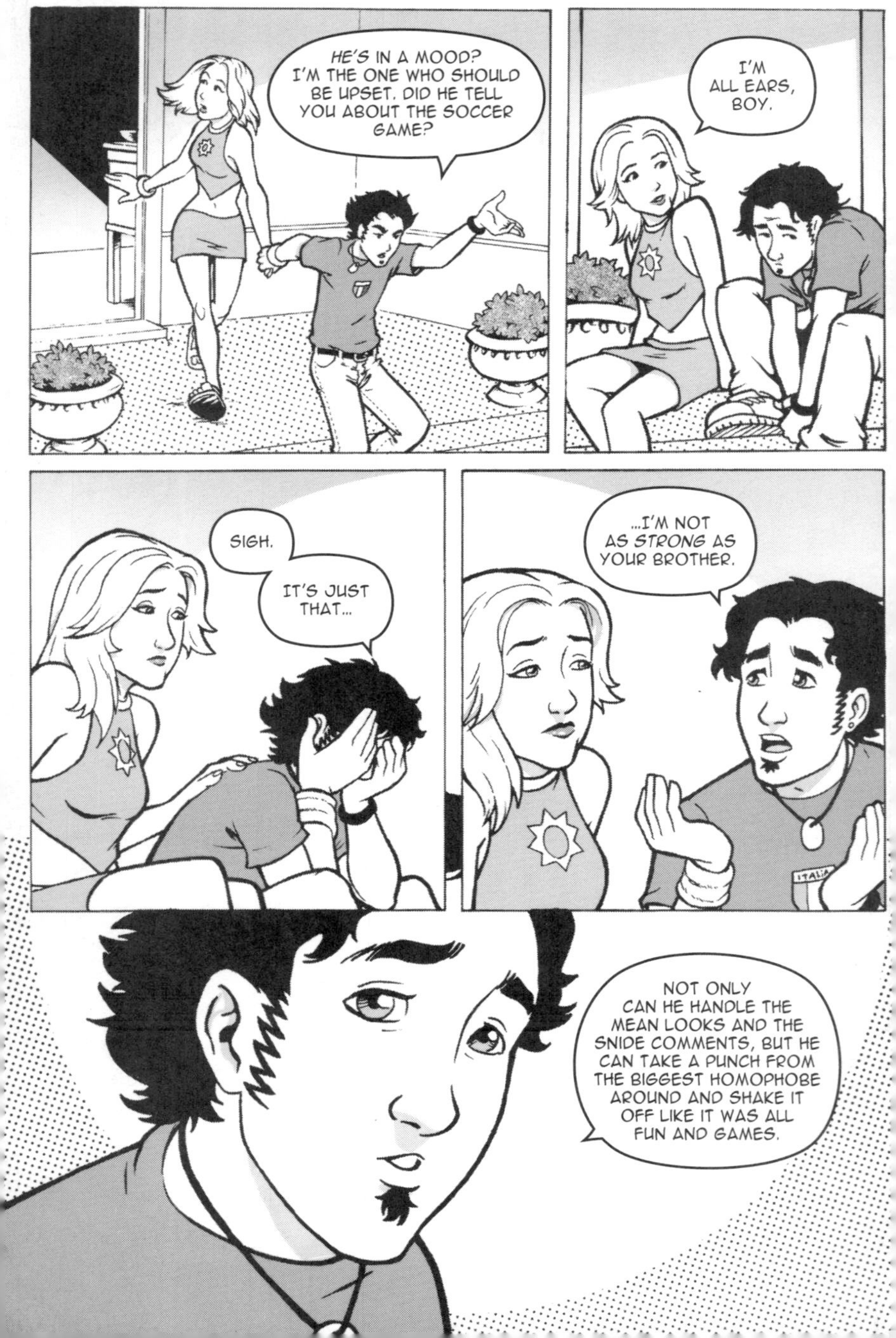
HE'S IN A MOOD? I'M THE ONE WHO SHOULD BE UPSET. DID HE TELL YOU ABOUT THE SOCCER GAME?
I'M ALL EARS, BOY.
SIGH.
IT'S JUST THAT...
...I'M NOT AS STRONG AS YOUR BROTHER.
NOT ONLY CAN HE HANDLE THE MEAN LOOKS AND THE SNIDE COMMENTS, BUT HE CAN TAKE A PUNCH FROM THE BIGGEST HOMOPHOBE AROUND AND SHAKE IT OFF LIKE IT WAS ALL FUN AND GAMES.

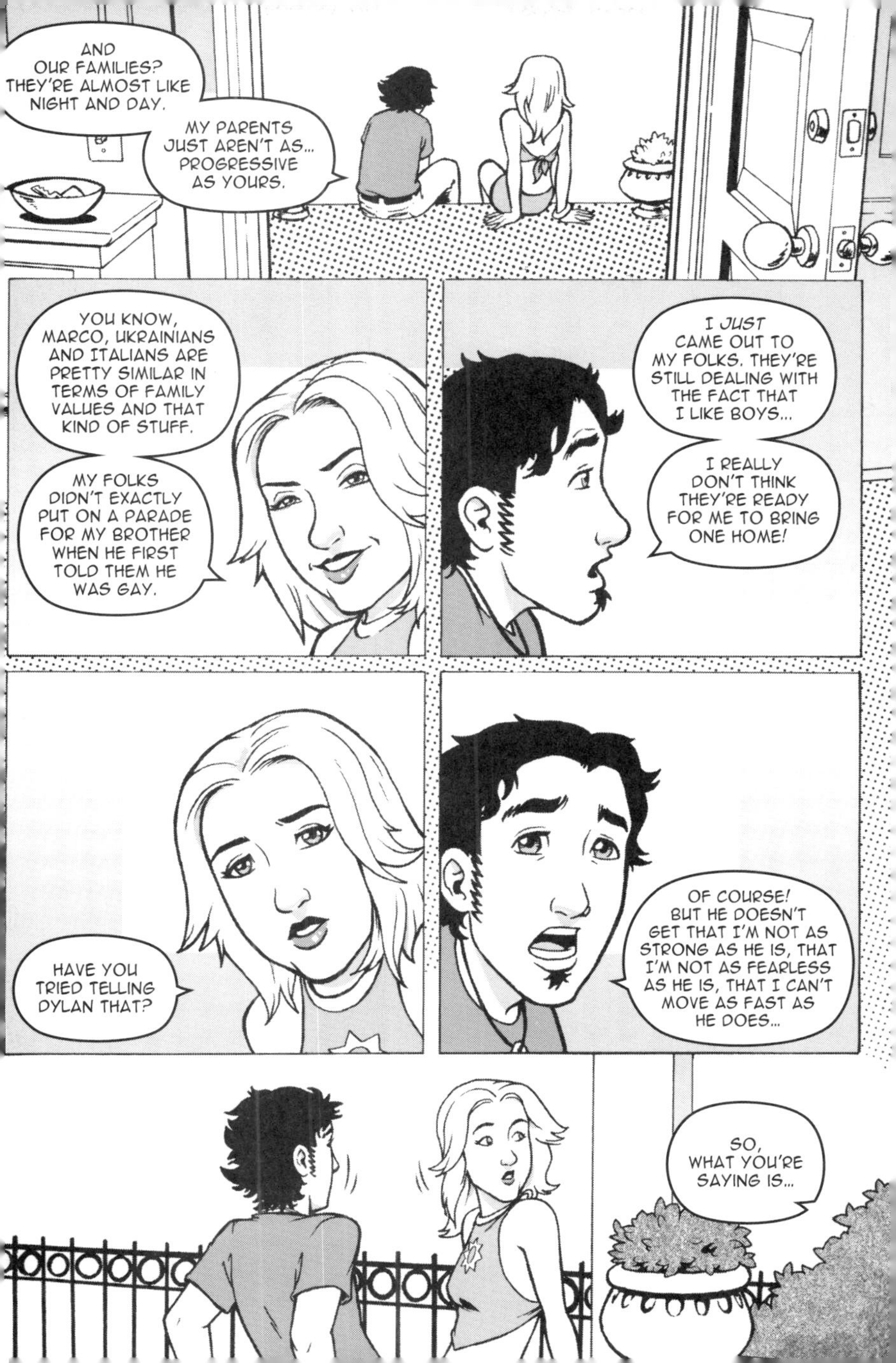
AND OUR FAMILIES? THEY'RE ALMOST LIKE NIGHT AND DAY.
MY PARENTS JUST AREN'T AS... PROGRESSIVE AS YOURS.
YOU KNOW, MARCO, UKRAINIANS AND ITALIANS ARE PRETTY SIMILAR IN TERMS OF FAMILY VALUES AND THAT KIND OF STUFF.
MY FOLKS DIDN'T EXACTLY PUT ON A PARADE FOR MY BROTHER WHEN HE FIRST TOLD THEM HE WAS GAY.
I *JUST* CAME OUT TO MY FOLKS. THEY'RE STILL DEALING WITH THE FACT THAT I LIKE BOYS...
I REALLY DON'T THINK THEY'RE READY FOR ME TO BRING ONE HOME!
HAVE YOU TRIED TELLING DYLAN THAT?
OF COURSE! BUT HE DOESN'T GET THAT I'M NOT AS STRONG AS HE IS, THAT I'M NOT AS FEARLESS AS HE IS, THAT I CAN'T MOVE AS FAST AS HE DOES...
SO, WHAT YOU'RE SAYING IS...

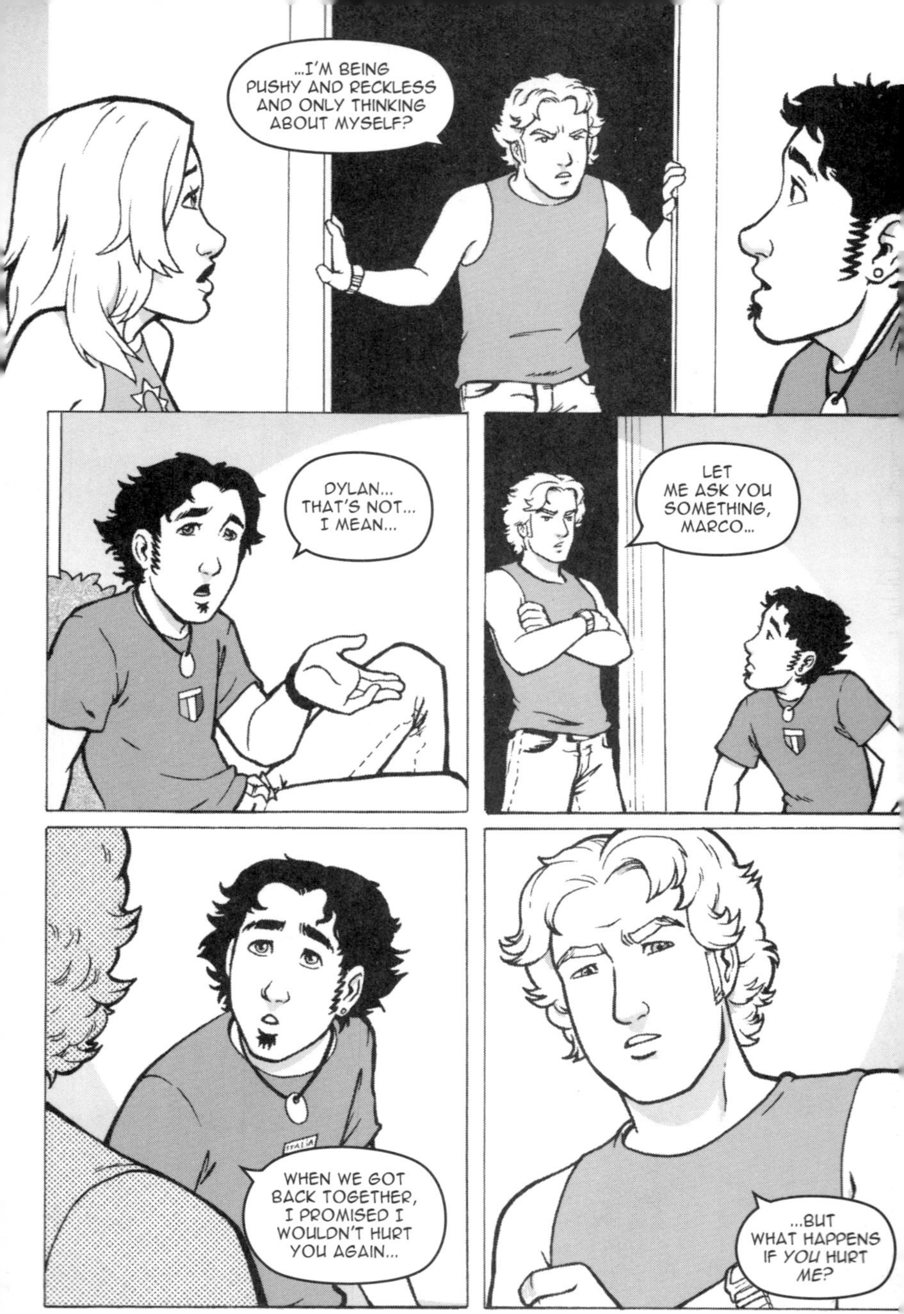
...I'M BEING PUSHY AND RECKLESS AND ONLY THINKING ABOUT MYSELF?
DYLAN... THAT'S NOT... I MEAN...
LET ME ASK YOU SOMETHING, MARCO...
WHEN WE GOT BACK TOGETHER, I PROMISED I WOULDN'T HURT YOU AGAIN...
...BUT WHAT HAPPENS IF *YOU* HURT ME?

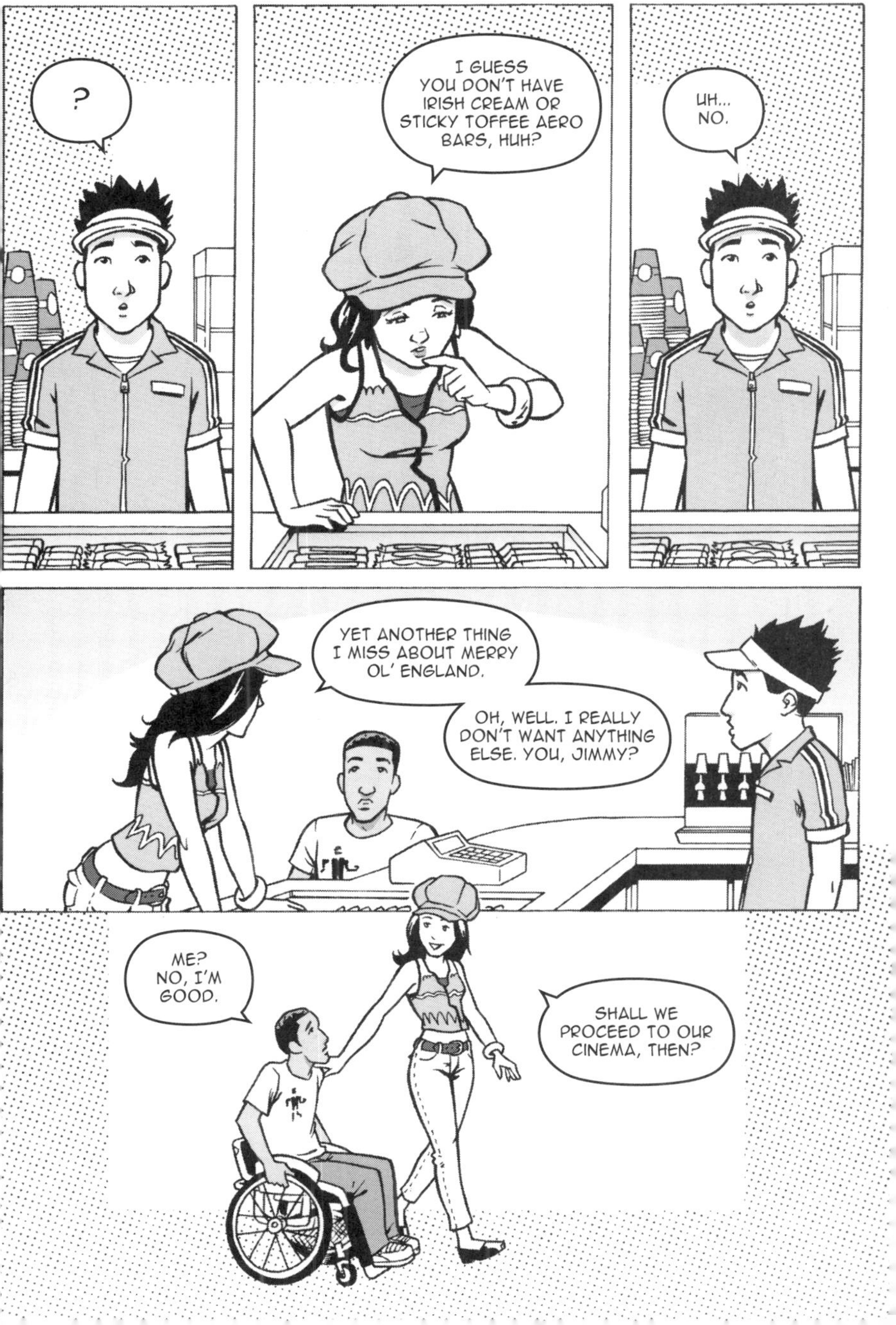
?
I GUESS YOU DON'T HAVE IRISH CREAM OR STICKY TOFFEE AERO BARS, HUH?
UH... NO.
YET ANOTHER THING I MISS ABOUT MERRY OL' ENGLAND.
OH, WELL. I REALLY DON'T WANT ANYTHING ELSE. YOU, JIMMY?
ME? NO, I'M GOOD.
SHALL WE PROCEED TO OUR CINEMA, THEN?

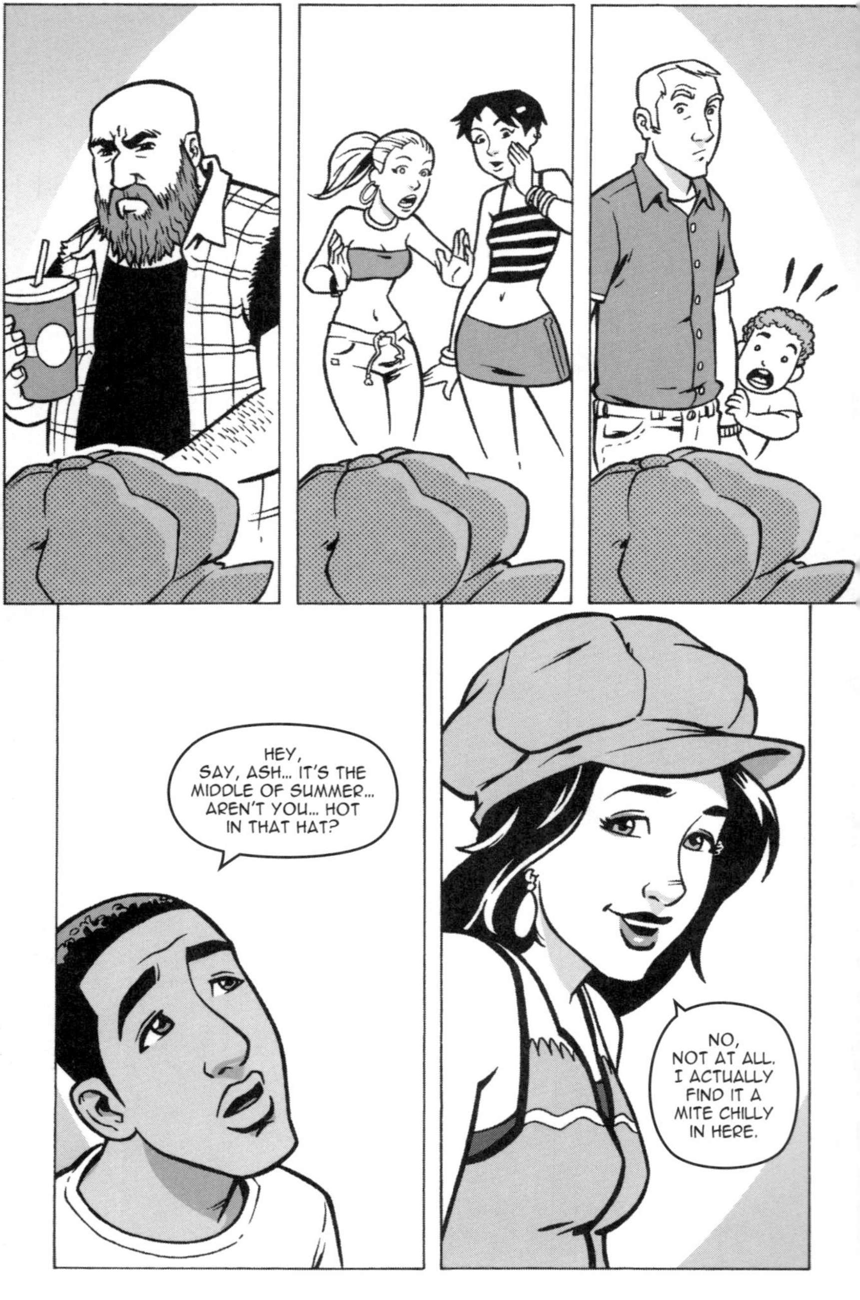
HEY, SAY, ASH... IT'S THE MIDDLE OF SUMMER... AREN'T YOU... HOT IN THAT HAT?
NO, NOT AT ALL. I ACTUALLY FIND IT A MITE CHILLY IN HERE.

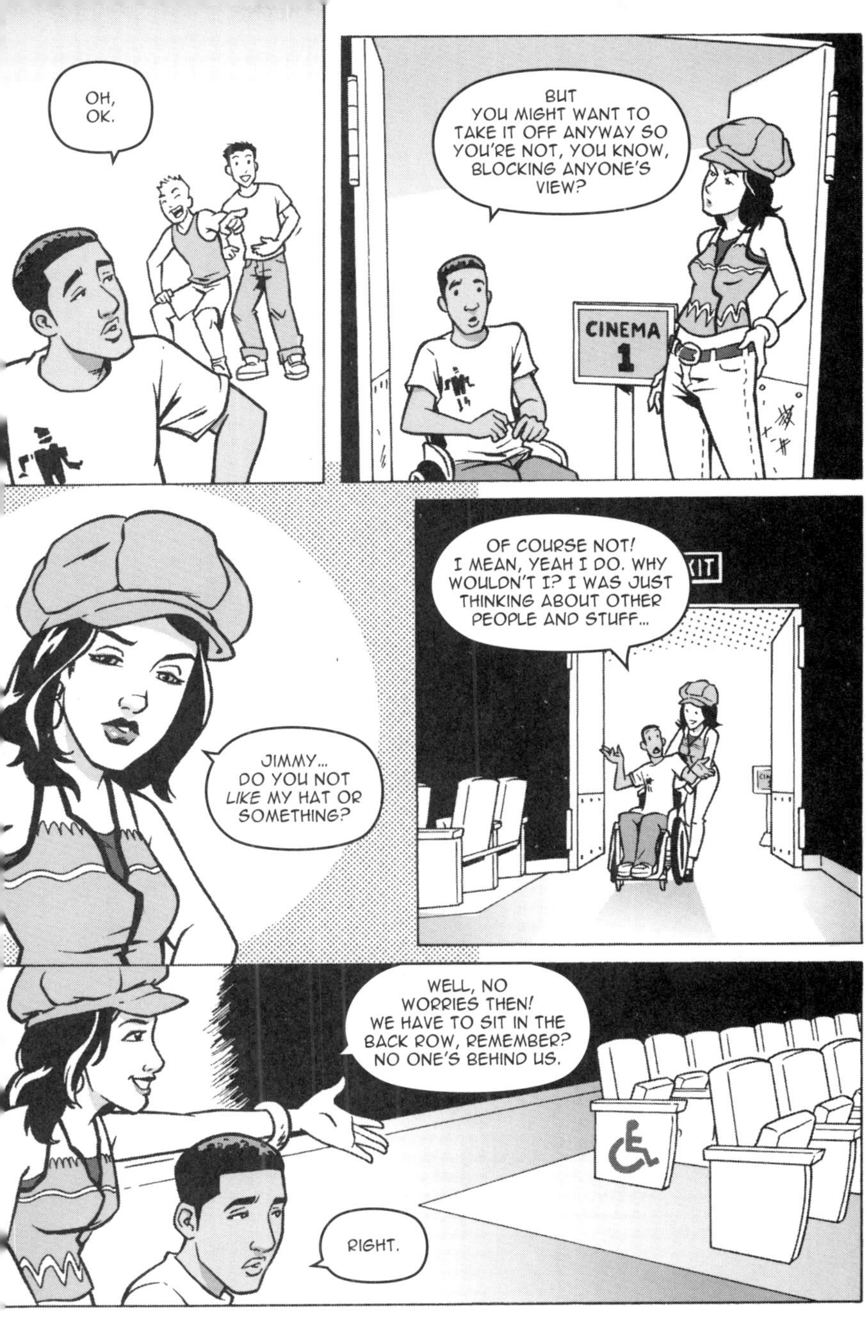
OH, OK.
BUT YOU MIGHT WANT TO TAKE IT OFF ANYWAY SO YOU'RE NOT, YOU KNOW, BLOCKING ANYONE'S VIEW?
CINEMA 1
JIMMY... DO YOU NOT LIKE MY HAT OR SOMETHING?
OF COURSE NOT! I MEAN, YEAH I DO. WHY WOULDN'T I? I WAS JUST THINKING ABOUT OTHER PEOPLE AND STUFF...
WELL, NO WORRIES THEN! WE HAVE TO SIT IN THE BACK ROW, REMEMBER? NO ONE'S BEHIND US.
RIGHT.

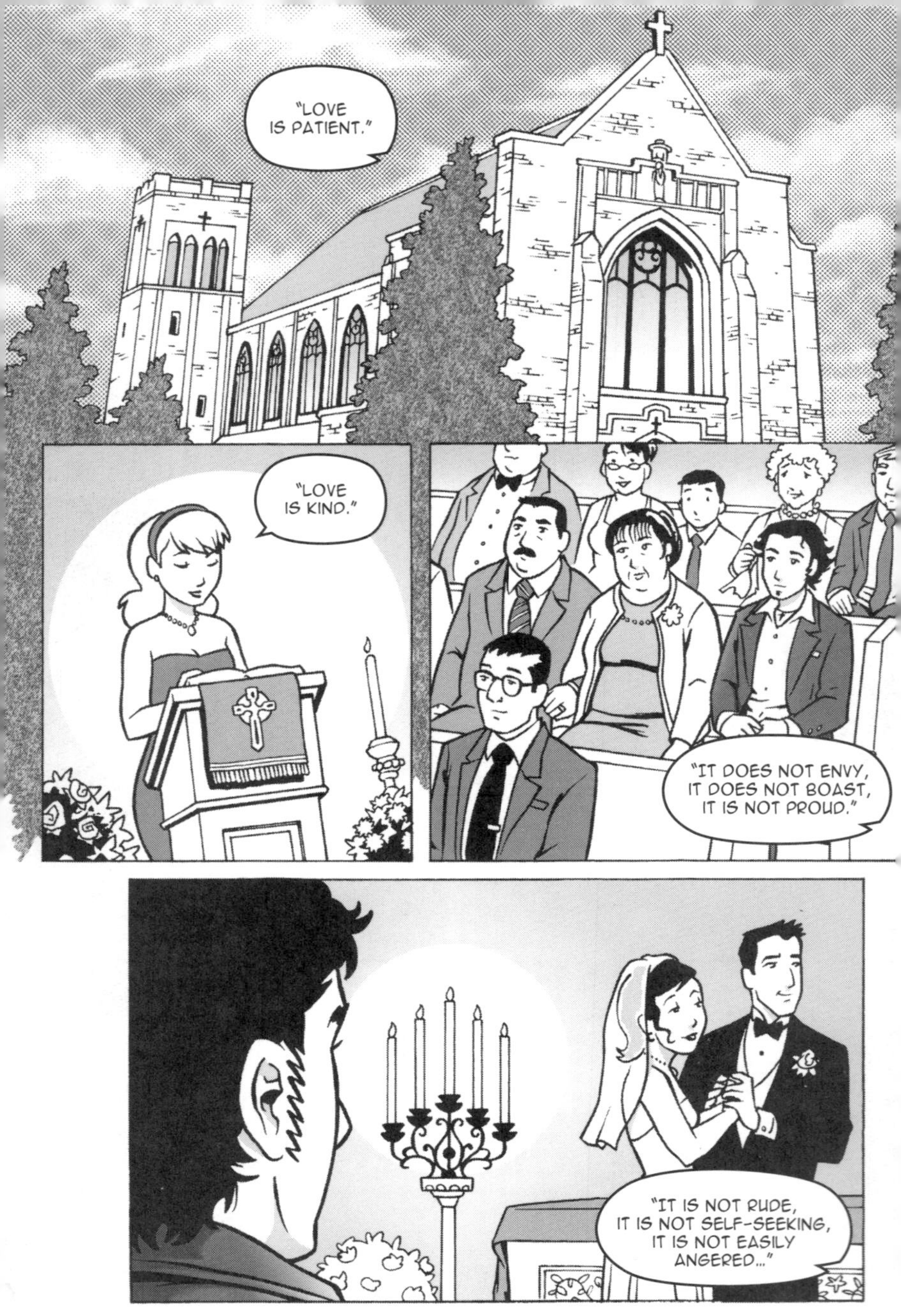
"LOVE IS PATIENT."
"LOVE IS KIND."
"IT DOES NOT ENVY, IT DOES NOT BOAST, IT IS NOT PROUD."
"IT IS NOT RUDE, IT IS NOT SELF-SEEKING, IT IS NOT EASILY ANGERED..."

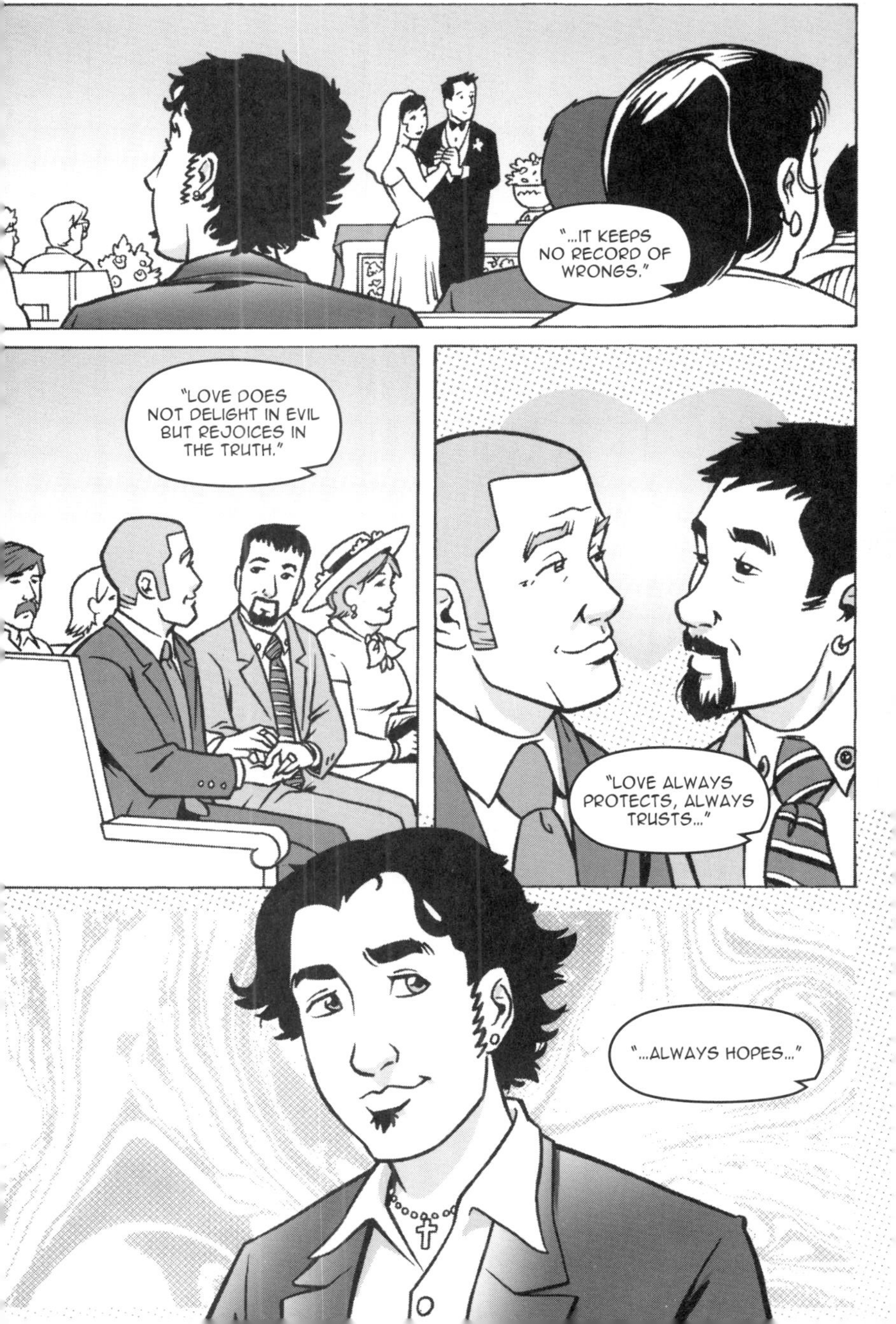
"...IT KEEPS NO RECORD OF WRONGS."
"LOVE DOES NOT DELIGHT IN EVIL BUT REJOICES IN THE TRUTH."
"LOVE ALWAYS PROTECTS, ALWAYS TRUSTS..."
"...ALWAYS HOPES..."

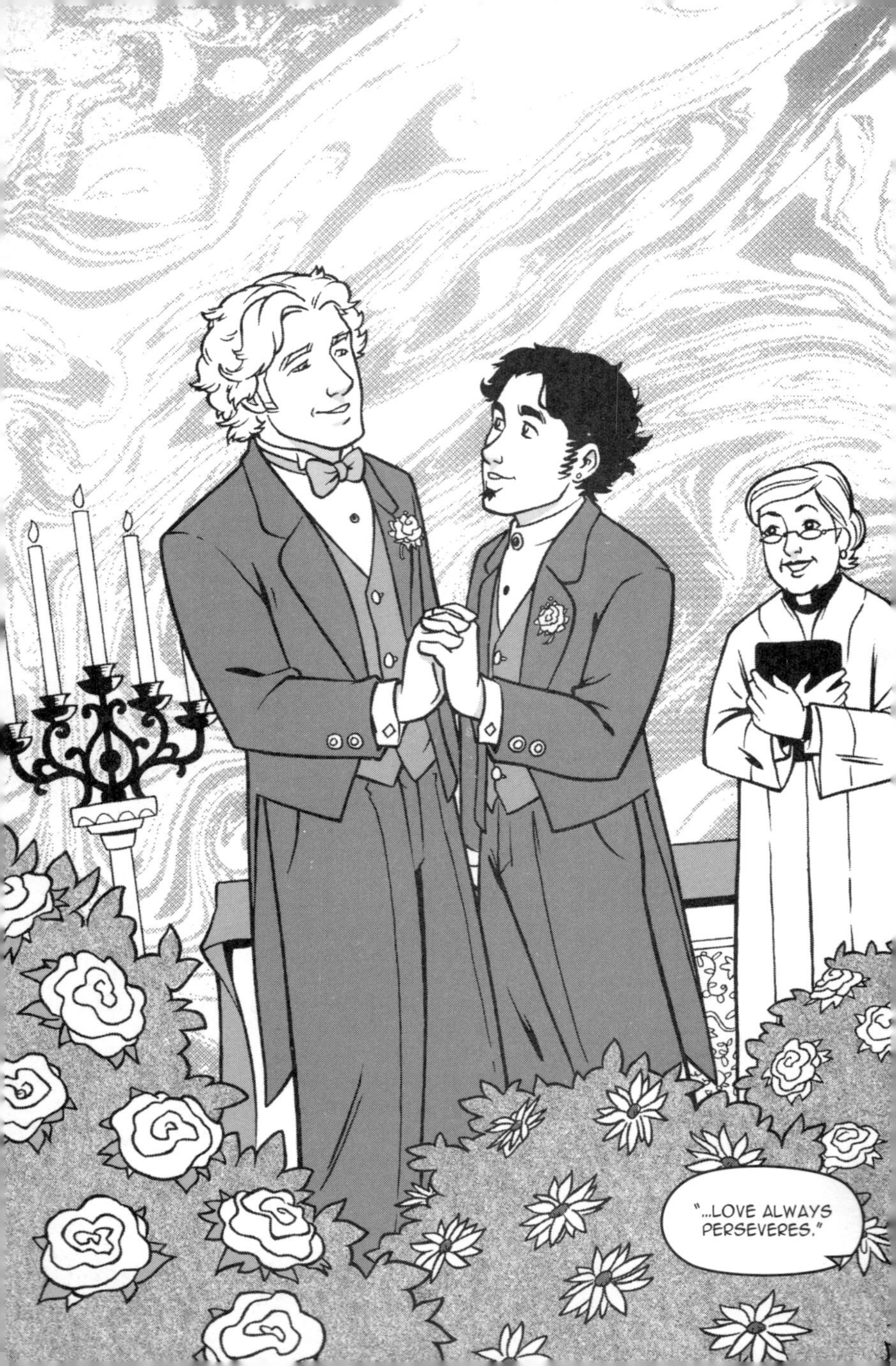
"...LOVE ALWAYS PERSEVERES."

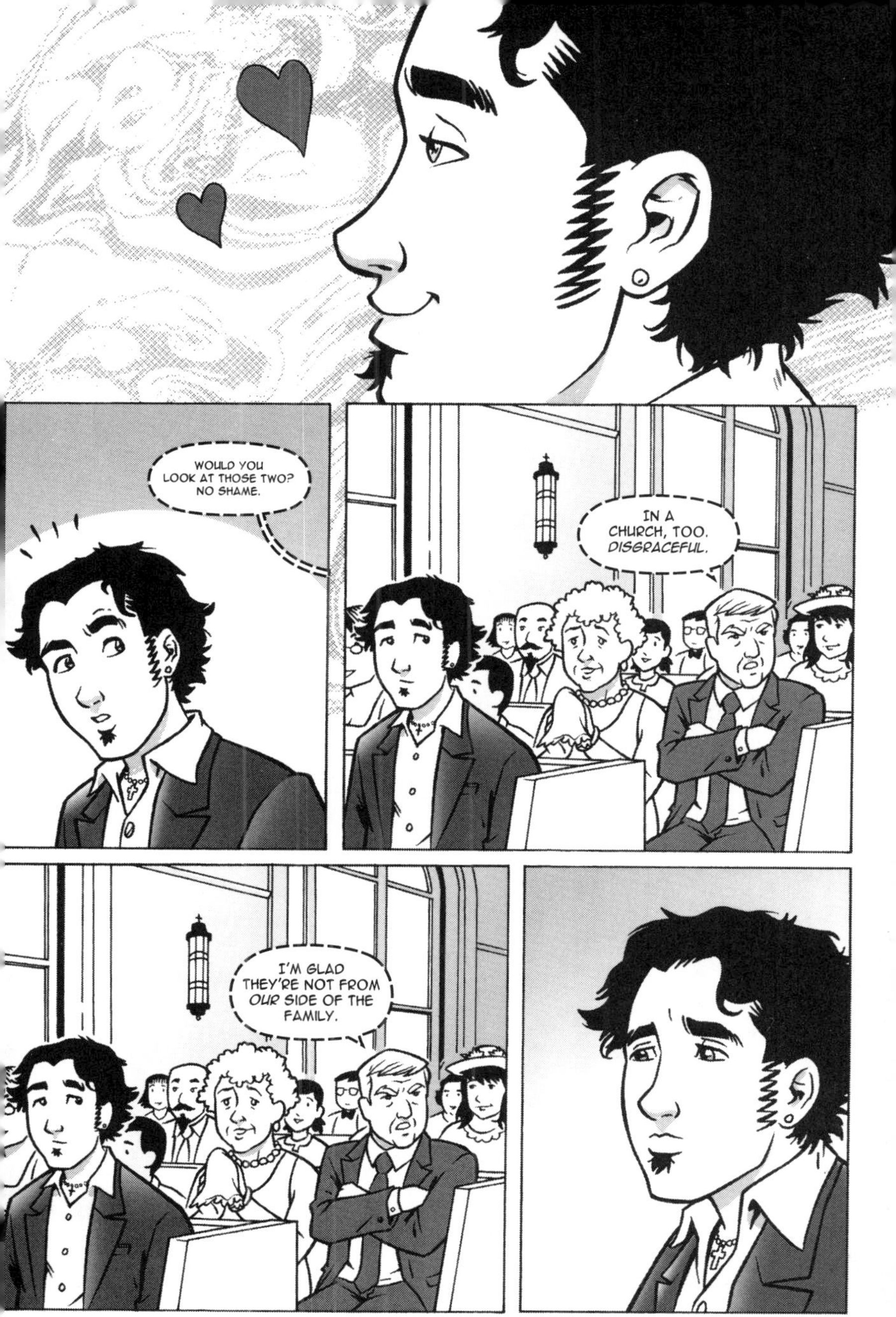
WOULD YOU LOOK AT THOSE TWO? NO SHAME.
IN A CHURCH, TOO. *DISGRACEFUL.*
I'M GLAD THEY'RE NOT FROM *OUR* SIDE OF THE FAMILY.

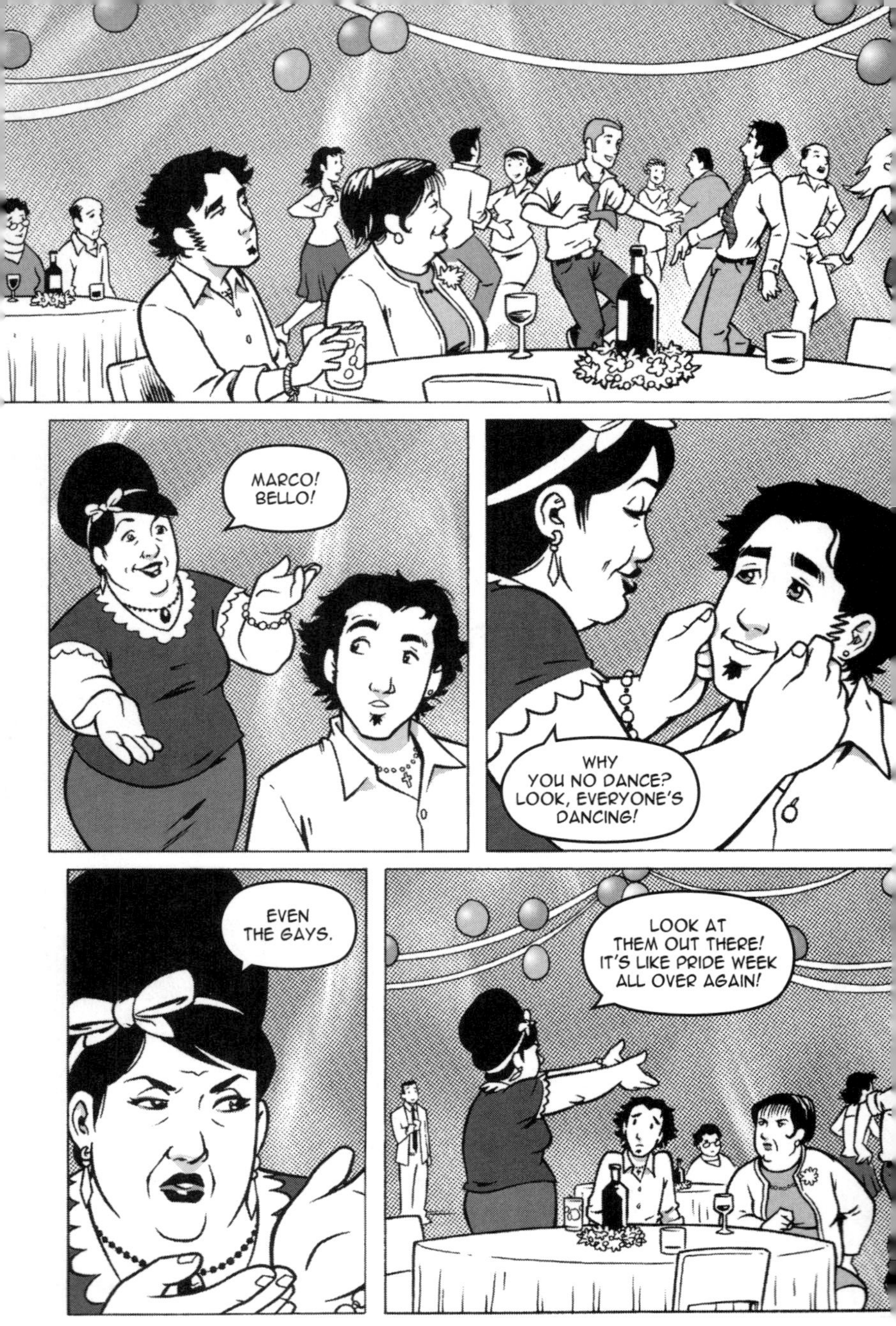
MARCO! BELLO!
WHY YOU NO DANCE? LOOK, EVERYONE'S DANCING!
EVEN THE GAYS.
LOOK AT THEM OUT THERE! IT'S LIKE PRIDE WEEK ALL OVER AGAIN!

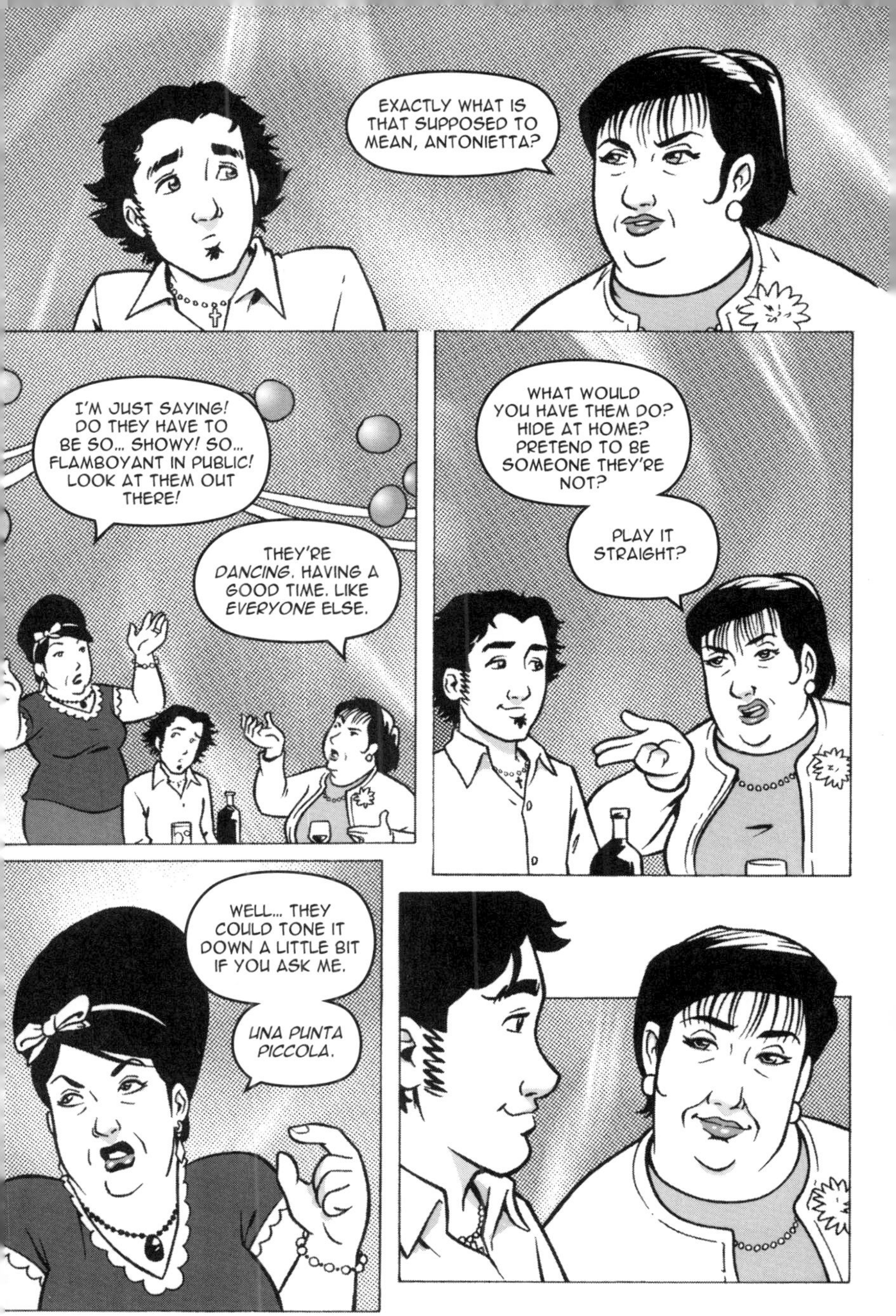
EXACTLY WHAT IS THAT SUPPOSED TO MEAN, ANTONIETTA?
I'M JUST SAYING! DO THEY HAVE TO BE SO... SHOWY! SO... FLAMBOYANT IN PUBLIC! LOOK AT THEM OUT THERE!
THEY'RE *DANCING*. HAVING A GOOD TIME. LIKE *EVERYONE* ELSE.
WHAT WOULD YOU HAVE THEM DO? HIDE AT HOME? PRETEND TO BE SOMEONE THEY'RE NOT?
PLAY IT STRAIGHT?
WELL... THEY COULD TONE IT DOWN A LITTLE BIT IF YOU ASK ME.
UNA PUNTA PICCOLA.

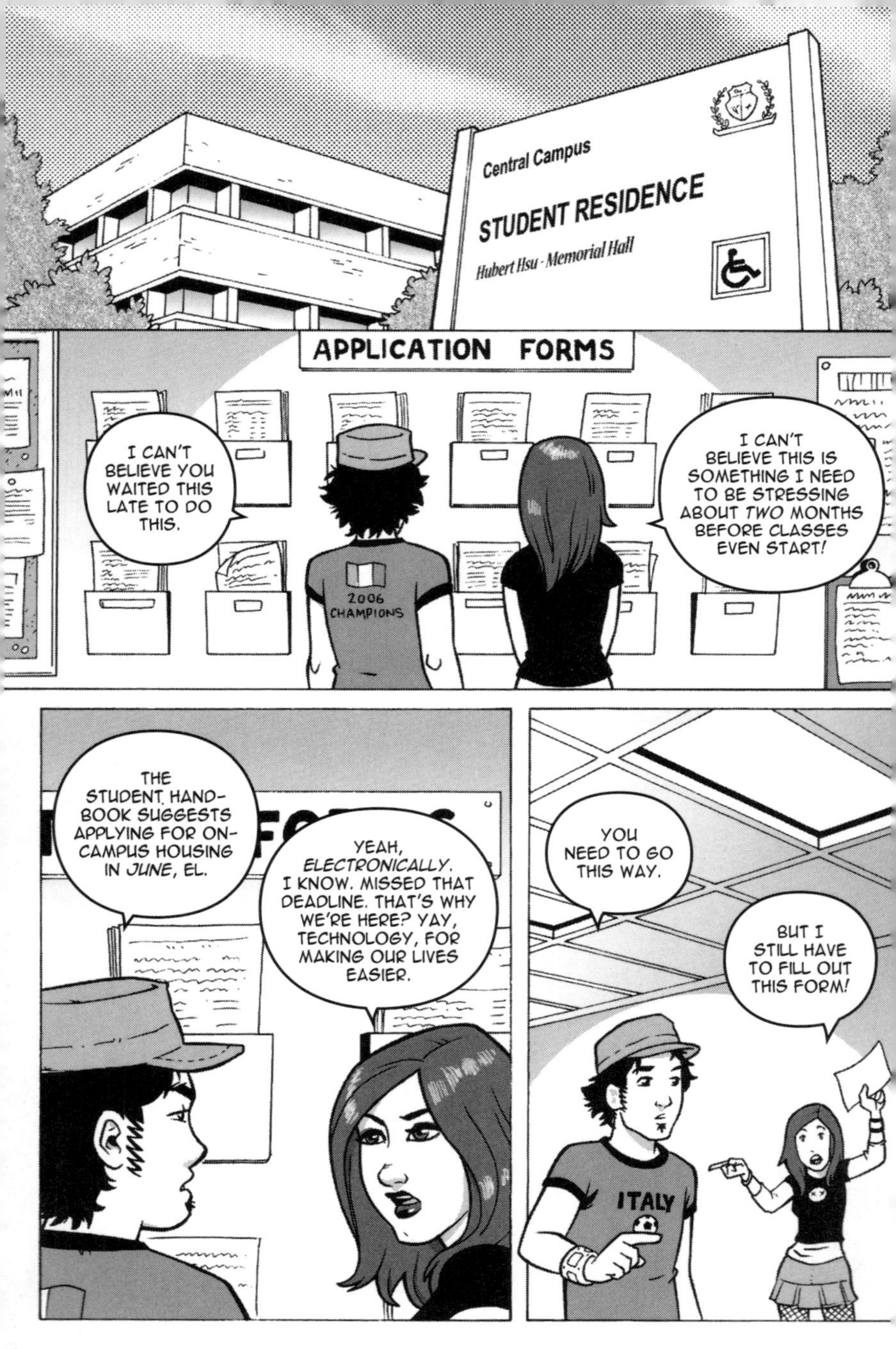
Central Campus
STUDENT RESIDENCE
Hubert Hsu · Memorial Hall
APPLICATION FORMS
I CAN'T BELIEVE YOU WAITED THIS LATE TO DO THIS.
2006 CHAMPIONS
I CAN'T BELIEVE THIS IS SOMETHING I NEED TO BE STRESSING ABOUT *TWO* MONTHS BEFORE CLASSES EVEN START!
THE STUDENT HAND-BOOK SUGGESTS APPLYING FOR ON-CAMPUS HOUSING IN *JUNE*, EL.
YEAH, *ELECTRONICALLY*. I KNOW. MISSED THAT DEADLINE. THAT'S WHY WE'RE HERE? YAY, TECHNOLOGY, FOR MAKING OUR LIVES EASIER.
YOU NEED TO GO THIS WAY.
BUT I STILL HAVE TO FILL OUT THIS FORM!
ITALY

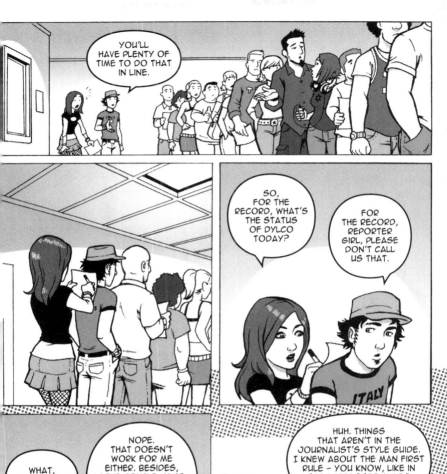

YOU'LL HAVE PLENTY OF TIME TO DO THAT IN LINE.

SO, FOR THE RECORD, WHAT'S THE STATUS OF DYLCO TODAY?

FOR THE RECORD, REPORTER GIRL, PLEASE DON'T CALL US THAT.

WHAT, YOU PREFER "MARLAN"?

NOPE. THAT DOESN'T WORK FOR ME EITHER. BESIDES, IN THE COUPLE NAME-SMOOSHING GAME, THE SMOOSHED NAME CAN'T BE A REAL NAME LIKE MARLAN.

HUH. THINGS THAT AREN'T IN THE JOURNALIST'S STYLE GUIDE. I KNEW ABOUT THE MAN FIRST RULE – YOU KNOW, LIKE IN "BENNIFER," "TOMKAT," "BRANGELINA"...

BUT WHAT IF IT'S TWO GUYS LIKE YOU AND DYLAN? OR...

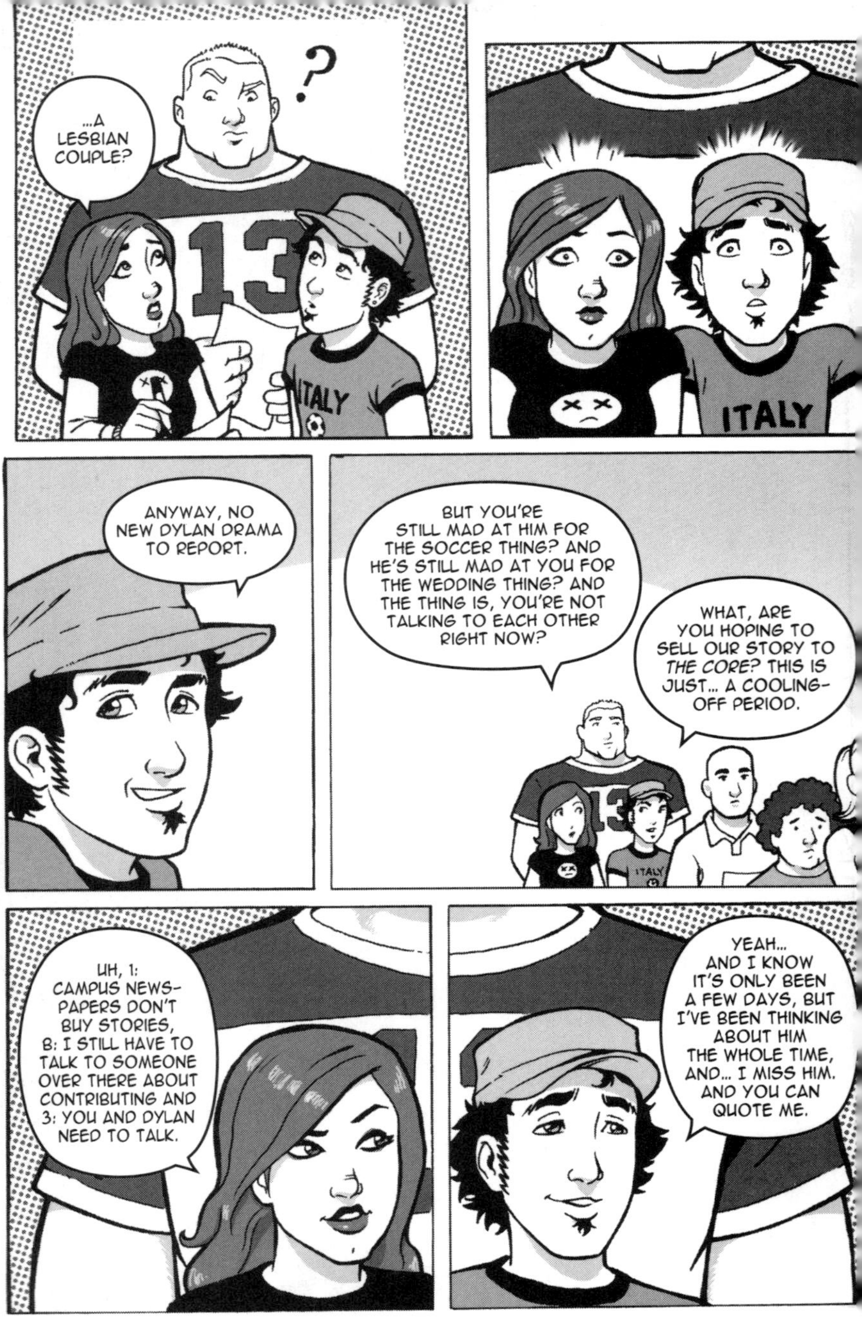
...A LESBIAN COUPLE?
?
13
ITALY
ITALY
ANYWAY, NO NEW DYLAN DRAMA TO REPORT.
BUT YOU'RE STILL MAD AT HIM FOR THE SOCCER THING? AND HE'S STILL MAD AT YOU FOR THE WEDDING THING? AND THE THING IS, YOU'RE NOT TALKING TO EACH OTHER RIGHT NOW?
WHAT, ARE YOU HOPING TO SELL OUR STORY TO *THE CORE*? THIS IS JUST... A COOLING-OFF PERIOD.
UH, 1: CAMPUS NEWS-PAPERS DON'T BUY STORIES, B: I STILL HAVE TO TALK TO SOMEONE OVER THERE ABOUT CONTRIBUTING AND 3: YOU AND DYLAN NEED TO TALK.
YEAH... AND I KNOW IT'S ONLY BEEN A FEW DAYS, BUT I'VE BEEN THINKING ABOUT HIM THE WHOLE TIME, AND... I MISS HIM. AND YOU CAN QUOTE ME.

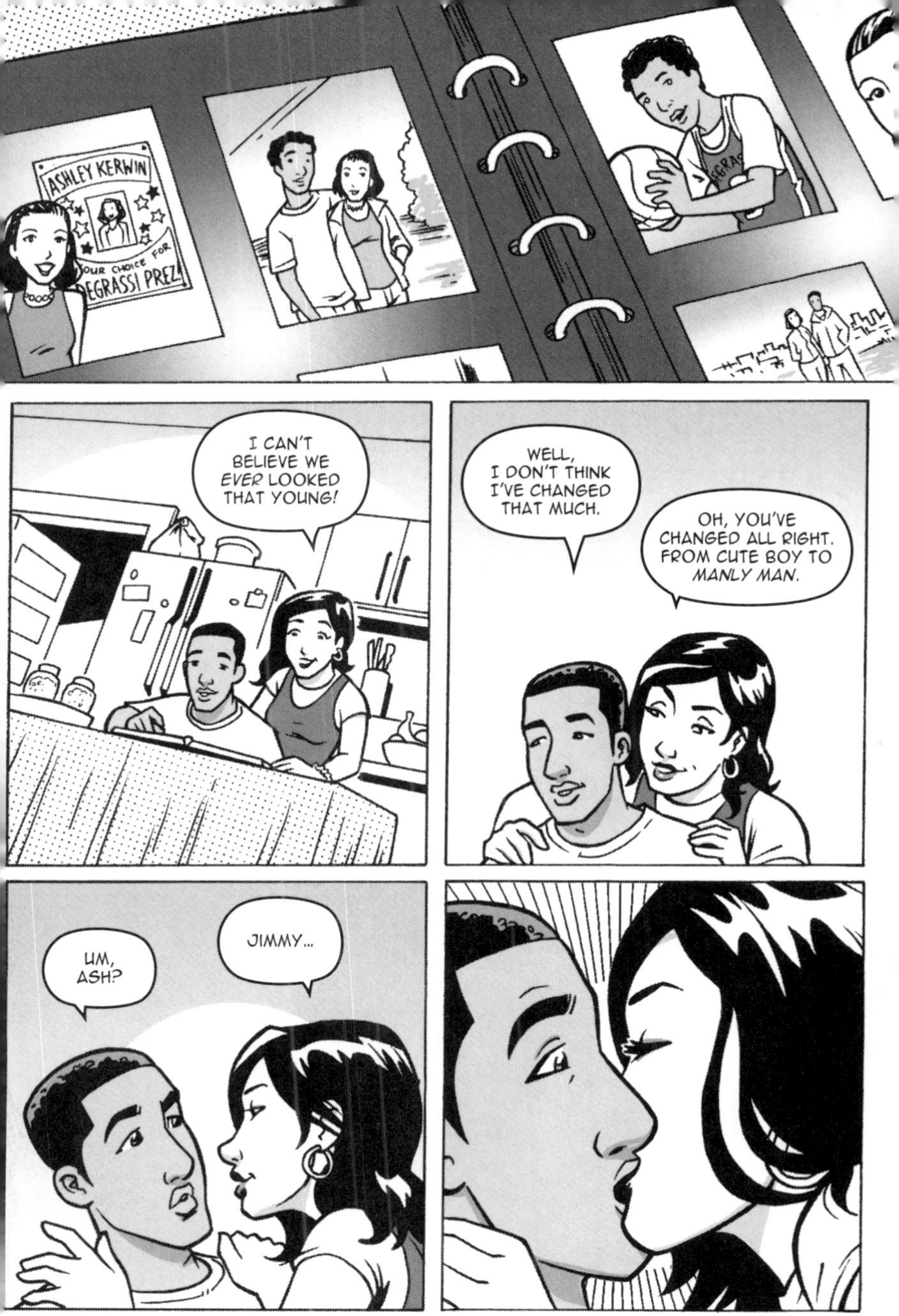
ASHLEY KERWIN
OUR CHOICE FOR
EGRASSI PREZ!
I CAN'T BELIEVE WE *EVER* LOOKED THAT YOUNG!
WELL, I DON'T THINK I'VE CHANGED THAT MUCH.
OH, YOU'VE CHANGED ALL RIGHT. FROM CUTE BOY TO *MANLY MAN*.
UM, ASH?
JIMMY...

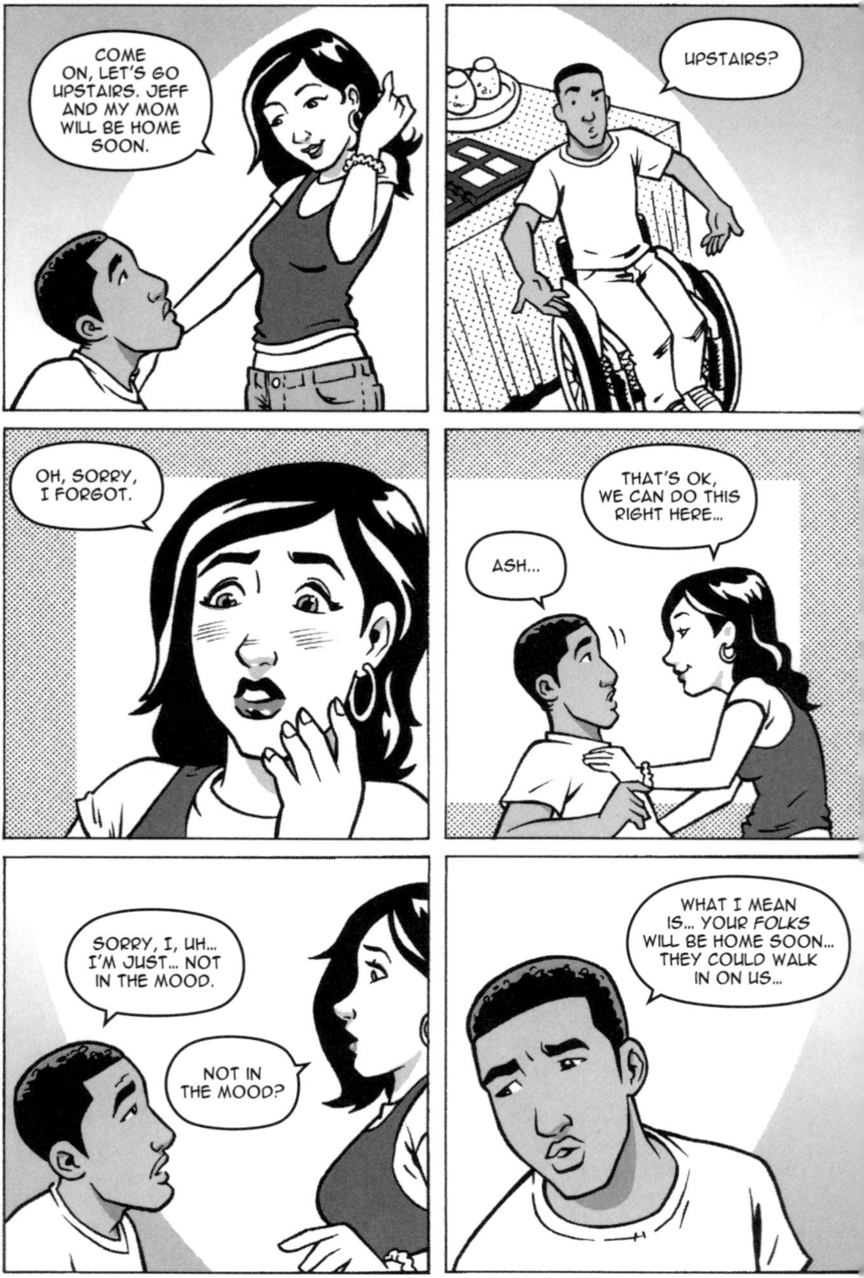
COME ON, LET'S GO UPSTAIRS. JEFF AND MY MOM WILL BE HOME SOON.
UPSTAIRS?
OH, SORRY, I FORGOT.
THAT'S OK, WE CAN DO THIS RIGHT HERE...
ASH...
SORRY, I, UH... I'M JUST... NOT IN THE MOOD.
NOT IN THE MOOD?
WHAT I MEAN IS... YOUR *FOLKS* WILL BE HOME SOON... THEY COULD WALK IN ON US...

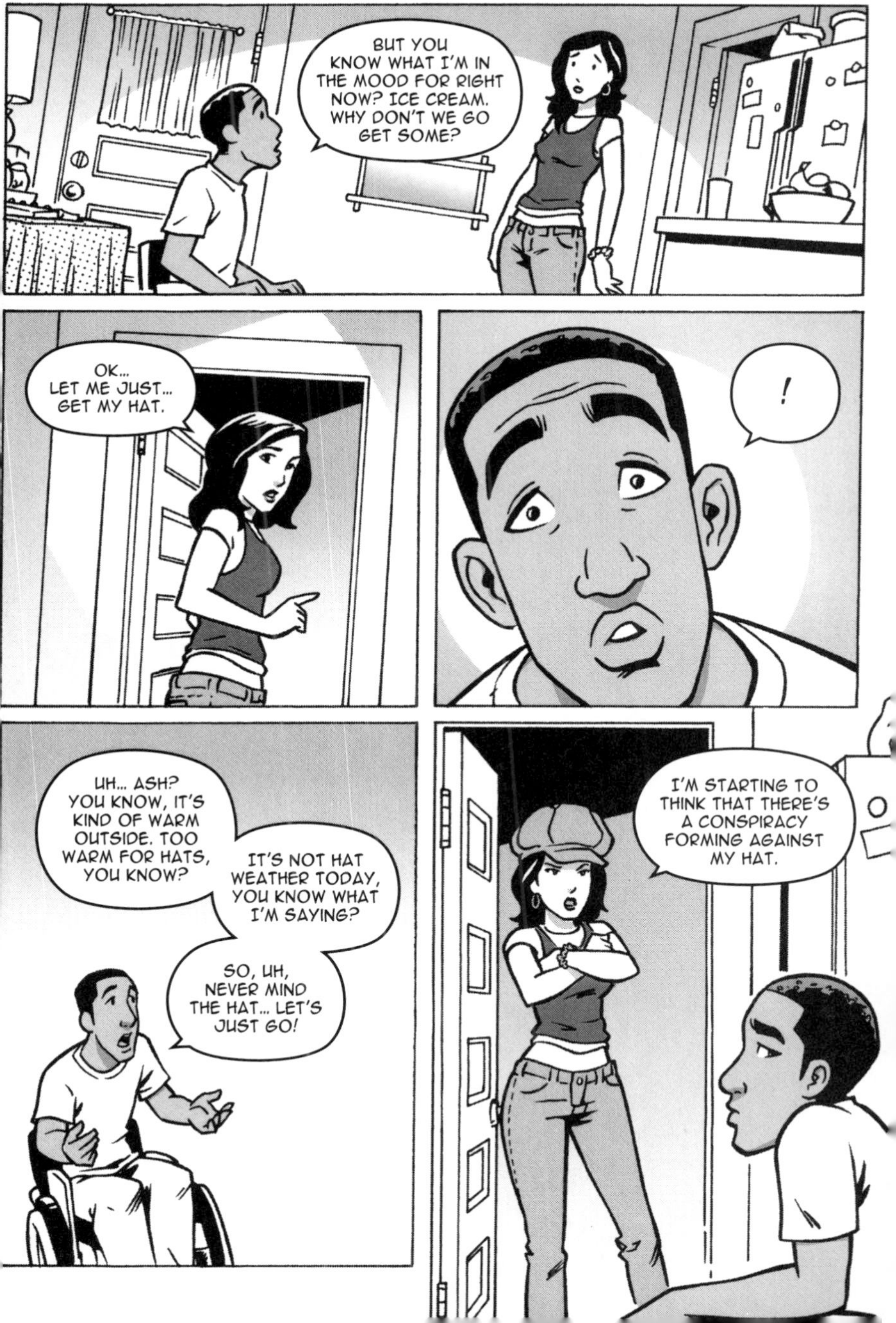
BUT YOU KNOW WHAT I'M IN THE MOOD FOR RIGHT NOW? ICE CREAM. WHY DON'T WE GO GET SOME?
OK... LET ME JUST... GET MY HAT.
!
UH... ASH? YOU KNOW, IT'S KIND OF WARM OUTSIDE. TOO WARM FOR HATS, YOU KNOW?
IT'S NOT HAT WEATHER TODAY, YOU KNOW WHAT I'M SAYING?
SO, UH, NEVER MIND THE HAT... LET'S JUST GO!
I'M STARTING TO THINK THAT THERE'S A CONSPIRACY FORMING AGAINST MY HAT.

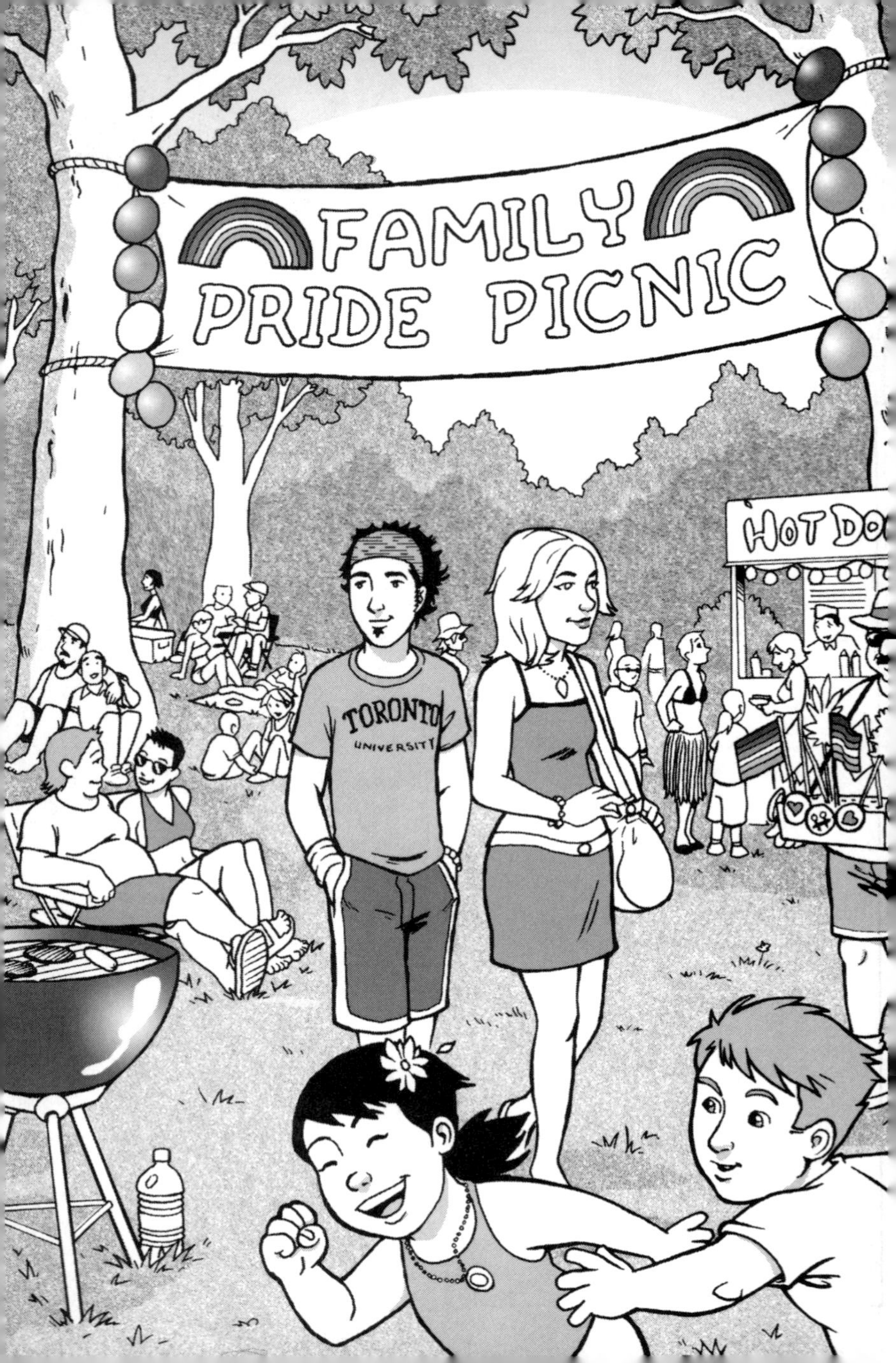
FAMILY PRIDE PICNIC
HOT DO
TORONTO UNIVERSITY

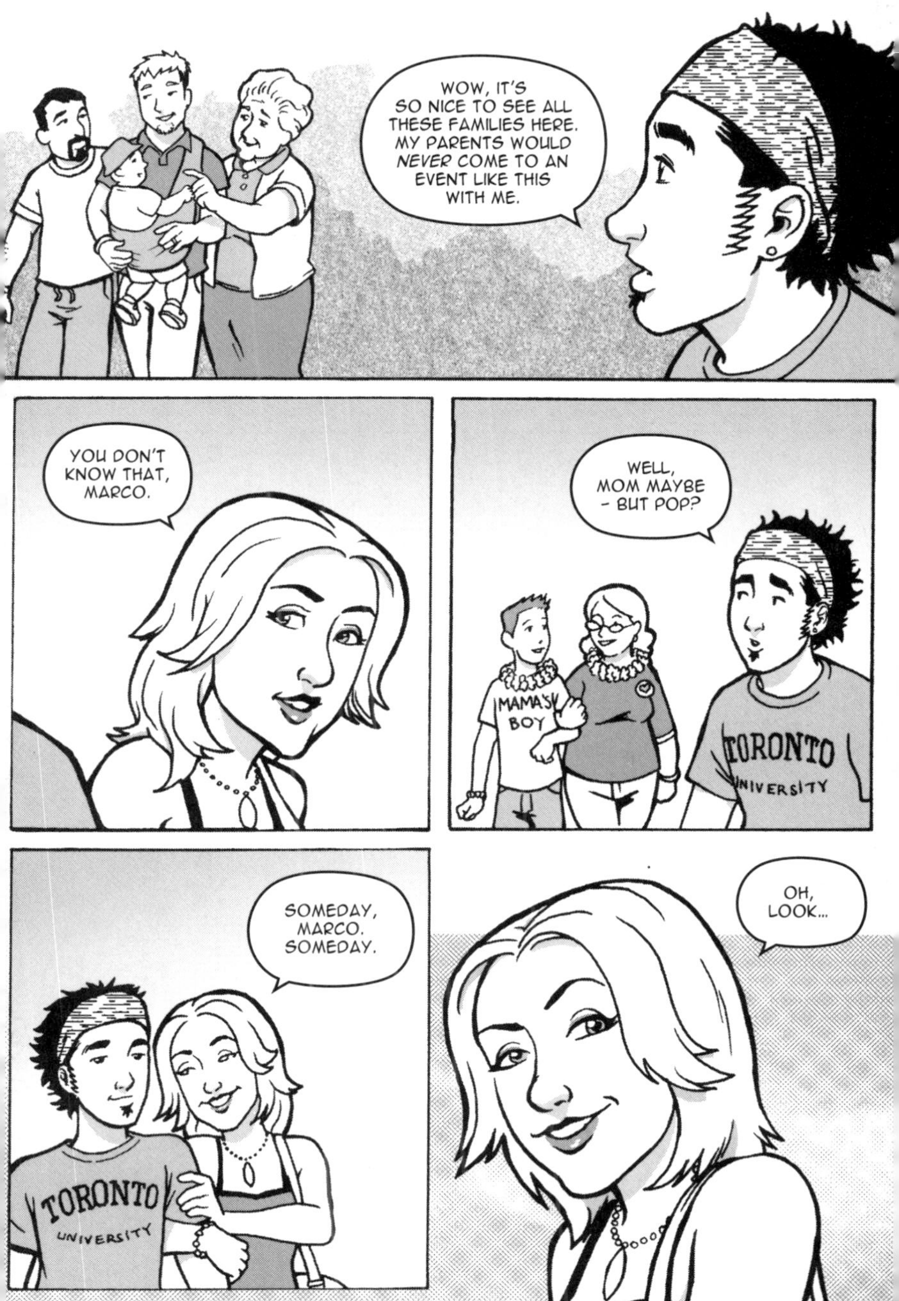
WOW, IT'S SO NICE TO SEE ALL THESE FAMILIES HERE. MY PARENTS WOULD *NEVER* COME TO AN EVENT LIKE THIS WITH ME.
YOU DON'T KNOW THAT, MARCO.
WELL, MOM MAYBE - BUT POP?
MAMA'S BOY
TORONTO UNIVERSITY
SOMEDAY, MARCO. SOMEDAY.
TORONTO UNIVERSITY
OH, LOOK...

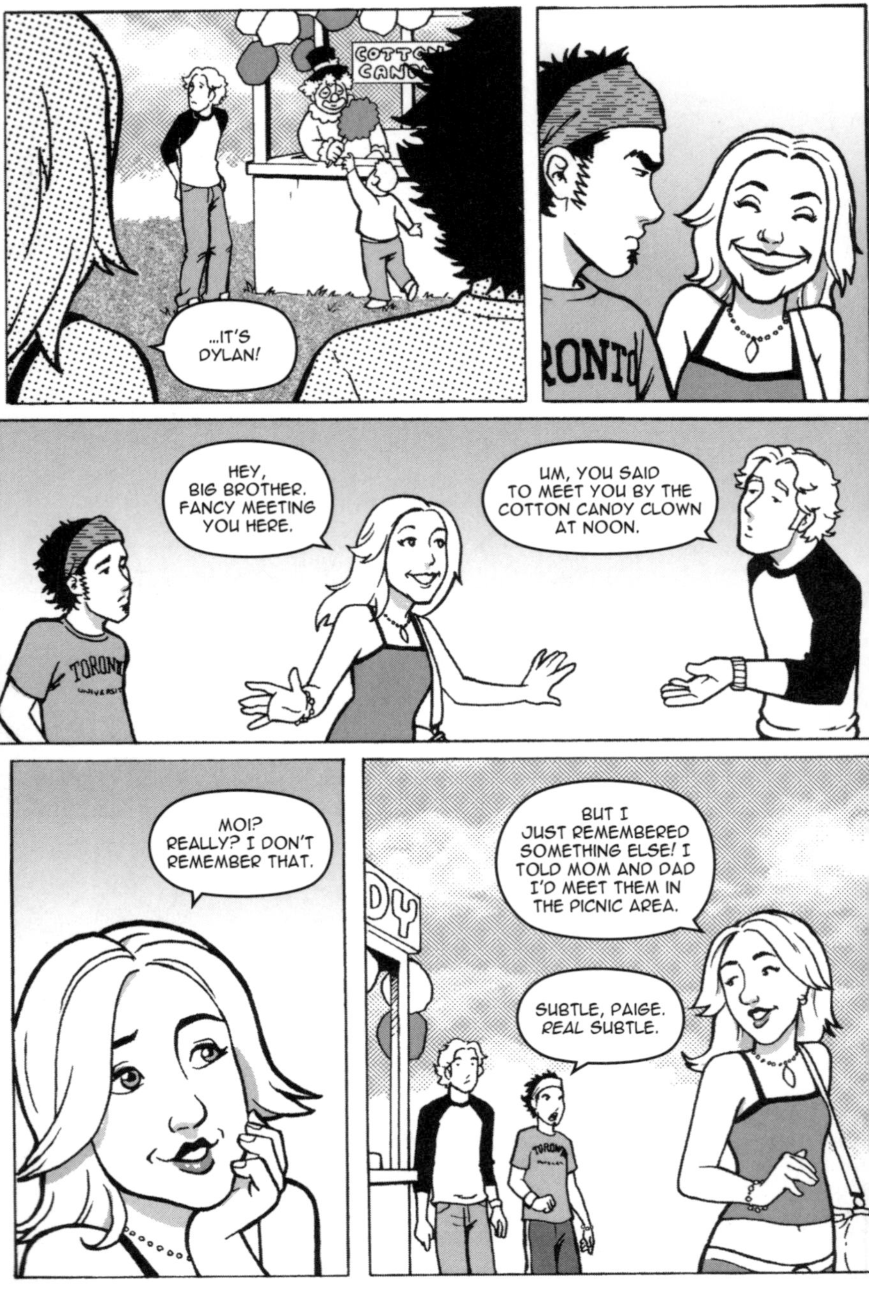
COTTON CANDY
...IT'S DYLAN!
TORONTO
HEY, BIG BROTHER. FANCY MEETING YOU HERE.
UM, YOU SAID TO MEET YOU BY THE COTTON CANDY CLOWN AT NOON.
TORONTO UNIVERSITY
MOI? REALLY? I DON'T REMEMBER THAT.
DY
BUT I JUST REMEMBERED SOMETHING ELSE! I TOLD MOM AND DAD I'D MEET THEM IN THE PICNIC AREA.
SUBTLE, PAIGE. REAL SUBTLE.
TORONTO

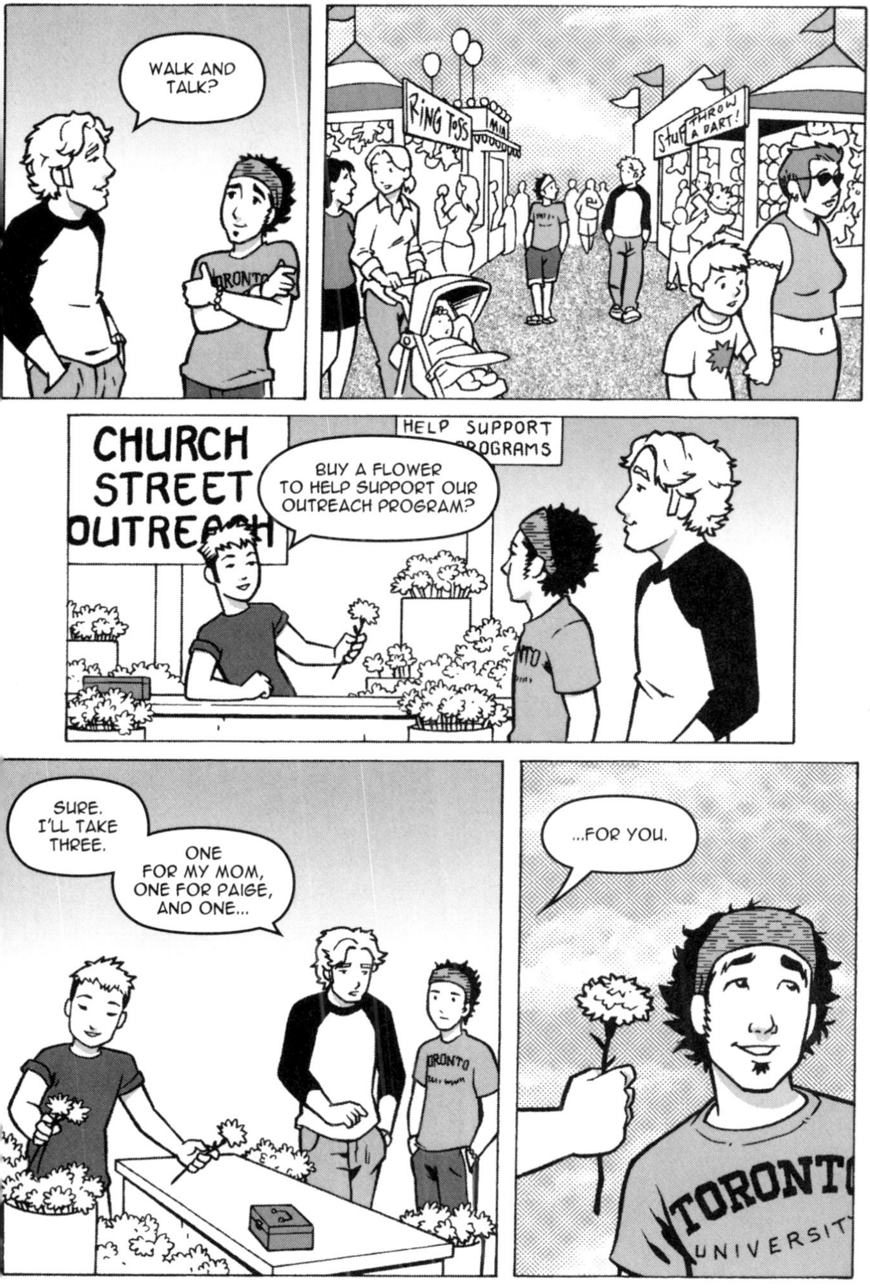
WALK AND TALK?
RING TOSS
THROW A DART!
CHURCH STREET
HELP SUPPORT
BUY A FLOWER TO HELP SUPPORT OUR OUTREACH PROGRAM?
SURE. I'LL TAKE THREE.
ONE FOR MY MOM, ONE FOR PAIGE, AND ONE...
...FOR YOU.
TORONTO

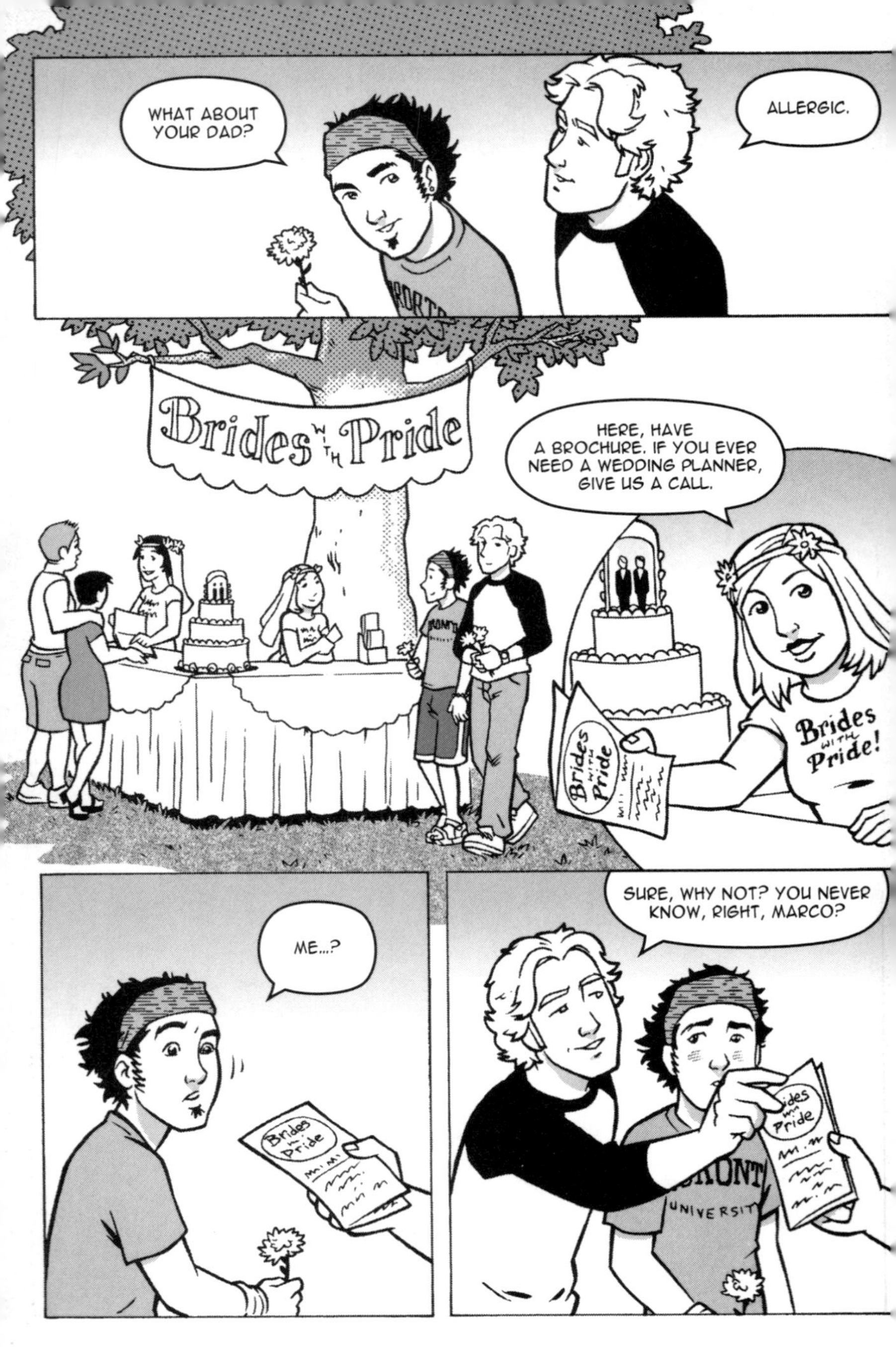
WHAT ABOUT YOUR DAD?
ALLERGIC.
Brides WITH Pride
HERE, HAVE A BROCHURE. IF YOU EVER NEED A WEDDING PLANNER, GIVE US A CALL.
Brides WITH Pride
Brides WITH Pride!
ME...?
SURE, WHY NOT? YOU NEVER KNOW, RIGHT, MARCO?

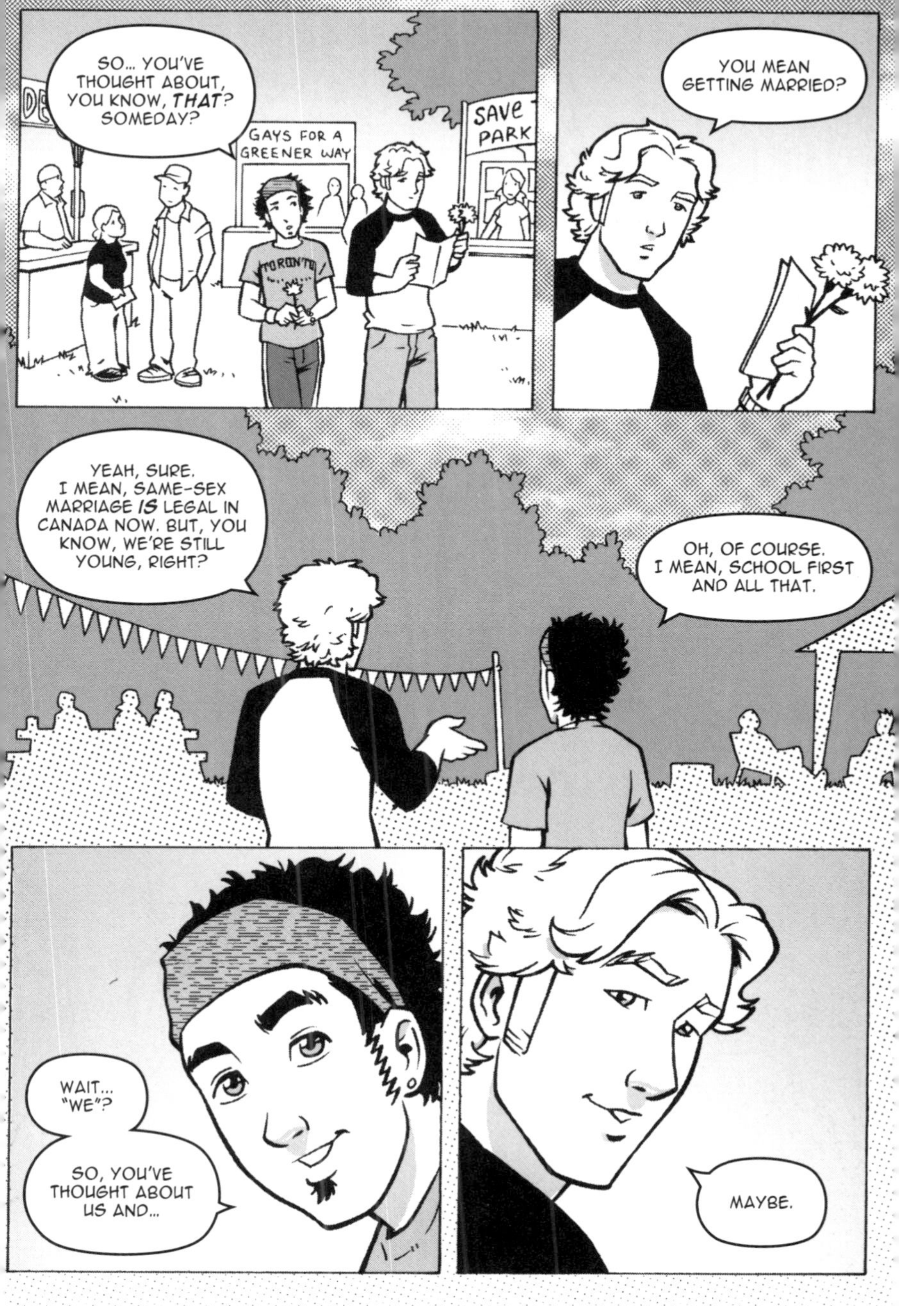
SO... YOU'VE THOUGHT ABOUT, YOU KNOW, ***THAT***? SOMEDAY?
GAYS FOR A GREENER WAY
SAVE PARK
TORONTO
YOU MEAN GETTING MARRIED?
YEAH, SURE. I MEAN, SAME-SEX MARRIAGE ***IS*** LEGAL IN CANADA NOW. BUT, YOU KNOW, WE'RE STILL YOUNG, RIGHT?
OH, OF COURSE. I MEAN, SCHOOL FIRST AND ALL THAT.
WAIT... "WE"?
SO, YOU'VE THOUGHT ABOUT US AND...
MAYBE.

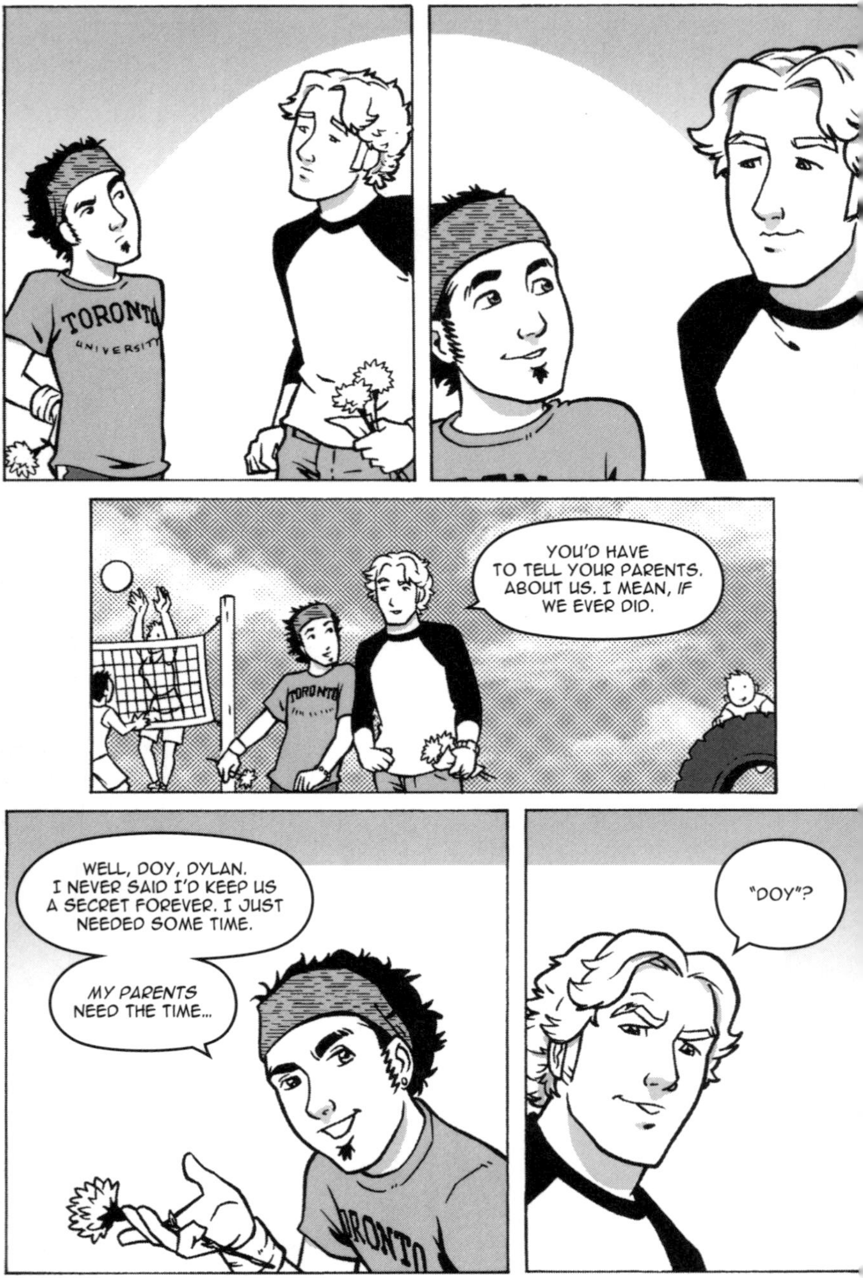
TORONTO UNIVERSITY
YOU'D HAVE TO TELL YOUR PARENTS. ABOUT US. I MEAN, *IF* WE EVER DID.
WELL, DOY, DYLAN. I NEVER SAID I'D KEEP US A SECRET FOREVER. I JUST NEEDED SOME TIME.
MY PARENTS NEED THE TIME...
"DOY"?

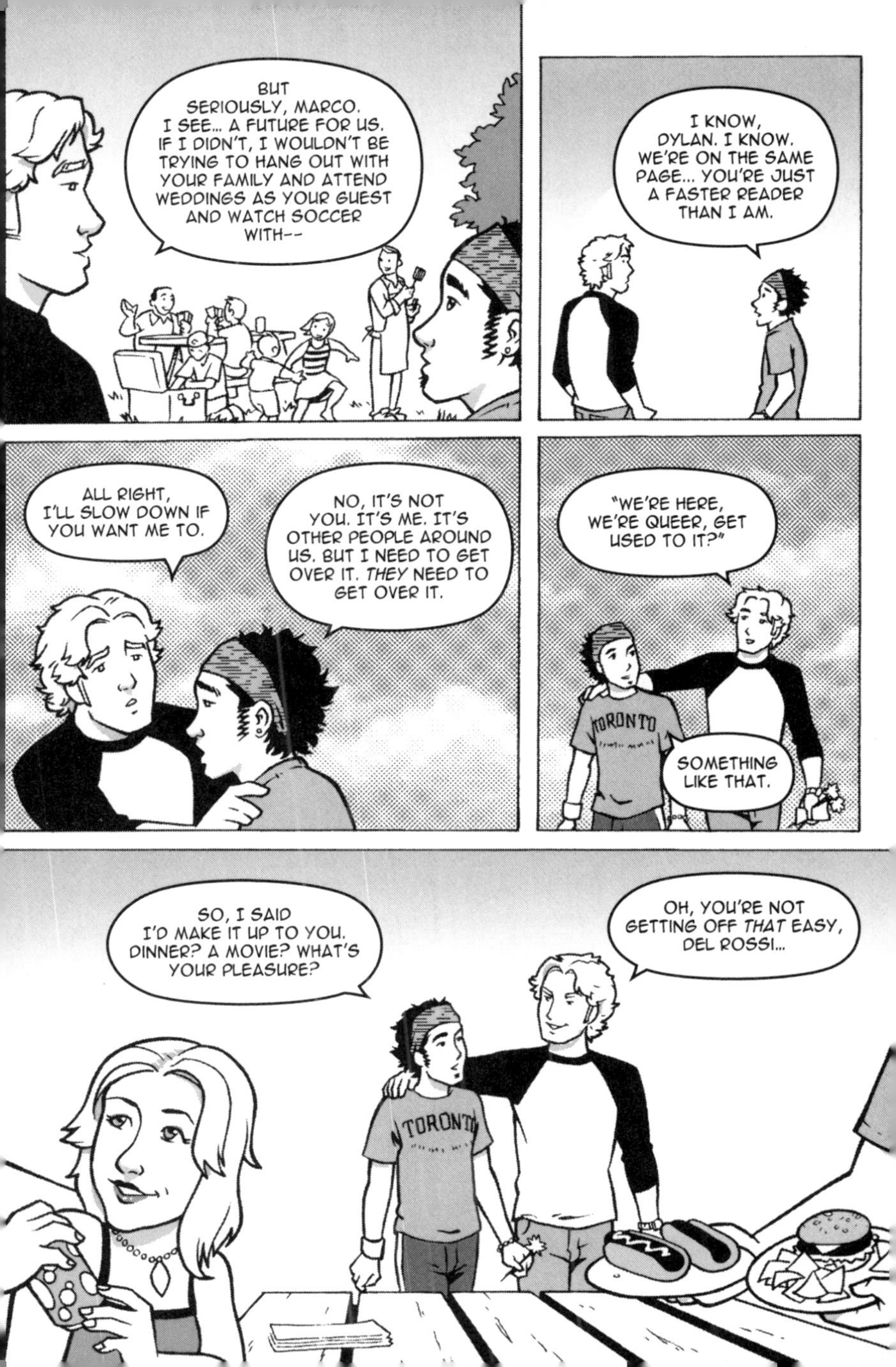
BUT SERIOUSLY, MARCO. I SEE... A FUTURE FOR US. IF I DIDN'T, I WOULDN'T BE TRYING TO HANG OUT WITH YOUR FAMILY AND ATTEND WEDDINGS AS YOUR GUEST AND WATCH SOCCER WITH--
I KNOW, DYLAN. I KNOW. WE'RE ON THE SAME PAGE... YOU'RE JUST A FASTER READER THAN I AM.
ALL RIGHT, I'LL SLOW DOWN IF YOU WANT ME TO.
NO, IT'S NOT YOU. IT'S ME. IT'S OTHER PEOPLE AROUND US. BUT I NEED TO GET OVER IT. *THEY* NEED TO GET OVER IT.
"WE'RE HERE, WE'RE QUEER, GET USED TO IT?"
TORONTO
SOMETHING LIKE THAT.
SO, I SAID I'D MAKE IT UP TO YOU. DINNER? A MOVIE? WHAT'S YOUR PLEASURE?
OH, YOU'RE NOT GETTING OFF *THAT* EASY, DEL ROSSI...
TORONTO

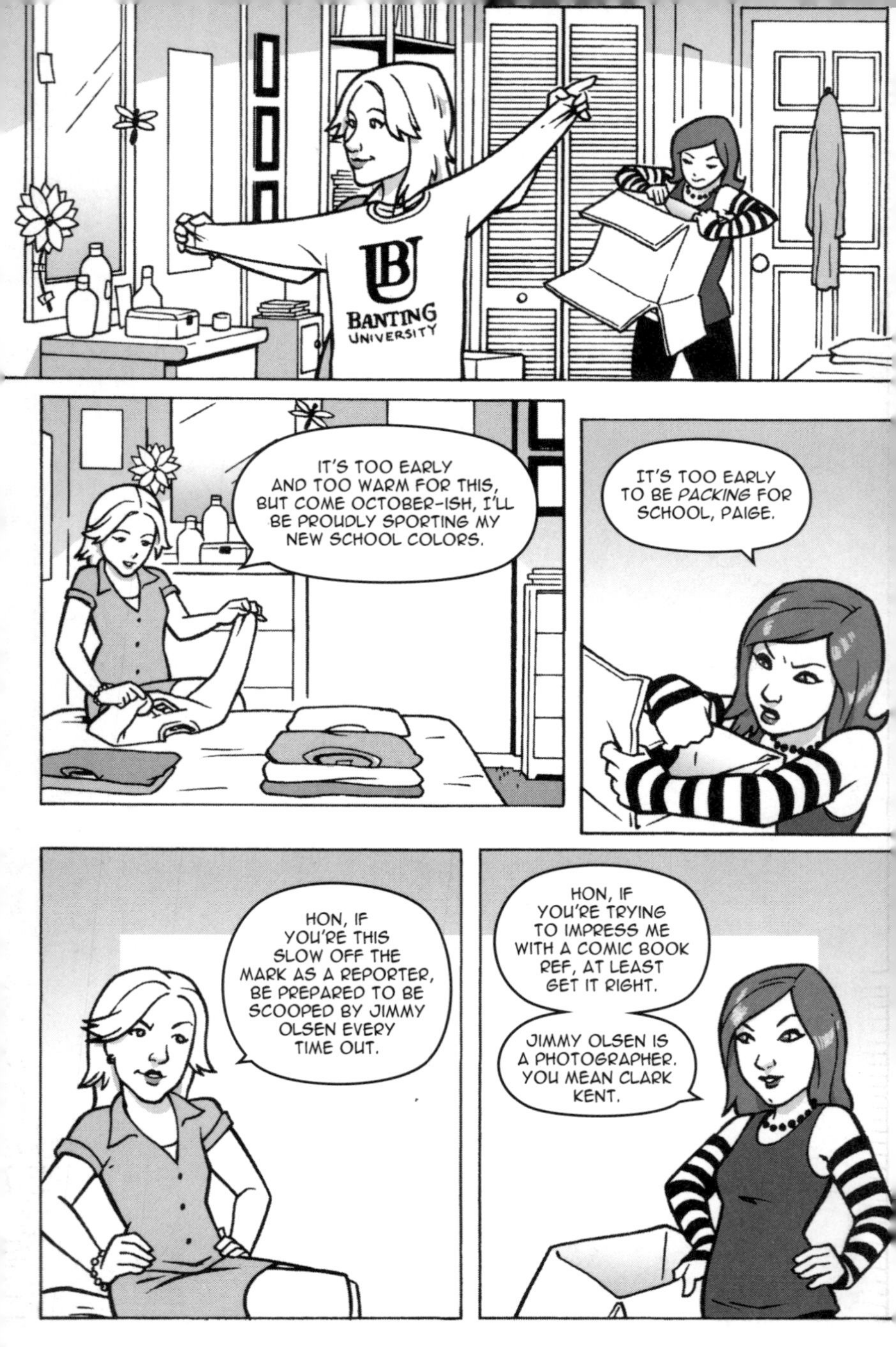

UB
BANTING
UNIVERSITY
IT'S TOO EARLY AND TOO WARM FOR THIS, BUT COME OCTOBER-ISH, I'LL BE PROUDLY SPORTING MY NEW SCHOOL COLORS.
IT'S TOO EARLY TO BE *PACKING* FOR SCHOOL, PAIGE.
HON, IF YOU'RE THIS SLOW OFF THE MARK AS A REPORTER, BE PREPARED TO BE SCOOPED BY JIMMY OLSEN EVERY TIME OUT.
HON, IF YOU'RE TRYING TO IMPRESS ME WITH A COMIC BOOK REF, AT LEAST GET IT RIGHT.
JIMMY OLSEN IS A PHOTOGRAPHER. YOU MEAN CLARK KENT.

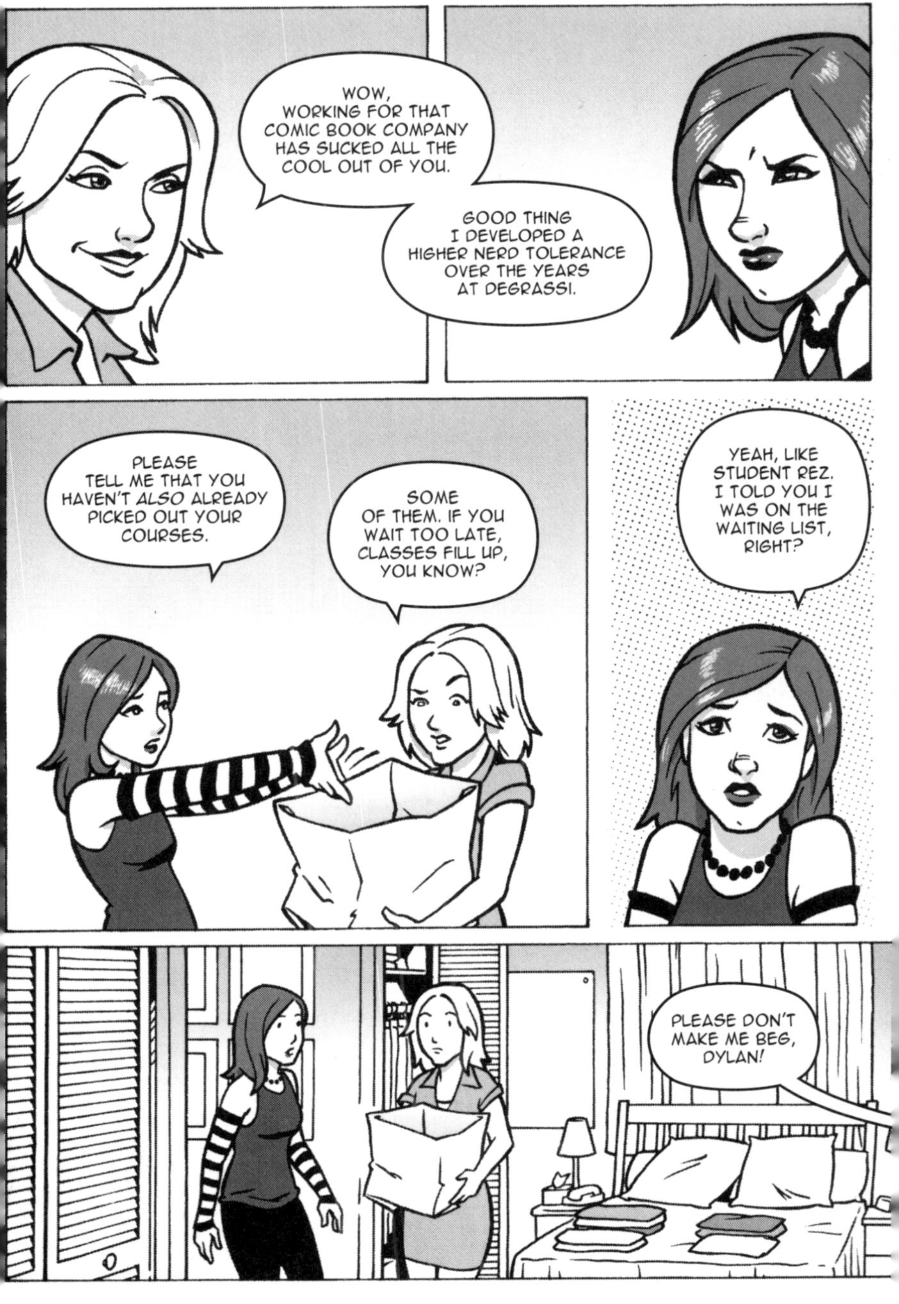
WOW, WORKING FOR THAT COMIC BOOK COMPANY HAS SUCKED ALL THE COOL OUT OF YOU.
GOOD THING I DEVELOPED A HIGHER NERD TOLERANCE OVER THE YEARS AT DEGRASSI.
PLEASE TELL ME THAT YOU HAVEN'T *ALSO* ALREADY PICKED OUT YOUR COURSES.
SOME OF THEM. IF YOU WAIT TOO LATE, CLASSES FILL UP, YOU KNOW?
YEAH, LIKE STUDENT REZ. I TOLD YOU I WAS ON THE WAITING LIST, RIGHT?
PLEASE DON'T MAKE ME BEG, DYLAN!

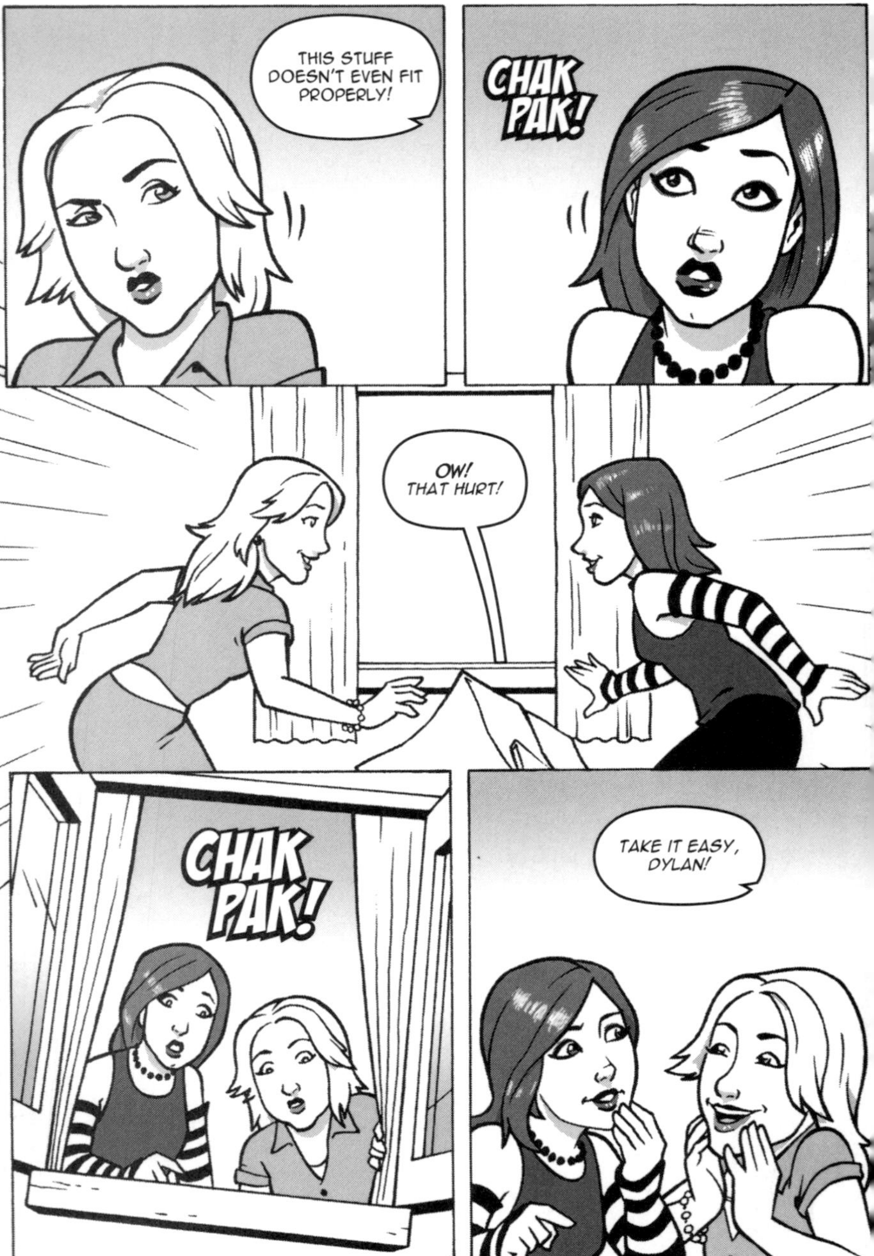
THIS STUFF DOESN'T EVEN FIT PROPERLY!
CHAK PAK!
OW! THAT HURT!
CHAK PAK!
TAKE IT EASY, DYLAN!

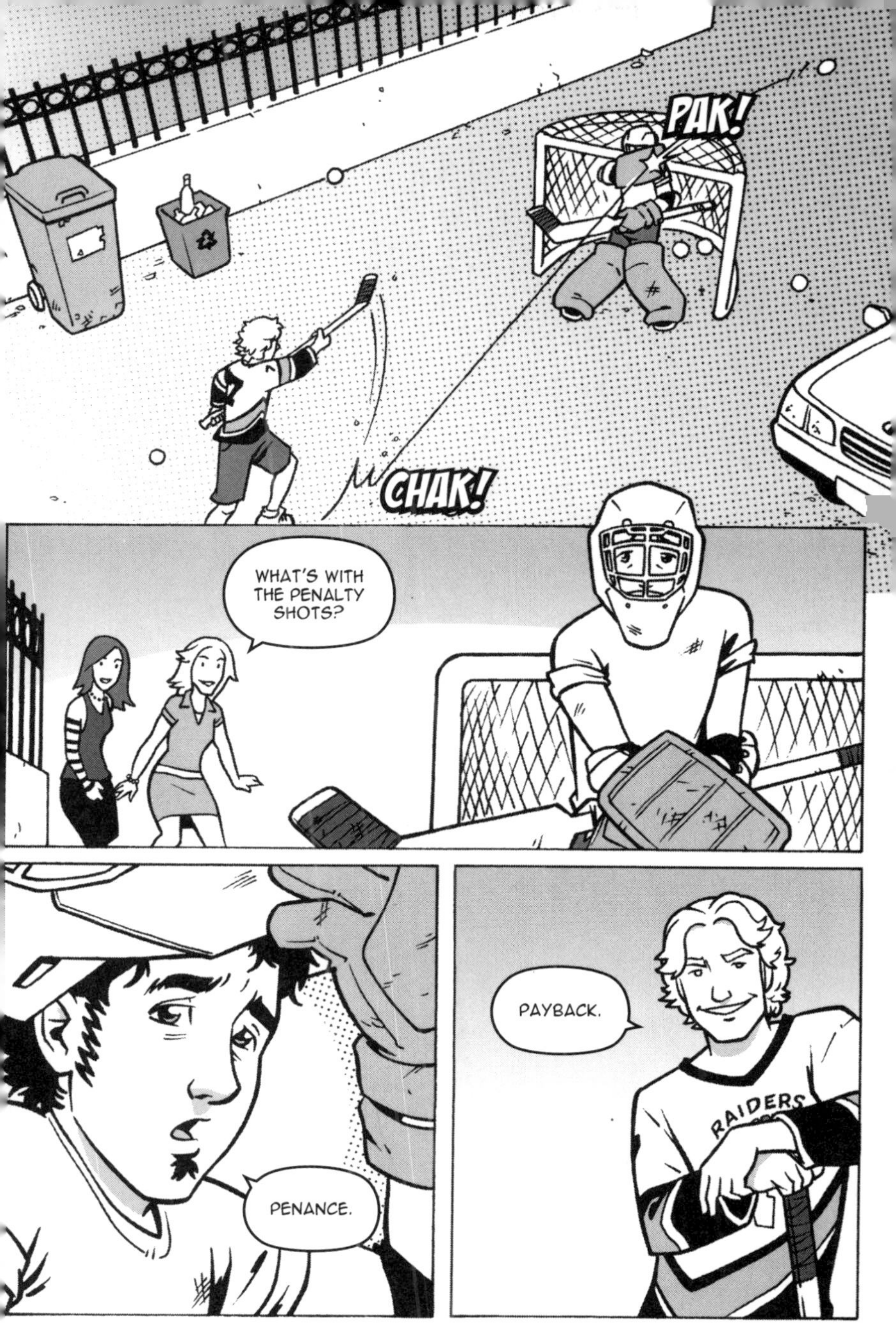
PAK!
CHAK!
WHAT'S WITH THE PENALTY SHOTS?
PENANCE.
PAYBACK.
RAIDERS

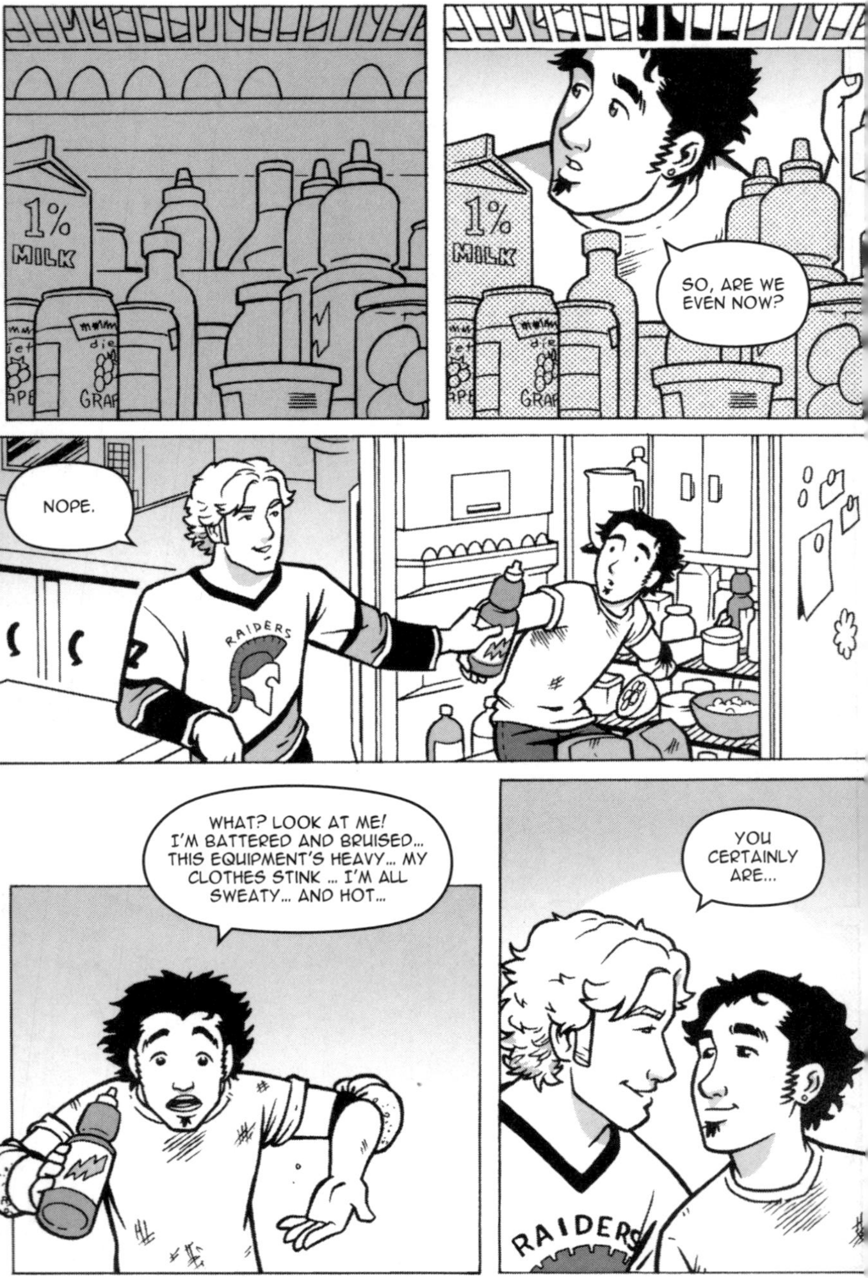
1% MILK
SO, ARE WE EVEN NOW?
NOPE.
RAIDERS
WHAT? LOOK AT ME! I'M BATTERED AND BRUISED... THIS EQUIPMENT'S HEAVY... MY CLOTHES STINK ... I'M ALL SWEATY... AND HOT...
YOU CERTAINLY ARE...
RAIDERS

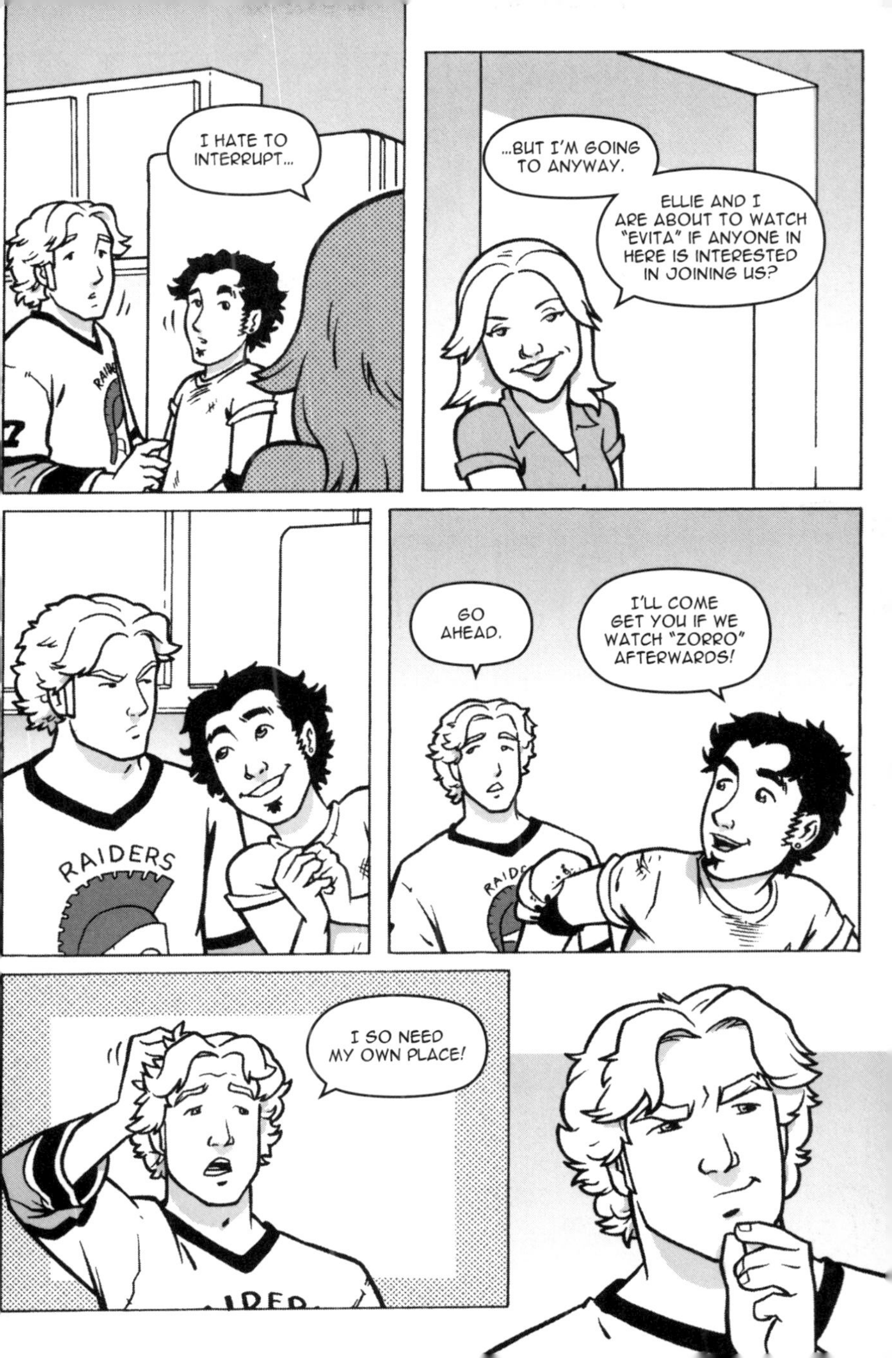

I HATE TO INTERRUPT...
...BUT I'M GOING TO ANYWAY.
ELLIE AND I ARE ABOUT TO WATCH "EVITA" IF ANYONE IN HERE IS INTERESTED IN JOINING US?
GO AHEAD.
I'LL COME GET YOU IF WE WATCH "ZORRO" AFTERWARDS!
I SO NEED MY OWN PLACE!

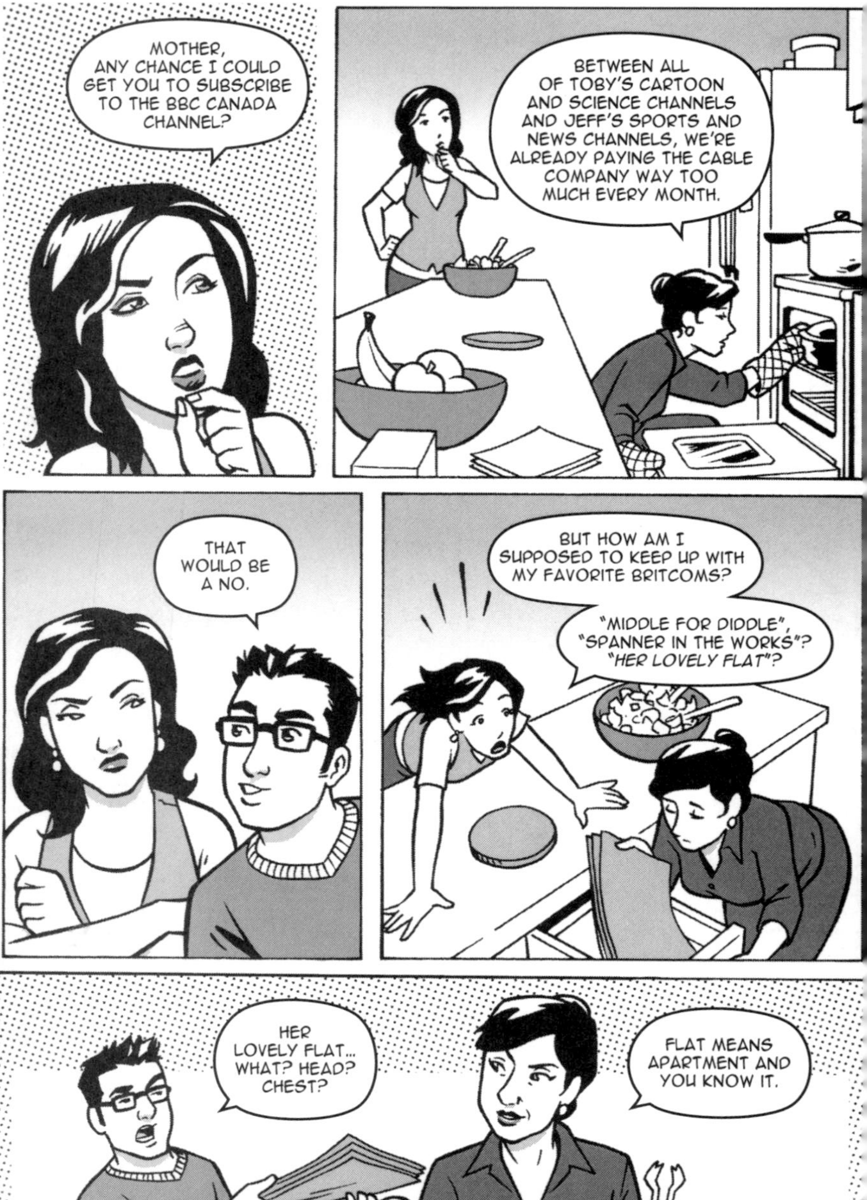
MOTHER, ANY CHANCE I COULD GET YOU TO SUBSCRIBE TO THE BBC CANADA CHANNEL?
BETWEEN ALL OF TOBY'S CARTOON AND SCIENCE CHANNELS AND JEFF'S SPORTS AND NEWS CHANNELS, WE'RE ALREADY PAYING THE CABLE COMPANY WAY TOO MUCH EVERY MONTH.
THAT WOULD BE A NO.
BUT HOW AM I SUPPOSED TO KEEP UP WITH MY FAVORITE BRITCOMS?
"MIDDLE FOR DIDDLE", "SPANNER IN THE WORKS"? "*HER LOVELY FLAT*"?
HER LOVELY FLAT... WHAT? HEAD? CHEST?
FLAT MEANS APARTMENT AND YOU KNOW IT.

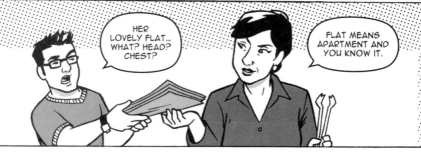

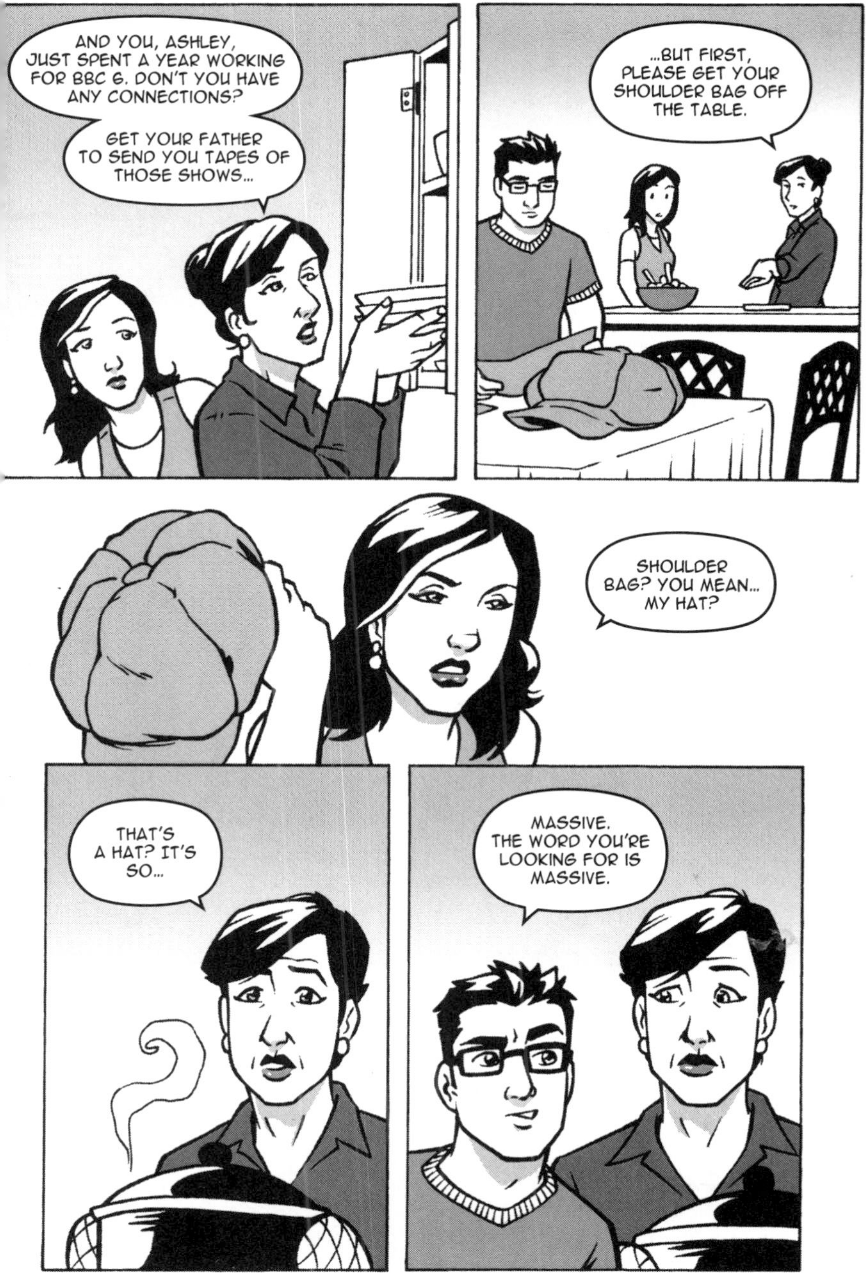
AND YOU, ASHLEY, JUST SPENT A YEAR WORKING FOR BBC 6. DON'T YOU HAVE ANY CONNECTIONS?
GET YOUR FATHER TO SEND YOU TAPES OF THOSE SHOWS...
...BUT FIRST, PLEASE GET YOUR SHOULDER BAG OFF THE TABLE.
SHOULDER BAG? YOU MEAN... MY HAT?
THAT'S A HAT? IT'S SO...
MASSIVE. THE WORD YOU'RE LOOKING FOR IS MASSIVE.

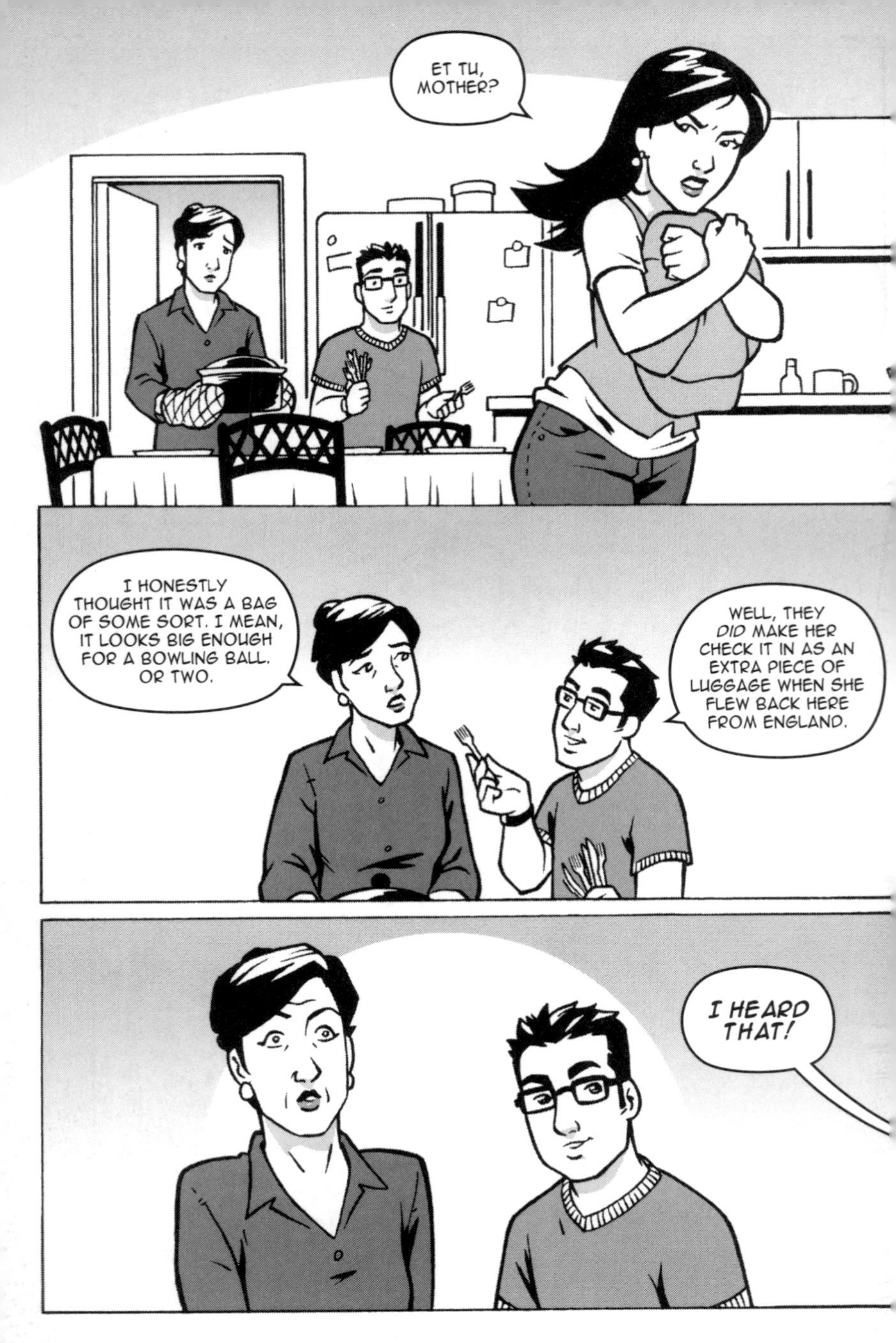
ET TU, MOTHER?
I HONESTLY THOUGHT IT WAS A BAG OF SOME SORT. I MEAN, IT LOOKS BIG ENOUGH FOR A BOWLING BALL. OR TWO.
WELL, THEY *DID* MAKE HER CHECK IT IN AS AN EXTRA PIECE OF LUGGAGE WHEN SHE FLEW BACK HERE FROM ENGLAND.
I HEARD THAT!

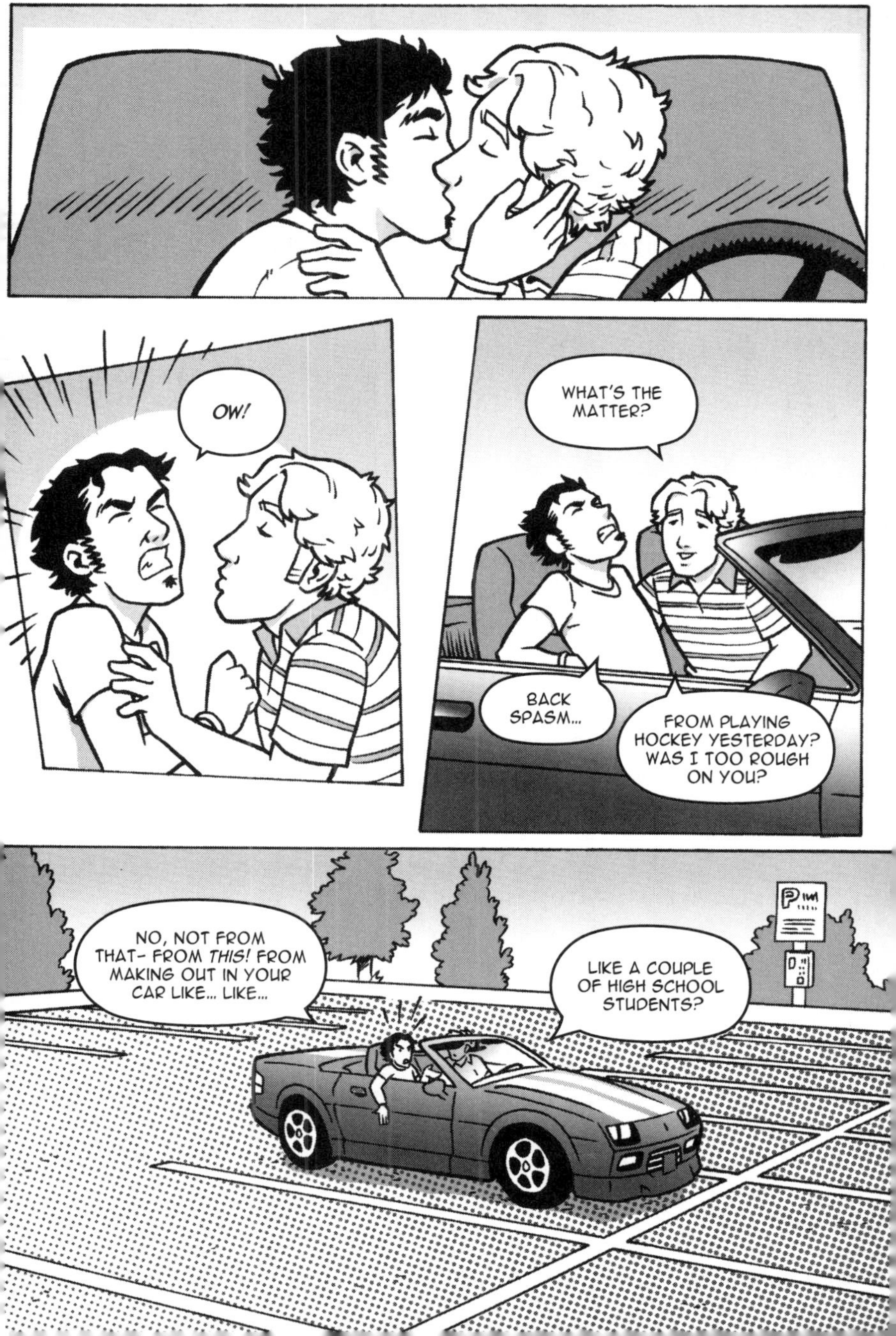
OW!
WHAT'S THE MATTER?
BACK SPASM...
FROM PLAYING HOCKEY YESTERDAY? WAS I TOO ROUGH ON YOU?
NO, NOT FROM THAT- FROM *THIS!* FROM MAKING OUT IN YOUR CAR LIKE... LIKE...
LIKE A COUPLE OF HIGH SCHOOL STUDENTS?

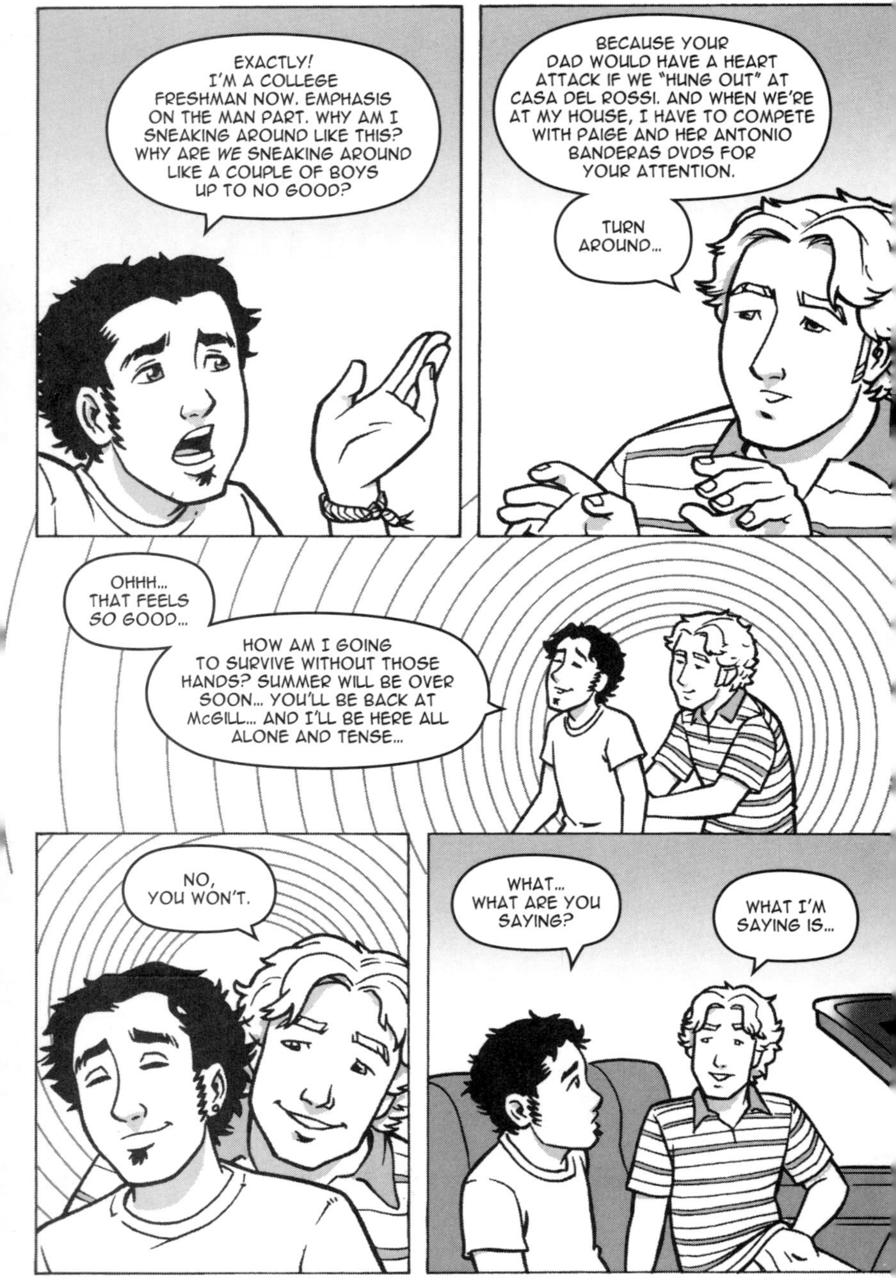
EXACTLY! I'M A COLLEGE FRESHMAN NOW. EMPHASIS ON THE MAN PART. WHY AM I SNEAKING AROUND LIKE THIS? WHY ARE *WE* SNEAKING AROUND LIKE A COUPLE OF BOYS UP TO NO GOOD?
BECAUSE YOUR DAD WOULD HAVE A HEART ATTACK IF WE "HUNG OUT" AT CASA DEL ROSSI. AND WHEN WE'RE AT MY HOUSE, I HAVE TO COMPETE WITH PAIGE AND HER ANTONIO BANDERAS DVDS FOR YOUR ATTENTION.
TURN AROUND...
OHHH... THAT FEELS *SO* GOOD...
HOW AM I GOING TO SURVIVE WITHOUT THOSE HANDS? SUMMER WILL BE OVER SOON... YOU'LL BE BACK AT McGILL... AND I'LL BE HERE ALL ALONE AND TENSE...
NO, YOU WON'T.
WHAT... WHAT ARE YOU SAYING?
WHAT I'M SAYING IS...

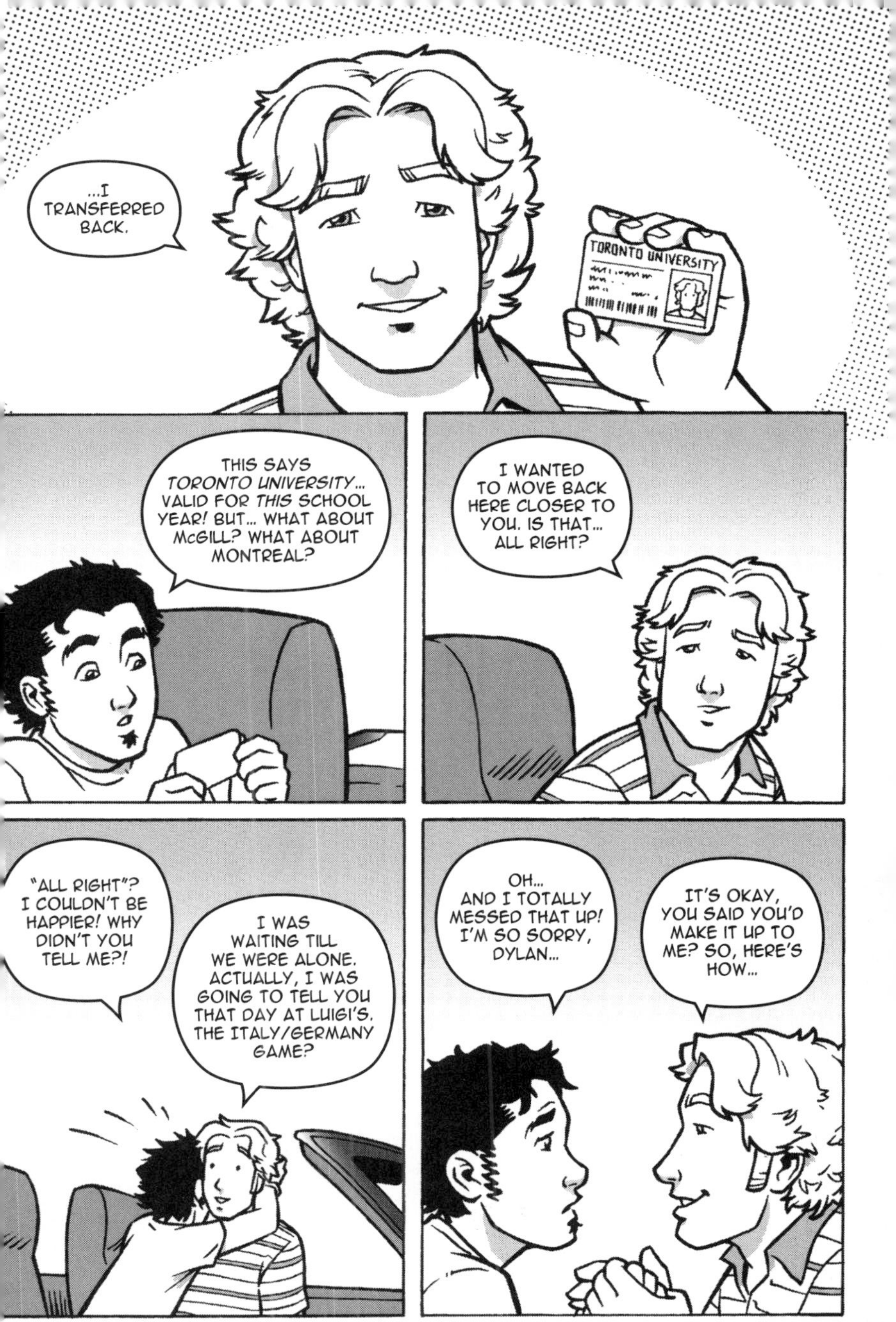
...I TRANSFERRED BACK.
TORONTO UNIVERSITY
THIS SAYS *TORONTO UNIVERSITY*... VALID FOR *THIS* SCHOOL YEAR! BUT... WHAT ABOUT McGILL? WHAT ABOUT MONTREAL?
I WANTED TO MOVE BACK HERE CLOSER TO YOU. IS THAT... ALL RIGHT?
"ALL RIGHT"? I COULDN'T BE HAPPIER! WHY DIDN'T YOU TELL ME?!
I WAS WAITING TILL WE WERE ALONE. ACTUALLY, I WAS GOING TO TELL YOU THAT DAY AT LUIGI'S. THE ITALY/GERMANY GAME?
OH... AND I TOTALLY MESSED THAT UP! I'M SO SORRY, DYLAN...
IT'S OKAY, YOU SAID YOU'D MAKE IT UP TO ME? SO, HERE'S HOW...

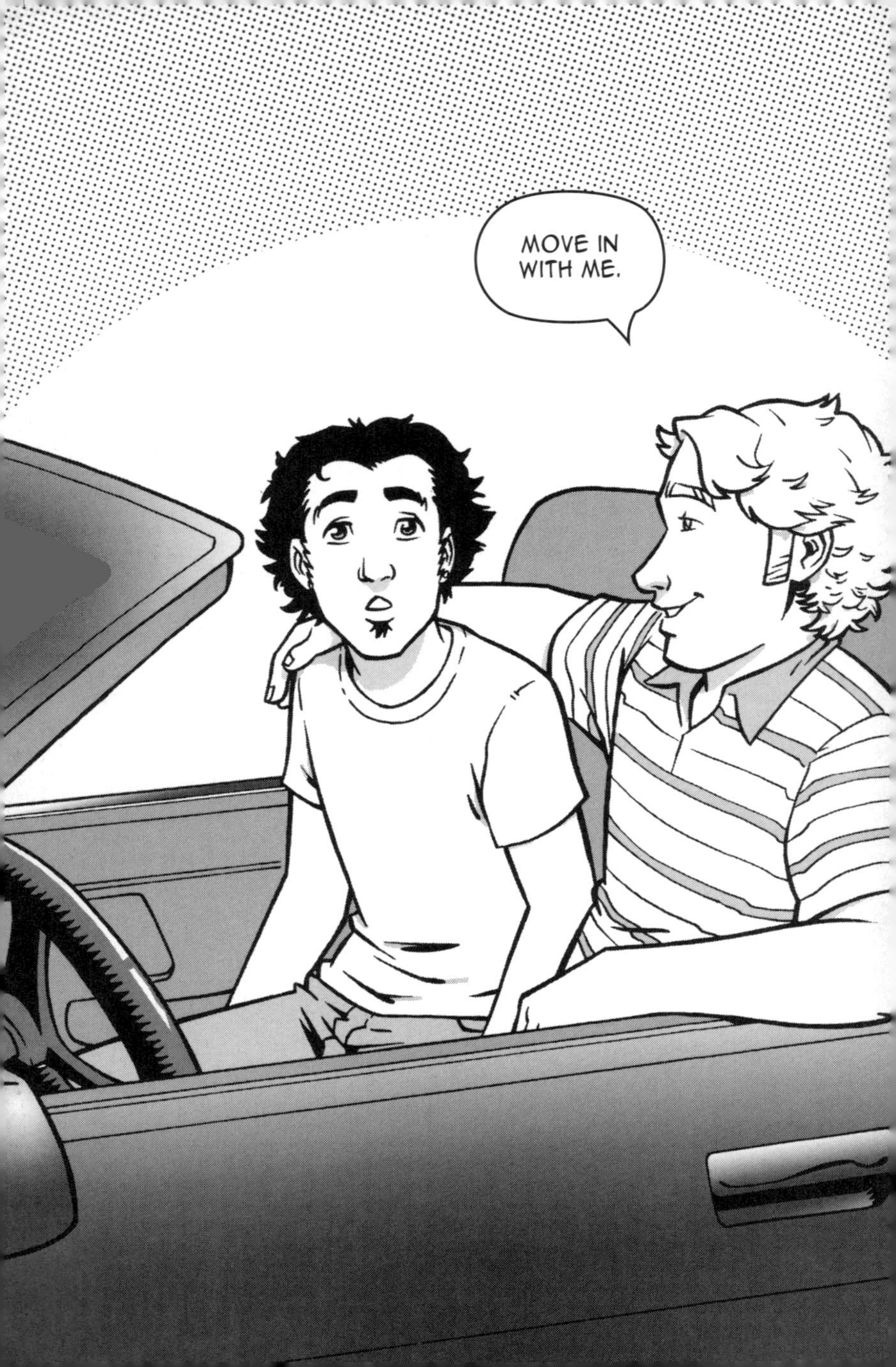
MOVE IN WITH ME.

ACT 2

"We can go when we want to,
The night is young and so am I,
And we can dress real neat
from our hats to our feet,
And surprise 'em with the victory cry.

Say, we can act if we want to,
If we don't nobody will,
And you can act real rude and
totally removed,
And I can act like an imbecile."
— Men Without Hats

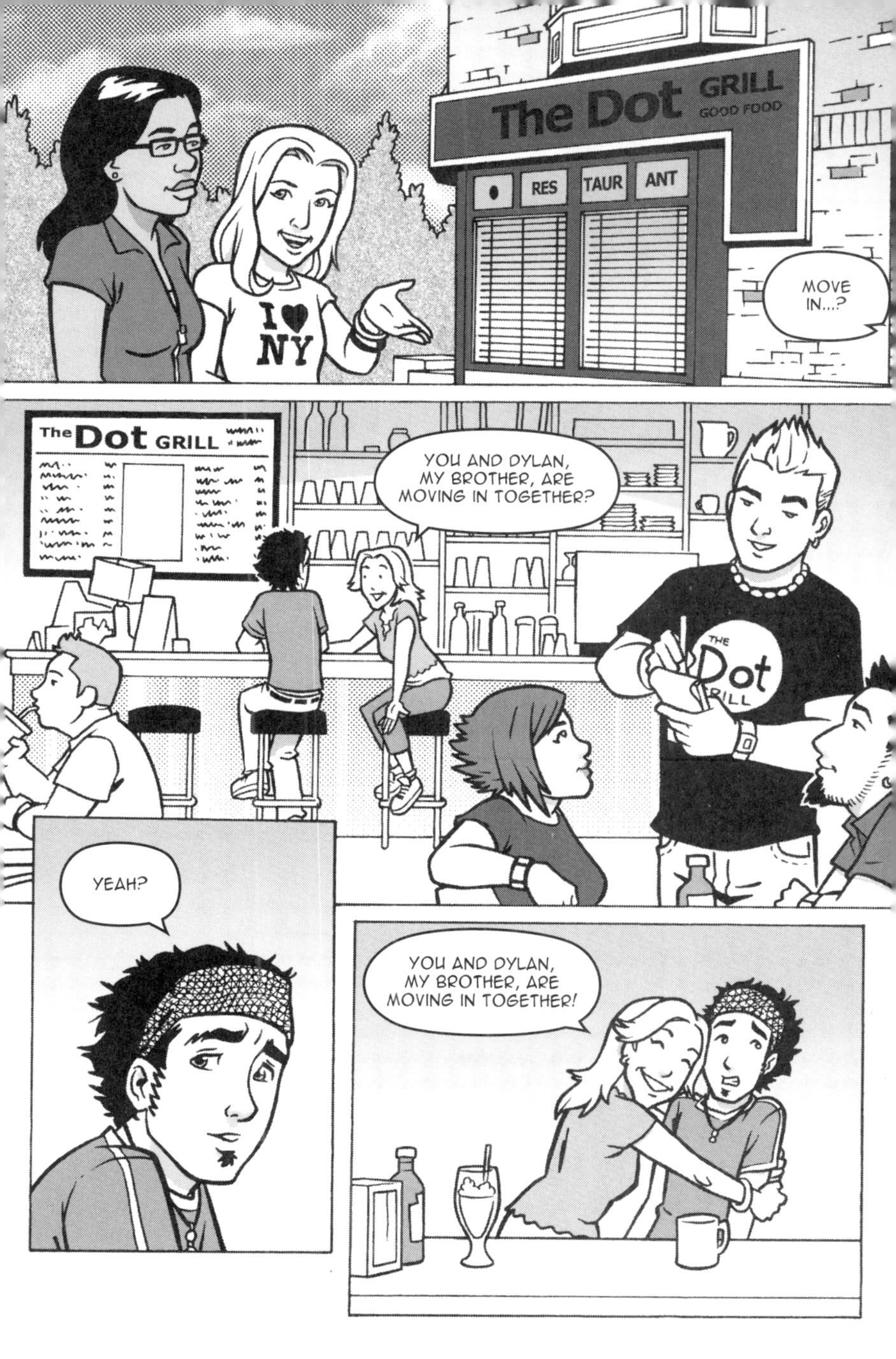

The Dot GRILL
GOOD FOOD
RES TAUR ANT
I ♥ NY
MOVE IN...?
The Dot GRILL
YOU AND DYLAN, MY BROTHER, ARE MOVING IN TOGETHER?
THE Dot GRILL
YEAH?
YOU AND DYLAN, MY BROTHER, ARE MOVING IN TOGETHER!

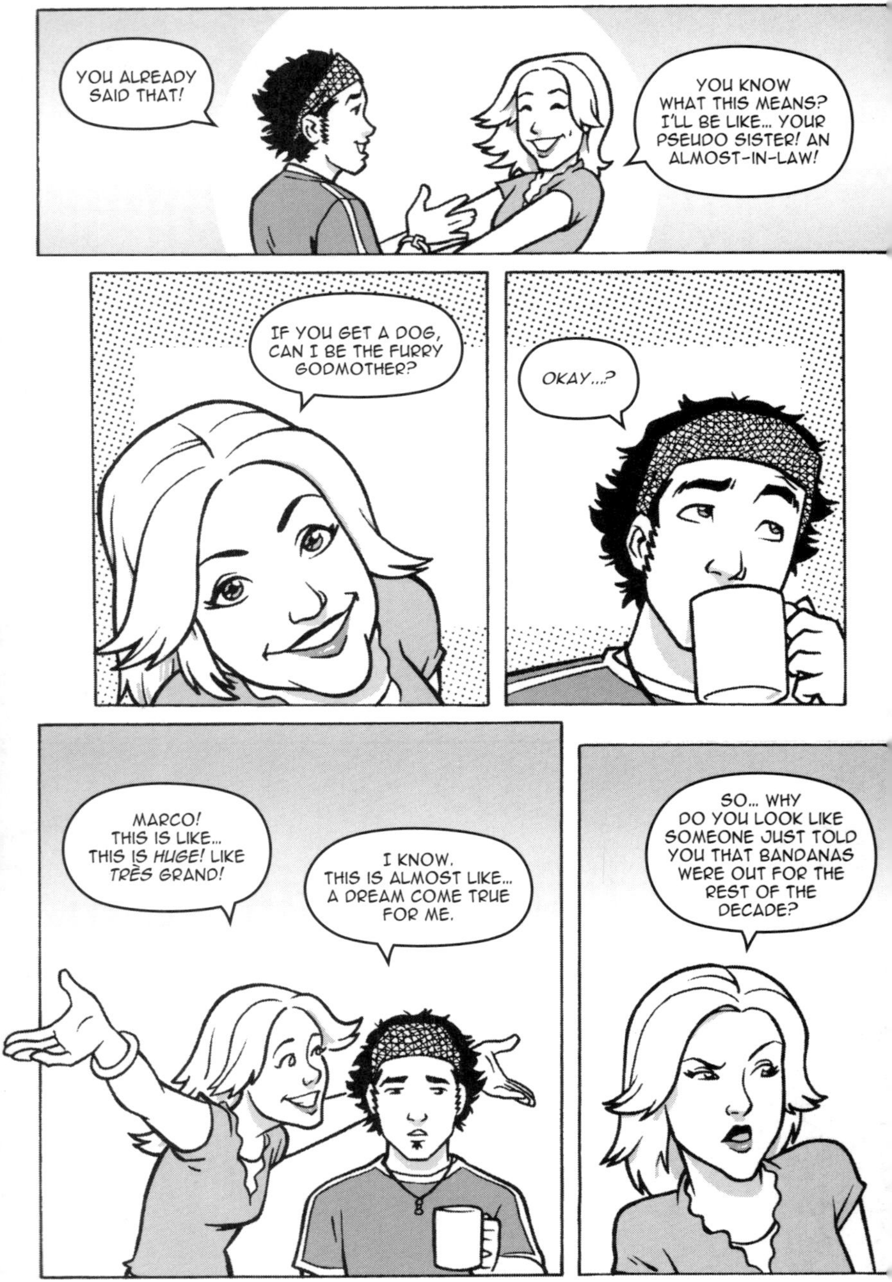
YOU ALREADY SAID THAT!
YOU KNOW WHAT THIS MEANS? I'LL BE LIKE... YOUR PSEUDO SISTER! AN ALMOST-IN-LAW!
IF YOU GET A DOG, CAN I BE THE FURRY GODMOTHER?
OKAY...?
MARCO! THIS IS LIKE... THIS IS *HUGE!* LIKE *TRÈS* GRAND!
I KNOW. THIS IS ALMOST LIKE... A DREAM COME TRUE FOR ME.
SO... WHY DO YOU LOOK LIKE SOMEONE JUST TOLD YOU THAT BANDANAS WERE OUT FOR THE REST OF THE DECADE?

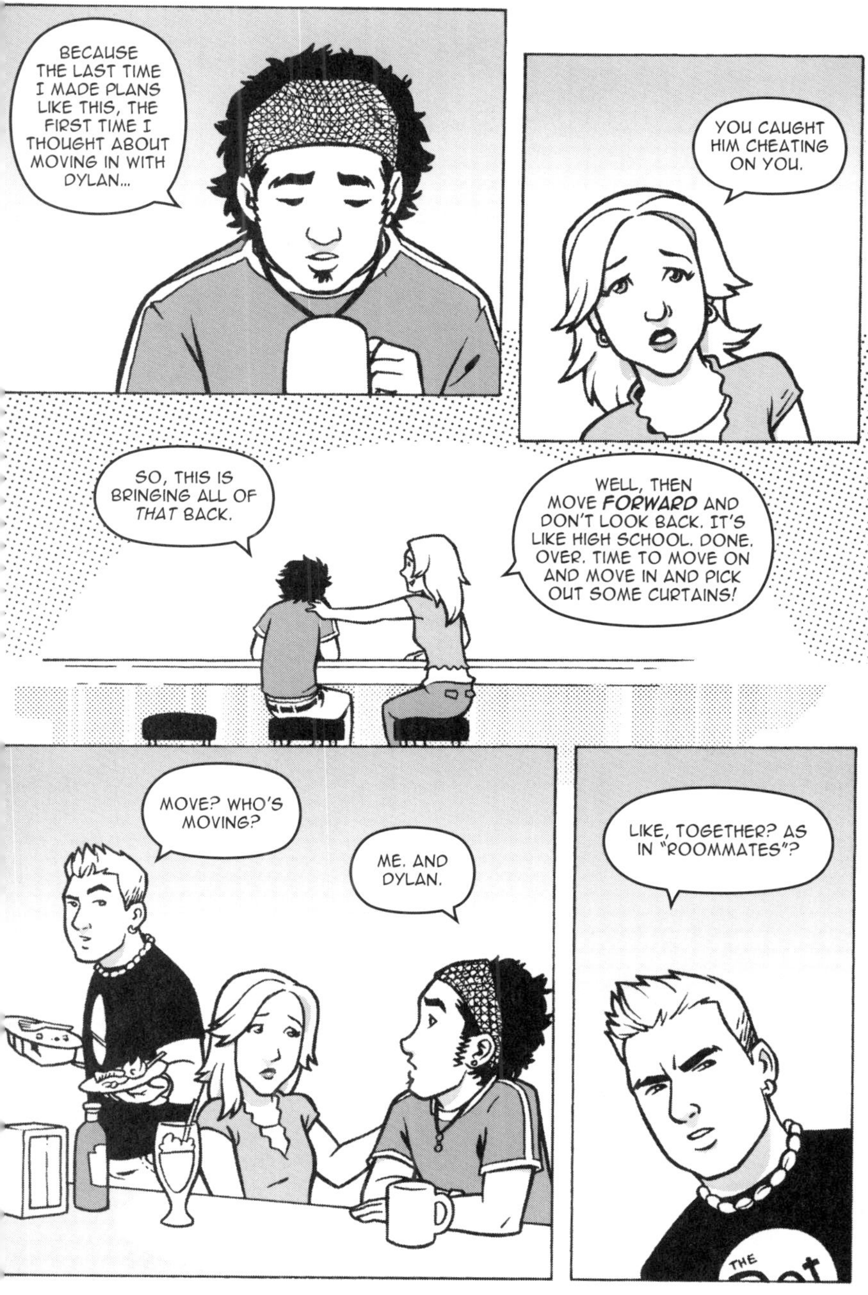
BECAUSE THE LAST TIME I MADE PLANS LIKE THIS, THE FIRST TIME I THOUGHT ABOUT MOVING IN WITH DYLAN...
YOU CAUGHT HIM CHEATING ON YOU.
SO, THIS IS BRINGING ALL OF *THAT* BACK.
WELL, THEN MOVE ***FORWARD*** AND DON'T LOOK BACK. IT'S LIKE HIGH SCHOOL. DONE. OVER. TIME TO MOVE ON AND MOVE IN AND PICK OUT SOME CURTAINS!
MOVE? WHO'S MOVING?
ME. AND DYLAN.
LIKE, TOGETHER? AS IN "ROOMMATES"?
THE

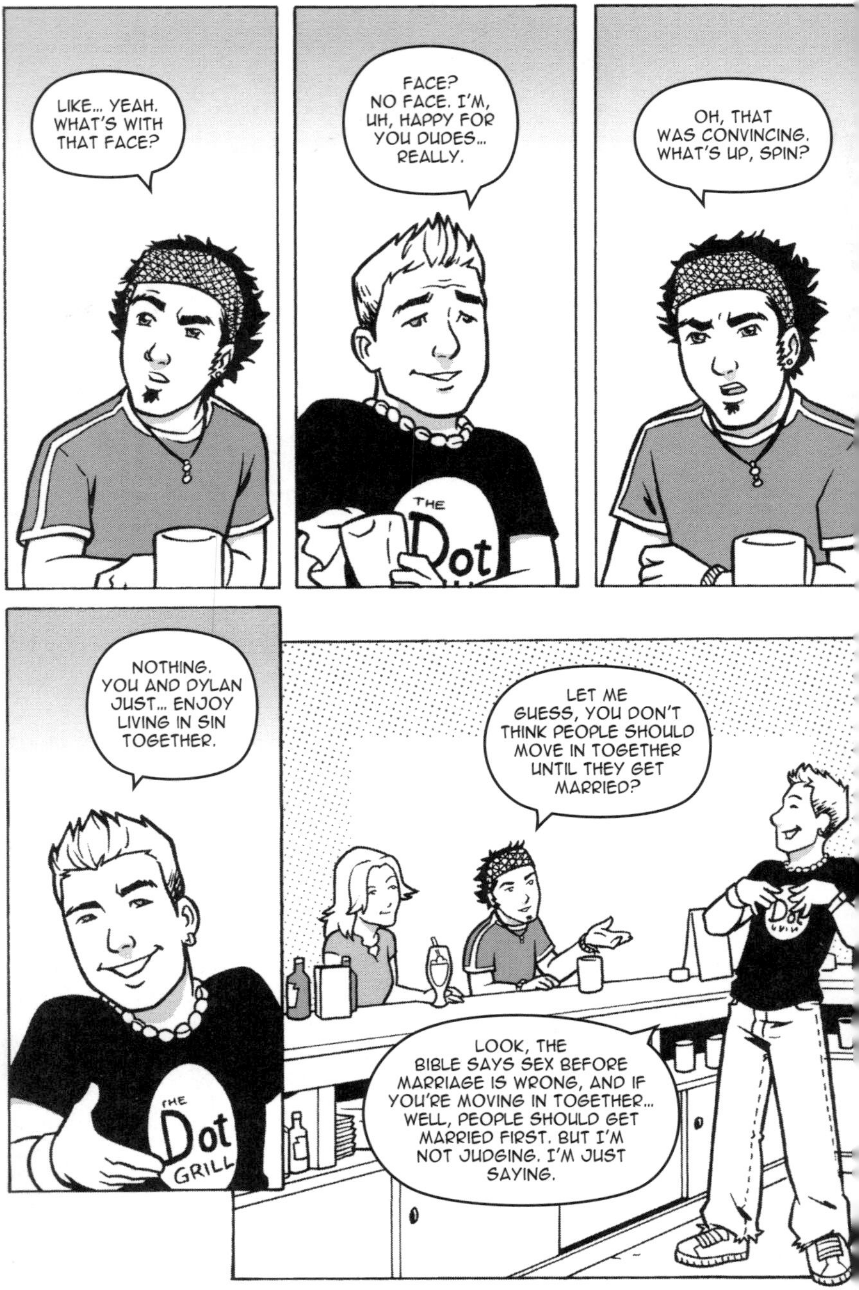
LIKE... YEAH. WHAT'S WITH THAT FACE?
FACE? NO FACE. I'M, UH, HAPPY FOR YOU DUDES... REALLY.
OH, THAT WAS CONVINCING. WHAT'S UP, SPIN?
NOTHING. YOU AND DYLAN JUST... ENJOY LIVING IN SIN TOGETHER.
LET ME GUESS, YOU DON'T THINK PEOPLE SHOULD MOVE IN TOGETHER UNTIL THEY GET MARRIED?
LOOK, THE BIBLE SAYS SEX BEFORE MARRIAGE IS WRONG, AND IF YOU'RE MOVING IN TOGETHER... WELL, PEOPLE SHOULD GET MARRIED FIRST. BUT I'M NOT JUDGING. I'M JUST SAYING.

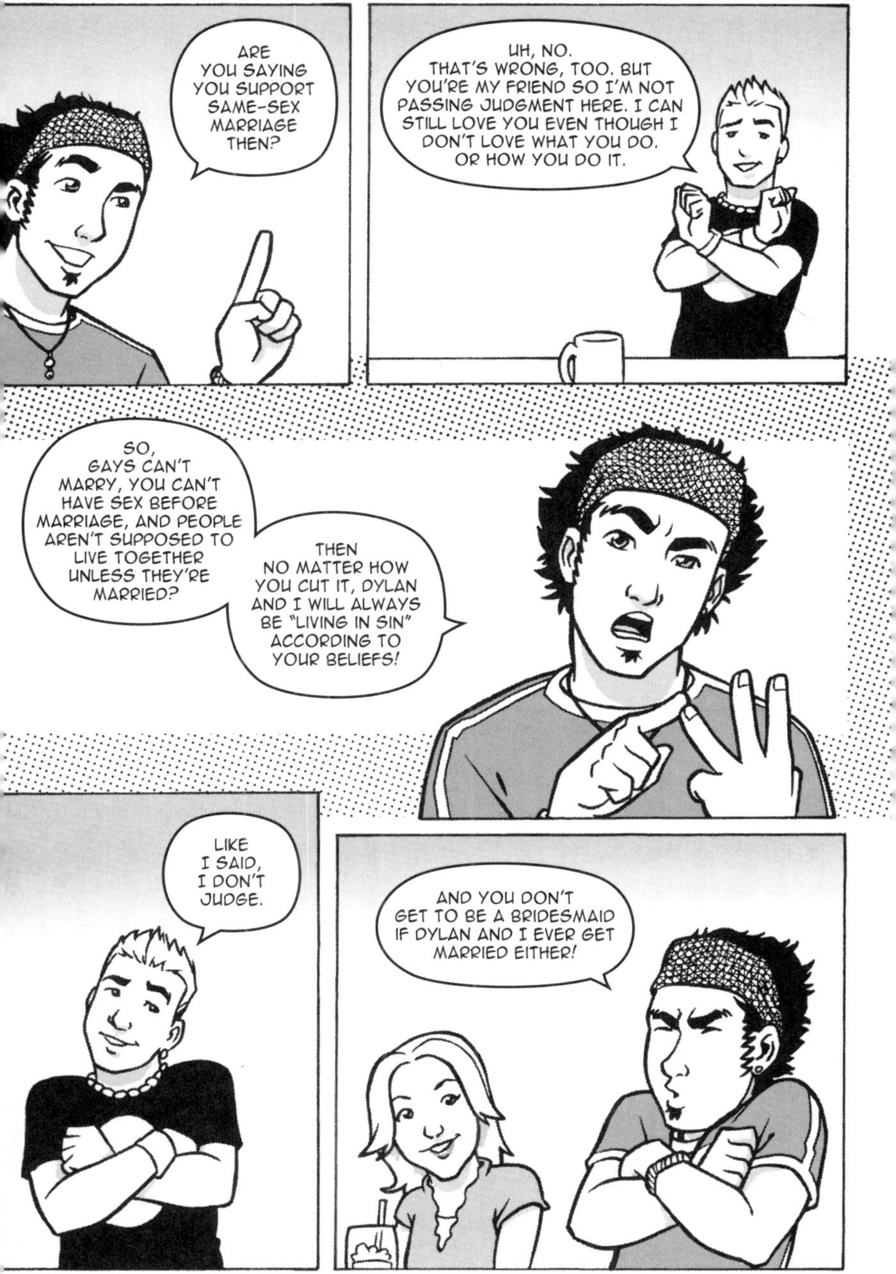
ARE YOU SAYING YOU SUPPORT SAME-SEX MARRIAGE THEN?
UH, NO. THAT'S WRONG, TOO. BUT YOU'RE MY FRIEND SO I'M NOT PASSING JUDGMENT HERE. I CAN STILL LOVE YOU EVEN THOUGH I DON'T LOVE WHAT YOU DO. OR HOW YOU DO IT.
SO, GAYS CAN'T MARRY, YOU CAN'T HAVE SEX BEFORE MARRIAGE, AND PEOPLE AREN'T SUPPOSED TO LIVE TOGETHER UNLESS THEY'RE MARRIED?
THEN NO MATTER HOW YOU CUT IT, DYLAN AND I WILL ALWAYS BE "LIVING IN SIN" ACCORDING TO YOUR BELIEFS!
LIKE I SAID, I DON'T JUDGE.
AND YOU DON'T GET TO BE A BRIDESMAID IF DYLAN AND I EVER GET MARRIED EITHER!

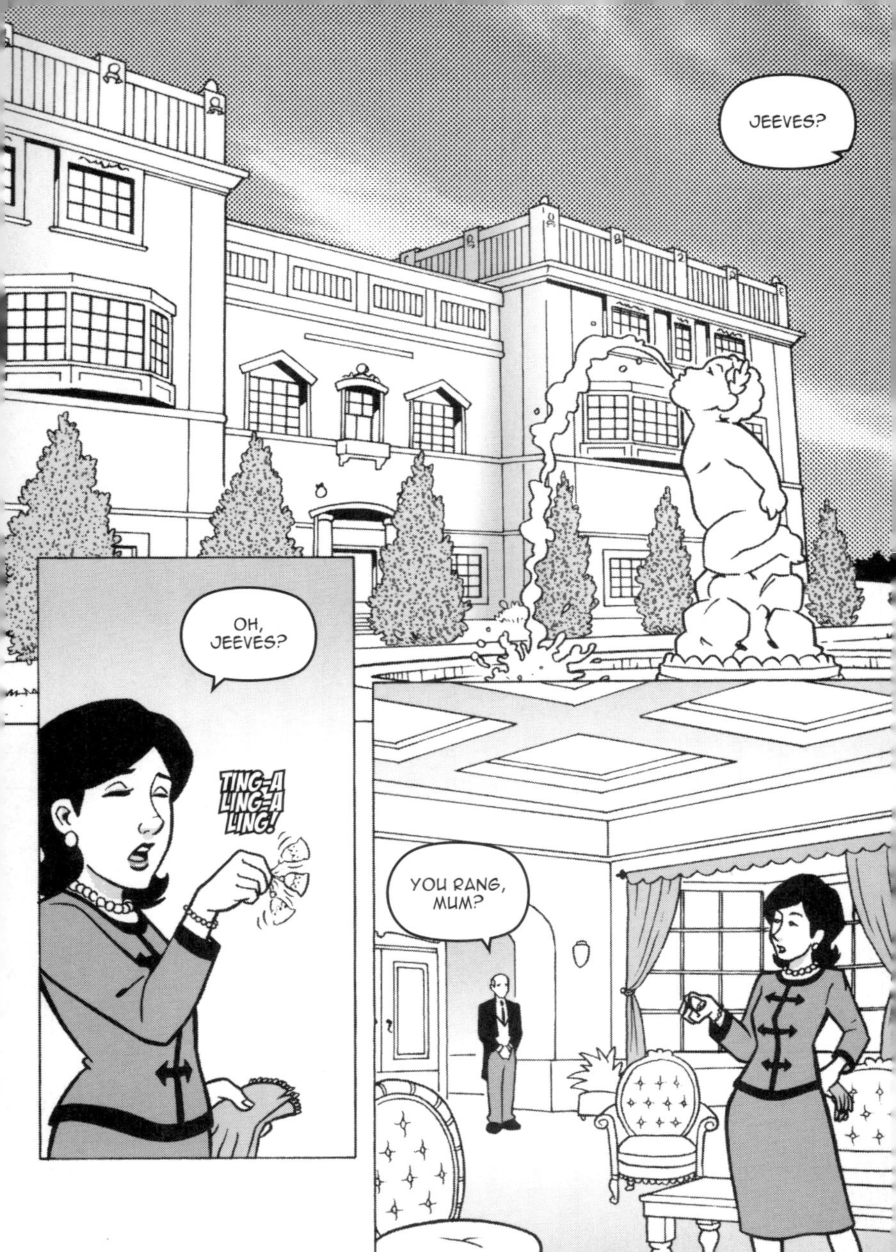
JEEVES?
OH, JEEVES?
TING-A LING-A LING!
YOU RANG, MUM?

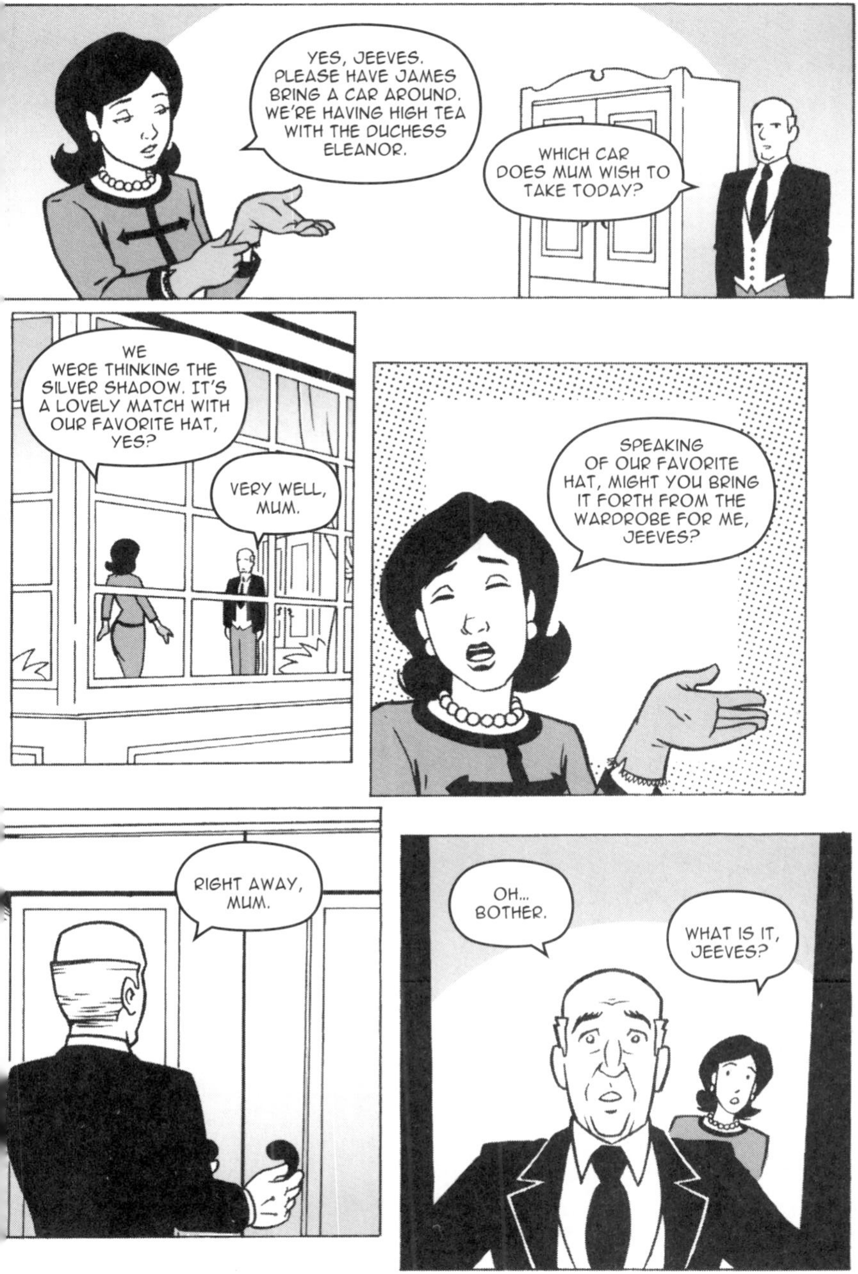
YES, JEEVES. PLEASE HAVE JAMES BRING A CAR AROUND. WE'RE HAVING HIGH TEA WITH THE DUCHESS ELEANOR.
WHICH CAR DOES MUM WISH TO TAKE TODAY?
WE WERE THINKING THE SILVER SHADOW. IT'S A LOVELY MATCH WITH OUR FAVORITE HAT, YES?
VERY WELL, MUM.
SPEAKING OF OUR FAVORITE HAT, MIGHT YOU BRING IT FORTH FROM THE WARDROBE FOR ME, JEEVES?
RIGHT AWAY, MUM.
OH... BOTHER.
WHAT IS IT, JEEVES?

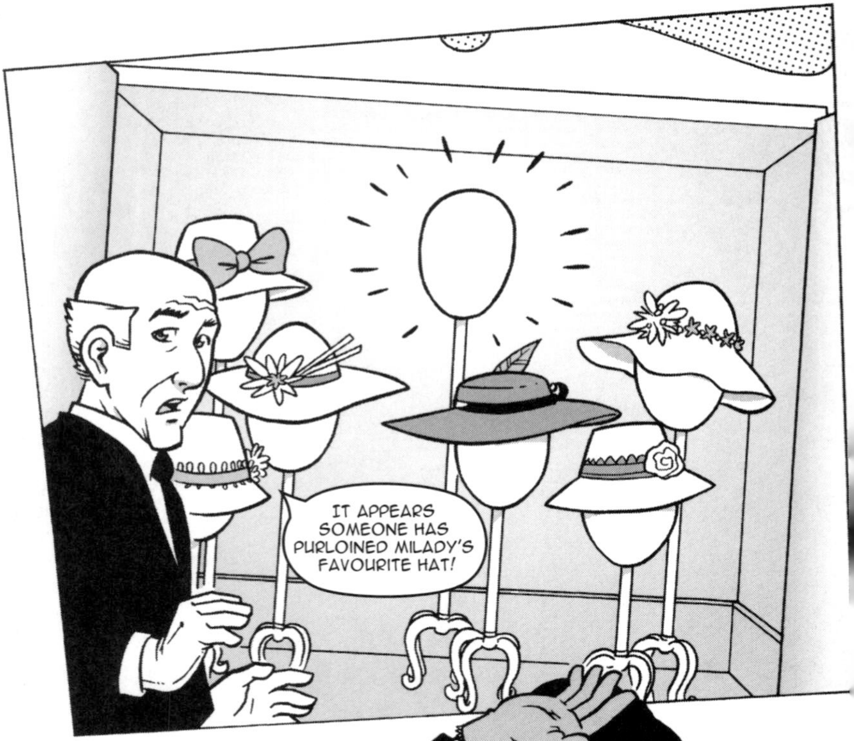
IT APPEARS SOMEONE HAS PURLOINED MILADY'S FAVOURITE HAT!

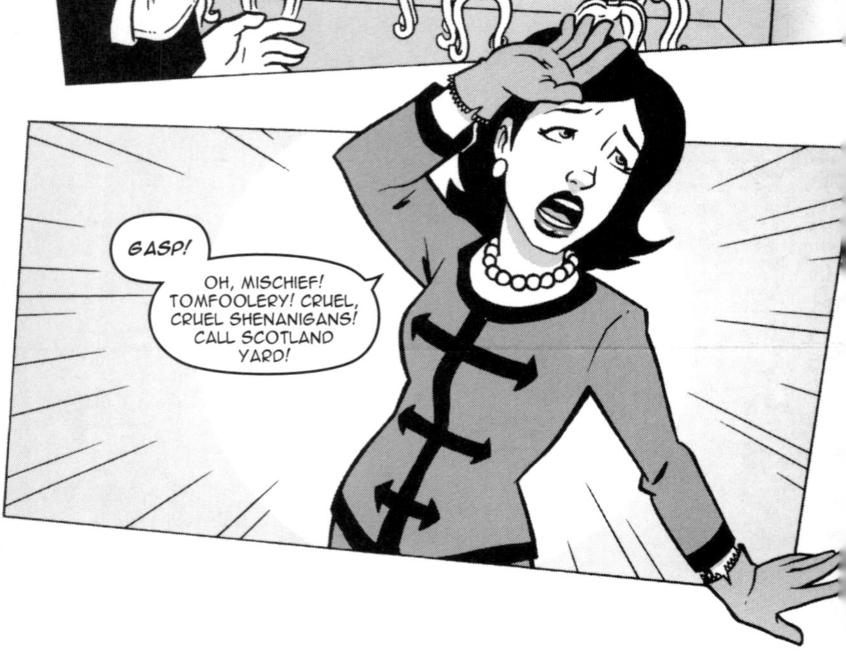
GASP!
OH, MISCHIEF! TOMFOOLERY! CRUEL, CRUEL SHENANIGANS! CALL SCOTLAND YARD!

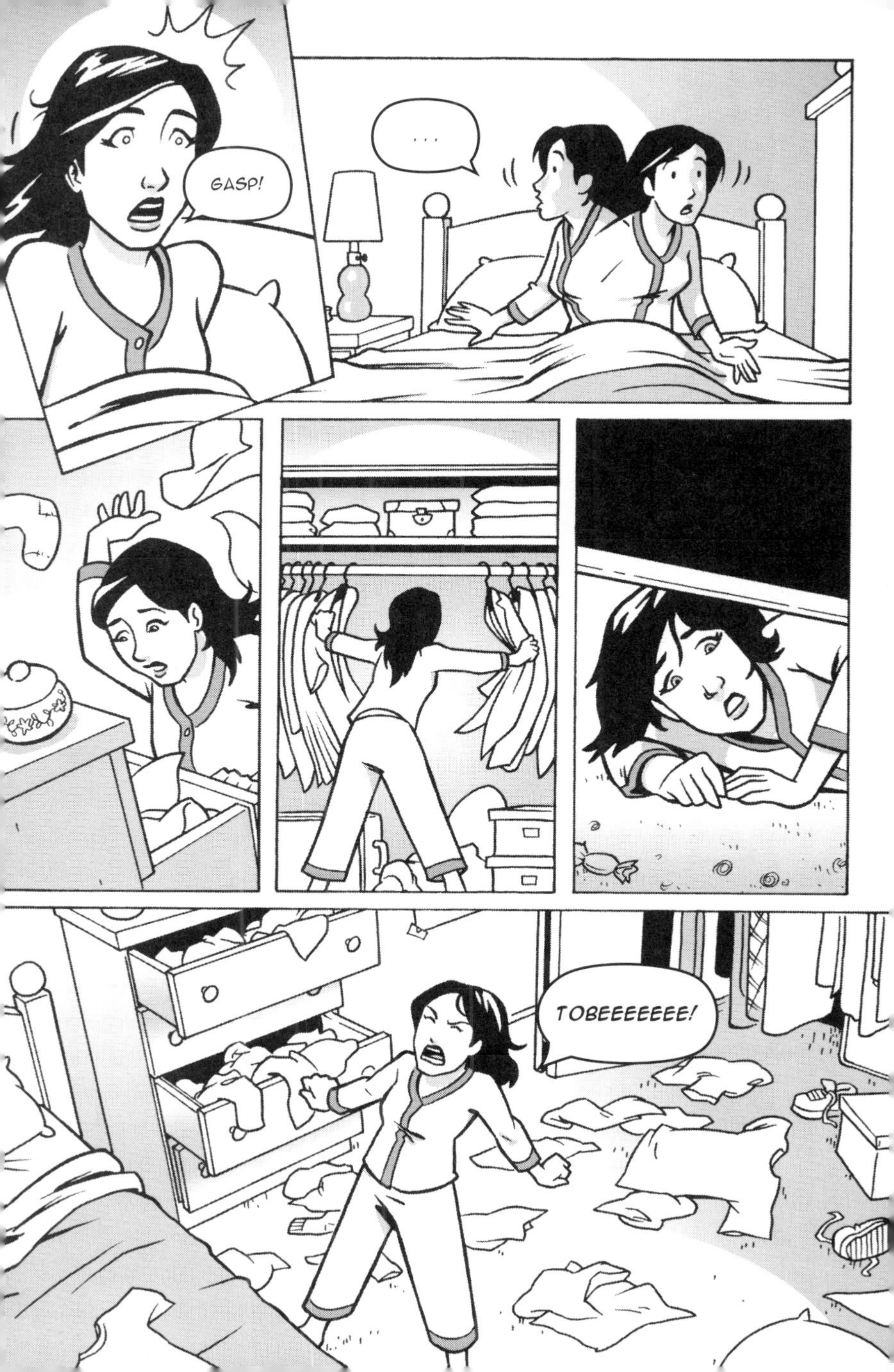
GASP!
. . .
TOBEEEEEEEE!

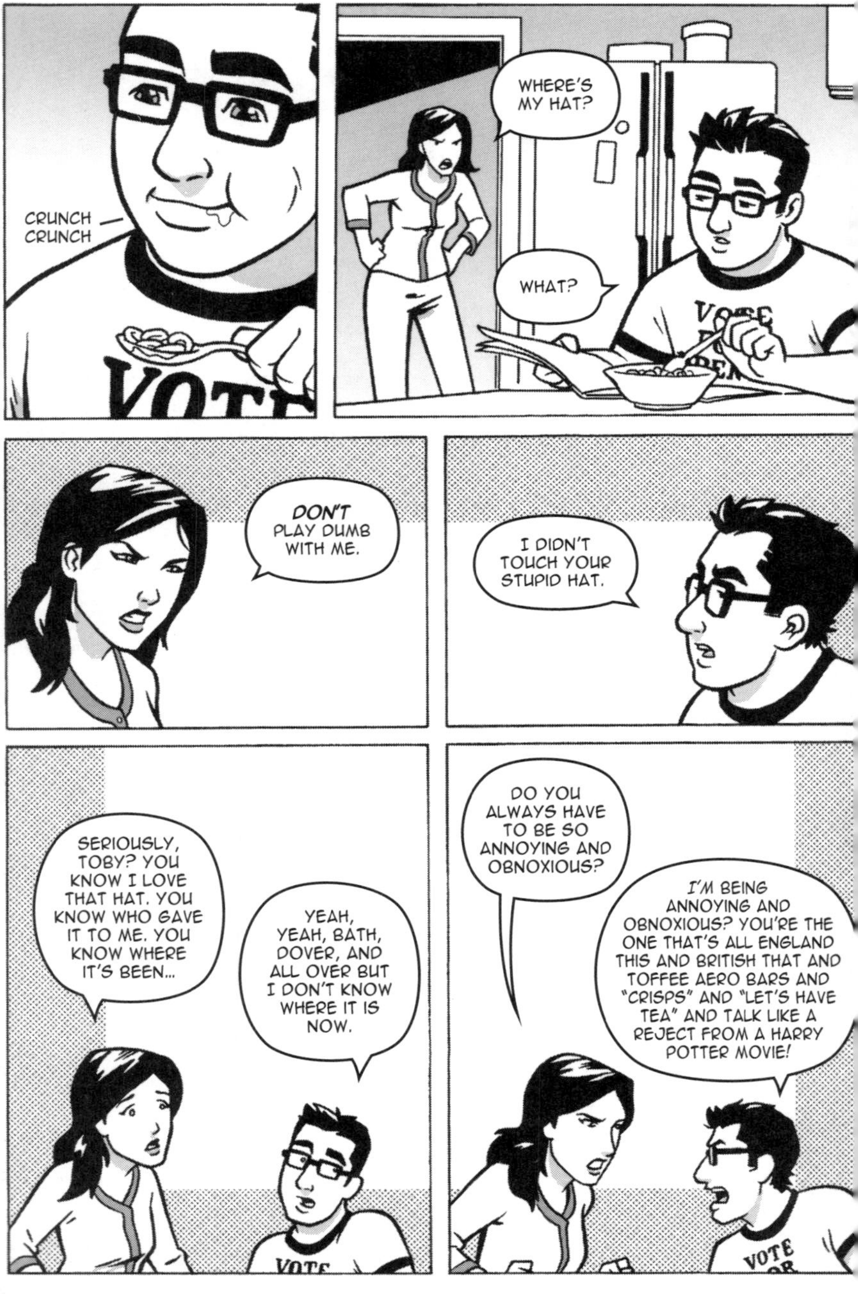
CRUNCH CRUNCH
VOTE
WHERE'S MY HAT?
WHAT?
DON'T PLAY DUMB WITH ME.
I DIDN'T TOUCH YOUR STUPID HAT.
SERIOUSLY, TOBY? YOU KNOW I LOVE THAT HAT. YOU KNOW WHO GAVE IT TO ME. YOU KNOW WHERE IT'S BEEN...
YEAH, YEAH, BATH, DOVER, AND ALL OVER BUT I DON'T KNOW WHERE IT IS NOW.
DO YOU ALWAYS HAVE TO BE SO ANNOYING AND OBNOXIOUS?
I'M BEING ANNOYING AND OBNOXIOUS? YOU'RE THE ONE THAT'S ALL ENGLAND THIS AND BRITISH THAT AND TOFFEE AERO BARS AND "CRISPS" AND "LET'S HAVE TEA" AND TALK LIKE A REJECT FROM A HARRY POTTER MOVIE!
VOTE

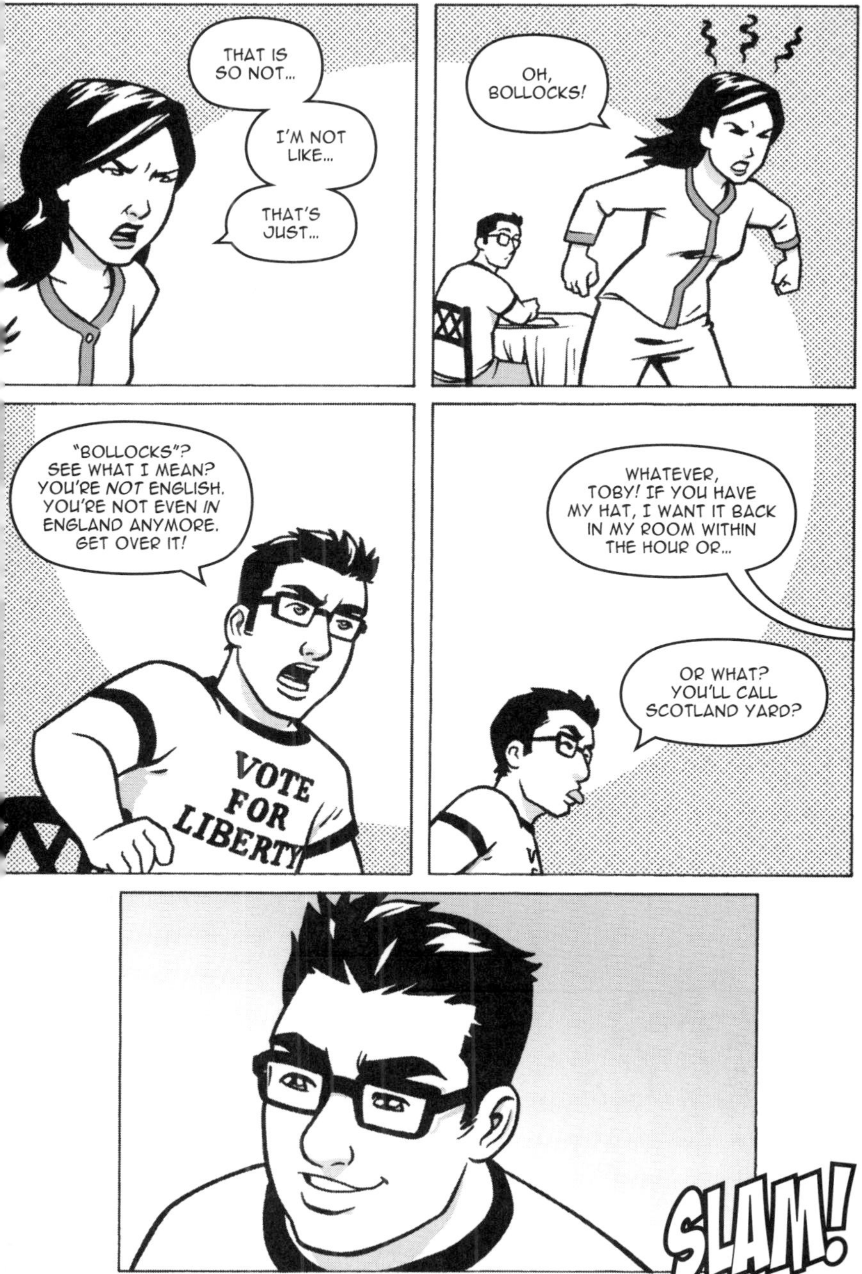
THAT IS SO NOT...
I'M NOT LIKE...
THAT'S JUST...
OH, BOLLOCKS!
"BOLLOCKS"? SEE WHAT I MEAN? YOU'RE *NOT* ENGLISH. YOU'RE NOT EVEN *IN* ENGLAND ANYMORE. GET OVER IT!
VOTE FOR LIBERTY
WHATEVER, TOBY! IF YOU HAVE MY HAT, I WANT IT BACK IN MY ROOM WITHIN THE HOUR OR...
OR WHAT? YOU'LL CALL SCOTLAND YARD?
SLAM!

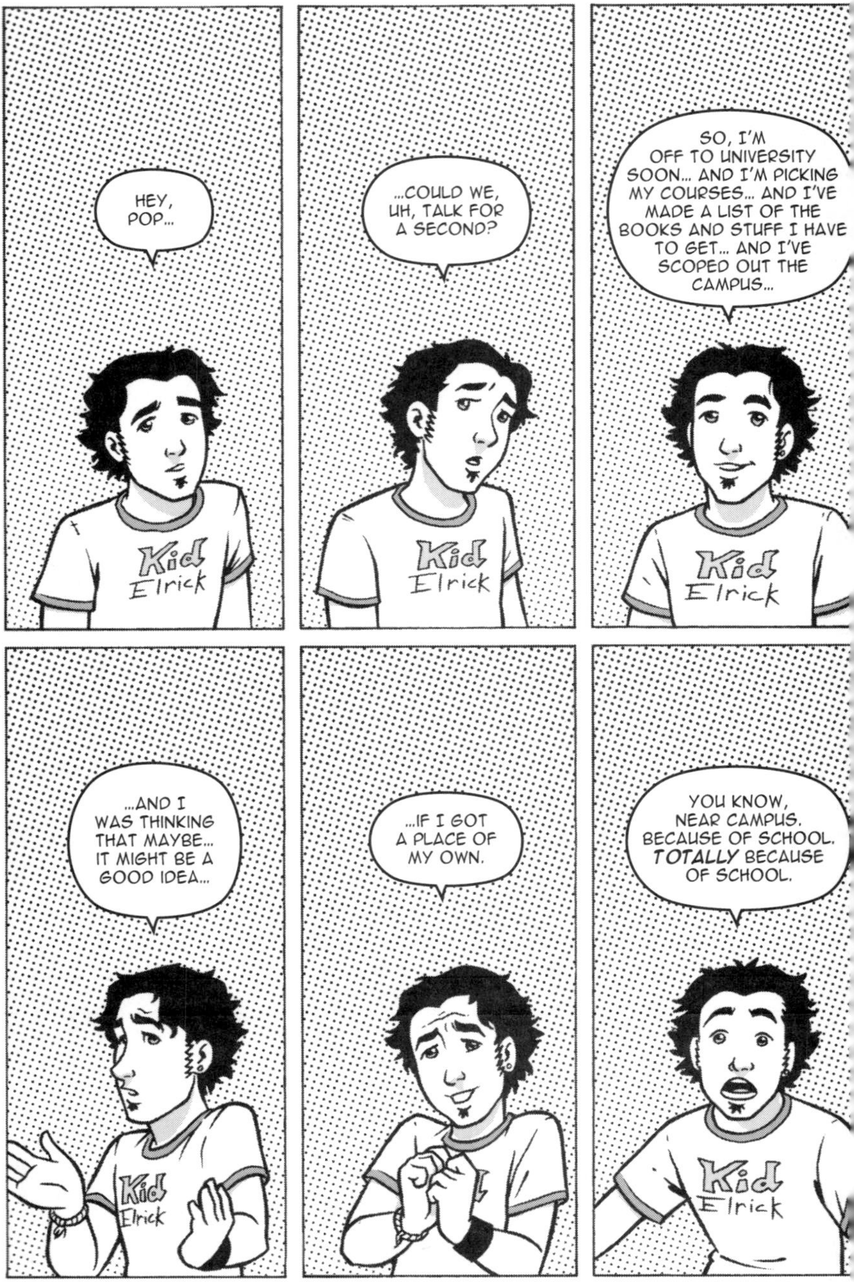
HEY, POP...
...COULD WE, UH, TALK FOR A SECOND?
SO, I'M OFF TO UNIVERSITY SOON... AND I'M PICKING MY COURSES... AND I'VE MADE A LIST OF THE BOOKS AND STUFF I HAVE TO GET... AND I'VE SCOPED OUT THE CAMPUS...
...AND I WAS THINKING THAT MAYBE... IT MIGHT BE A GOOD IDEA...
...IF I GOT A PLACE OF MY OWN.
YOU KNOW, NEAR CAMPUS. BECAUSE OF SCHOOL. *TOTALLY* BECAUSE OF SCHOOL.
Kid Elrick

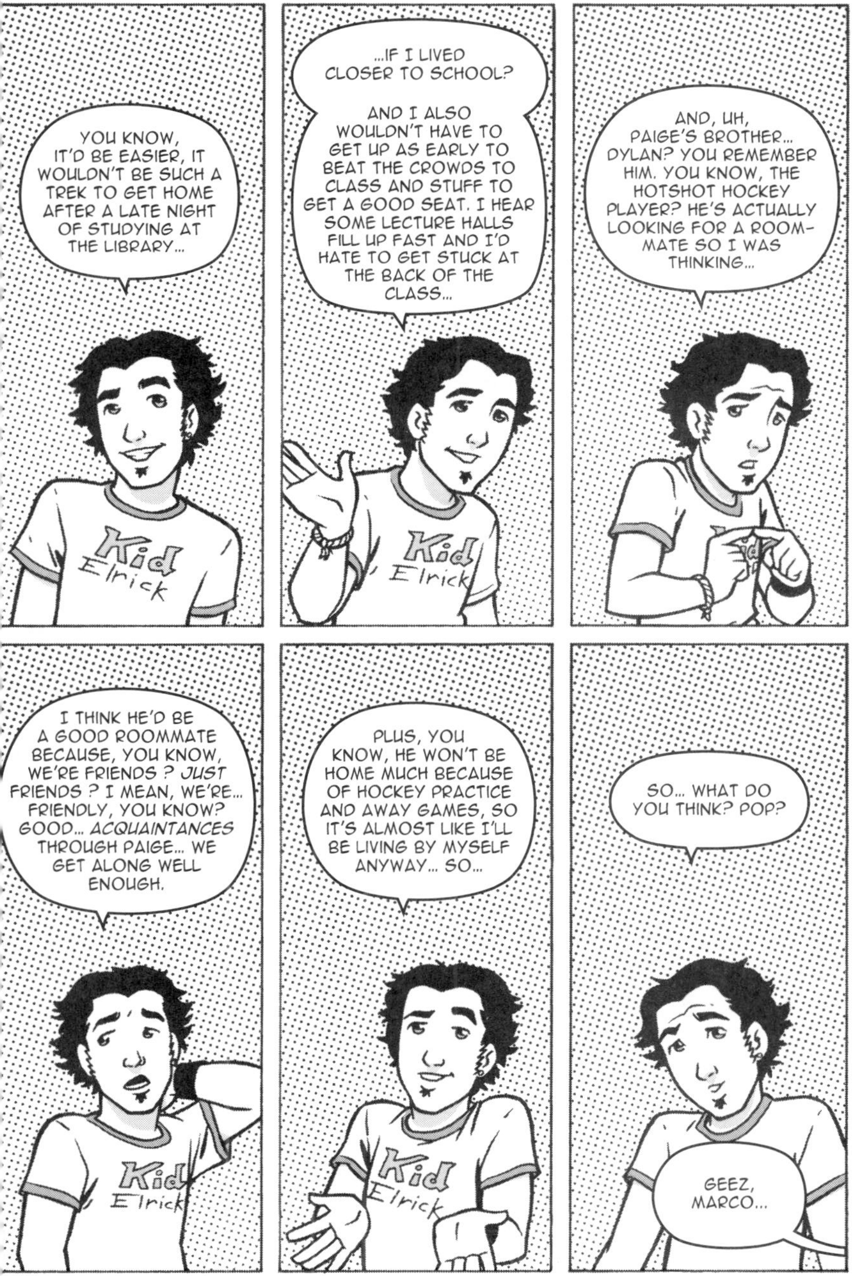
YOU KNOW, IT'D BE EASIER, IT WOULDN'T BE SUCH A TREK TO GET HOME AFTER A LATE NIGHT OF STUDYING AT THE LIBRARY...
...IF I LIVED CLOSER TO SCHOOL?
AND I ALSO WOULDN'T HAVE TO GET UP AS EARLY TO BEAT THE CROWDS TO CLASS AND STUFF TO GET A GOOD SEAT. I HEAR SOME LECTURE HALLS FILL UP FAST AND I'D HATE TO GET STUCK AT THE BACK OF THE CLASS...
AND, UH, PAIGE'S BROTHER... DYLAN? YOU REMEMBER HIM. YOU KNOW, THE HOTSHOT HOCKEY PLAYER? HE'S ACTUALLY LOOKING FOR A ROOM-MATE SO I WAS THINKING...
I THINK HE'D BE A GOOD ROOMMATE BECAUSE, YOU KNOW, WE'RE FRIENDS ? *JUST* FRIENDS ? I MEAN, WE'RE... FRIENDLY, YOU KNOW? GOOD... *ACQUAINTANCES* THROUGH PAIGE... WE GET ALONG WELL ENOUGH.
PLUS, YOU KNOW, HE WON'T BE HOME MUCH BECAUSE OF HOCKEY PRACTICE AND AWAY GAMES, SO IT'S ALMOST LIKE I'LL BE LIVING BY MYSELF ANYWAY... SO...
SO... WHAT DO YOU THINK? POP?
GEEZ, MARCO...

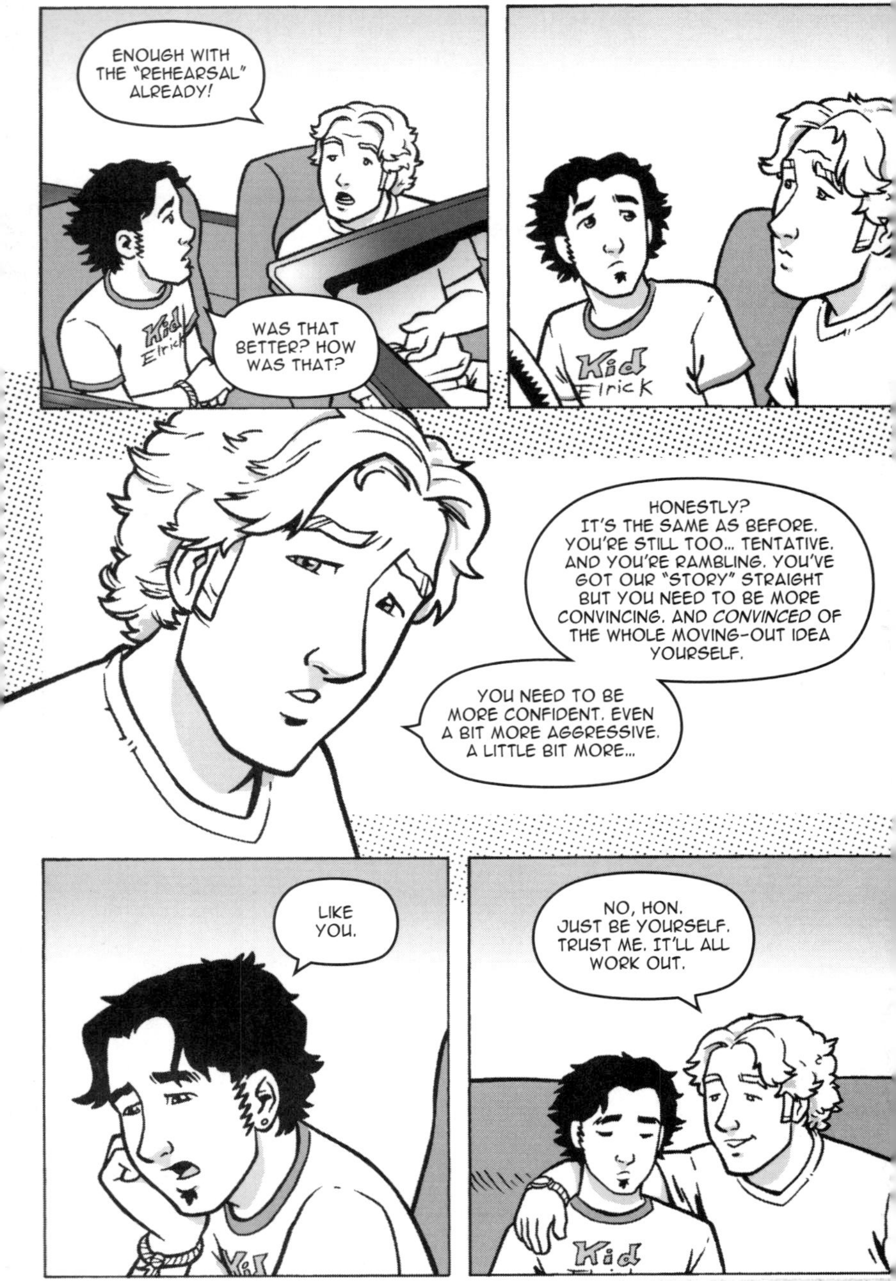
ENOUGH WITH THE "REHEARSAL" ALREADY!
Kid Elrick
WAS THAT BETTER? HOW WAS THAT?
Kid Elrick
HONESTLY? IT'S THE SAME AS BEFORE. YOU'RE STILL TOO... TENTATIVE. AND YOU'RE RAMBLING. YOU'VE GOT OUR "STORY" STRAIGHT BUT YOU NEED TO BE MORE CONVINCING. AND *CONVINCED* OF THE WHOLE MOVING-OUT IDEA YOURSELF.
YOU NEED TO BE MORE CONFIDENT. EVEN A BIT MORE AGGRESSIVE. A LITTLE BIT MORE...
LIKE YOU.
NO, HON. JUST BE YOURSELF. TRUST ME. IT'LL ALL WORK OUT.
Kid

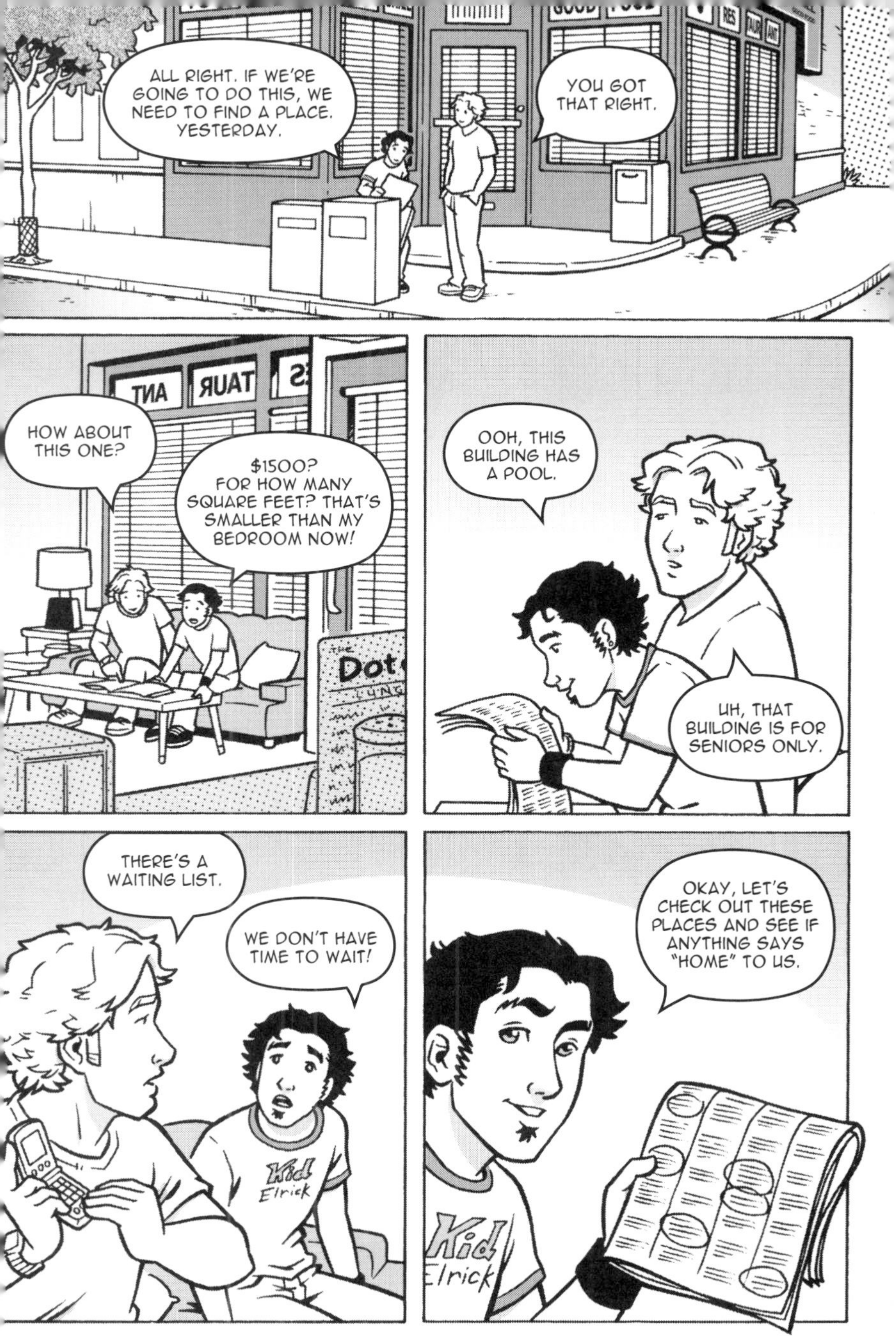
ALL RIGHT. IF WE'RE GOING TO DO THIS, WE NEED TO FIND A PLACE. YESTERDAY.
YOU GOT THAT RIGHT.
RES TAUR ANT
HOW ABOUT THIS ONE?
$1500? FOR HOW MANY SQUARE FEET? THAT'S SMALLER THAN MY BEDROOM NOW!
OOH, THIS BUILDING HAS A POOL.
UH, THAT BUILDING IS FOR SENIORS ONLY.
THERE'S A WAITING LIST.
WE DON'T HAVE TIME TO WAIT!
Kid Elrick
OKAY, LET'S CHECK OUT THESE PLACES AND SEE IF ANYTHING SAYS "HOME" TO US.

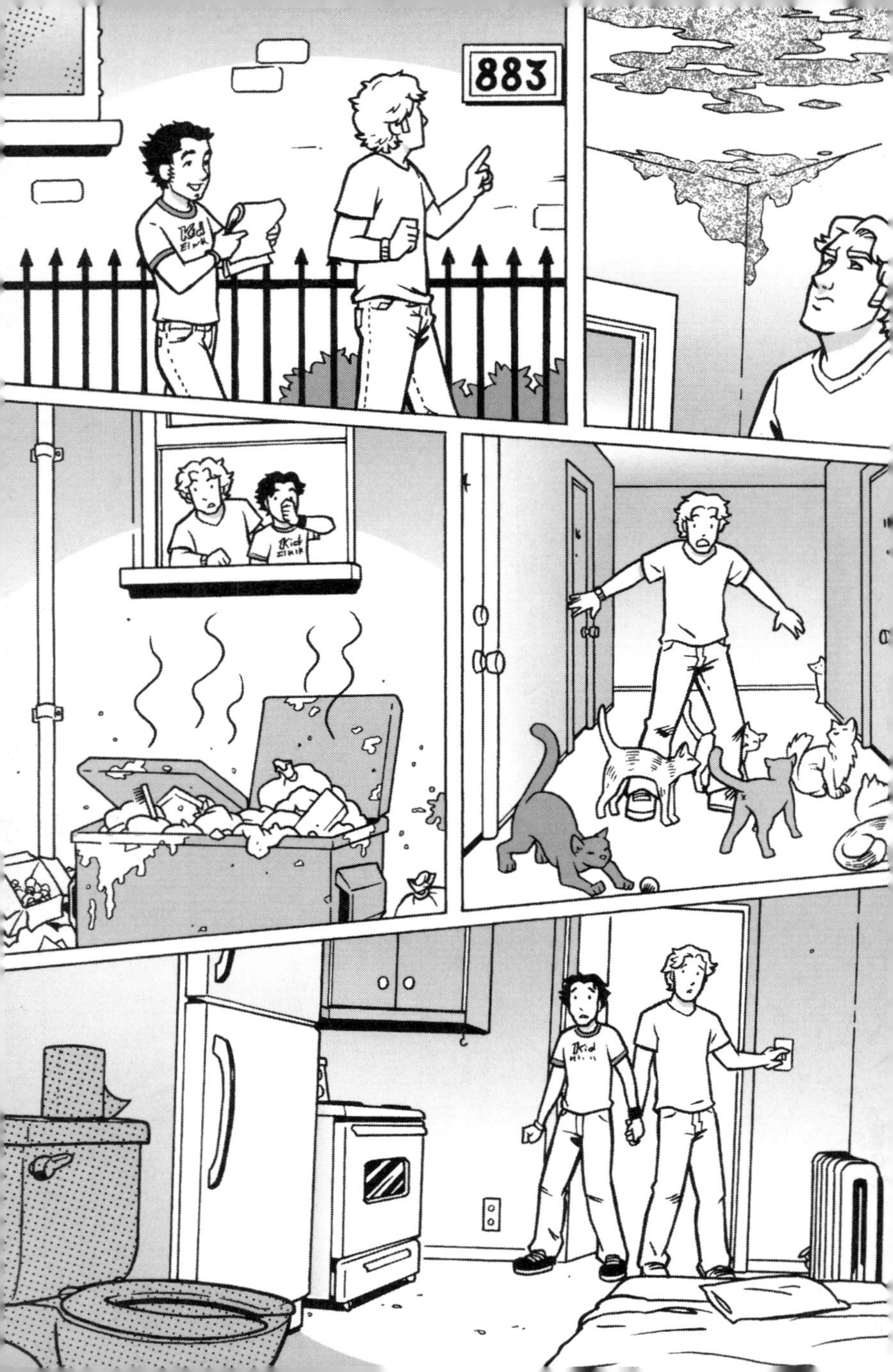
883

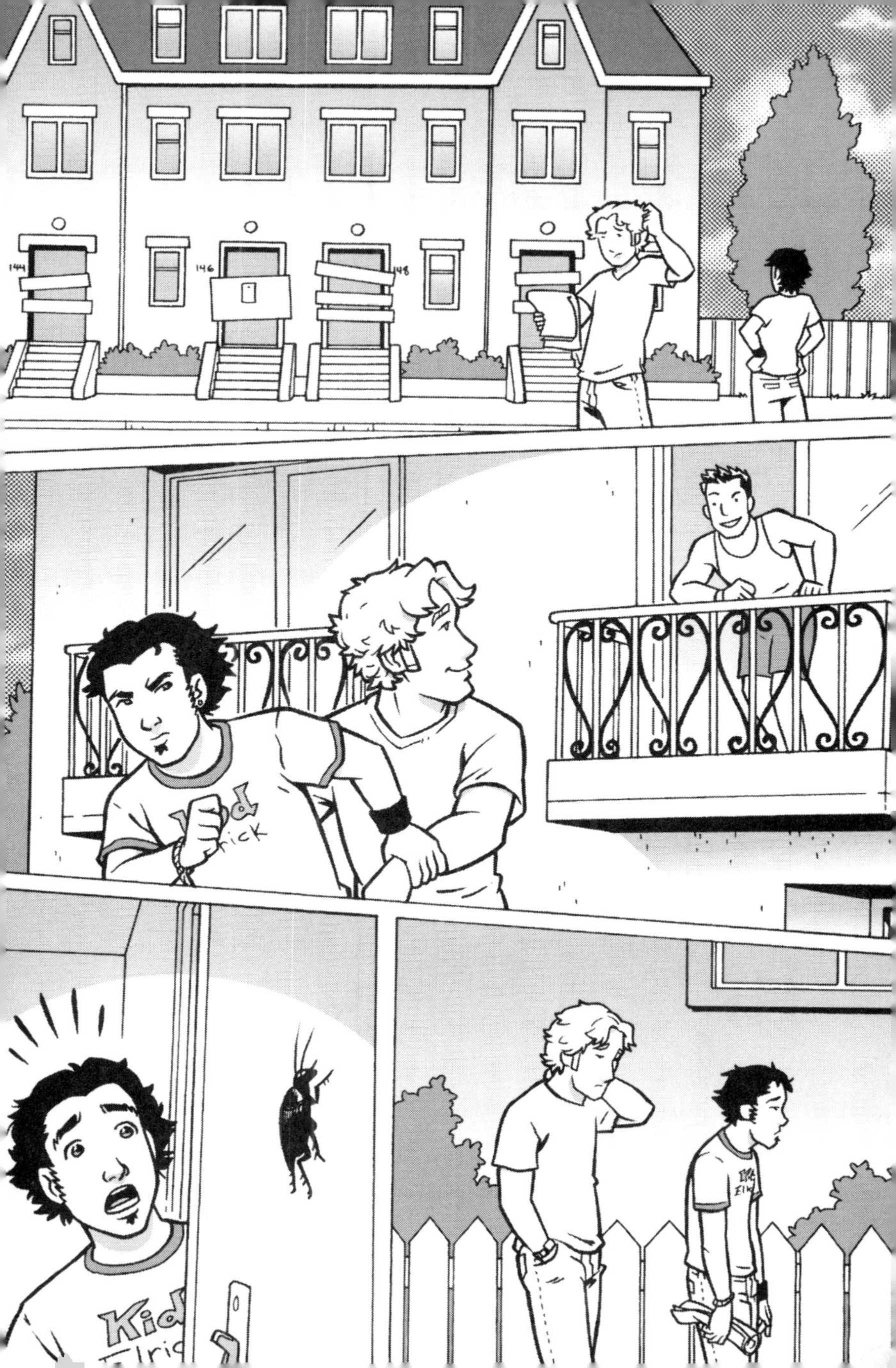
144
146
148
Kid

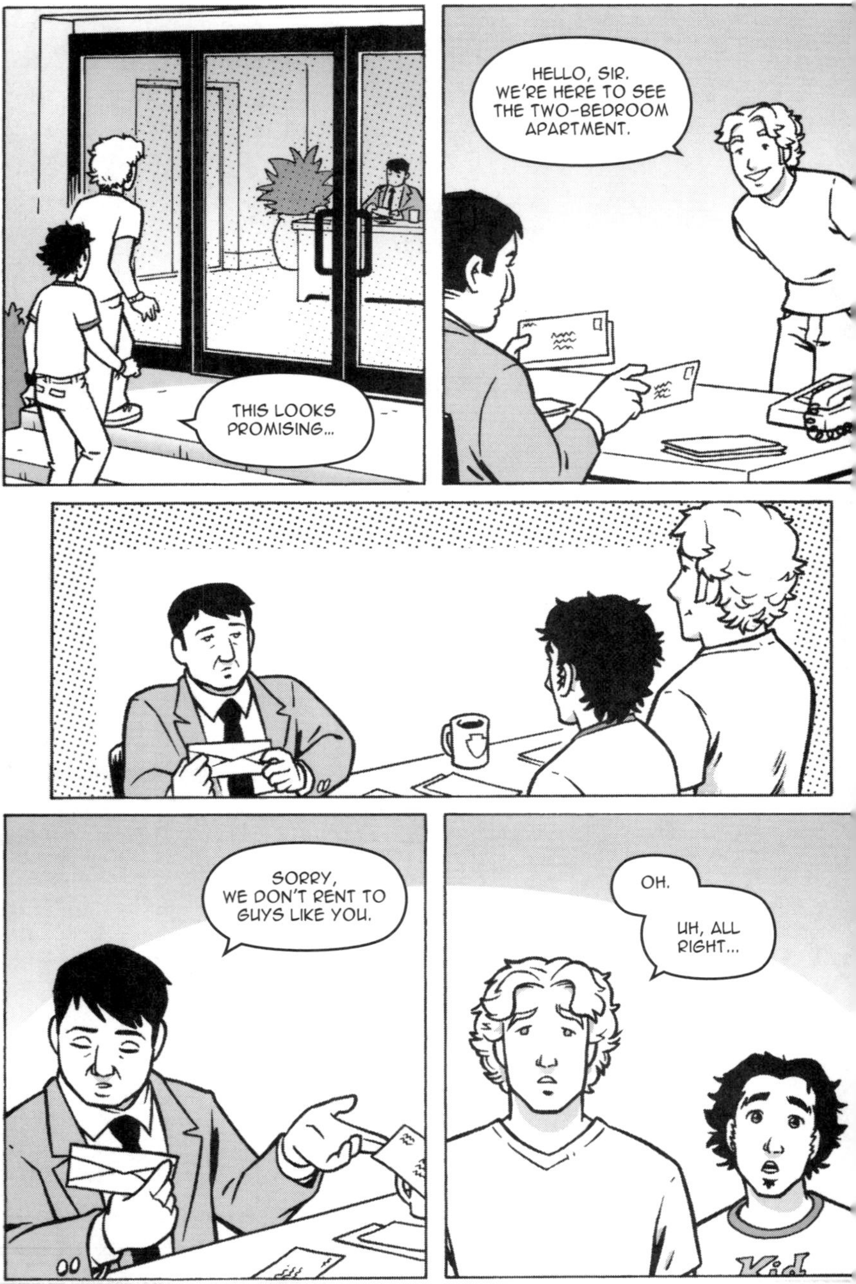
THIS LOOKS PROMISING...
HELLO, SIR. WE'RE HERE TO SEE THE TWO-BEDROOM APARTMENT.
SORRY, WE DON'T RENT TO GUYS LIKE YOU.
OH.
UH, ALL RIGHT...

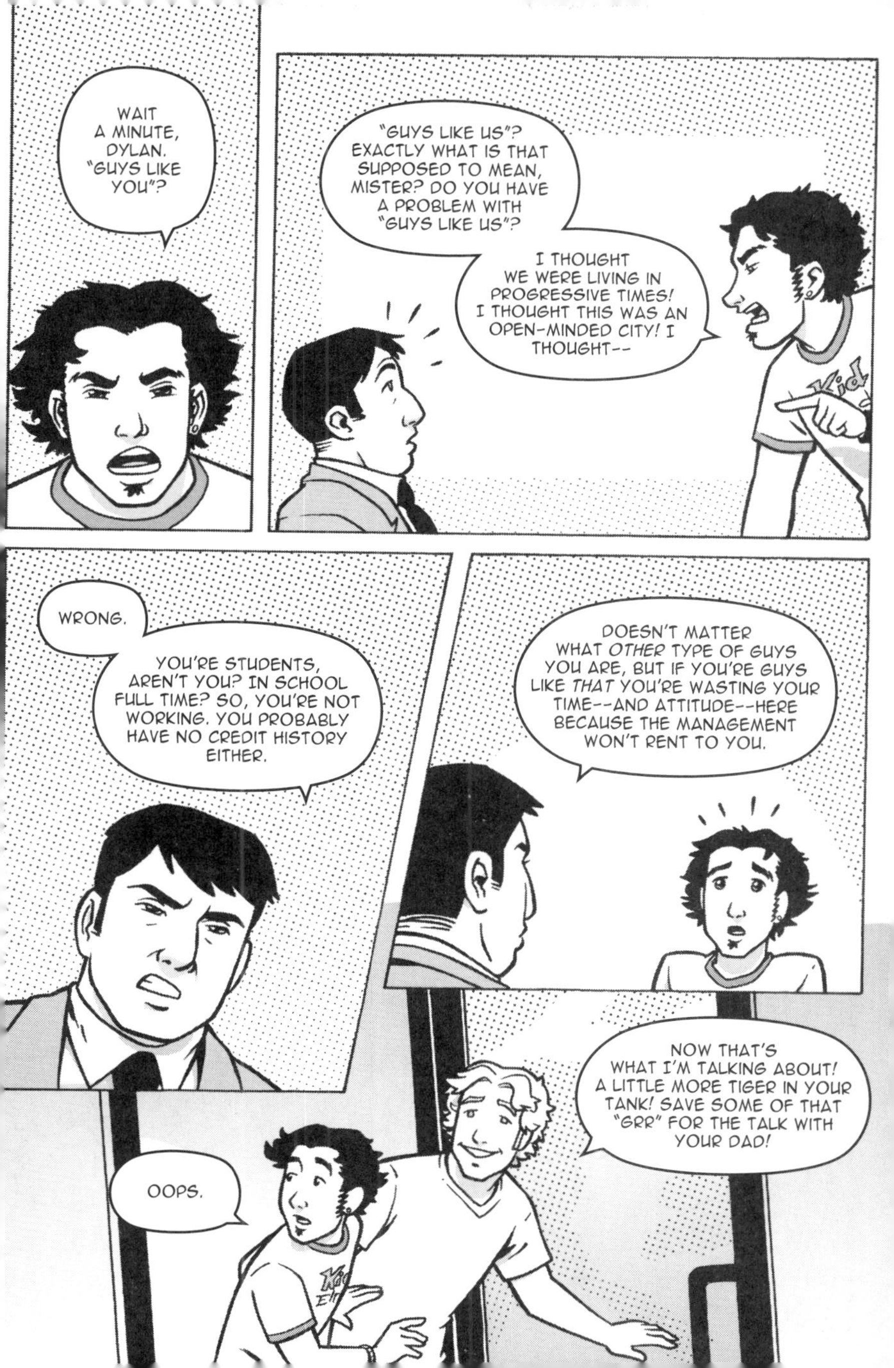
WAIT A MINUTE, DYLAN. "GUYS LIKE YOU"?
"GUYS LIKE US"? EXACTLY WHAT IS THAT SUPPOSED TO MEAN, MISTER? DO YOU HAVE A PROBLEM WITH "GUYS LIKE US"?
I THOUGHT WE WERE LIVING IN PROGRESSIVE TIMES! I THOUGHT THIS WAS AN OPEN-MINDED CITY! I THOUGHT--
WRONG.
YOU'RE STUDENTS, AREN'T YOU? IN SCHOOL FULL TIME? SO, YOU'RE NOT WORKING. YOU PROBABLY HAVE NO CREDIT HISTORY EITHER.
DOESN'T MATTER WHAT *OTHER* TYPE OF GUYS YOU ARE, BUT IF YOU'RE GUYS LIKE *THAT* YOU'RE WASTING YOUR TIME--AND ATTITUDE--HERE BECAUSE THE MANAGEMENT WON'T RENT TO YOU.
OOPS.
NOW THAT'S WHAT I'M TALKING ABOUT! A LITTLE MORE TIGER IN YOUR TANK! SAVE SOME OF THAT "GRR" FOR THE TALK WITH YOUR DAD!

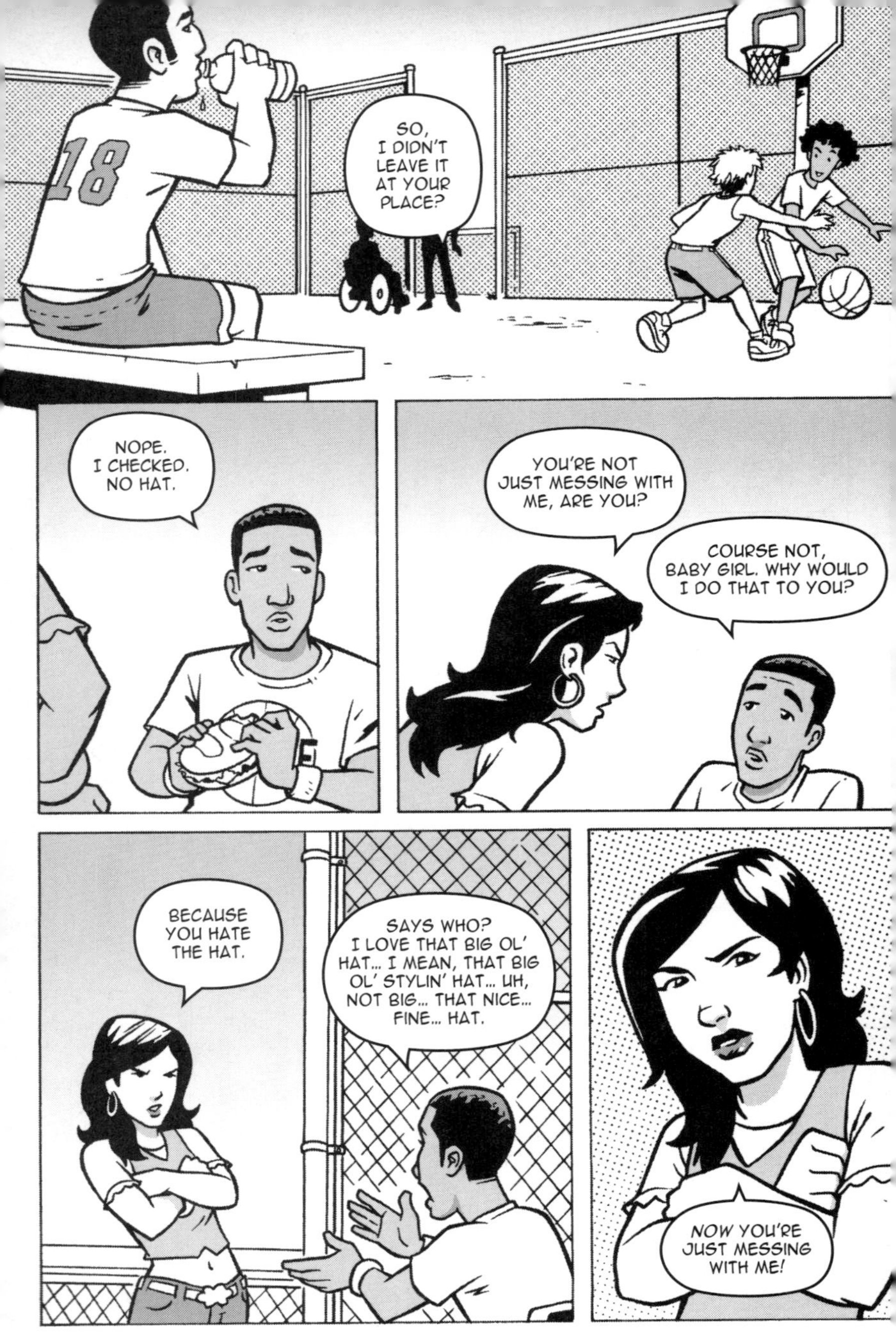
SO, I DIDN'T LEAVE IT AT YOUR PLACE?
NOPE. I CHECKED. NO HAT.
YOU'RE NOT JUST MESSING WITH ME, ARE YOU?
COURSE NOT, BABY GIRL. WHY WOULD I DO THAT TO YOU?
BECAUSE YOU HATE THE HAT.
SAYS WHO? I LOVE THAT BIG OL' HAT... I MEAN, THAT BIG OL' STYLIN' HAT... UH, NOT BIG... THAT NICE... FINE... HAT.
NOW YOU'RE JUST MESSING WITH ME!

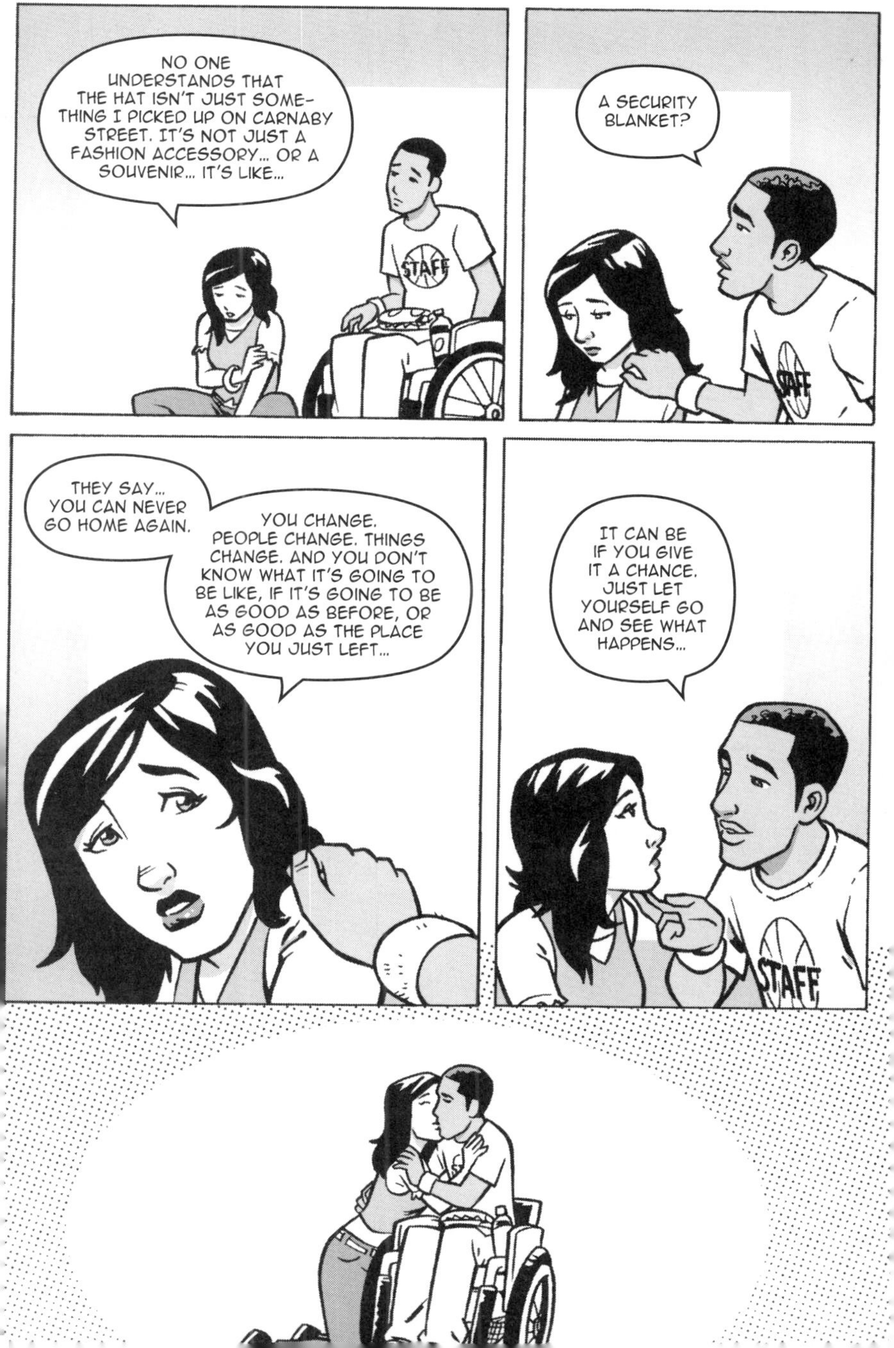
NO ONE UNDERSTANDS THAT THE HAT ISN'T JUST SOME-THING I PICKED UP ON CARNABY STREET. IT'S NOT JUST A FASHION ACCESSORY... OR A SOUVENIR... IT'S LIKE...
A SECURITY BLANKET?
THEY SAY... YOU CAN NEVER GO HOME AGAIN.
YOU CHANGE. PEOPLE CHANGE. THINGS CHANGE. AND YOU DON'T KNOW WHAT IT'S GOING TO BE LIKE, IF IT'S GOING TO BE AS GOOD AS BEFORE, OR AS GOOD AS THE PLACE YOU JUST LEFT...
IT CAN BE IF YOU GIVE IT A CHANCE. JUST LET YOURSELF GO AND SEE WHAT HAPPENS...

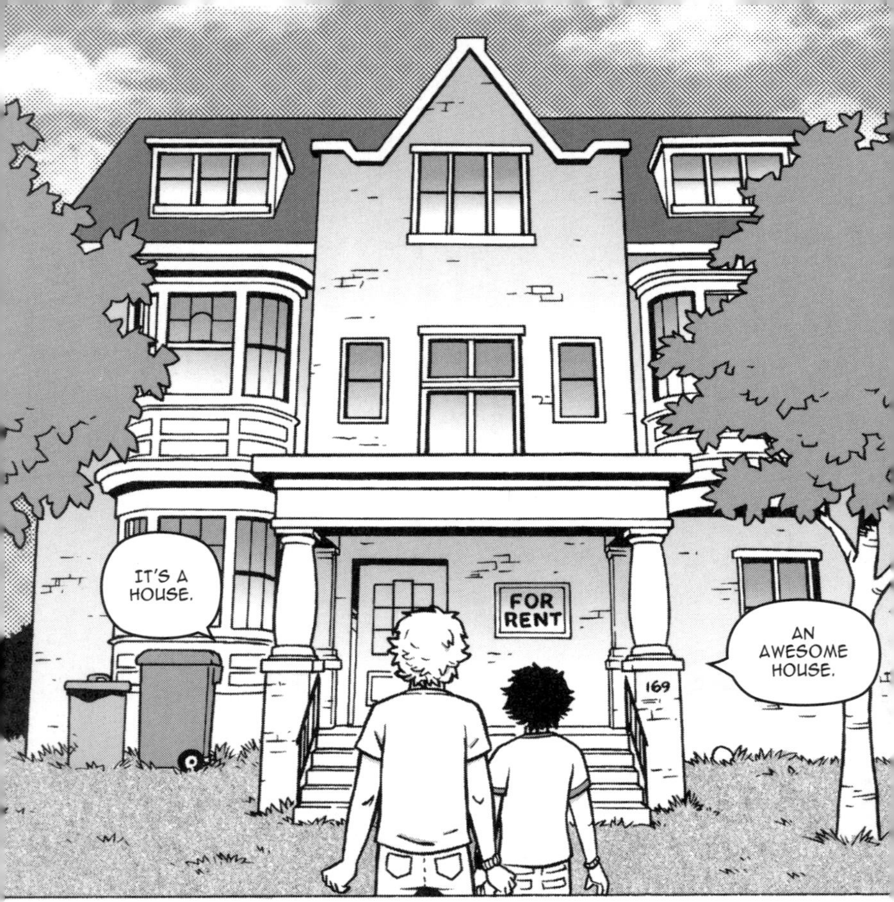
IT'S A HOUSE.
AN AWESOME HOUSE.
FOR RENT
169
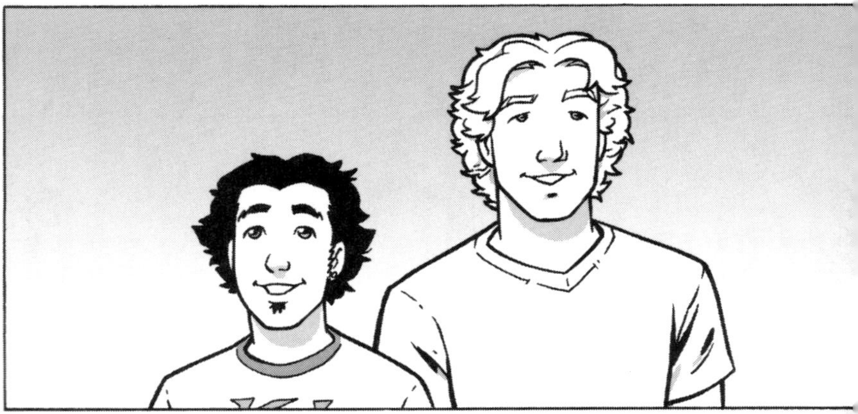

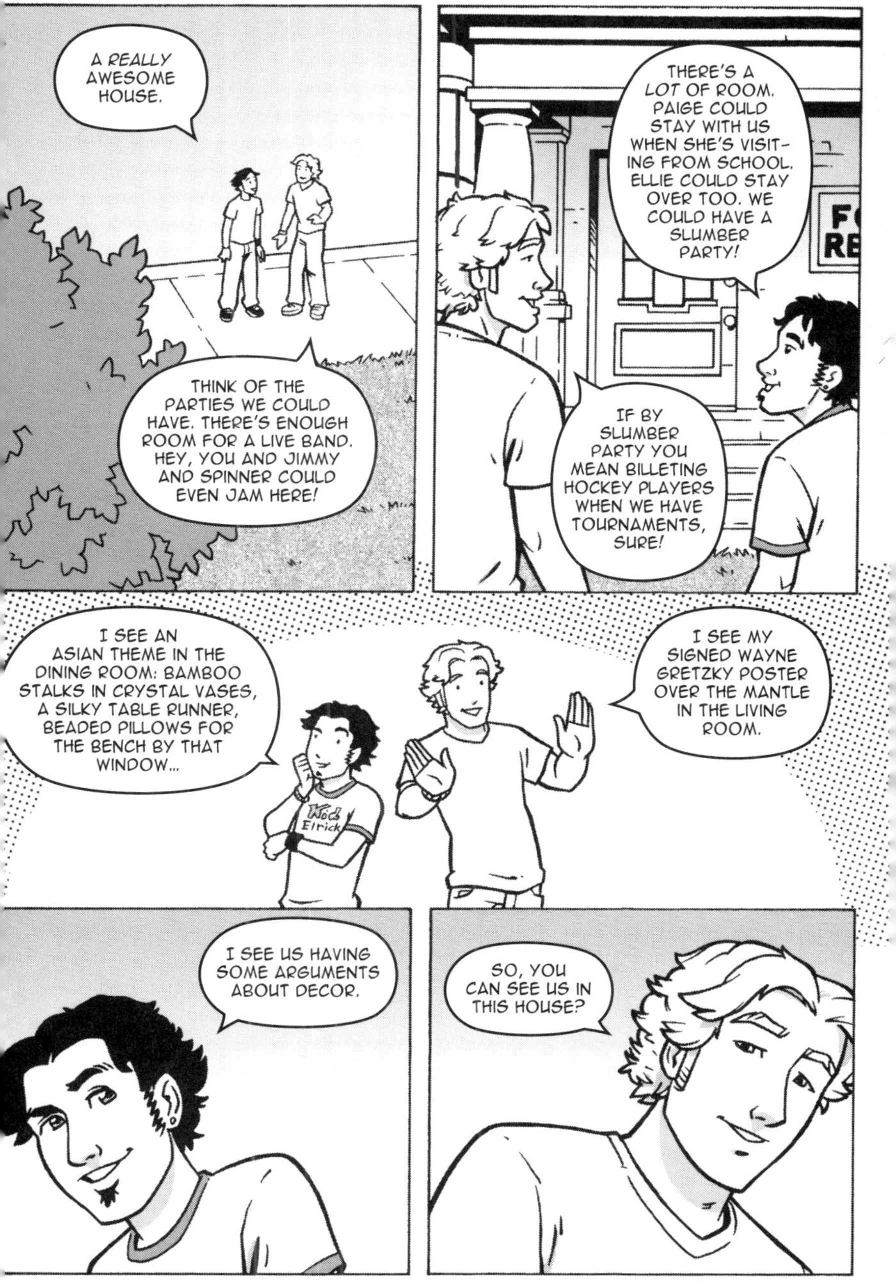
A REALLY AWESOME HOUSE.
THINK OF THE PARTIES WE COULD HAVE. THERE'S ENOUGH ROOM FOR A LIVE BAND. HEY, YOU AND JIMMY AND SPINNER COULD EVEN JAM HERE!
THERE'S A LOT OF ROOM. PAIGE COULD STAY WITH US WHEN SHE'S VISITING FROM SCHOOL. ELLIE COULD STAY OVER TOO. WE COULD HAVE A SLUMBER PARTY!
IF BY SLUMBER PARTY YOU MEAN BILLETING HOCKEY PLAYERS WHEN WE HAVE TOURNAMENTS, SURE!
I SEE AN ASIAN THEME IN THE DINING ROOM: BAMBOO STALKS IN CRYSTAL VASES, A SILKY TABLE RUNNER, BEADED PILLOWS FOR THE BENCH BY THAT WINDOW...
I SEE MY SIGNED WAYNE GRETZKY POSTER OVER THE MANTLE IN THE LIVING ROOM.
I SEE US HAVING SOME ARGUMENTS ABOUT DECOR.
SO, YOU CAN SEE US IN THIS HOUSE?

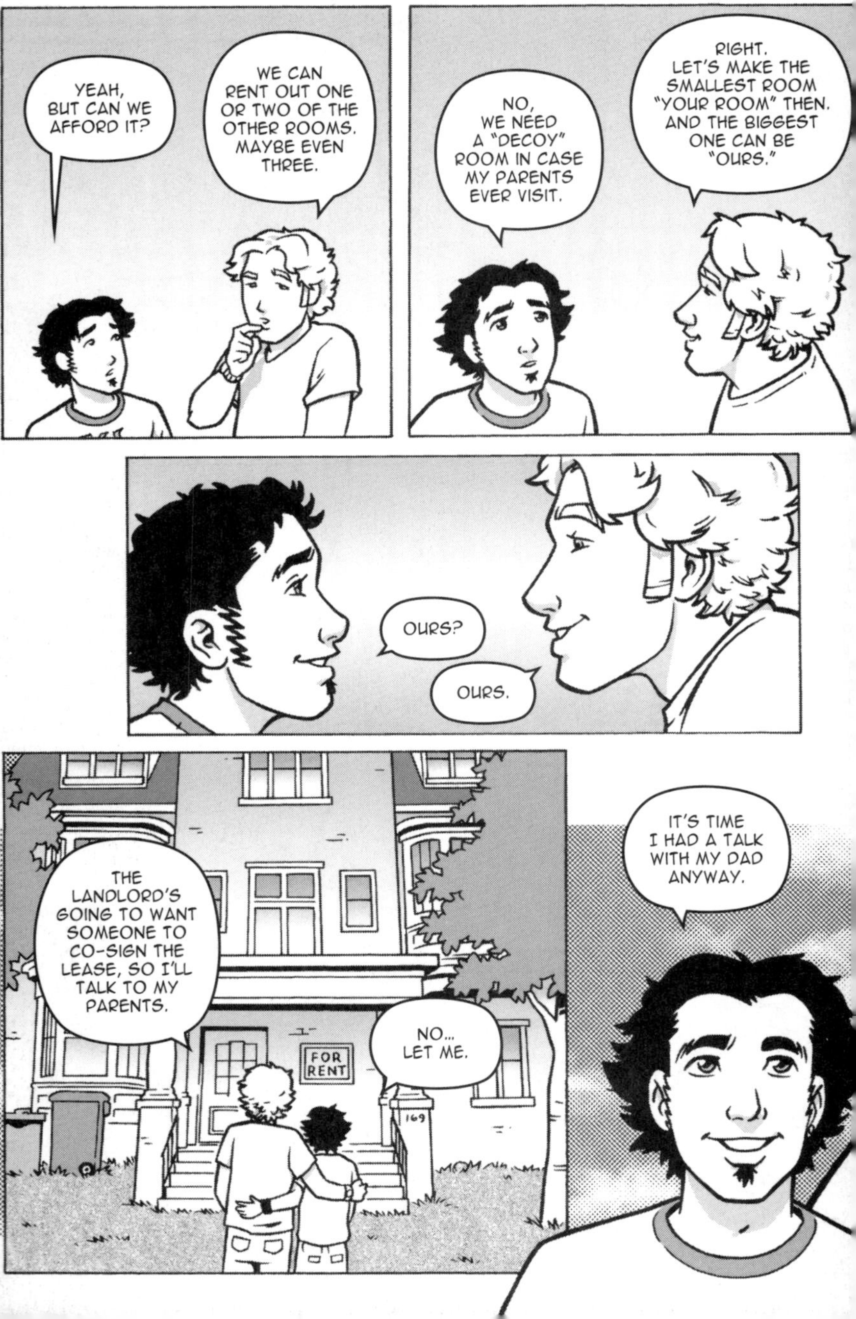
YEAH, BUT CAN WE AFFORD IT?
WE CAN RENT OUT ONE OR TWO OF THE OTHER ROOMS. MAYBE EVEN THREE.
NO, WE NEED A "DECOY" ROOM IN CASE MY PARENTS EVER VISIT.
RIGHT. LET'S MAKE THE SMALLEST ROOM "YOUR ROOM" THEN. AND THE BIGGEST ONE CAN BE "OURS."
OURS?
OURS.
THE LANDLORD'S GOING TO WANT SOMEONE TO CO-SIGN THE LEASE, SO I'LL TALK TO MY PARENTS.
FOR RENT
169
NO... LET ME.
IT'S TIME I HAD A TALK WITH MY DAD ANYWAY.

ACT 3

"You miss 100% of the shots you never take."

— Wayne Gretzky

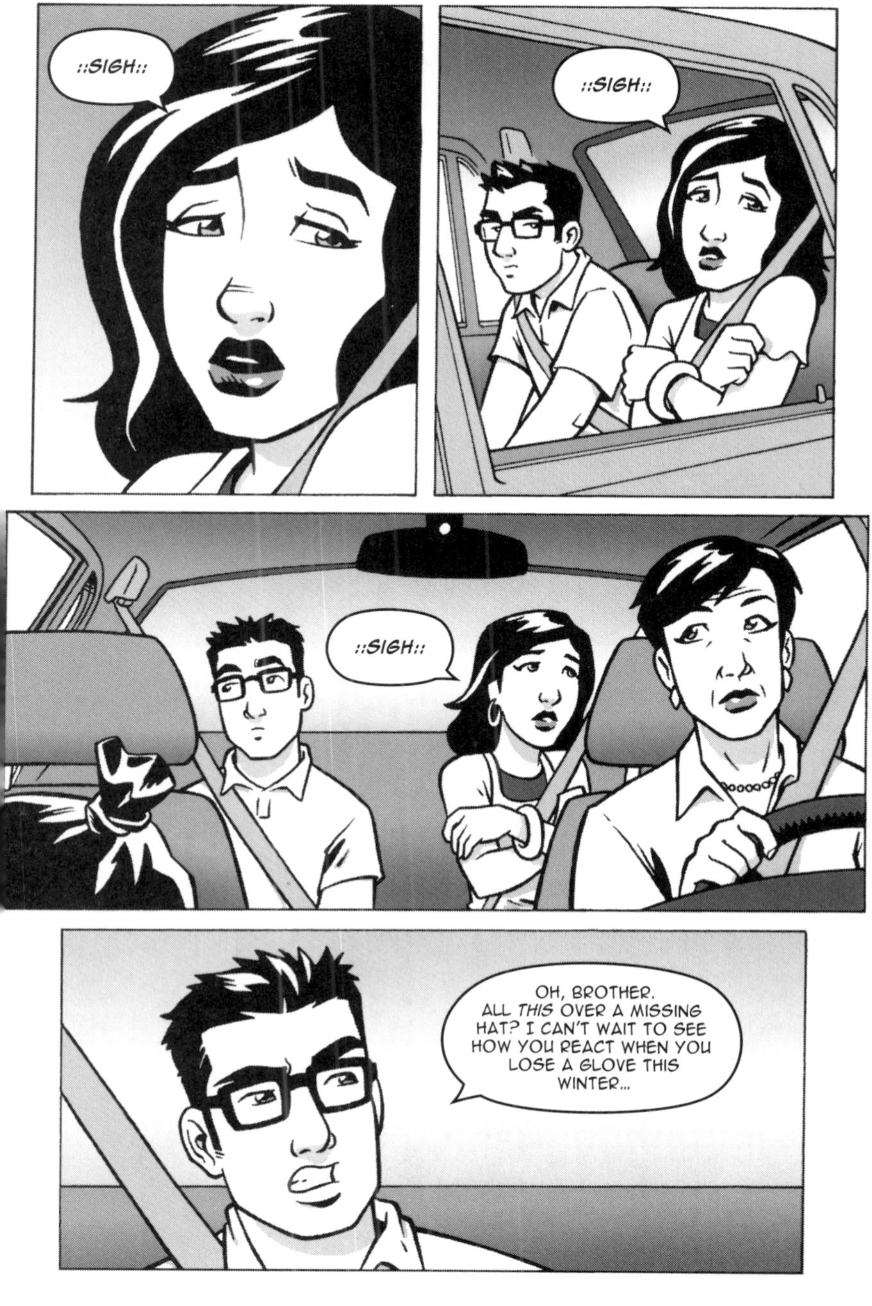
::SIGH::
::SIGH::
::SIGH::
OH, BROTHER. ALL *THIS* OVER A MISSING HAT? I CAN'T WAIT TO SEE HOW YOU REACT WHEN YOU LOSE A GLOVE THIS WINTER...

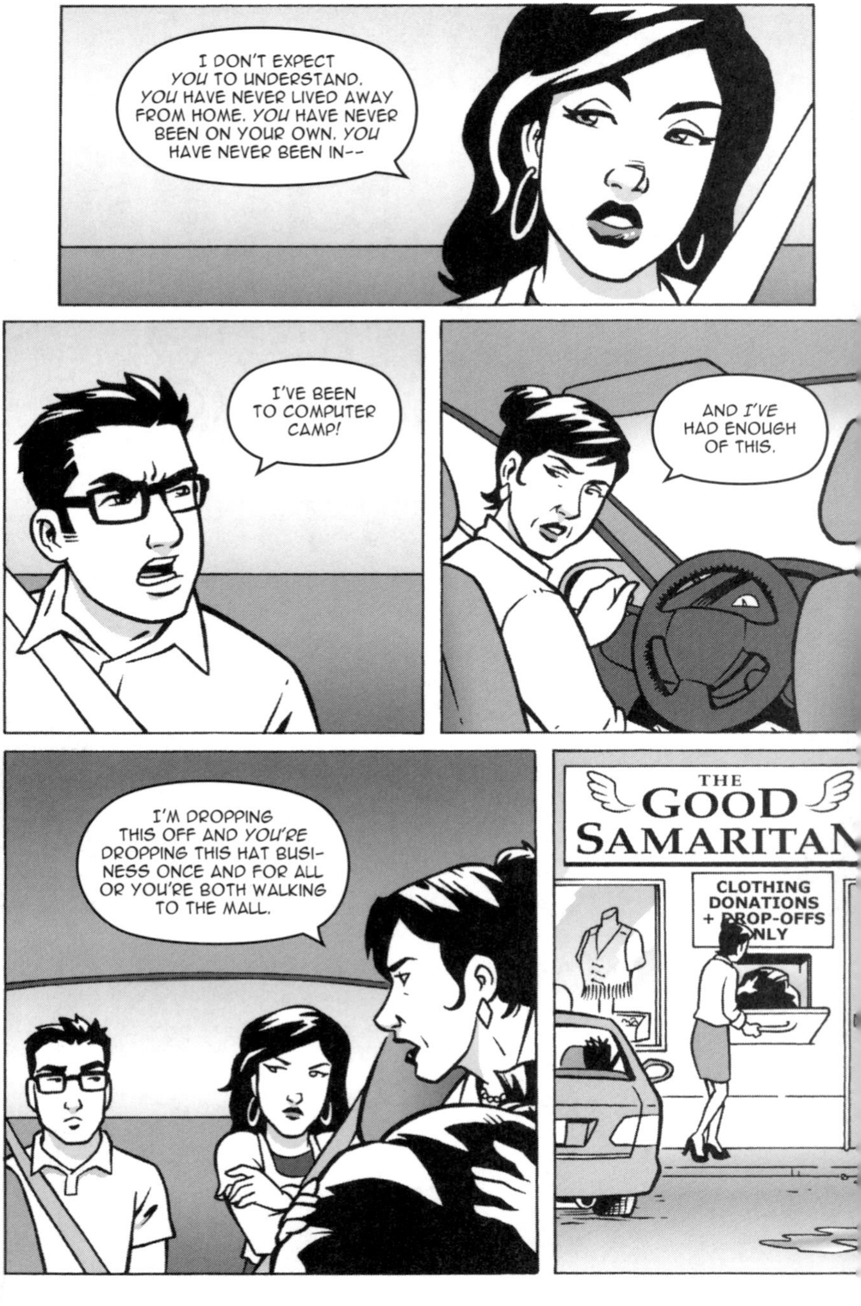
I DON'T EXPECT *YOU* TO UNDERSTAND. *YOU* HAVE NEVER LIVED AWAY FROM HOME. *YOU* HAVE NEVER BEEN ON YOUR OWN. *YOU* HAVE NEVER BEEN IN--
I'VE BEEN TO COMPUTER CAMP!
AND *I'VE* HAD ENOUGH OF THIS.
I'M DROPPING THIS OFF AND *YOU'RE* DROPPING THIS HAT BUSINESS ONCE AND FOR ALL OR YOU'RE BOTH WALKING TO THE MALL.
THE GOOD SAMARITAN
CLOTHING DONATIONS + DROP-OFFS ONLY

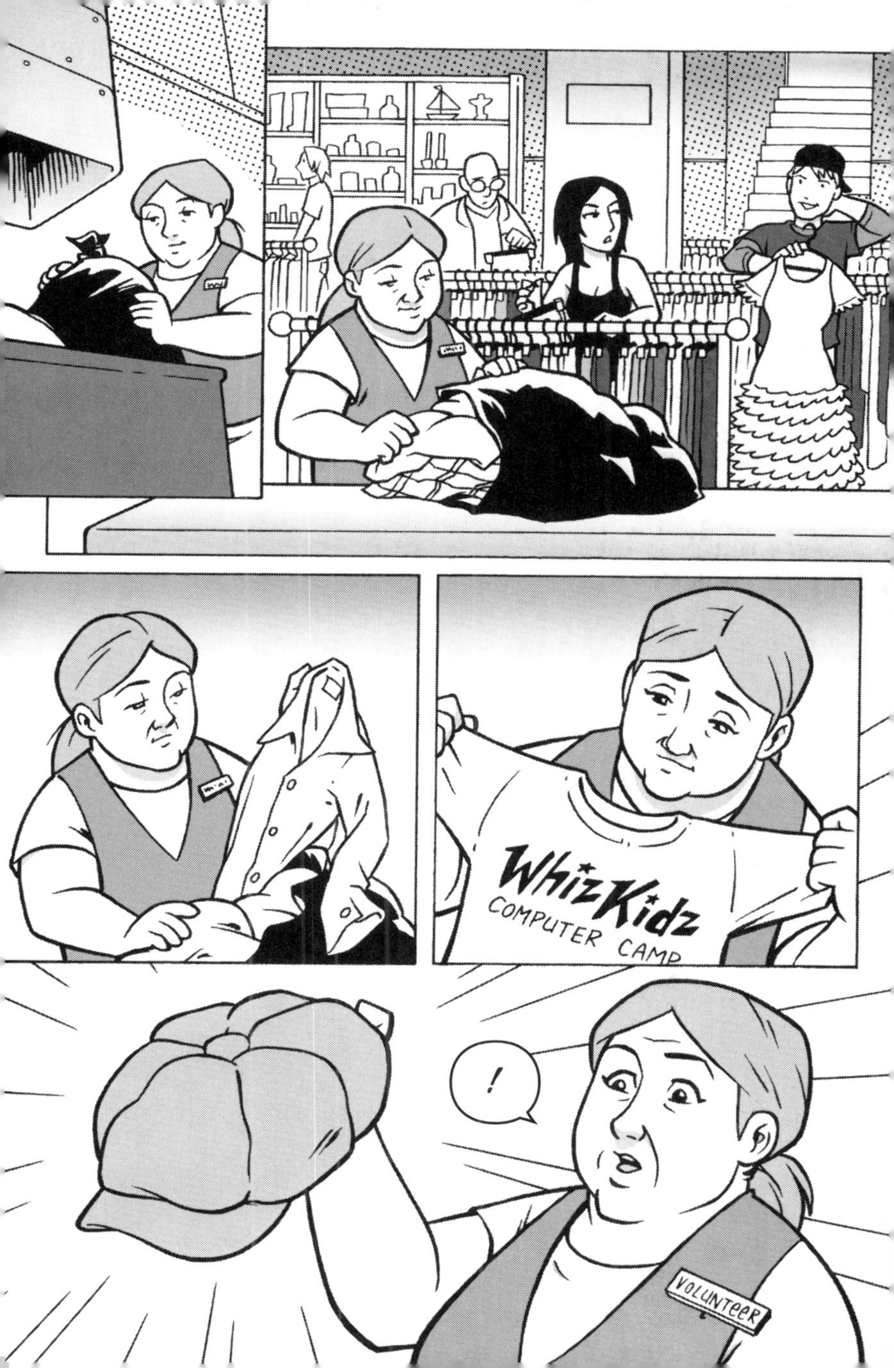
WhizKidz
COMPUTER CAMP
!
VOLUNTEER

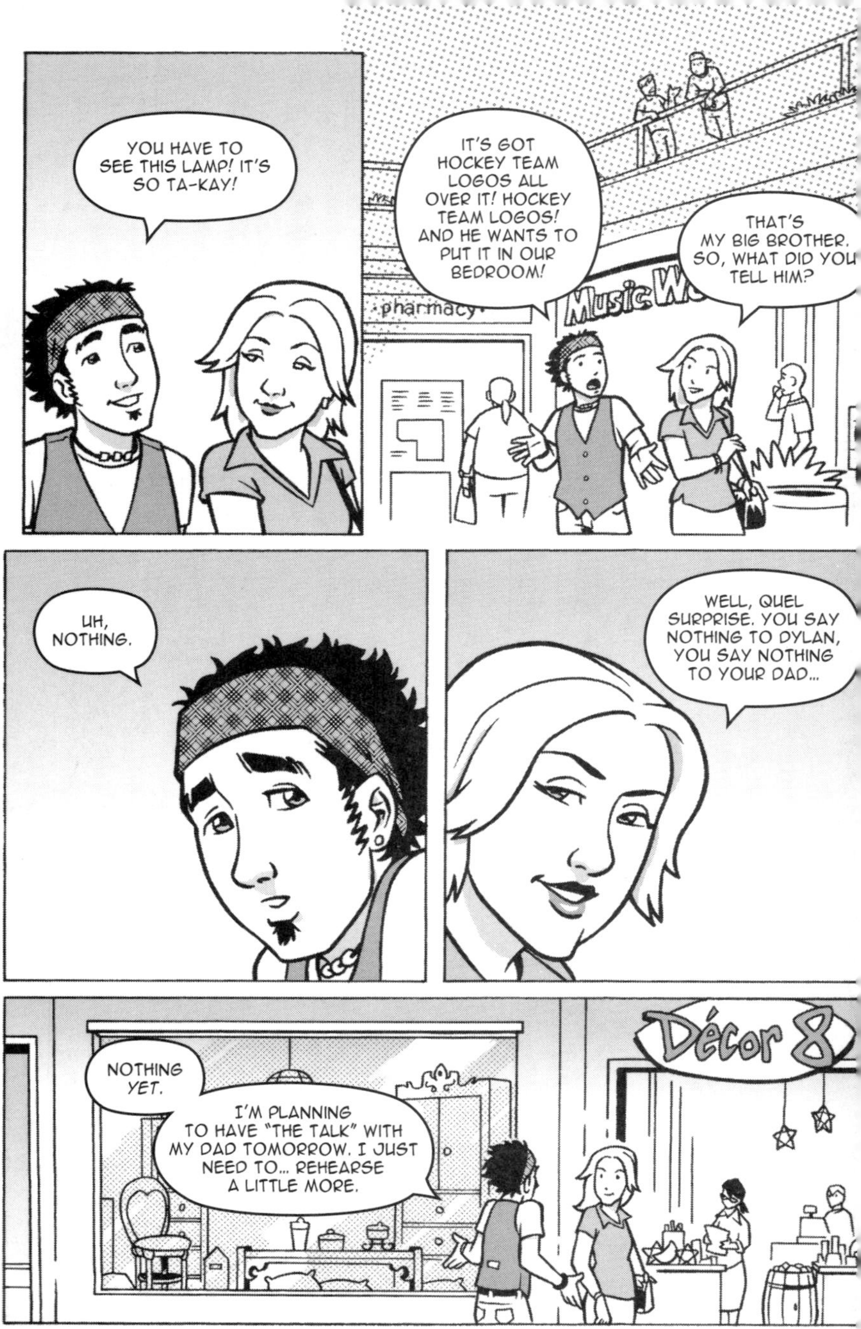
YOU HAVE TO SEE THIS LAMP! IT'S SO TA-KAY!
IT'S GOT HOCKEY TEAM LOGOS ALL OVER IT! HOCKEY TEAM LOGOS! AND HE WANTS TO PUT IT IN OUR BEDROOM!
pharmacy
Music W
THAT'S MY BIG BROTHER. SO, WHAT DID YOU TELL HIM?
UH, NOTHING.
WELL, QUEL SURPRISE. YOU SAY NOTHING TO DYLAN, YOU SAY NOTHING TO YOUR DAD...
Décor 8
NOTHING *YET.*
I'M PLANNING TO HAVE "THE TALK" WITH MY DAD TOMORROW. I JUST NEED TO... REHEARSE A LITTLE MORE.

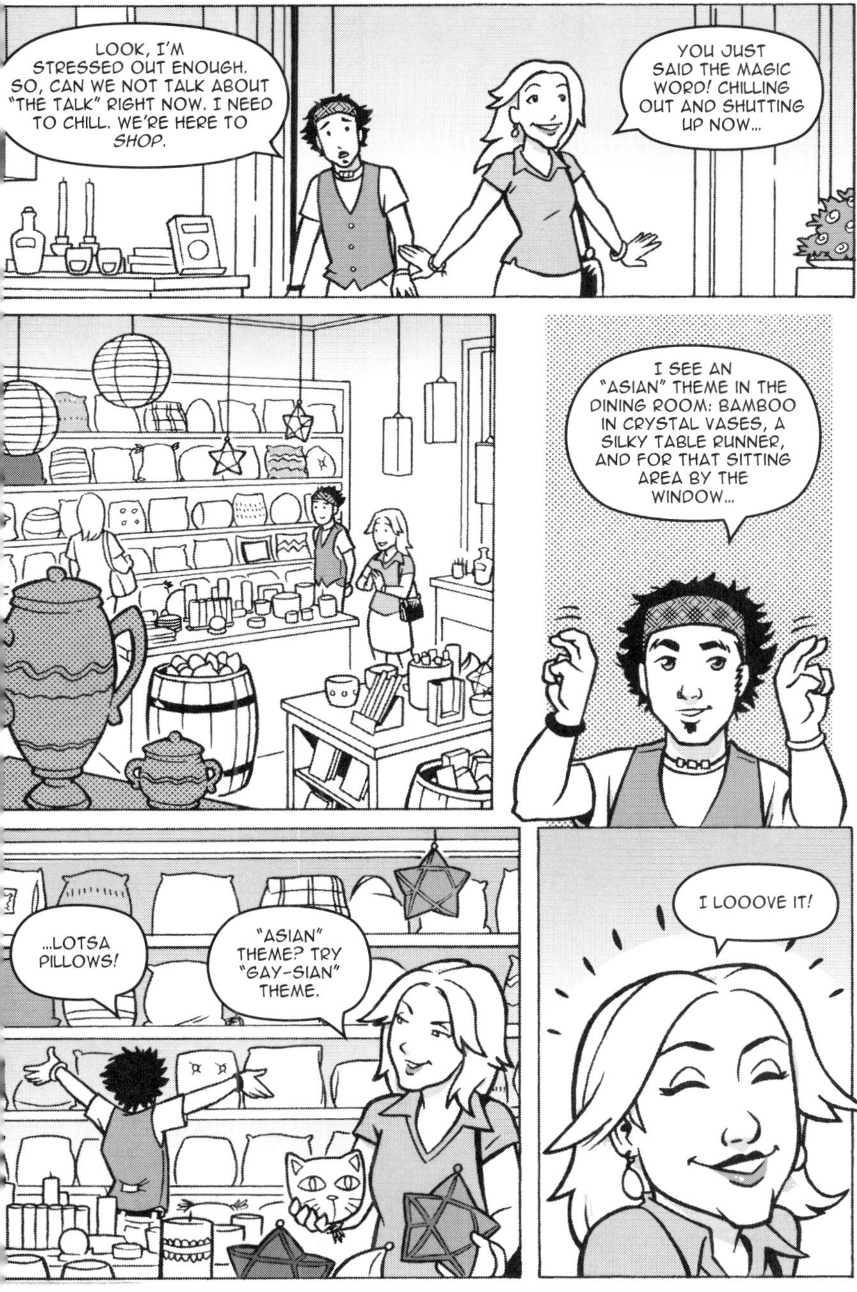
LOOK, I'M STRESSED OUT ENOUGH. SO, CAN WE NOT TALK ABOUT "THE TALK" RIGHT NOW. I NEED TO CHILL. WE'RE HERE TO *SHOP*.
YOU JUST SAID THE MAGIC WORD! CHILLING OUT AND SHUTTING UP NOW...
I SEE AN "ASIAN" THEME IN THE DINING ROOM: BAMBOO IN CRYSTAL VASES, A SILKY TABLE RUNNER, AND FOR THAT SITTING AREA BY THE WINDOW...
...LOTSA PILLOWS!
"ASIAN" THEME? TRY "GAY-SIAN" THEME.
I LOOOVE IT!

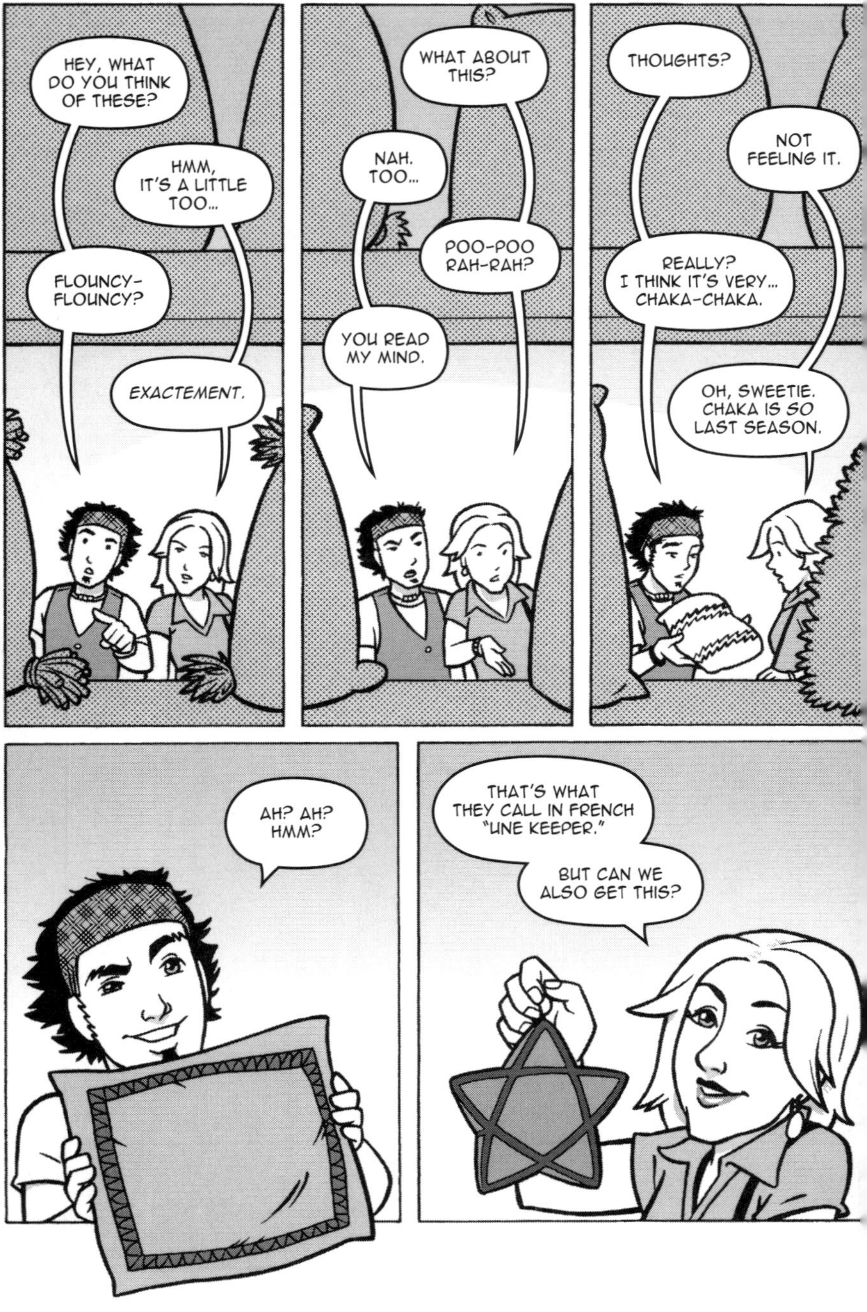
HEY, WHAT DO YOU THINK OF THESE?
HMM, IT'S A LITTLE TOO...
FLOUNCY-FLOUNCY?
EXACTEMENT.
WHAT ABOUT THIS?
NAH. TOO...
POO-POO RAH-RAH?
YOU READ MY MIND.
THOUGHTS?
NOT FEELING IT.
REALLY? I THINK IT'S VERY... CHAKA-CHAKA.
OH, SWEETIE. CHAKA IS *SO* LAST SEASON.
AH? AH? HMM?
THAT'S WHAT THEY CALL IN FRENCH "UNE KEEPER."
BUT CAN WE ALSO GET THIS?

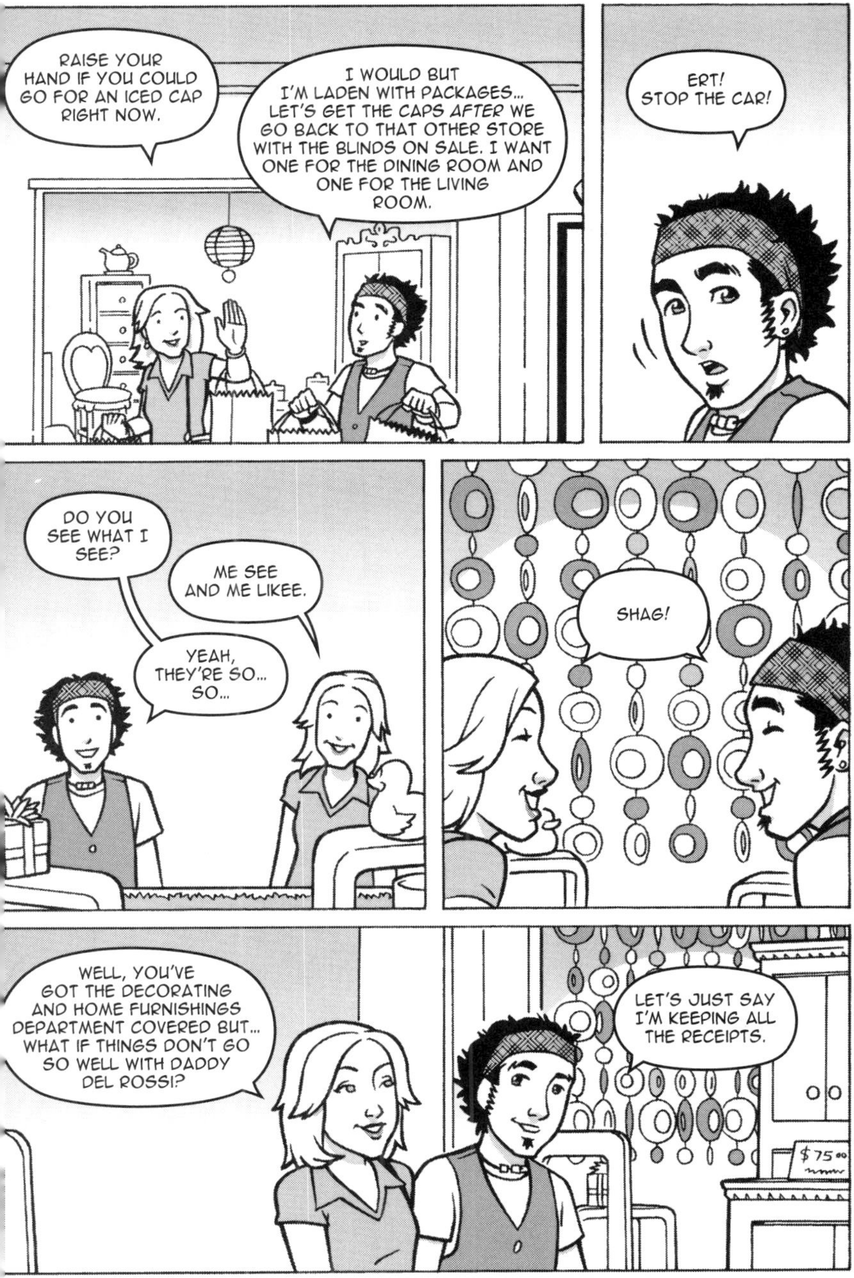
RAISE YOUR HAND IF YOU COULD GO FOR AN ICED CAP RIGHT NOW.
I WOULD BUT I'M LADEN WITH PACKAGES... LET'S GET THE CAPS *AFTER* WE GO BACK TO THAT OTHER STORE WITH THE BLINDS ON SALE. I WANT ONE FOR THE DINING ROOM AND ONE FOR THE LIVING ROOM.
ERT! STOP THE CAR!
DO YOU SEE WHAT I SEE?
ME SEE AND ME LIKEE.
YEAH, THEY'RE SO... SO...
SHAG!
WELL, YOU'VE GOT THE DECORATING AND HOME FURNISHINGS DEPARTMENT COVERED BUT... WHAT IF THINGS DON'T GO SO WELL WITH DADDY DEL ROSSI?
LET'S JUST SAY I'M KEEPING ALL THE RECEIPTS.
$75.00

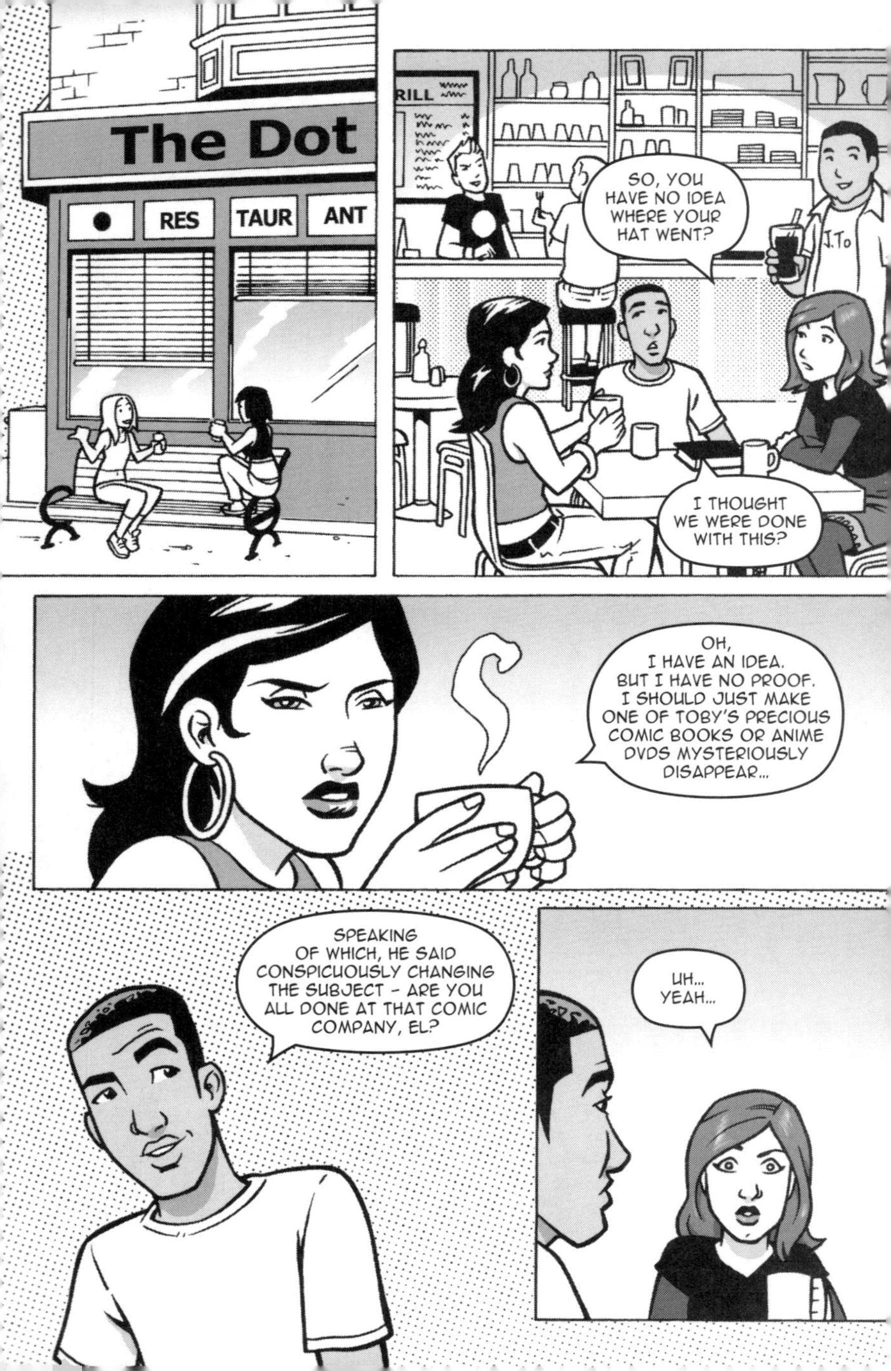
The Dot
RES TAUR ANT
SO, YOU HAVE NO IDEA WHERE YOUR HAT WENT?
J.To
I THOUGHT WE WERE DONE WITH THIS?
OH, I HAVE AN IDEA. BUT I HAVE NO PROOF. I SHOULD JUST MAKE ONE OF TOBY'S PRECIOUS COMIC BOOKS OR ANIME DVDS MYSTERIOUSLY DISAPPEAR...
SPEAKING OF WHICH, HE SAID CONSPICUOUSLY CHANGING THE SUBJECT - ARE YOU ALL DONE AT THAT COMIC COMPANY, EL?
UH... YEAH...

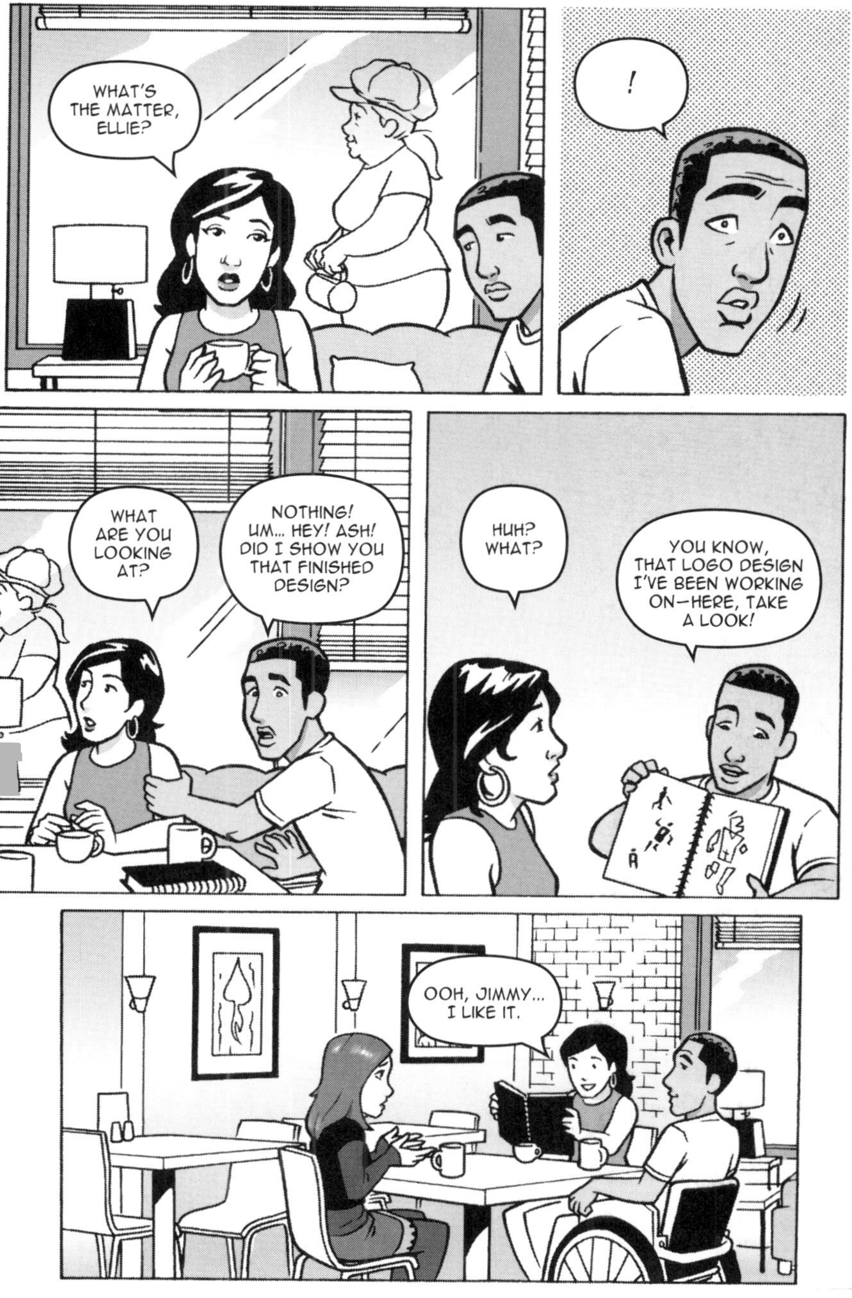
WHAT'S THE MATTER, ELLIE?
!
WHAT ARE YOU LOOKING AT?
NOTHING! UM... HEY! ASH! DID I SHOW YOU THAT FINISHED DESIGN?
HUH? WHAT?
YOU KNOW, THAT LOGO DESIGN I'VE BEEN WORKING ON—HERE, TAKE A LOOK!
OOH, JIMMY... I LIKE IT.

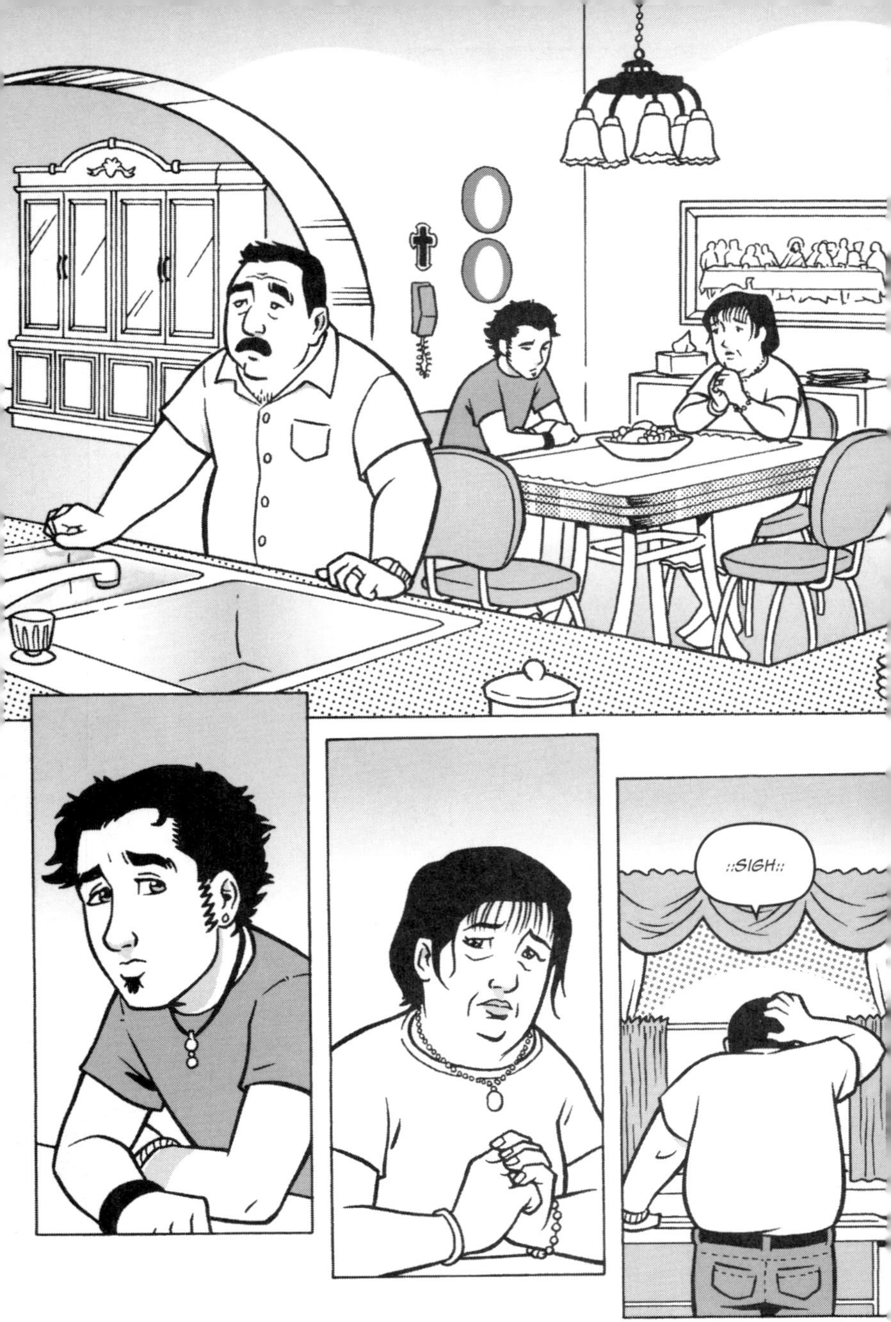
::SIGH::

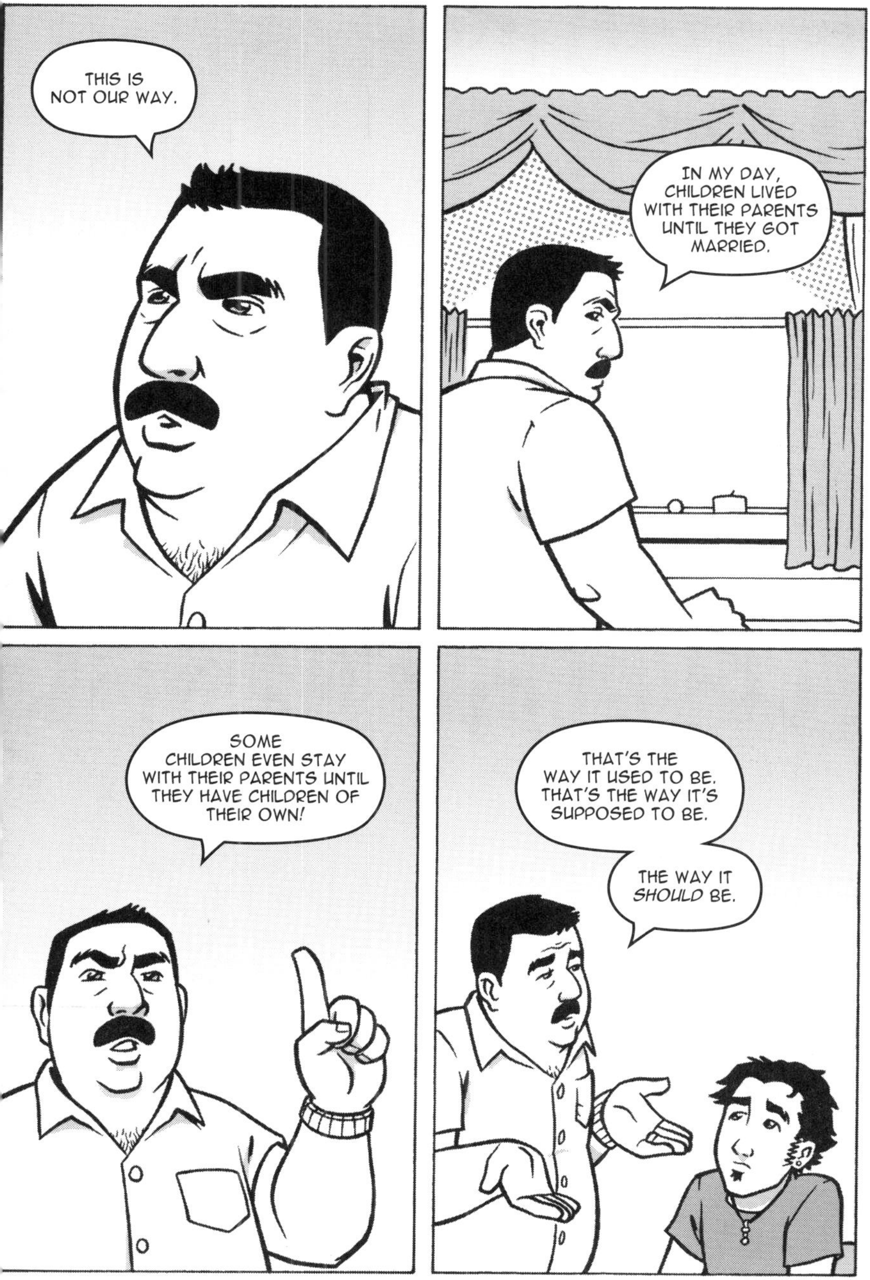
THIS IS NOT OUR WAY.
IN MY DAY, CHILDREN LIVED WITH THEIR PARENTS UNTIL THEY GOT MARRIED.
SOME CHILDREN EVEN STAY WITH THEIR PARENTS UNTIL THEY HAVE CHILDREN OF THEIR OWN!
THAT'S THE WAY IT USED TO BE. THAT'S THE WAY IT'S SUPPOSED TO BE.
THE WAY IT *SHOULD* BE.

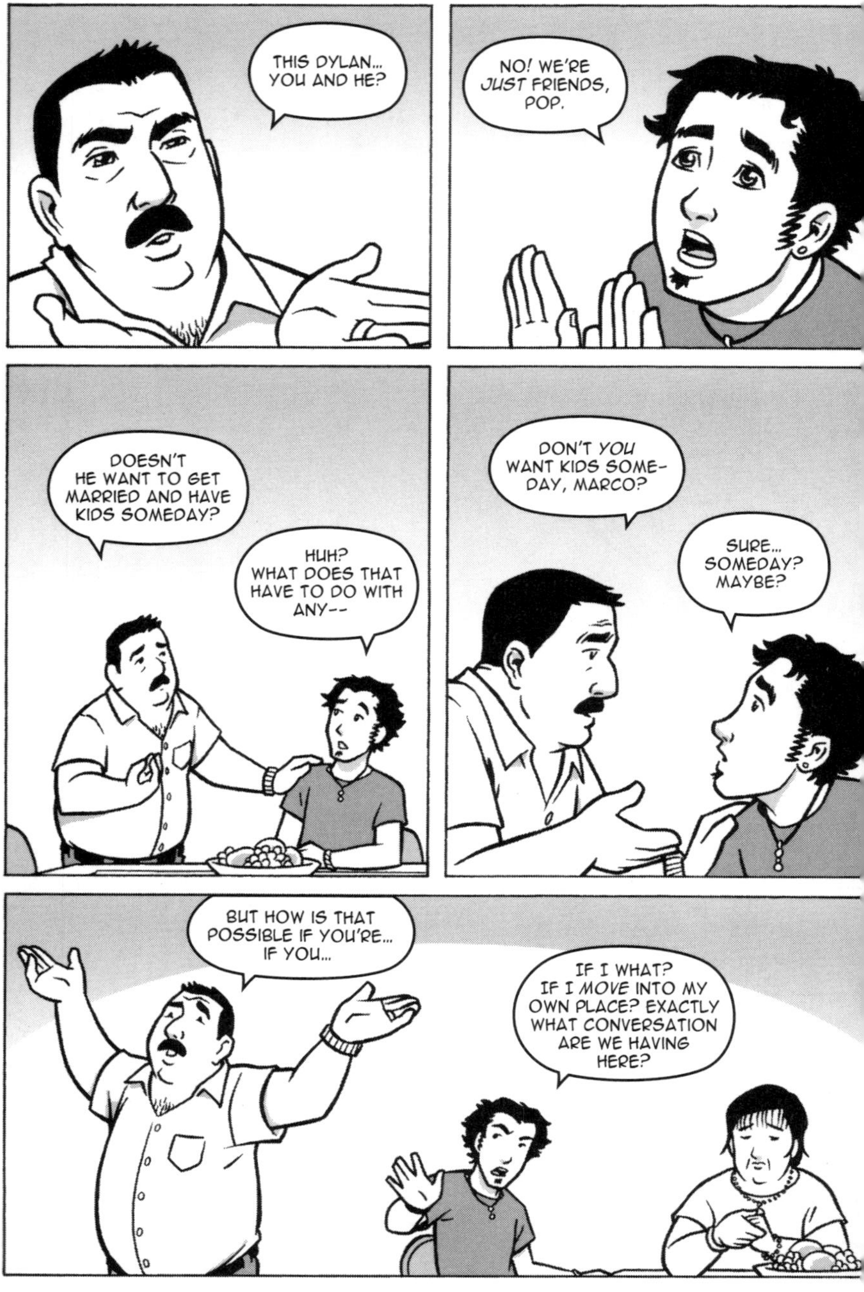
THIS DYLAN... YOU AND HE?
NO! WE'RE *JUST* FRIENDS, POP.
DOESN'T HE WANT TO GET MARRIED AND HAVE KIDS SOMEDAY?
HUH? WHAT DOES THAT HAVE TO DO WITH ANY--
DON'T *YOU* WANT KIDS SOME-DAY, MARCO?
SURE... SOMEDAY? MAYBE?
BUT HOW IS THAT POSSIBLE IF YOU'RE... IF YOU...
IF I WHAT? IF I *MOVE* INTO MY OWN PLACE? EXACTLY WHAT CONVERSATION ARE WE HAVING HERE?

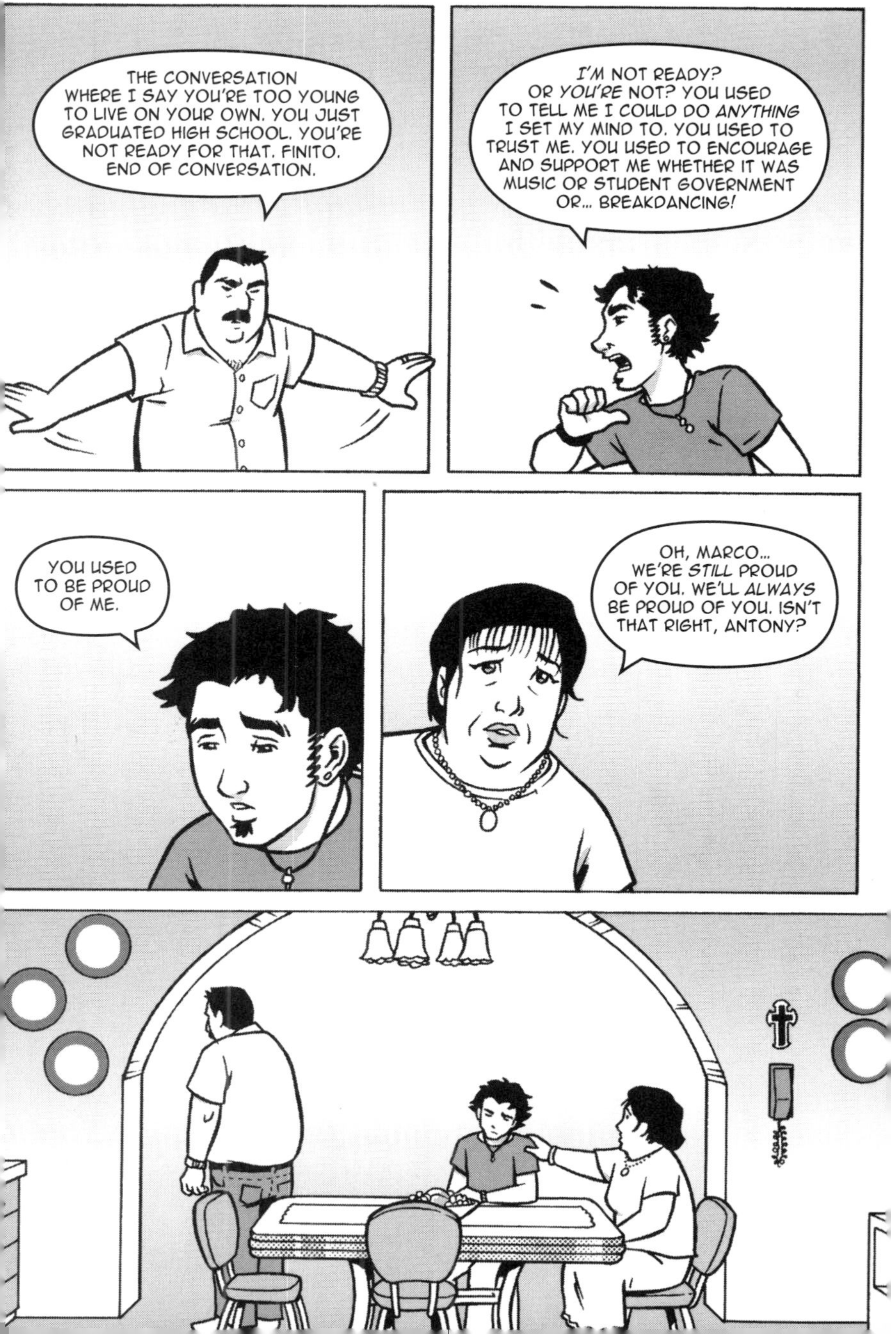
THE CONVERSATION WHERE I SAY YOU'RE TOO YOUNG TO LIVE ON YOUR OWN. YOU JUST GRADUATED HIGH SCHOOL. YOU'RE NOT READY FOR THAT. FINITO. END OF CONVERSATION.
I'M NOT READY? OR *YOU'RE* NOT? YOU USED TO TELL ME I COULD DO *ANYTHING* I SET MY MIND TO. YOU USED TO TRUST ME. YOU USED TO ENCOURAGE AND SUPPORT ME WHETHER IT WAS MUSIC OR STUDENT GOVERNMENT OR... BREAKDANCING!
YOU USED TO BE PROUD OF ME.
OH, MARCO... WE'RE *STILL* PROUD OF YOU. WE'LL *ALWAYS* BE PROUD OF YOU. ISN'T THAT RIGHT, ANTONY?

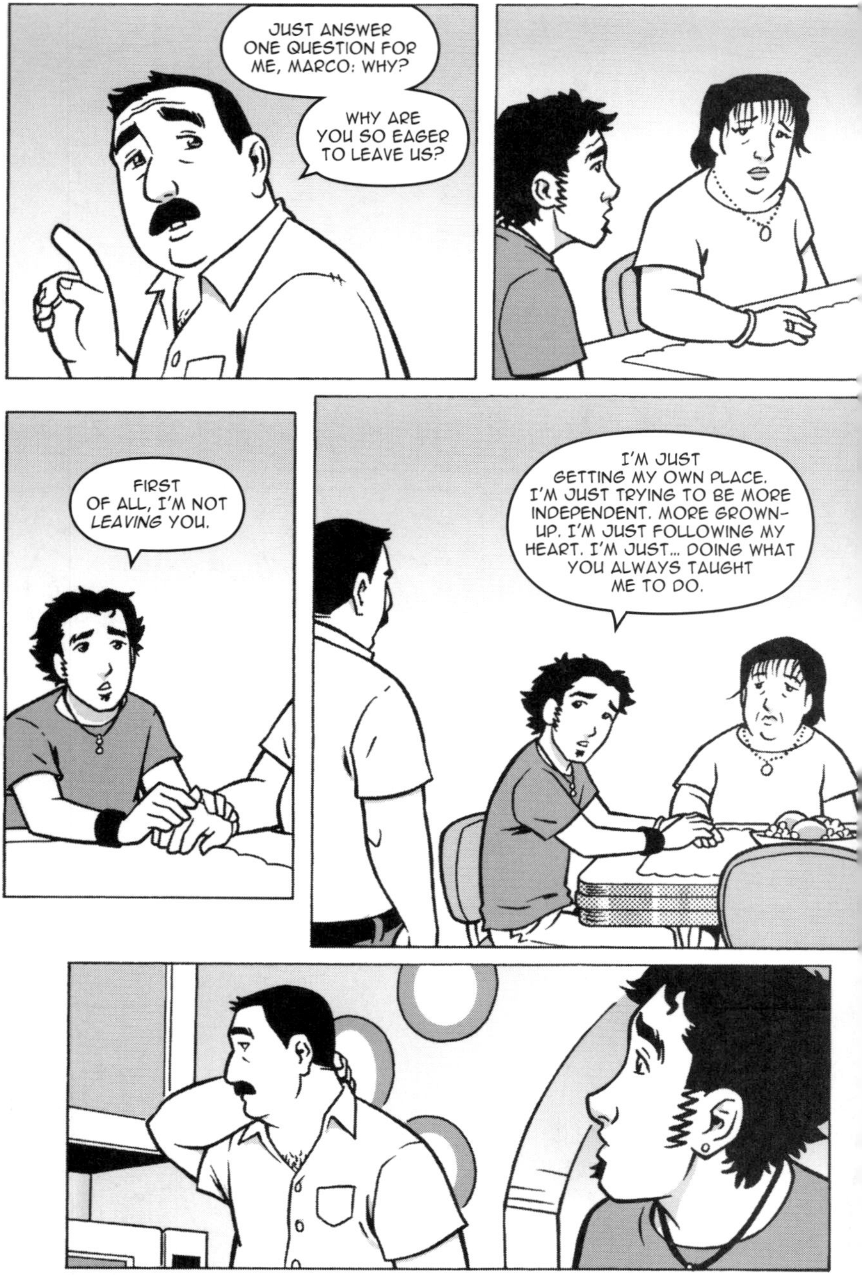

JUST ANSWER ONE QUESTION FOR ME, MARCO: WHY?
WHY ARE YOU SO EAGER TO LEAVE US?
FIRST OF ALL, I'M NOT *LEAVING* YOU.
I'M JUST GETTING MY OWN PLACE. I'M JUST TRYING TO BE MORE INDEPENDENT. MORE GROWN-UP. I'M JUST FOLLOWING MY HEART. I'M JUST... DOING WHAT YOU ALWAYS TAUGHT ME TO DO.

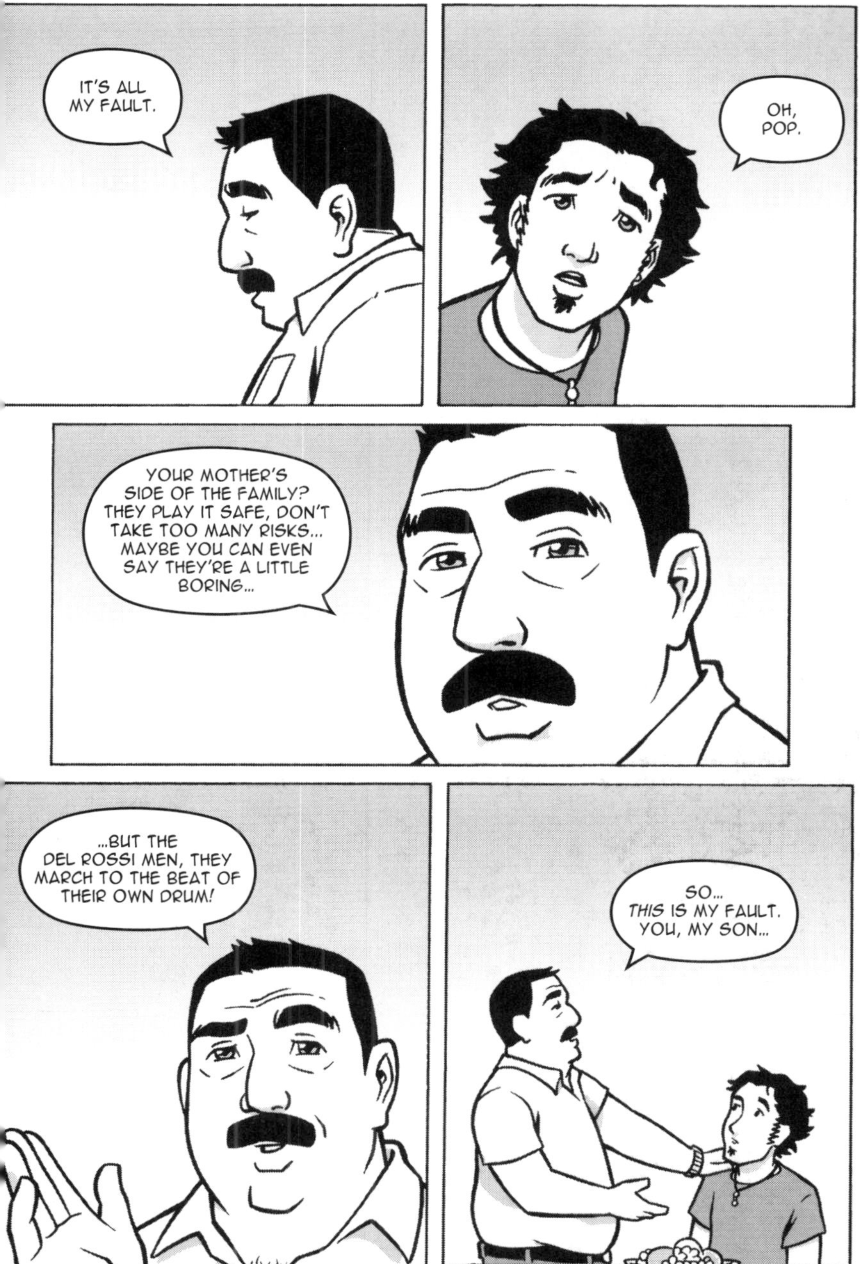
IT'S ALL MY FAULT.
OH, POP.
YOUR MOTHER'S SIDE OF THE FAMILY? THEY PLAY IT SAFE, DON'T TAKE TOO MANY RISKS... MAYBE YOU CAN EVEN SAY THEY'RE A LITTLE BORING...
...BUT THE DEL ROSSI MEN, THEY MARCH TO THE BEAT OF THEIR OWN DRUM!
SO... THIS IS MY FAULT. YOU, MY SON...

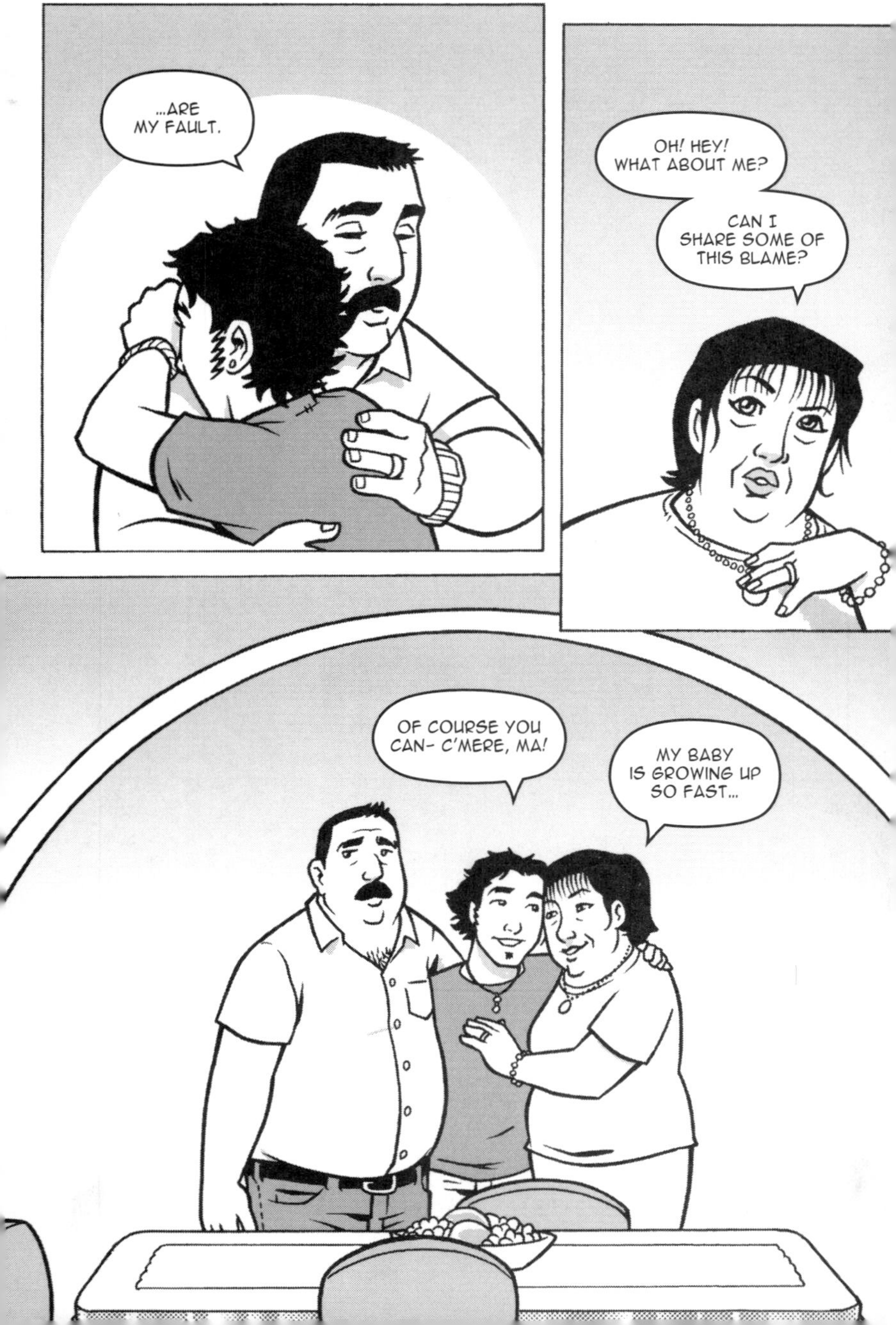
...ARE MY FAULT.
OH! HEY! WHAT ABOUT ME?
CAN I SHARE SOME OF THIS BLAME?
OF COURSE YOU CAN- C'MERE, MA!
MY BABY IS GROWING UP SO FAST...

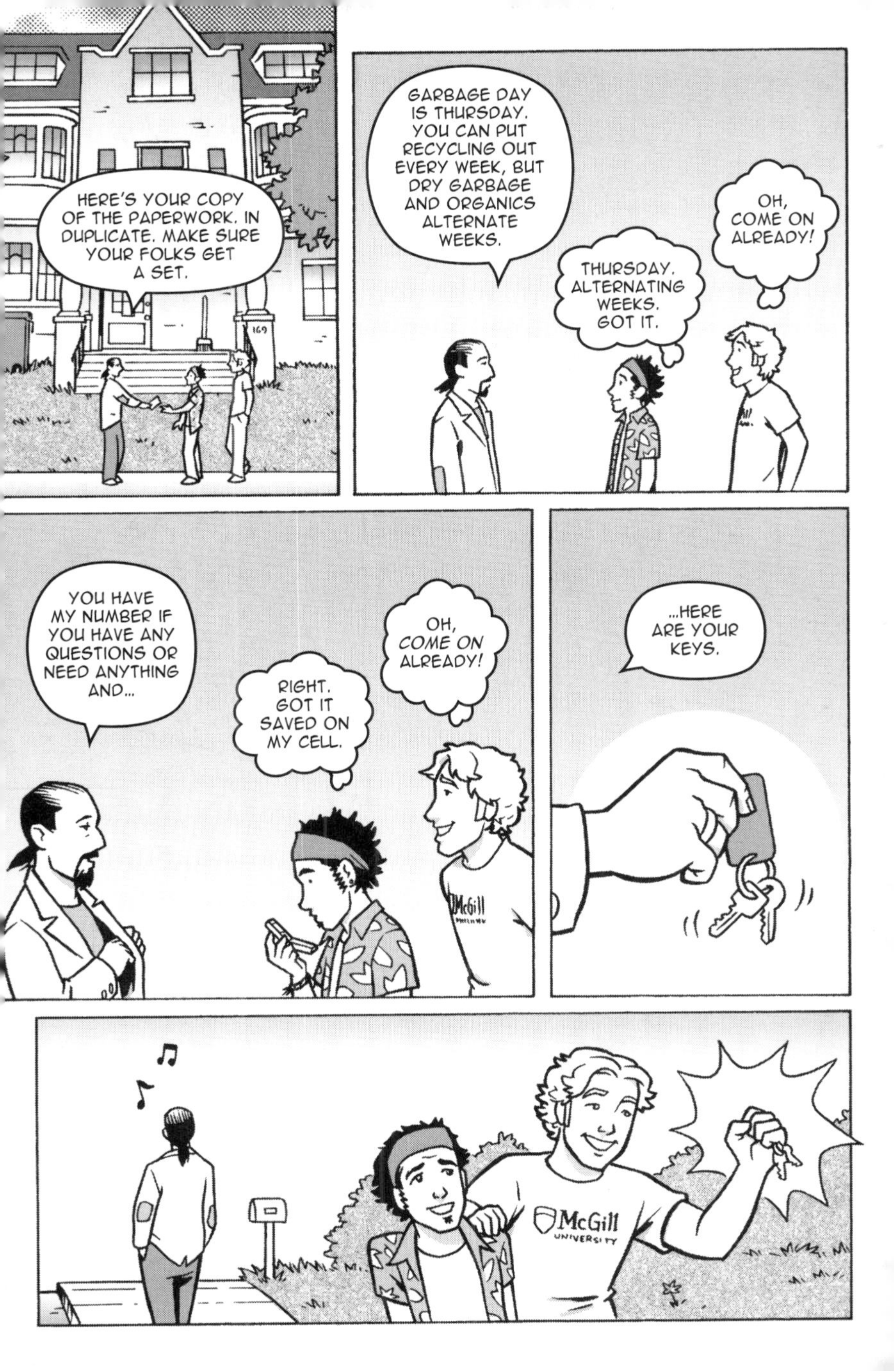
HERE'S YOUR COPY OF THE PAPERWORK. IN DUPLICATE. MAKE SURE YOUR FOLKS GET A SET.
169
GARBAGE DAY IS THURSDAY. YOU CAN PUT RECYCLING OUT EVERY WEEK, BUT DRY GARBAGE AND ORGANICS ALTERNATE WEEKS.
THURSDAY. ALTERNATING WEEKS. GOT IT.
OH, COME ON ALREADY!
YOU HAVE MY NUMBER IF YOU HAVE ANY QUESTIONS OR NEED ANYTHING AND...
RIGHT. GOT IT SAVED ON MY CELL.
OH, *COME ON* ALREADY!
McGill
...HERE ARE YOUR KEYS.
McGill UNIVERSITY

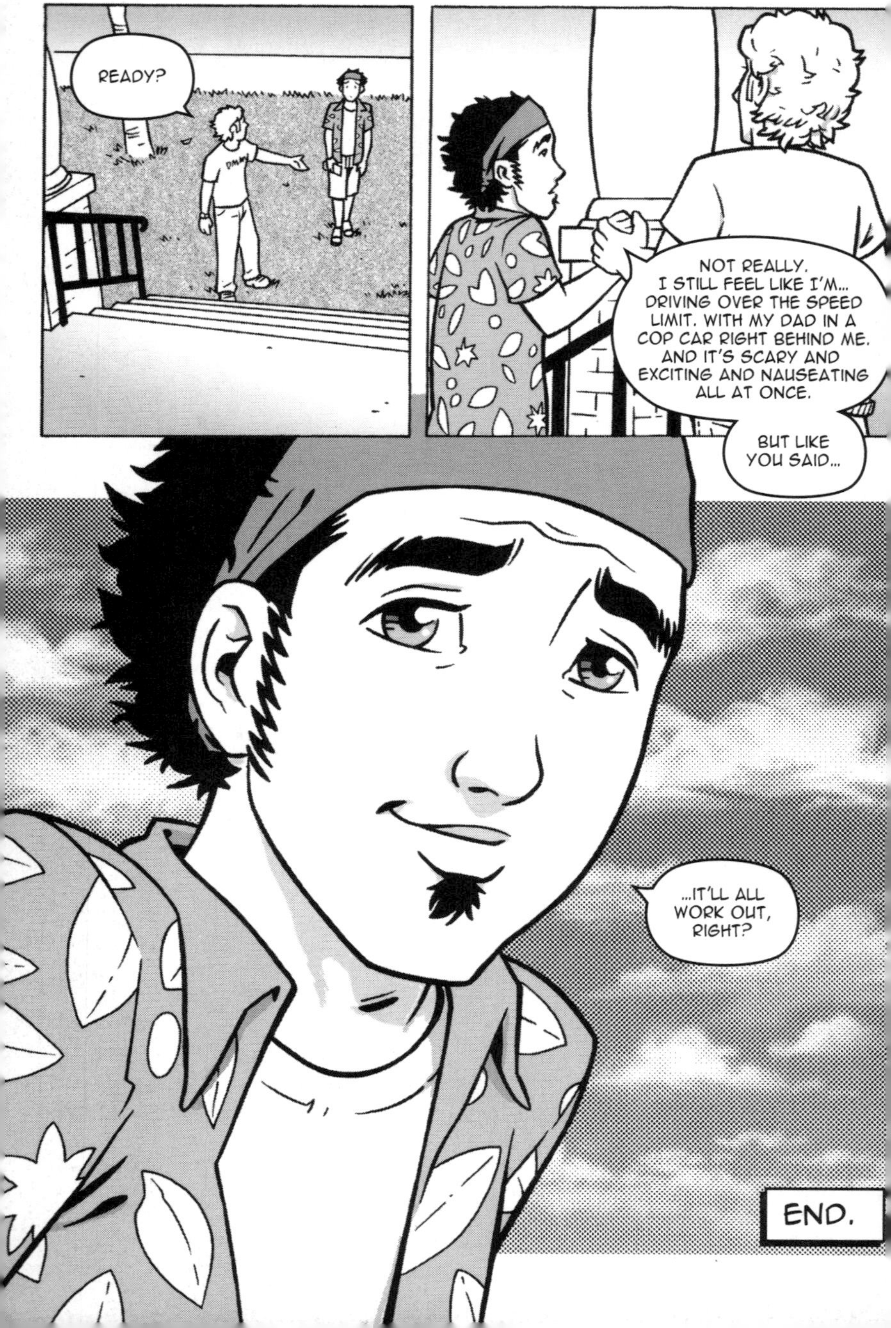
READY?
NOT REALLY. I STILL FEEL LIKE I'M... DRIVING OVER THE SPEED LIMIT. WITH MY DAD IN A COP CAR RIGHT BEHIND ME. AND IT'S SCARY AND EXCITING AND NAUSEATING ALL AT ONCE.
BUT LIKE YOU SAID...
...IT'LL ALL WORK OUT, RIGHT?
END.

The darkest, most intense season of Degrassi

Director's Cut Ultimate Box Set Now Available!
Packed with extras including
deleted scenes, bloopers, and much more!

www.dodegrassi.com

THE CREATORS

J. TORRES writes **NINJA SCROLL** and **TEEN TITANS GO** for DC Comics, and also contributes to **BATMAN STRIKES** and **LEGION OF SUPER HEROES IN THE 31ST CENTURY**. His other graphic novels include **ALISON DARE**, **DAYS LIKE THIS**, **SIDEKICKS** and the award-winning **LOVE AS A FOREIGN LANGUAGE**.

STEVE ROLSTON is the writer/artist of the "slacker noir" graphic novel **ONE BAD DAY**. He has also illustrated a wide range of comics, including **THE ESCAPISTS, POUNDED, MEK** and the Eisner Award-winning **QUEEN & COUNTRY**.

Inking
Jeff Wasson

Additional Inking
Mychal Allen

Toning
Julian Lawrence

Lettering
Chris Butcher

Cover Art
Ed Northcott

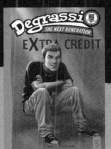

ACKNOWLEDGMENTS

My gratitude and appreciation to everyone at Epitome, Madison, Fenn, Simon & Schuster and Pearson Education Canada who helped make *Extra Credit* possible — with special thanks to Linda Schuyler, Stephen Stohn and Christopher Jackson for the hall passes; Brendon Yorke, James Hurst, Aaron Martin, Kate Miles Melville and Sean Reycraft for letting me copy their notes; Stephanie Cohen and Shernold Edwards for helping me with my homework; and Hye-Young Im for going to the prom with me. Also, thanks to Diana Sullada and Wanda Nowakowska for helping me get through those finals. Last but not least, thanks to Steve for being the Ellie to my Marco! — ***J. Torres***

First off, I'd like to thank the mighty J. Torres for letting this *Degrassi* fan become a *Degrassi* artist and for giving me such a great script to work with. Thanks also to Diana Sullada and Wanda Nowakowska at Madison; and to Christopher Jackson and everyone at Epitome who helped me along the way. Much gratitude to Jeff Wasson, Julian Lawrence and Christopher Butcher for their solid work on the book and for being so cool. And eternal thanks to Sabina and my family for helping me get this far. — ***Steve Rolston***

Madison Press Books would like to thank Linda Schuyler, Stephen Stohn, Christopher Jackson, Stephanie Cohen and Shernold Edwards at Epitome Pictures for their support and crucial feedback. We would also like to thank the cast of *Degrassi: The Next Generation*.

Degrassi THE NEXT GENERATION
EXTRA CREDIT

was produced by **Madison Press Books**

Art Director Diana Sullada
Editorial Director Wanda Nowakowska
Production Manager Sandra L. Hall

Vice President, Finance & Production Susan Barrable
President & Publisher Oliver Salzmann